"Serpents o
and
"The Magigals Mystery"

TWO CLASSIC ADVENTURES OF

THE Shadow ™

by Walter B. Gibson
writing as Maxwell Grant

plus **"Death Comes to the Magician"**
by Sidney Slon

Foreword by Mark Wilson

with New Historical Essays by
Anthony Tollin and Will Murray

Published by Sanctum Productions for
NOSTALGIA VENTURES, INC.
P.O. Box 231183; Encinitas, CA 92023-1183

International Standard Book Numbers:
ISBN 1-932806-79-2   13 digit 978-1-932806-79-3

First printing: October 2007

Series editor: Anthony Tollin
P.O. Box 761474
San Antonio, TX 78245-1474
sanctumotr@earthlink.net

Consulting editor: Will Murray

Copy editor: Joseph Wrzos

Cover and photo restoration: Michael Piper

The editor gratefully acknowledges the magical contributions of the Reverend William Raushcher, Nick Ruggiero, Sidney Radner, Susan and David Siegel, Massimo Marini and Geoffrey Wynkoop in the preparation of this volume.

Nostalgia Ventures, Inc.
P.O. Box 231183; Encinitas, CA 92023-1183

Visit The Shadow at www.shadowsanctum.com and www.nostalgiatown.com.

THE Shadow ™

Volume 12

CONTENTS

Two Complete Novels From The Shadow's Private Annals As told to Maxwell Grant

Thrilling Tales and Features

Cover art by George Rozen
Interior illustrations by Edd Cartier and Paul Orban

A MANY TALENTED MAN OF MAGIC *by Mark Wilson*

I first met Walter Gibson in 1968, when he opened the door at his Eddyville home in upstate New York and said: *"Hello, Mark Wilson. It's about time we got together."* That was one of the nicest things I had ever heard in my life. Walter was then, and is even more so now, a legendary figure to those of us who love the Art of Magic.

You see, magic is not only my profession, but also my hobby and my recreation. When we go on vacation, it's always to a magic convention. Magic helped me woo and win my beautiful wife, the lovely Nani Darnell Wilson; has taken my family and me around the world; blessed us with several network and syndicated television series; and provided a nice income over the years, which put our two sons through college, and much more. Magic has been an all-consuming, lifelong addiction, for which Walter Gibson has been a major supplier. His many novels, books, pamphlets, comic books, radio shows and articles have provided information and inspiration, not just for me, but for all of the magicians in the world. I believe an intensive analysis of Walter Gibson's total written works will show that there are few, if any, who surpass him in either quantity or quality of printed pages concerning magic.

That last statement is also true of pulp fiction novels, for which Walter certainly holds the record. In his heyday, everyone in this country knew Walter's alter ego, The Shadow. That would include all the teenage boys, as I was then; everyone of any age who bought those wonderful pulp volumes that came out twice each month with captivating action covers, which they purchased at their local newsstand, and those who listened every week to the exciting Sunday afternoon radio shows, which everybody did then. All of us were well aware of the mysterious man in the slouch hat and long black cape, The Shadow. Perhaps the greatest magic worked by Walter Gibson was his introduction of a now-legendary character whose special magic has endured for three quarters of a century!

I first became acquainted with the name Walter Gibson because he had written many of the books sold at the magic shop where I worked, Douglas Magic Land, in Dallas, Texas. Mr. Douglas had hired me as the magic demonstrator, because the young man who had held that job for several years had volunteered for the Seabees and gone off to fight World War II. I was twelve years old when I was hired, and Mr. Douglas paid me $2.50 a day. Of much more importance to me was, I could now buy the magic and the books in the shop at wholesale.

When I first explored all those wonderful magic tricks I would be demonstrating and hopefully selling to folks who would come in to our little "land of magic," I discovered that many of the most popular books were written by Walter Gibson. I later learned he had been the ghostwriter for, or coauthor with, many of the greatest magicians in the world, including such legends as Houdini, Thurston, Raymond, Blackstone and Dunninger.

When this exceptional man I had admired all my life had said, *"Hello, Mark. It's about time we got together,"* those words proved to me that my life to date had not been totally wasted.

Then Walter was kind enough to give me a tour of his house, a large three-story, built well before the Civil War. There were books everywhere. There were overflowing bookcases on every wall, piles of books stacked on the floor, on tables, on chairs, in the hall, in the bedroom, in the living room, everywhere. I was even more impressed when Walter explained that each room contained a specific category of volumes. "This is the gambling book room with information about all forms of wagering: the games of roulette, dice, poker, blackjack, horse racing, mahjong, everything from chess to spin the bottle."

Another room concerned spiritualism and its many variations, another one mind reading, still another parapsychology. The list goes on, because this was a huge house. And then we reached the largest and most cluttered of all which, as you would guess, was one of three magic rooms, where we had our first meeting.

I nervously explained to Walter my desire to write an all-inclusive instruction book covering many areas of the art of magic, designed for those who were sincerely interested in learning and who would promise never to reveal any of the secrets they learned to the uninitiated. I was delighted when Walter agreed with my goals and said he would be happy to help me reach them. The other result of our get-together was even more important to me, because Walter and I became friends. A few weeks later, I arranged for his first visit to my facility in Los Angeles, where our friendship became even greater.

The book we discussed evolved into *The Mark Wilson Complete Course in Magic,* first published in 1975. It had some 500 pages, for which the written content had taken over four years, and thoroughly explained the 300 magic tricks it encompassed. In the book's production, we had shot over 10,000 photographs, from which we selected the best. These were relayed to the two full-time artists I had hired, and they took two years to render the more than 2,000 line drawing illustrations in the book. The end result was exactly what I had envisioned, and was well accepted by magicians and laymen alike. The book has now been issued in many editions in English, and has also been published in French,

Italian, Chinese and Russian. The total number of copies printed is somewhere near 850,000. I believe that makes it the most popular single book of magic instruction ever written. As coauthor, Walter Gibson played an important part in that success.

As our friendship grew, I enjoyed each meeting with Walter more and more. He had an incredible memory, evidenced by things he would say, such as: "I was walking down the street in downtown Philadelphia with Thurston in 1925 when he said to me—" Then Walter would tell me of one of his amazing experiences or some other insightful or humorous event. Not only was Walter a wonderful storyteller, he would also happily answer any question I might ask. And what better person for me to ask than Walter? Because he knew almost everything, about almost everybody, in almost every category in the world in which I was interested. Each of his revelations would be interspersed with other related events, backstories, anecdotes about other famous magicians who were involved, or whatever. Shortly before the conclusion, Walter would say, "Now the point of all this is—" and then give his powerful, clever and often funny ending to that episode. I have thought many times since that Walter was the best man in the world for me to invite to dinner.

From the collection of Nick Ruggiero

Mark Wilson and Walter B. Gibson

Let me tell you of another example. As a teenager I had watched the Senior Blackstone perform his famous Tire Illusion. When I was fortunate enough to purchase the Tire Illusion at auction after Harry Sr.'s death, Walter told me how that effect had been inspired by one of The Shadow's exciting adventures. In the novel, our Man of Mystery had hidden from the bad guys in a stack of tires. When they discovered where he was and began firing at him, he was able to shoot back from between the tires while being protected from their return fire within his circular rubber fortress. When the heavies took The Shadow's hiding place apart, he had vanished! Except for the gunfire, that was an almost exact description of the first half of the Blackstone Tire Illusion. I had never realized before that my coauthor of the *Complete Course* had been the inspiration for one of the most baffling illusions of that time. This was an insight into Walter's continuously clever thinking. He had been coming up with these unique concepts twice a month for many years.

During Walter's later years, his tremendous contributions to the magic community were finally honored. In 1971, the Academy of Magical Arts presented him a literary fellowship recognizing "the high standards he has maintained over the years in his writing on the subject of magic." Walter was inducted into the Society of American Magicians' Hall of Fame in 1976, joining an elite group that included his friends Houdini, Raymond, Thurston and Blackstone.

On March 10, 1979, it was my pleasure to host Walter Gibson as he was awarded the Academy of Magical Arts' Masters Fellowship at the Variety Arts Theatre in Los Angeles. After a show headlined by David Copperfield, Harry Anderson and Doug Henning, Walter received the award that had previously been presented to such greats as Cardini, Dai Vernon and his lifelong friend, Dunninger.

Walter Gibson's outstanding contributions to our wonderful world of magic will be with us for many generations to come. As the years go by, I recall Walter's first greeting. Now I hope that sometime in the future, if I play my cards right, we will meet again and he will say to me, *"Hello, Mark. I thought it was about time we got together again."* But if I know Walter Gibson, it will be a much better line.

Happy Magic!
Mark Wilson

Named one of the ten top American magicians of the 20th century by Magic Magazine, *Mark Wilson starred in the* Magic Land of Allakazam *(network television's first magic series), six* Magic Circus *specials, the* Magic of Mark Wilson *syndicated series and four HBO magic specials. Wilson produced the Hall of Magic pavilion at the 1964-65 New York World's Fair, and served as magic consultant on* Circus of the Stars *and Bill Bixby's* The Magician *series. The world's most honored magician is on the Board of Directors of Hollywood's Magic Castle.*

The Shadow is ensnared by the mystic power of the East, when

Serpents Of Siva

entangle him in their deadly coils!

CHAPTER I
WALLS OF DEATH

THE taxicab swung from the avenue, rolled past the lighted front of a big apartment house. With that, the bleak darkness of the side street engulfed it, save for the twinkle of the cab's taillight that formed a feeble, fading dot.

A chill wind swept that forgotten street, like the icy fingers of a death-devil clutching for human prey. The gust whistled, whimpered through the open windows of the cab, but the lone passenger did not notice it.

He was too busy, craning toward the blackish tomblike fronts of brownstone houses. His squinty eyes were looking for a number, while his pudgy lips muttered oaths because he could not see it.

They were all alike, these houses—old, dingy, almost forgotten, in a portion of Manhattan so neglected that even the street lamps were inadequate.

A Complete Book-length Novel from the Private Annals of The Shadow

Then,
like a rift in
that monotonous
wall line, came the spot
that the passenger wanted.
He snarled for the driver to stop
the cab. It halted in front of a door that
had a light above it. That glow came through
a glass transom that bore the house number.

by Maxwell Grant

The passenger alighted. He paid the driver and ascended the high steps. Fumbling in the darkness, he found a bell button. When he pressed it, his ears caught a melancholy response from a distant bell. There was something ghostly in its tone; it seemed as rusted as the clank of ancient chains.

A chill caught the visitor. He glanced along the street; the lights from that back corner looked faraway. He was impressed by the grim solitude of these steps; for only that light above the door showed life. The houses on each side were stark and vacant; ghoulish vaults that squeezed this ancient mansion between their barren walls.

There was the grate of a bolt, the screech of hinges. The door swung inward; though the way was partly blocked, the visitor shouldered through. Anything was better than that chilly outside darkness, where the wind warned with its whispers.

Reaching the hallway, the visitor stood in the light. His peaked face showed sallow, with its squinty eyes and twitchy lips. Those marks, however, were due to dissipation; for the visitor was youthful. In that last quality, he differed from the man who had admitted him.

Turning toward the vestibule through which he had shoved his way, the visitor saw a white-haired man with wrinkled face, whose eyes made little beads. Lips were withery beneath a high-bridged nose. The old man's attire was of simple black, including the thin bow tie that showed against his pointed collar.

The sallow visitor managed a smile.

"Hello," he greeted, in a hoarse voice. "My name is Jack Sarmon. I've come to see Morton Mayland."

The old man gave a dry smile. It didn't please Sarmon. He had no liking for flunkies who thought themselves important. He squinted shrewdly, waiting his chance to show this fellow his place.

"May I inquire," clucked the old man, "just why you wish to see Mr. Mayland?"

"Sure," returned Sarmon. "I want to talk to his granddaughter, Lucille. I've heard the old man raises a squawk about people coming to see her. But he won't, in my case. Not when he knows why I'm here."

The white-haired man made no reply. He reached for the visitor's hat and coat, hung them on a hook beside the stairway. Beckoning, he conducted Sarmon up the stairs. Steps creaked as they ascended; along the way, Sarmon saw clusters of cobwebs. Then came a long hall; finally, a door.

The old man knocked; held his head tilted, until he received a reply. Opening the door, he motioned the visitor through.

JACK SARMON stepped into a well-lighted, comfortably furnished living room, to face a girl who had risen to receive him. She was alone in the room—a fact that puzzled Sarmon, particularly when he recognized her.

The girl was Lucille Mayland. She looked beautiful when Sarmon faced her; in fact, her appearance was more striking than he had remembered. That, perhaps, was due to her well-chosen costume.

Lucille Mayland was a pronounced brunette; her black hair had a ravenish glisten, against which her skin showed very white and clear. Her costume, tonight, consisted of black lounging pajamas with sandal slippers to match. That getup was admirably suited to her.

Sarmon saw darkish eyes beneath thin-penciled brows; a nose that was thin but well-formed; lips that had just the right ruddiness, above an oval chin. There was calmness in Lucille's manner; she evidenced it in her low-modulated voice.

"Hello, Jack!" Lucille placed a long, black cigarette holder to her lips, puffed a slow curl of smoke. "You have come to tell me something about Courtney Renshell?"

Sarmon nodded. He couldn't find his voice right then.

"Whatever it is"—Lucille was frigid—"I do not care to hear it. I am no longer interested in anything that concerns Mr. Renshell!"

"I am, though!" blurted Sarmon. "I've got a lot of things I want to talk to Court about. He's a good friend of mine—"

"Then why not see him yourself?"

"Because he's disappeared! I just found it out, yesterday, when I came in unexpectedly from Chicago."

Lucille shrugged. She turned away, to extinguish her cigarette in an ash tray. Sarmon followed her, speaking in persistent tone.

"You've got to listen, Lucille!" he insisted. "You were engaged to Court. What's broken it up, I don't know—but, certainly, you ought to have some regard for him. Matters aren't right, I tell you!"

The statement did not change Lucille's attitude. Sarmon became excited.

"Something's happened to Court!" he added. "His apartment is cleaned out—empty—and something more." The young man lowered his tone. "There was a big box shipped out of there. The janitor said it looked like a coffin—"

A sound interrupted. It was the *click* of the door. Sarmon turned about, to view the white-haired man who had admitted him. The fellow approached, chuckling to himself. Sarmon protested to Lucille.

"What's the idea of this?" he demanded. "Does this flunky have to butt into our conversation?"

There was a flash of Lucille's eyes as she turned.

"This gentleman," she told Sarmon, "happens to be my grandfather. We have no servant in this house."

Sarmon gaped. He tried to mumble an apology.

Old Morton Mayland did not seem to want one. He chuckled, as though he regarded the mistake as a joke. With clawlike hand, he clapped Sarmon on the back.

"Come along, young man," said Mayland, dryly. "I can explain this problem for you."

THEY went out, closing the door to leave Lucille alone. On the stairway, Mayland produced a folded paper. He opened it, with the comment:

"A letter that Courtney Renshell wrote to me."

Sarmon read the letter. It was dated a week ago, from Havana. It stated bluntly that Renshell had not visited Lucille before his departure, because he felt that she did not care to see him.

"Just another tiff," cackled Mayland. "They have had them frequently, you know."

Sarmon nodded. He spoke reflectively, as they descended the stairs.

"Havana," recalled Sarmon. "Court was there six months ago. I wonder why he went back?"

"The climate," suggested Mayland. "Or perhaps—"

Sarmon caught the wise chuckle in the old man's tone.

"A girl down there?" Sarmon shook him head. "No, I don't think Court would go for a Cuban senorita. Listen, Mr. Mayland; you heard what I said upstairs. I still think that something is wrong. I'm going to find out more about that box that was shipped from Court's apartment."

They were at the foot of the stairs. Mayland smiled and bowed good-night. Sarmon went to the rear of the hallway, to get his hat and coat. He heard the old man's footsteps shuffling upward.

Evidently, Mayland wanted him to show himself out. That didn't bother Sarmon; what did trouble him was the fact that he couldn't find his hat and coat. He thought that he had seen Mayland put them on a hook; but they were no longer there.

Groping in the darkness at the rear wall, Sarmon found nothing but the smoothness of the woodwork. He turned about, intending to go to the stairs and call up for Mayland. He changed that intention before he had moved three steps.

A sound caused Sarmon's shift of policy. It was much like the sound that he had heard upstairs: the *click* of a door. But there was no door in this rear hallway; none that the visitor could see. The fact puzzled him, and his bewilderment was the beginning of a final confusion.

Something slicked from the darkness behind him. A lash, thinner than the slenderest of whips, slithered about the young man's neck. He sped his hands to his throat, but Sarmon's sallow lips could not give the cry that his vocal cords sought to produce.

The thin cord tightened. Sarmon's eyes bulged. His gargle was almost soundless, for it was deep in his tortured throat. His knees caved; his body sagged to the floor, slumping softly.

With one last upward look, Jack Sarmon saw a darkish face, barely distinguishable in the hallway gloom. He heard a hiss, low, snakish, fearsome. An instant later, all went black; the victim's ears were tormented with a roar that split his head. Those were his last living sensations.

The snakish hiss was repeated.

Hands came from an opened panel at the rear of the hall. The dead form of Jack Sarmon was eased through. With padded tread, the murderer followed, his body contorted in reptilian fashion.

THERE was a brief interval. A man stepped from the panel, muffled in Sarmon's coat, the victim's hat upon his head. With direct stride, the man went out through the hall and opened the front door. He slammed it, as he stepped out into the night.

Timed to that slam came the click of the closing panel, as unseen hands drew it shut.

The door slam must have been heard upstairs. Old Morton Mayland came down with brisk steps. He reached the front door, opened it an inch. Outside, he discerned the man in hat and overcoat, under the dim glow of a street light, beckoning for a cab at the corner.

Mayland closed the front door and bolted it. His smile was cryptic as he returned upstairs.

Walls of doom had taken their toll. In this sinister mansion, isolated by the companion houses that sided it, Jack Sarmon, the unwanted visitor, had found swift death.

Whatever the circumstances surrounding the disappearance of Courtney Renshell, the missing man's friend would not investigate them!

CHAPTER II
ACROSS THE SOUND

THE reserved manner that Lucille Mayland displayed was not caused by the somber setting of her grandfather's home. She showed the same pose elsewhere; even when a member of a gay group.

That was evident the next afternoon, when Lucille sat by the rail of a trim yacht that was slicing through the waters of Long Island Sound.

There were a dozen in the party; and their chat was trivial. The talk concerned the dory races that they had watched from the Regatta Club, on the north shore. Most of the other spectators had gone back to New York by car or train; but this crowd had accepted the yacht owner's invitation to return by way of Long Island Sound.

Seated almost alone, Lucille seemed ignorant of the fact that she made a most attractive picture. Though her manner was the same, her appearance was quite different from the night before. She was wearing a white yachting costume, instead of the black attire. She seemed out of place amid this talkative group.

There was a young man who observed that fact.

He, too, was silent and restrained; and with good reason. He had not taken this trip for fun. Serious matters lay at stake; he was hoping for a glimpse of them.

The young man's name was Harry Vincent. He was the trusted agent of a personage called The Shadow, mysterious crime-fighter whose very name struck terror to the underworld.

Conversation was not turning the way that Harry wanted. That was why he had taken a gradual interest in Lucille. She seemed the sort who would respond if serious subjects came under discussion. Those subjects, however, were the very ones that remained taboo on this occasion.

The yacht veered; spray splashed across the rail. Someone pointed toward a smaller craft that was plowing some distance ahead, almost lost in the hazy dusk that was settling over the Long Island shore.

"There's Rodney Welk," remarked the pointer. "He's been pacing us all the way across."

"He's showing good speed in that little cabin ship of his," came another person's comment. "No wonder! He's traveling alone."

There was a bitterness to the comment that did not pass unnoticed. It opened a brisk discussion concerning Rodney Welk; brought out facts that Harry Vincent already knew.

Welk was a wealthy young man who had a distinct aversion to companionship; probably because he had been bothered by money-seekers who claimed to be his friends. He had been at the boat races during the afternoon; as usual, he had embarked alone in his little cabin cruiser.

Rumor had it, too, that Welk cared as little for his relatives as he did for his friends. All that, however, was understandable to the persons in Harry's group. Most of them had money and were anxious to keep it. At heart, they sympathized with Rodney Welk, who had more than they and, therefore, encountered greater problems.

There was a pause; then someone added:

"It is dangerous, though, for a chap like Welk to travel alone. One never knows when accidents may occur."

A HUSH gripped the little group; after it, subdued whispers passed. Those whispers rose to murmurs, that developed into conversation. With the tension broken, persons were discussing the very subject that they had avoided. Harry Vincent was hearing what he wanted.

These people were mentioning recent accidents, wherein members of their own social set had met with death. One man, wealthy like Welk, had been killed in an automobile crash. Another, older, and also wealthy, had been found dead at his Berkshire hunting lodge. That death had been due to the accidental discharge of the man's own shotgun.

There was also the case of a wealthy widow, who had made a trip to inspect an old house that she owned. A stairway had collapsed, plunging her to death.

Mention of those cases chilled the yachting party. Some members became uneasy, tried to change the topic; but the talk had advanced too far. There were a few who found a thrill in this discourse of death.

Harry Vincent was a silent listener. He hoped for some rift in the conversation; some suggestion that something might lie behind those supposed accidents. That idea, however, did not occur to the group.

It had occurred to The Shadow. That was why Harry was aboard the yacht.

Back at the Regatta Club, The Shadow, himself, was sounding the opinions of other persons. The Shadow was there in the guise of Lamont Cranston, a reputed millionaire. In fact, it was Cranston who had introduced Harry to this smart set.

Long ago, Harry had identified The Shadow with Cranston; but he had also deemed that the personality was simply a disguise. Who The Shadow actually was, remained a mystery to Harry; but there was never any question regarding The Shadow's theories.

The Shadow suspected crime behind those recent deaths. The motive would logically be profit, since all the victims were wealthy. It happened, however, that the affairs of the dead persons were in excellent order. The only people who had gained wealth were legitimate heirs, who had no connection with the deaths.

One point, nevertheless, had impressed The Shadow.

The principal heirs, in each case, were persons of a similar type. All were quiet, reserved; possessed of a self-sufficient manner. They were persons like Lucille Mayland. Nothing could disturb the calmness of their pose.

Woven through the fabric of this social set were others of that sort; human threads who shared some common secret. The Shadow, with Harry aiding, intended to learn what subtle cause lay beneath that surface.

CHANCE had placed Lucille under Harry's observation. This was his opportunity to learn more regarding the girl. Already, Lucille was showing definite reactions. While others either gloried or shuddered at the talk of death, Lucille remained calmly indifferent.

Harry saw the girl produce a cigarette case from a pocket of her yachting jacket. Another object came with the case; it slipped from Lucille's fingers

As a mongoose whips a cobra —as a cowboy throws a wild steer—as a lion springs on its unwary prey—so, too, does The Shadow attack the hordes of crime and thwart their evil ends! Master of Darkness—Crime-fighter Extraordinary—The Shadow, by wits and thundering automatic, overawes those who seek to break the law and those already beyond its pale!

In his never-ceasing campaign to deal justice to crooks and honest citizens alike, The Shadow at times assumes the role of Lamont Cranston, globe-trotting millionaire. With this disguise, The Shadow

THE SHADOW

makes his ends to meet, unbeknownst to denizens of the underworld.

Assisting The Shadow in his perpetual battle with the underworld are a retinue of aides—men who owe their lives to The Shadow and for whom they gladly do his slightest bidding:

Burbank is the contact man between The Shadow and his aides; through him go all orders and information. Rutledge Mann gives invaluable service to the Master of Darkness through his "front" of insurance broker. Harry Vincent is very close to The Shadow, and acts in many cases as his advance man. To Moe Shrevnitz goes the honor of transporting the Crime Master to battle—in his taxicab. Clyde Burke, reporter on the "Classic," furnishes The Shadow with "inside" information and advance news.

Cliff Marsland and "Hawkeye" are purported tough underworld characters; but, in reality, they are aides of The Shadow. When physical strength is needed the Master of Darkness calls on Jericho, giant African, whose muscular power is equalled only by his willingness to fight crime.

These, then, are the aides of The Shadow, characters who are willing to subject themselves to the Master of Darkness because they realize in him a superior force counteractant to crime.

and fell on the seat beside her. Harry reached over to pick up the object. Lucille clutched it first.

That object was a tiny golden image, as curious as any that Harry had ever seen.

No larger than a small paperweight, the little figure had three heads, each studded with several jeweled eyes. A dozen arms gave the body a spidery appearance; about the figure's triple throat was a carved chain that looked like a miniature necklace.

Before Harry could make out the details of the necklace, Lucille had dropped the little image in her pocket. She brought out a long white cigarette holder; turned to Harry and asked for a light.

While he was flicking his lighter, Harry questioned, in tone as quiet as Lucille's:

"What of these accidents? Do they trouble you, Miss Mayland? Some of our friends"—Harry smiled slightly, as he spoke—"seem to think there is a hoodoo close at hand."

Lucille puffed her cigarette. Her eyes met Harry's with a gaze that penetrated. In low, precise tone, Lucille declared:

"Death is feared only by those who do not understand it."

"True enough," agreed Harry. Then: "You understand death, Miss Mayland?"

"I understand that fear brings evil consequences," responded Lucille, "of the very sort that one wishes to avoid. That can apply to death. Therefore, I neither fear death, nor discuss it."

"That must take a lot of effort," remarked Harry, lightly. "I would need something to help my mind fix itself on that idea. Some lucky charm, for instance. I used to carry one of those things, once—"

Harry paused. It wasn't the closeness of Lucille's gaze that halted him. Harry had seen something farther away, beyond the yacht's rail. It was a white shape, yawing crazily against the darkened background of the Long Island shore.

Somebody else saw the same sight; exclaimed the very thought that had struck Harry.

"Look out there!" came the cry. "Welk's cruiser, running in circles! What's come over the fool? He'll capsize before he knows it!"

THE yacht's captain had spied the cruiser's behavior. Bells clanged; the yacht made for the veering craft. Previous talk was forgotten; everyone was agog, except Lucille. They could hear the beat of the circling cruiser's motor, when they neared it; but the tiny deck was vacant.

The yacht's crew put a small boat overboard. It cut through the choppy sea, trying to clip the cruiser's course. Harry heard the comment that Welk must have gone down into the cabin. That seemed probable; but foolhardy.

The thought gripped Harry that something much worse could have happened. That proved true.

The boat crew boarded the cruiser, after a lucky grab. They stopped the motor; kept the cruiser broadside to the waves, while the yacht arrived close enough to hook alongside.

Harry was among the first to clamber over the yacht's rail and drop to the cruiser's deck.

The next task was to find Welk. They headed down through the cockpit, into the little cabin. There, they saw empty bunks on each side. Toward the bow was an entrance to a little forecastle, where a lantern hung above a stack of boxes.

"Canned goods," Harry heard someone say. "Welk stocked up for a cruise."

None of the boxes was very large. They were stacked squarely against the front of the forecastle, with no space beyond them. There wasn't a place where Welk could be. The searchers went on deck to report.

There was only one answer to the mystery: Rodney Welk had gone overboard from the tiller of his cruiser. Someone recalled that there had been a rope on deck, attached to an anchor. That equipment was absent. It could account for Welk's disappearance.

The yacht's radio was flashing the news ashore, while the crew took the cruiser in tow. Harry and a few others remained on the cruiser's deck, discussing the theory that Welk had accidentally entangled in the anchor rope, to take an overboard pitch.

Standing with his arms upon the cabin, Harry looked ahead, toward the stern of the towing yacht. Through his mind thrummed the ominous conversation that had preceded Welk's disappearance. Those persons who thought Welk unwise to cruise alone had spoken prophetic words.

Among those figures on the yacht was Lucille Mayland. She was too distant for Harry to see her face; but he remembered the look she had given him, when she disclaimed her own fear of death. Harry wondered what Lucille would say now.

For the disappearance of Rodney Welk was another case of death—as sudden, as awe-inspiring as those other fatal occurrences which had been classed as accidents. So strange, in fact, that Harry Vincent could not regard it as an accident at all.

Welk's death was murder, the latest in an insidious chain. Somehow—Harry could not shake the belief—it linked with something that concerned Lucille Mayland, and the tiny, three-headed image that the girl carried.

Only one living person could solve such a maze of riddles.

That being was The Shadow!

CHAPTER III
SERPENTS HISS

WHEN Welk's cabin cruiser docked beside an old, weather-battered pier, a swarthy man of stocky build was waiting there. He had an official appearance and Harry Vincent recognized him. The man was Inspector Joe Cardona, of the New York police.

This portion of Long Island was within the New York City limits. The yacht's wireless call had been relayed to police headquarters. Cardona had made a quick trip here from Manhattan.

Cardona was something of a crime detector, in his blunt, direct fashion. Any report of strange death struck him as murder, until he had investigated it. Harry saw him craning as he walked along the pier.

In the dusk, Cardona examined every portion of the cruiser's hull, from the sharp-cut bow to the wide stern, where the name *Wanderer* appeared in shiny gilt letters.

The ace inspector came aboard, to quiz the men who stood there. He recognized Harry Vincent; recalled that he was a friend of Lamont Cranston. Since Cranston, in turn, was a friend of the police commissioner, Cardona was pleased. He figured that he would acquire reliable testimony regarding Welk's disappearance.

Harry and the others answered Cardona's questions. No one had seen Welk go overboard. The cruiser had been too distant, the visibility too poor. All statements began with a description of the boat's odd behavior.

Accompanied by Harry, Cardona went down into the cabin; then into the lantern-lighted forecastle. He studied the stacks of boxes; looked into every cranny. That done, he returned to the deck and made some notations in a little book. Abruptly, the ace asked:

"What was it somebody said about an anchor rope?"

Harry explained the theory. Cardona examined the deck and made measurements. The theory satisfied him.

"All that's left," said Cardona, bluntly, "is to drag for Welk's body."

That work was already under way. Out in the Sound, tiny lights were bobbing amid the rising mist. Prompt grappling should bring good results, if coiled ropes had dragged Welk to the bottom. There would be plenty of opportunity for the hooks to catch the rope, if not the drowned man's body.

Cardona boarded a little boat with an outboard motor. The craft chugged out to join the grapplers.

HARRY VINCENT found himself alone on the pier beside the *Wanderer.*

The others had gone back to the yacht, which was moored some fifty yards from shore. It was silent along the rickety dock, and very dark, for night had set in rapidly. The lick of wavelets disturbed the stillness; twinkling lights showed from the Sound.

But Harry was oblivious to those impressions. All about him, he felt silence and blackness.

From far out on the Sound, a searchlight cut the mist, its path dimmed before it reached the shore. Some other craft was coming across the Sound, perhaps bringing new passengers who had attended the boat races.

Harry did not notice it, but the incoming power boat was making a wide circuit to another old pier, nearly two hundred yards away.

Two ideas gripped Harry Vincent. First, that he should remain close to the *Wanderer,* on the chance that The Shadow would soon arrive; second, that even Cardona's belief that Welk's death was accidental might not be correct.

Those two ideas linked. By staying near the *Wanderer,* Harry could assure The Shadow that nothing had changed aboard the little cruiser since Cardona had inspected it. To Harry, that vigil promised to be nothing more than mere routine.

Harry was mistaken.

The boat from the Sound was docking at its remote pier, when Harry became conscious of something very close at hand. There were sounds past the stern of the *Wanderer;* thumps that indicated a low-lying boat moving in from the darkness.

Scrapes followed; enough to tell that persons were climbing to the pier. A flashlight blinked; its glow was instantly stifled. Harry heard a low-growled curse.

Whoever these persons were, it might not be wise to meet them. There was no time for Harry to hurry to the shore end of the pier, even if he had been inclined to do so. A hiding place was a logical preference; and Harry knew a good one. That spot was the cabin of the *Wanderer.*

One minute later, Harry had finished a silent scramble across the cruiser's deck and down the steps to the cabin. He was hunched behind an open door at the end of one of the sleeping bunks.

Cabin and forecastle both had small portholes. They were open; but they produced no sounds nor lights, either from the dock or the water. Harry decided that the scraping boat had touched at the wrong pier, and was moving on its way. He started to come from his hiding place.

A sound stopped him. It was from the deck—an evil, ghoulish noise that sounded far from human. As nearly as Harry could picture it, the sound was a snake's hiss.

THE venomous tone riveted Harry's mind, although he instinctively shifted back into his hiding place, glad that he had not been discovered. The hiss was repeated, as snakish as before, but this time, Harry was convinced that a first impression was correct.

That hiss was not a chance challenge from the darkness. It was a signal; repeated for some definite purpose.

A few seconds later, the sibilant call was answered. The muffled reply came from the one spot that Harry least expected: from the forecastle, where the lighted lantern hung!

It seemed incredible that anyone could have sneaked aboard the *Wanderer*. Duty, plus the sensation of a hidden menace, urged Harry to creep from his hiding place. He kept well away from the cockpit door; near a porthole, he fancied that he heard a movement on the deck. Satisfied that the man on the deck had shifted away, Harry concentrated on the forecastle.

Peering from the darkness of the cabin, he saw the forecastle as empty as before. There wasn't a spot where even a snake could be—not with those boxes packed so close against the front wall.

Harry was ready to doubt all that his ears had heard, when his eyes produced new evidence.

There was motion in the forecastle; it came from a stack of boxes. One container was shifting upward, under pressure from beneath. The motion lay in the lower box. Harry thought of snakes again, for the walls of the box quivered as if pressed from inside by coils.

The end of the box swung outward on a hinge. Something brownish wriggled into the light. Harry was treated to a sight so incredible that only his knowledge of danger made him credit it.

The thing that came from the box was human; it became more so, as it unlimbered. Spidery arms clutched the box front; long gangling legs stretched to the floor; bare brown feet padded softly. A spindly figure stretched to its full height.

The creature from the box was a Hindu; so emaciated that his scanty garb looked baggy. His wasted face was apish, with lips so drawn that the hiss must have come from between his teeth. He was, in a sense, a human reptile, for his thin limbs were as restless and as twisty as those of a serpent. His

eyes, moreover, had a snake's glitter. Harry noted that when the creature turned.

The Hindu had literally packed himself into the special box, with a skill that outmatched any contortionist that Harry had ever seen. The man's egress from the box was another marvel, so astonishing that Harry was too amazed to budge.

Had those snaky eyes looked into the cabin, they would have spotted The Shadow's agent. Fortunately for Harry, the uncoiled Hindu was otherwise concerned.

The snakish creature turned about; pressed the front of the opened box back into place. He was making it appear to be an ordinary box of canned goods, from which the contents had for some reason been removed.

The Hindu did that task carefully, with no degree of haste. That was a break for Harry.

Shoving his hand to the hip where he carried an automatic, Harry eased back toward the door beyond the bunks. He was crouched there when the snakish Hindu came creeping through the cabin. Harry heard hissed breath, scarcely audible, when the fellow stopped close by the door.

This man was Welk's murderer!

OF that, there was no doubt. In this emergency, it was Harry's job to apprehend him. Caution, alone, compelled Harry to await the Hindu's next move. Harry saw gritted teeth glisten in the dim reflection of the light from the forecastle.

Those teeth ejected another hiss. The sound was not answered. The Hindu crept toward the companionway.

Satisfied that the man on the deck had gone, Harry made a lunge from his hiding place. It was a silent surge; but the Hindu sensed it. He spun about, rapid as a dervish, made a wide fling away from Harry's clutch. A sleek arm slipped from Harry's fingers.

Given a larger space, the coily Hindu would have easily nullified Harry's attack; but the cabin was too small for the snakish tactics to succeed. Pouncing sideways, Harry trapped the wiry man beside a bunk; he jabbed the gun muzzle against the Hindu's thin-skinned ribs.

It seemed a sure capture, until Harry heard a padded thud behind him. It was his turn to wheel; too late.

A second Hindu, almost the twin of the first, had sprung from the steps. He was the one who had produced the outside signal; he had not departed, as Harry supposed. He was making a long spring, his scrawny arms above his head forming an oval frame for his grinning monkeyish face. Between his hands he held the ends of a slender cord.

The Hindu by the bunk made a grab for Harry's gun hand. Before The Shadow's agent could fire, the man from the deck finished his swoop. The thin cord looped around Harry's neck; he felt the same effects that had been Jack Sarmon's, only the night before.

There was a gurgle deep in Harry's throat. His hands numbed; the gun went from his grip. A crackle roared through his ears; his bulging eyes seemed to view those murderous attackers as brown-faced demons. With all that, a hideous thought beat through Harry's brain.

He knew what these murderers were. They were dacoits—fanatics who strangled victims without mercy. Each was a follower of Hindu thuggee, of that evil caste who consider murder by the cord to be a deed of virtue!

Harry's head went backward. His eyes were fixed upon that short companionway that led down from the deck. Like Jack Sarmon, last night's victim, Harry experienced a surge of blackness, that swept upon his vision like a blotting being of life.

It was the forerunner of death, that blackness; but doom was not for Harry Vincent. As Harry's tortured eyelids went shut, he heard snarls in the dizzy whirls about him. He slumped; but the pressure from his throat was gone. His fingers could feel his flesh; the cord was no longer there!

Lashing bodies struck Harry's shoulder. He rolled sidewards, toward a bunk; opened his eyes, in the direction of the forecastle. There, he saw the dacoits struggling viciously with a black-cloaked fighter who was swinging them about like puppets. Harry remembered that downward surge of blackness.

That had been a living attack, directed against the murderers who held Harry in their clutch.

It had marked the advent of a rescuer.

The Shadow!

CHAPTER IV
BATTLE FROM WITHOUT

In those first quick minutes, Harry had no strength to aid his chief against the dacoits. Even the stuffy air of the cabin was sweet to Harry's lungs. He needed long drafts of it, to revive sufficiently for battle.

Dimly, Harry groped for his gun; he found it while The Shadow whipped back and forth, flinging the wiry dacoits from side to side. They were tenacious fighters, those Hindus, even against The Shadow's power.

For some reason, The Shadow did not fire. He preferred silent conflict, as he swung a gun from one gloved fist, while his free hand plucked at wriggling foemen. The dacoits, in their turn, wanted escape; and all the while, they were dodging sudden swings from The Shadow's gun.

At last, one Hindu flayed at The Shadow's arms, while the other dived to make an attack from The Shadow's back. On his feet, Harry wobbled in to give aid. It proved unnecessary.

The Shadow's gun hand came downward from the grip of brownish fingers. The weight of an automatic glanced from the dacoit's skull, sent the murderer slumping. With a quick twist, The Shadow whipped clear of a cord that was flicking about his neck. He caught his second opponent with a downward grab; straightening, he pitched the fellow backward over his shoulders.

Harry had seen that whip-snap move before. With it, The Shadow could send a two-hundred-pound man on a long, hard plunge. The dacoit, with only half that poundage, traveled like a thing of straw.

Arms flinging wide, he sailed through the door to the forecastle; crashed headfirst against the stacked boxes. The containers tumbled; they buried the dacoit in a deluge.

That crash made The Shadow forget the dacoits. In quick-rasped whisper, he gave a command to Harry; then headed for the companionway, with his agent close behind. There were pounding noises on the deck; flashlights shone, as The Shadow reached the cockpit.

Men from the little boat—that Harry had heard scraping while on the dock—had listened to the finish of the battle in the cabin of the *Wanderer.* They had boarded the cruiser to aid the beaten dacoits.

They were battlers of a different sort, this crew, as their oaths told. They were mobbies from the Manhattan waterfront; and, like The Shadow, they wanted silent battle when they recognized their foe.

Knives flashed in the glow; went out of sight as flashlights were extinguished. Those blades were slashing for The Shadow.

Attackers thought they had a sure victim. They had not reckoned with the speed of The Shadow's upward surge. As knives went wide, he was out of the cockpit. On the deck, he was slugging into the midst of scummy battlers, dropping them right and left.

Sounds told the result to Harry, when he reached the cockpit. He knew that it would be useless, perhaps suicidal, to enter that fray. The Shadow had an advantage; for every man was his foeman. Crooks, meanwhile, were at loss with their knives, fearing that they might down their own clan-members, instead of The Shadow.

Harry's chance was to cut off reserves. He sprang for the dock; landed upon a crouching enemy and gave the hoodlum a blow that sent him sprawling from the dock. There were splashes, too, from the other side of the cruiser, as The Shadow sent men reeling overboard.

A minute more, the battle would have ended, when a flashlight suddenly flickered on the dock. The beam showed a pair of sweatered rowdies; they sprang for the person with the light. Harry heard a gasp as the glowing torch went upward. In the light's focus, Harry saw a face.

The newcomer was a girl. Harry recognized Lucille Mayland!

HARRY did not stop to wonder why Lucille had arrived here. Nor did he reason that the mobsters had no need to harm the girl, once they had deprived her of the flashlight. He gave a warning yell, as he took a long bound forward.

Both enemies flung Lucille across the dock, then turned to deal with Harry. In the last flick from the flashlight, they saw Harry's gun. They yanked revolvers of their own.

An automatic tongued from the *Wanderer*'s deck. It was The Shadow's gun; picking his aim in the last instant of light, he winged the first of Harry's attackers. As Harry grappled with the other water rat, The Shadow followed to the dock.

Slashing hard with his own gun, Harry felt the stroke go wide. Down came the crook's revolver; blinding stars cluttered around Harry. Above him, he heard a report: The Shadow's gun again. This time, it was a bullet for the killer who had downed Harry and was about to riddle him with slugs.

Guns crackled from the deck of the *Wanderer.* With gunfire started, the remnants of the boarding crew cared no more for silence. They were out to get The Shadow; but finding him in that blanket of darkness was too much for them.

The Shadow shoved Harry against the side of the *Wanderer,* to keep him away from bullets. With a weird, low-toned laugh, The Shadow voiced an answer to the wild barrage; though the mirth taunted their ears, the attackers could not guess the direction from which it had come.

Their first knowledge of The Shadow's actual location came when his big guns spoke. He was a dozen yards along the dock, well away from their misguided aim. But his enemies were clustered where the whiteness of the deck made a background.

There were howls, groans, as crooks spilled under The Shadow's withering fire. The rest hurtled to the far side of the *Wanderer,* where their low-lying boat—a rakish powerboat—had pulled alongside. That craft roared away, keeping the hull of the cabin cruiser as barrier, through which The Shadow could not fire.

Changing direction, The Shadow arrived beside Harry. He looked through the portholes of the *Wanderer.* The lantern showed the forecastle; The Shadow used a flashlight to view the cabin. Both were empty.

The bounding dacoits had recovered from the hard treatment that The Shadow had given them. They had wormed out through the tiny portholes, to drop aboard the powerboat. They were away with the survivors of the waterfront crew.

HARRY VINCENT was too groggy to realize all that followed. Those events were handled entirely by The Shadow. A boat came sweeping up to hail the pier; a loud voice shouted "Ahoy!" as someone suddenly switched on a searchlight.

The flooding glow showed Harry, as it swept along the side of the *Wanderer;* but the gleam never reached The Shadow. He had recognized the raucous tone of the shout; he knew, too, that the boat's arrival was a ruse.

If that crew had come along to help matters, they would have followed the fleeing powerboat. This was a cover-up outfit, acting with the crowd that had fled. The Shadow spoiled their game by a single shot squarely for the searchlight's glowing orb.

The light was extinguished by that bullet. Loud-ripped oaths accompanied the clatter of glass. The Shadow's laugh responded; his guns spurted for the darkness, lower than the spot where the light had gleamed.

The second boat whipped away, while its crew fired useless bullets against the sides of the *Wanderer* and into the rotted planking of the dock.

There were new shouts, from other sources. Calls from the yacht moored in the Sound; cries from along the shore. Lights bobbed from the mist, where Cardona and others on the water had heard the burst of battle.

The Shadow readied Harry for a quick departure. As Harry rallied, The Shadow's keen eyes noted the other side of the dock. There, a white-clad witness to the fray was coming from shelter. Lucille Mayland had found a spot of safety, to remain there throughout that last battle.

The girl groped for her flashlight. Finding it, she played it on the very spot where she had seen Harry, close beside the *Wanderer.* Harry was gone.

Lucille turned the light shoreward; she flickered it there, too late. There was no one at the land end of the pier. Guided by The Shadow, Harry had left the scene.

Calmly, Lucille swung the light toward the dock itself, then to the deck of the cabin cruiser. She saw sprawled figures there; heard savage snarls as wounded men tried to rise. Then footsteps pounded the planking of the dock. People from the shore had arrived to learn the cause of trouble.

SHORTLY afterward, Lucille Mayland was star witness when Joe Cardona arrived to learn what had happened. Her story was convincing and direct.

She had come ashore from the yacht, she said, and had been passing by the dock when she heard a scuffle there. She had started out to investigate the trouble, and had walked into the thick of gunfire.

"You were lucky, Miss Mayland," declared Cardona, in a tone that showed admiration for the girl's nerve. "It looks like a couple of mobs were on the job. What they were after is something I've got to find out."

Cardona boarded the *Wanderer* with a pair of detectives, to gather up the wounded prisoners. Lucille, on shore, received the congratulations of the group from the yacht. They agreed with Cardona, that her escape had been fortunate.

Lucille accepted those congratulations with her usual calmness. Of all those present, she alone was not excited. Coolly, the girl surveyed the group, noting all persons present. Her lips showed the slightest of smiles when she noted that Harry Vincent was not among her friends.

As they waited on the shore, Lucille Mayland drew an object from her pocket, held it concealed between her fondling fingers. She retained her smile, unnoticed in the darkness.

The object that Lucille held was that tiny, three-headed image with the jeweled eyes and many arms.

That curious golden figure linked with the battle that Lucille had witnessed. The fact that the girl owned such an image was to tell much to The Shadow.

CHAPTER V
HARRY MAKES PLANS

IN his checkup of matters along the shorefront, Joe Cardona learned that a speedboat had docked shortly before trouble began aboard the *Wanderer*. Cardona decided to learn more regarding that unknown craft; he headed for the pier where it lay.

To his surprise, Cardona found Lamont Cranston aboard; with the millionaire was Harry Vincent.

Cranston, it seemed, had made the trip across the Sound. He had heard the firing that took place along the dock beside the *Wanderer*; but he had lacked opportunity to reach the cabin cruiser.

Cranston was a hawk-faced individual, whose features were almost masklike. His manner, like his appearance, was impassive. Sometimes he had a way of implying statements, without making them. That was true on this occasion. He let Cardona believe that Harry Vincent had arrived at the speed boat immediately after it docked.

Cardona asked no questions on that score. It was apparent that he did not suspect Harry's part in the battle on the *Wanderer*. That, in turn, gave The Shadow cause for some keen speculation.

The Shadow knew that Cardona had already talked to Lucille Mayland. The girl had seen Harry during the fight. Possibly, she had not recognized him. It was more likely that she *had* recognized him, but had chosen not to mention the fact.

The latter situation, if it existed, could prove of value to The Shadow; particularly as he had received a complete report from Harry, before Cardona arrived.

They walked along the shore with Cardona. Harry showed no ill effects from the recent skirmish, although his head was aching badly. He felt steadier when they joined the group beside the *Wanderer;* he smiled, as he nodded to Lucille.

The girl's dark eyes fixed upon Harry. That glance was observed by Cranston. The Shadow knew instantly that Lucille was keeping silence. In Cranston's quiet tone, he mentioned that to Harry as soon as they had stepped aside. With that information, The Shadow gave brief instructions to his agent.

Most of the wounded mobsters had been removed; but there were two, less scathed than the others, who had been kept here at Cardona's order. The inspector quizzed them, while Cranston stood by. The story that they gave fitted with Cardona's theory regarding rival mobs.

THEY had been told, so they said, to pick up a cargo from a boat at this old dock. What was in the cargo, they didn't know; but Cardona suspected that the pair belonged to a crew of opium runners, though they wouldn't admit it.

They testified that they had run into unexpected trouble; and held to the opinion that they had been brought here by a hoax.

As they put it, there was always rivalry along the waterfront, with one outfit holding a grudge against another. Since Cardona knew that to be a fact the statement satisfied him; particularly after he completed a thorough inspection of the *Wanderer*.

Although some of the tumbled boxes were empty, none had been removed. In the midst of a hurried flight, no one would have wasted time unloading dope in parcels.

Though Cardona had a marked ability for playing hunches, he did not show it on this occasion. He apparently regarded Welk's death and the subsequent trouble on the *Wanderer* as coincidences. Working from the facts, that opinion was a logical one. From the size of the empty boxes in the forecastle, Cardona never guessed that one could have housed a murderer.

Moreover, boats were coming in from the Sound when Cardona completed his inspection. Grapplers had reclaimed the body of Rodney Welk, enmeshed in the anchor rope. They placed the corpse upon the pier, where a physician went through the formality of pronouncing the death a drowning case.

Only Lamont Cranston saw evidence of another cause, as he viewed the body in glare of electric lanterns.

Across Welk's bloated throat was a hairline that carried a ruddy tinge. It was the fading trace of the mark made by a dacoit's strangle cord.

Members of the yachting party had left for Manhattan. Only two remained. One was Lucille

Mayland, closest witness to the battle on the dock. The other was Harry Vincent, who had stayed because of Cranston's presence.

Occasionally, when glancing at Lucille, Harry had a feeling that the girl had something to say to him alone. Cranston had observed the same; it was he who paved the way to that opportunity.

He remarked that the police commissioner was coming to Long Island; that he would like to wait for him. So he offered Harry and Lucille use of his large limousine, parked near the landing place.

The two went aboard the big car. As soon as it pulled away, Cranston made a telephone call for a taxicab. A low laugh whispered from his lips, as he followed the same route into Manhattan. That repressed mirth was the tone of The Shadow.

IN the smooth-running limousine, Harry and Lucille were discussing the very topic that The Shadow expected. It was Lucille who opened the subject.

Acting Inspector Joe Cardona

"I owe you thanks, Mr. Vincent," she expressed, in a musical tone. "Your arrival on the pier was most fortunate."

"The thanks should be mine," returned Harry, politely. "I didn't want to be mixed with that brawl. You helped me out of a lot of bother by avoiding mention of my part."

"Let us say then, that our thanks are mutual."

"Yes. Our thanks to each other."

Lucille gave a mild laugh when she heard Harry's statement. They were riding along a lighted boulevard; Harry could see her head shake.

"Not thanks to each other"—Lucille's laugh had ended; her tone was serious—"but thanks from both of us, to Siva."

"To Siva?" Harry spoke as though puzzled, to cover his eagerness. "Who is Siva?"

"A strange and mighty power," replied Lucille, "who holds the keys to life and death. You saw the image of Siva, this afternoon, upon the yacht."

"You mean that little token that you dropped?"

"Yes. Here it is. Be careful of it."

Lucille placed the golden curio in Harry's hand. As he examined it, Harry remembered comments that Cranston had made, after hearing a description of the tiny figure. Cranston had identified it as a replica of the Hindu god Siva; a miniature of the many idols that represented that Oriental deity.

Not only that. In the fashion of Cranston, The Shadow had told Harry more. Lucille Mayland was not the only person who carried and valued one of these golden tokens. The Shadow had met others who seemed to regard them as mystic talismans.

"I spoke of death," recalled Lucille, in a faraway tone. "Of those who do not understand it. We, who follow Siva, know the truths of life and death."

Harry was so interested in the image, that he scarcely caught Lucille's words. He had noted the jeweled eyes and spiky arms; but he was puzzled over the carved necklace beneath the three heads of Siva. Lucille saw his interest.

"The necklace," she remarked, "consists of serpents and skulls. They represent life and death."

Serpents and skulls!

The contrast struck home to Harry. Those creatures on the *Wanderer* were like human serpents! One had disposed of Rodney Welk. The skull of death could stand for Welk!

Did Lucille recognize the grim significance of those symbols?

Harry looked toward the girl, in hope that she might betray an answer. Her eyes showed no flinch. Her lips were forming their half smile, as she plucked the Siva image from Harry.

"I am sorry," spoke Lucille, almost sadly, "to learn that you are not interested in Siva."

"I am," affirmed Harry, earnestly. "My apologies,

Miss Mayland. I was so intrigued by the image, that I scarcely heard your comment. You spoke of life and death—"

"Yes. Siva controls them. We, of Siva, are guarded against death. I was protected tonight, and so were you."

"But I carry no image of Siva—"

"This one was sufficient. Its charm fulfilled my wish that you—like myself—would experience no harm."

LUCILLE spoke the words with full belief. Harry hated to show agreement with such superstition; but it was his only course. His present duty was to learn all he could, in reference to the Siva cult, of which Lucille was obviously a member.

"It amazes me," spoke Harry, "that those who carry a miniature Siva can protect anyone they wish—"

"Only when the other person is close at hand," interposed Lucille. "The danger must be recognized, and visible."

"Then, unless we are together—"

"Siva cannot protect you. Unless you carry a charm of your own. Otherwise, you may become like—"

Lucille paused. Her lips showed bitterness. She glanced toward Harry, saw that his expression was sympathetic. Abruptly, Lucille asked:

"Do you know Courtney Renshell?"

Harry could not recall the name.

"He was my fiancé," explained Lucille. "It was Courtney who first took me to see Siva. I learned, later, that he considered the whole matter as a jest; but that was not until I had gained the belief which Courtney pretended.

"We quarreled because of Siva. Since then, I have not seen Courtney, nor have I heard from him. But I have seen Siva—often. I mean the real Siva."

The big car was rolling easily along a Manhattan avenue; for some reason, the chauffeur was making the trip a slow one. Harry noted the fact; guessed that it was at Cranston's order. The Shadow was giving Harry ample time to talk with Lucille.

"You have seen Siva!" Harry faked an awed tone. "The real Siva! What a privilege that must be."

"You would like to see Siva?" questioned Lucille. "Do you think that you could believe?"

"What else?" queried Harry. "After tonight, when I was rescued by some strange, mysterious power—"

"You heard it, too," put in Lucille. "That tone from the darkness—the voice of Siva!"

Harry nodded, realizing that through her blind belief in Siva, Lucille had supposed the laugh of The Shadow to be a manifestation of some supernatural presence. With that nod, Harry captured Lucille's full confidence.

The limousine turned a corner; it slid past the lighted front of an apartment house. Entering the obscurity of a blackened street, it halted before a grim old house, where a number shone from a dim transom over the huge front door.

"Tomorrow night," whispered Lucille, her fingers pressing Harry's hand. "Come here, alone. We shall go together, to see Siva. But say nothing to my grandfather!"

They stepped from the car. Harry accompanied Lucille up the brownstone steps, helped her unlock the big door. When he returned to the limousine, Harry felt a chill. Perhaps it was the rawness of the night; but, somehow, the sensation was linked with that somber old house, clamped between two dismal untenanted mansions.

When the limousine had gone, blackness glided from the obscurity of a house wall. A cloaked shape showed momentarily, near a street lamp; then merged with the night. The presence of that figure supplied another reason for the limousine's slow trip in from Long Island.

Harry Vincent had approached the home of Morton Mayland, a mansion where doom existed. During his brief pause there, he had been under a protection that had already proven itself more potent than the supposed power of Siva.

Harry's safety had been assured by The Shadow!

CHAPTER VI
PATHS IN THE NIGHT

INSPECTOR JOE CARDONA was a man who balanced speech with silence. Once he had voiced a theory, he became a clam. Cardona had found that such a system worked two ways. If his opinions proved correct, he could point to them. If they turned out wrong, the less that he had said the better.

That policy had become a habit with Cardona. He applied it to the death of Rodney Welk. The case was an accidental drowning; that settled it. As for the battle on the *Wanderer,* two mobs of water rats had chosen the cruiser's dock as their skirmish ground for the settlement of old scores. That was all.

It remained for the newspapers, particularly the tabloids, to see mystery behind the double event. They played up pictures of Welk, the *Wanderer,* and the pier; even the dory races at the Regatta Club. They went into the past histories of crooks who had been wounded in the gunfight.

All that was a laugh to Joe Cardona. He had spent a full afternoon at the hospital quizzing bandaged hoodlums, only to get the same answers that two of the lot had given him the night before. Nevertheless, Cardona was a trifle irked.

If the newspapers kept up all this hullabaloo what would the public think? Cardona didn't like rumors that had no facts to back them. It was tough enough, having unsolved crimes on the books, without a bunch of newshounds faking situations that did not exist.

Worst of all, when Cardona said nothing, reporters always took it that he knew a lot he did not care to tell. It made a bad mess while it lasted; still, silence was the only way to handle it. All this newspaper hokum would fade out after a few days. But, meanwhile, it was a nuisance.

Cardona had proof of that just before dinner time, when he received a message from the police commissioner. The commissioner wanted Cardona to call on some old fossil named Phineas Leeth, who lived at the Ritz Plaza. Leeth, it appeared, had bags of money, and was worried over what he termed the "Welk case."

As Cardona analyzed it, the old boy probably had the notion that wealthy people were getting a suicide complex, and wanted to be talked out of it.

IT was half past seven when Cardona sat with Leeth in the latter's richly furnished hotel suite. Leeth was a stoop-shouldered chap who sat crouched in his chair, a big walking stick close at hand, in case he wanted to hobble anywhere.

His face was long and droopy, his head completely bald. But his eyes, when they could shake their weariness, had a sparkle that made him look like an old eagle watching from its nest.

"About this Welk case," insisted Leeth, in a crisp tone. "Is there nothing, inspector, to support these newspaper rumors regarding it?"

Cardona shook his head; made a gesture with his hands.

"Odd. Very odd." Leeth didn't seem fully satisfied. Then: "Those wounded men, aboard the cabin cruiser—were they all Americans?"

"I guess you'd call them that," grunted Cardona, "although they've got a lot of funny names."

"Were any of them Orientals?"

"You mean Chinese? No, there wasn't a chink in the bunch. They don't run dope, Mr. Leeth; they smoke it."

Leeth shook his head wearily.

"I wasn't thinking of Chinese," he said. "I was interested in Hindus."

The thought struck Cardona as an odd one; so unusual that it interested him. He had seen enough of Leeth to recognize that the old man was no dummy. Joe put a direct query.

"We didn't run into any Hindus," he declared. "But what makes you ask about them?"

Leeth gave a relieved smile.

"That settles my chief worry," he declared. "Still"—he stroked his parchment chin—"I wonder about Renshell, and Sarmon."

"Who are they?"

Leeth explained. Renshell was a man whom he had met on several occasions; his full name was Courtney Renshell. Only recently, a young man named Jack Sarmon had visited Leeth. Claiming to be a friend of Renshell's, Sarmon declared that Renshell had disappeared.

"And today," finished Leeth, "Sarmon was to call here, without fail. He did not arrive."

Cardona was writing down the names. Suddenly, he asked: "Where do the Hindus fit into it?"

"They have no real connection," replied Leeth, "considering that you have no reports on them. It merely happens that I knew Courtney Renshell through our mutual interest in a cult devoted to the Hindu god, Siva."

From a vest pocket, Leeth produced a tiny Siva image, the exact duplicate of the one Lucille carried. He passed it to Cardona, who held it under lamplight, where the tiny jeweled eyes twinkled with a dazzling glitter.

"That talisman," announced Leeth, soberly, "protects any person who carries it. So we have been told by Singhar Bund, guardian of the mighty Siva statue."

"You mean that Singhar Bund runs the outfit?" demanded Cardona. "That he's got one of these three-headed freaks built on a large scale?"

Leeth nodded, wincing as he did. He didn't care for Cardona's description of Siva. Joe noted it; decided not to repeat the mistake. He asked where the cult met. Leeth told him the address. When Cardona asked when the next meeting was scheduled, Leeth replied:

"Tonight."

That news enthused Cardona. He asked Leeth if visitors could attend the meeting.

"They are always welcome," declared the long-faced man, "if they are brought by members, like myself. I feel sure that Singhar Bund will welcome you, inspector. I shall be pleased to introduce you."

"As myself?" queried Cardona. Then, answering his own question: "Not a chance! That would queer everything. You wait here half an hour, Mr. Leeth, until I come back. Then I'll be ready to go to that meeting with you."

WHILE Cardona was obtaining a shortcut direct to the Siva cult, another investigator was busy elsewhere. The Shadow was in his sanctum, studying a stack of information. That data included reports from agents, newspaper clippings, photographs, together with an assortment of other items.

Beneath a bluish light, long fingers inscribed outstanding facts concerning a list of names.

First were the names of persons who had died in supposed accidents, like Rodney Welk. With them were names of heirs who had received legacies from the wealthy victims. In every case, one heir was a person whose manner resembled that of Lucille Mayland.

Since Lucille was admittedly a member of the Siva cult, The Shadow checked on Morton Mayland. Here, the case differed. Lucille's grandfather was not wealthy. He spent money in odd fashions; but apparently curtailed other expenditures by doing so.

One quirk was his desire for isolation. He owned the house in which he lived; also those on each side of it. He refused, however, to rent or sell the adjacent houses, claiming that neighbors annoyed him.

Morton Mayland had an income that amounted to a few thousand dollars yearly. It came from a royalty on patented electrical appliances that he had invented. The patents were controlled by a manufacturer named Louis Bolingbroke, whose wealth ran into millions.

That, reports told, was a sore point with Mayland. The old man believed that Bolingbroke had swindled him. Old clippings told of lawsuits instituted by Mayland; in every case, they had gone against him.

Facts jotted down, The Shadow plucked earphones from the wall. A tiny light glowed; a methodical voice came across the wire:

"Burbank speaking."

Burbank, another secret agent of The Shadow, was his contact man.

"Instructions," then whispered The Shadow. "For Vincent—"

The instructions followed, to be relayed by Burbank. They included names and descriptions of persons that Harry might meet at the Siva meeting. Such word given, The Shadow hung up the earphones, snapped off the light.

There was a whispered laugh within the blotted sanctum: The Shadow's tone of departure.

WHEN Harry Vincent called at the Mayland residence, a half hour later, he was admitted by Morton Mayland, in person.

Like Jack Sarmon, Harry made the mistake of thinking the white-haired man was a servant, particularly when Mayland took his hat and coat, to hang them in the rear hall.

Those tiny eyes, peering from beside the high-bridged nose, made Harry wonder why so shrewd a person could be content with a menial position. He had the answer, when Lucille appeared from upstairs, to introduce her grandfather.

Mayland's manner changed instantly.

"May I ask you, Mr. Vincent?" he inquired, crabbedly, "where you and my granddaughter intend to go this evening?"

Lucille's dark eyes sent a warning look from past Mayland's shoulder. Harry scarcely noticed the glance. He had expected this question. He produced a pair of tickets to a theater. Mayland inspected them; sourly smiled his approval.

"I am pleased," he told Harry, in cackly tone, "to learn that Lucille has new and lighter interests than those which have previously attracted her. I hope that you shall call here often, Mr. Vincent."

Mayland's reference was a veiled hint regarding the Siva cult; for Lucille had forewarned Harry that her grandfather disapproved of her interest in that group. The old man's tone showed guardedness, as if he hoped that Harry had never heard of the Siva worshippers.

Opening the front door, Mayland bowed; then noted that Harry did not have his hat and coat. With beady eyes, the old man looked toward the cab that awaited Harry and Lucille. He remarked that he would escort Lucille to the cab, and wait there until Harry joined them.

The front door closed. Harry was alone in the shuddery hall. He felt its ominous clutch as he stepped to the deep recess, where his hat and coat hung. Alone, Harry turned abruptly when his ears caught a stifled click.

Harry saw nothing except blackness; but as he took his hat and coat, a panel moved behind him. A slight draft swept Harry's neck; the chill ran along his spine. Arms bundled in his coat, he swung roundabout.

Harry was unready for attack; at that moment, his position was worse than Sarmon's had been, two nights ago. Fortunately, no thrust came. The panel was shut; blackness alone occupied the corner near it.

Nervously, Harry headed for the front door, letting his coat settle on his shoulders as he went.

Half a minute after Harry's departure, the big door reopened; from outdoors came the throb of the starting taxi. Old Mayland stepped through the portal, closed it, and gave a canny look about the hallway.

Sharp though his tiny eyes were, Mayland saw nothing in that gloom. In shuffly fashion, he ascended the stairs. When the final creak of his footsteps had faded, there was motion in the hall below.

A figure took shape from the blackness, emerged to the center of the hall. Above cloaked shoulders were eyes that peered from beneath the brim of a slouch hat. They were keener eyes than Mayland's.

Again, Harry's visit to this house had been screened from danger. The lurker in Mayland's mansion was The Shadow!

CHAPTER VII
THE TEMPLE OF SIVA

THREE dozen persons were assembled in a fantastic room, where brass walls formed the background of a magnificent setting. The place was a veritable product of the Orient, transplanted to New York for the amazement of all who might view it.

Chairs and settees were of teakwood. Brass lota

jars stood upon carved tables. Most bizarre of all was the huge bronze statue, raised upon a dais, that overlooked the room.

The statue was an idol of Siva, larger than a life-size figure. Its three heads faced toward the assemblage; and each bronze countenance possessed a half-dozen jeweled eyes. The many outstretched hands held tridents, axes, sheaves of grain. Those symbolized that Siva was a power of both creation and destruction, who ruled on sea as well as land.

The necklace that adorned the mammoth Siva was composed of skulls and serpents. The death's-heads were nearly full size; the snakes were so realistic that their brass coils appeared to writhe, if a person watched them steadily.

Presiding over this temple was a steady-eyed Hindu, who wore a golden robe. His turban, of the same rare cloth, was marked by a diamond crescent: the symbol of Siva.

Harry Vincent was looking toward the Hindu, when he heard Lucille Mayland whisper the name:

"Singhar Bund."

Though Singhar Bund conducted the Siva cult, he was not the only Hindu present. There were half a dozen others; they were attired in baggy garments that covered scrawny bodies. Harry was not certain, but he believed that two of these could be the foemen who had battled The Shadow aboard the *Wanderer*.

"They are the yogi," undertoned Lucille. "Through meditation, they can unite with Siva, to gain power over all material things."

Harry was getting a rapid insight into the setup of the Siva cult. The whole affair was a fake, despite its splendor; and for nerve, Singhar Bund could outmatch any swindler that Harry had ever met.

Not one so-called yogi was genuine, in Harry's opinion. The Shadow had correctly classed them as dacoits; despite their fancy garb, they looked like murderous stranglers. But the camouflage was good enough to deceive all persons whose knowledge of India depended solely upon what Singhar Bund told them.

Singhar Bund was speaking; his words were in English, smooth and persuasive. He was describing miracles of the Orient; wonders that would be reproduced within this temple. The listeners were persons of intelligence, many of them Lucille's friends; yet they drank in the statements of Singhar Bund.

The promise that lay behind the gorgeous sham was that of life and happiness; freedom from all danger, to those who believed in Siva.

WHILE Singhar Bund continued his languorous lecture, Harry studied the surroundings. The temple had been easy of access. It was located on the second floor of a building that had stores on the street level. Perhaps some of the ground floor belonged to Singhar Bund; certainly, there was more space on the second floor than the area that the temple occupied.

Though the portals stood wide open, Harry observed that they were equipped with gates of solid brass; once shut, those would turn the place into a stronghold. There were corridors outside the temple; where they led, Harry had been unable to learn.

One curious feature of the room was that of alcoves in the walls. There were four of them: one in each side wall, the other pair separated by the platform where the Siva statue rested.

In the alcove in the left wall, Harry observed a long wide board, its surface studded with spikes that pointed upward. The alcove in the right wall housed a small platform with a large rod extending vertically from its center.

In the alcove to the left of the Siva statue, Harry saw a huge metal casket that looked like a sarcophagus; but it was upright, instead of lying flat, as coffins usually did. The casket had a huge lid, which at present seemed to be a door; for it was hinged at one side and equipped with hasps and padlocks at the other.

Singhar Bund ceased his discourse. The group began to buzz among themselves. Harry mentioned the alcoves; Lucille explained the objects that were placed there.

"The bed of spikes," she said, referring to the nail-studded board. "I have seen a yogi lie there for hours, unharmed by the sharp points."

Harry was not impressed. He had seen that stunt at sideshows. The greater the number of spikes, the less weight each received. Even a heavy man could lie on a hundred spikes without feeling jabs from the points.

"Tonight"—Lucille pointed to the alcove in the right wall—"Singhar Bund has promised a demonstration of Hindu levitation. A yogi will rise in the air above that little platform."

"What about the big casket to the left of the statue?" asked Harry.

"It is for the *samadhi,* or living burial," replied Lucille. "That will be the final test in the course of instruction. It will be demonstrated at a later meeting."

Harry looked to the right of the statue. The fourth alcove was empty; but its inner wall had a brass door.

"That leads to Singhar Bund's own sanctuary," declared Lucille. "It is where he spends his time in contemplation."

Harry's guess was that Singhar Bund spent part of his time counting the contributions that the cult received; the rest, in studying new lists of dupes. It was wise, however, not to mention that opinion to Lucille. She was completely sold on the Siva cult.

Taken at face value, the cult racket would be a hard one to break. People had a right to believe what they wanted, and to contribute funds if they so chose. But if murder lay behind the game, the story would be different.

In that case, Singhar Bund could be exposed as a criminal; and his flimflam would be ended. The one flaw was that murder had not yet been pinned on Singhar Bund. To make it a positive conviction, his dacoits would have to be caught in an act of crime, and their actions traced back to Singhar Bund, himself.

ONE of the Hindus had entered the alcove in the right wall. While Singhar Bund was announcing the yogi's coming test, Harry asked Lucille about the other persons present. The girl knew the names of most of them. Some that she mentioned were on The Shadow's list.

One, in particular, was a pinch-faced woman who watched proceedings through a lorgnette. Her name was Madeline Selvin; though Lucille did not seem to know it, the woman was a relation of Rodney Welk. Information that had reached The Shadow, indicated that Madeline Selvin would receive a large portion of Welk's money.

Lucille also pointed out an elderly, stooped man, whose face was droopy and tired-eyed. His name was Phineas Leeth, and he was very wealthy. His money, so Lucille said, had come from mines in Mexico. Leeth was one of the largest contributors to the Siva cult. In fact, he was one of very few cult members who had money in his own right.

There was another man who interested Harry; but Lucille did not know his name. He was old, with white beard and flowing hair, that gave him the appearance of a patriarch. Though he sat silent and huddled, his eyes were keen and watchful.

Harry was positive that he had seen the old codger somewhere before. He was still wondering about the bearded man's identity, when Singhar Bund called for attention.

Two Hindus had been holding a cloth in front of the alcove in the right wall. They removed it, to show a yogi seated in midair. His legs were crossed beneath him; his right hand rested lightly on the post that stood in the pedestal.

Awed gasps came from the throng when Singhar Bund took a sword and dramatically passed it all about the seated man. The curtain was replaced; soon afterward, the Hindu came from the alcove.

The trick did not baffle Harry. He had read up on the methods of Hindu fakirs, at The Shadow's order. Harry had noted that the Hindu wore a long-sleeved jacket, different from those of Singhar Bund's other helpers.

That sleeve hid a rod connecting with the post. Passing along the Hindu's arm, the rod enlarged into a supporting cradle at the Hindu's back. The trick was an old one in India; but it was still mysterious, when performed with all the claptrap that Singhar Bund knew how to provide.

The meeting had ended. One by one, the Siva believers were approaching the huge statue, each waiting at a respectful distance until the one ahead had gone. Lucille told Harry that this was a usual ceremony. She took her turn among the rest.

Harry observed that the scrawny Hindus were awaiting their turn. When the others had gone, they filed toward the Siva statue. One bowed; went his way. Another did the same.

It struck Harry that he could establish himself more firmly with Lucille, if he performed the ritual. Seized by a bold urge, he approached the statue, just as the final Hindu reached it.

Harry was less than ten feet distant when the Hindu bowed. He was close enough to catch a sound that others had not noticed. From the lips of the bowing Hindu, Harry heard a hiss. Though subdued, it had the exact tone of the signal that had been given aboard the *Wanderer!*

HARRY was right. These Hindus were dacoits. One of them was the man who had pitched Welk overboard. Whether the final Hindu was that killer, did not matter. Harry wanted to know why the fake yogi had given the dacoit's call on this occasion. The fellow was still bowed before the statue; he had a listening attitude. Harry took a step forward.

Instantly, his arm was gripped by fingers that had an iron clutch. A hand drew him backward with surprising strength. In contrast came a velvet voice, that purred in Harry's ear; but its tones were so close that Harry could not hear sounds from elsewhere.

"Good evening, my friend," spoke the voice. "You are a neophyte, a newcomer in our midst. But you are one, my vision tells me, who chooses to believe in Siva."

Harry turned to face the smooth-tongued Singhar Bund. He met eyes that shone with glistening stare from a well-formed countenance of oval shape. Thin, brownish lips had parted in a friendly smile; but Singhar Bund's expression was his usual sham.

The grip relaxed from Harry's wrist. Had he been alone with Singhar Bund, Harry would have expected the Hindu's fingers to reach for his neck. Under present circumstances, Singhar Bund was forced to retain his oily pose.

The Hindu's eyes sidelonged toward the Siva statue. The last dacoit had gone. With a bow of his turbaned head, Singhar Bund conducted Harry to the image. After they stood in contemplation, Singhar Bund presented Harry with a miniature Siva figure, like the one that Lucille carried.

Harry rejoined Lucille. She was pleased because he had received a token from Singhar Bund; but

CLIFF MARSLAND

she was anxious to reach the theater before the show ended. She was sure that her grandfather would question her regarding the play.

They reached the street and took a taxi. It was difficult for Harry to realize that he was really in Manhattan, after the spell of the Siva temple. But as they rode along, he weighed the facts that he had gained.

Harry would have a real report for The Shadow, regarding both the Siva cult and its controller, Singhar Bund. Harry had learned much tonight; but chance had provided him with a highlight—namely, that signal given at the Siva statue.

Though Harry could not guess the reason for the dacoit's murderous call, he was confident that The Shadow would divine its purpose.

CHAPTER VIII
SINGHAR BUND SPEAKS

ALL the members of the Siva cult had not left the upstairs temple at the time when Harry and Lucille departed. Among those who remained was Phineas Leeth; bent low over his cane, the mine owner was chatting with others of the group.

Another person present was the white-bearded man who had captured Harry's attention. He was much interested in the temple. With slow gait, he went from alcove to alcove, peering with his quick-darting eyes.

The bearded man was looking at the big casket near the Siva statue, when a person approached

him. He turned to meet Singhar Bund. The Hindu showed the same suave pose that he had used with Harry.

"The burial tomb," spoke Singhar Bund, referring to the casket. "Imprisoned there, an ordinary mortal would soon die for want of air; but a yogi, placed in the hypnotic state that we term *samadhi,* can live indefinitely.

"The trance state represents the highest form of yogi concentration. That is why I have reserved the living burial for the final demonstration in this series of meetings. I hope, sir, that you will be present to witness it."

The old man nodded, as though he anticipated the event. Motioning toward the casket, he wheezed a question:

"Why the padlocks?"

"To prove that the yogi never leaves his tomb," smiled Singhar Bund. "There are always skeptics who doubt that these demonstrations are genuine. We find it necessary to convince them."

While his smooth voice purred, Singhar Bund kept steady eyes upon the bearded man. The visitor had no other question, so Singhar Bund put one of his own.

"Would you like to see some authentic photographs of yogi miracles?" he asked. "I have a collection, brought from India. They are in my private grotto."

He gestured toward the doorway beyond the Siva statue. The bearded man nodded his acceptance of the invitation.

The grotto lay beyond a heavy brass door. It proved much smaller than the temple, although its paneled walls were also of metal. The ceiling was arched, but low; the room was packed with exquisite furnishings.

Singhar Bund motioned the bearded man to a chair that looked as ornate as a rajah's throne.

"Why should we deal in pretense?" purred Singhar Bund. "You would be more comfortable without your disguise, Inspector Cardona!"

THE bearded man gave a start. A grunt came from his lips. After a moment's hesitation, he plucked away the white whiskers. Peeling the shocky wig from his head, he revealed himself as the person named by Singhar Bund.

"How did you figure who I was?" demanded Cardona, abruptly. "I've never met you, so far as I can remember."

"Your beard was obviously a false one," replied Singhar Bund. "I would advise you to obtain a better one. The wig, though, is excellent."

"You haven't answered my question," persisted Cardona. "I'll admit that the Santa Claus outfit looks like a fake. But that didn't tell you whose face was behind the bushes."

Singhar Bund smiled placidly.

"Much is known to those who serve Siva," he declared. "Should you be too skeptical to accept that explanation, let us say that I solved your identity through simple deduction. You will grant that any person coming to this meeting in disguise, could logically be taken for a police investigator."

Cardona granted that much.

"Very well," concluded Singhar Bund. "But why should such an investigator need a disguise at all? There is but one answer. He would have to be a person so definitely in the public eye, that he would fear recognition.

"There are very few police officials to whom that would apply. You are one of those few, inspector." Singhar Bund bowed with smug courtesy. "Moreover, you top the list. That is why I named you."

The explanation satisfied Cardona. While hearing it, Joe was choosing his next step. He had, at least, gained one benefit. He had penetrated to the private room that formed Singhar Bund's headquarters. Cardona decided to press that advantage.

"There's some questions I'd like to ask," he declared, "about this racket of yours."

"A racket?" Singhar Bund arched his thin eyebrows, as though he had never heard the term. "I do not understand, inspector. My Siva cult is a legitimate organization. Its meetings are not only orderly, they are attended by persons of culture and refinement. If you have come here on a complaint, I can assure you that it is unwarranted."

"I've come to inquire about two people," put in Cardona, bluntly. "One is named Courtney Renshell; the other is Jack Sarmon. I'd like to know where they are."

Singhar Bund pondered.

"I recall Renshell," he declared. "For a while, he was a *chela*—the name we give to true followers of Siva. But worldly matters interfered. Renshell became a skeptic. He has not attended the past few meetings. As for Sarmon, the name is unfamiliar."

SINGHAR BUND lifted a small, padded hammer; he tapped a bronze gong. A scrawny Hindu appeared from the temple; Cardona heard Singhar Bund babble words in Hindustani. Among them was the name of Phineas Leeth.

The Hindu servitor was gone for nearly a minute; when he reappeared, he ushered Leeth into the grotto. Pausing in his hobble, Leeth stared at Cardona. His tired eyes showed surprise, then chagrin, when they noted the absence of Cardona's disguise.

"Be at ease, Mr. Leeth," purred Singhar Bund. "I am not angered because you brought Inspector Cardona here. I merely wish to know whether he came at your request, or his own."

Leeth admitted that he had called Cardona.

Singhar Bund inquired if the matter concerned Courtney Renshell. Leeth replied in the affirmative. Singhar Bund opened the deep drawer of a thick-legged table. He found a typewritten card, that he handed to Cardona.

"This is all that I know regarding Renshell," assured Singhar Bund. "His name; his address; his attendance record. But the other man—Sarmon"— Singhar Bund looked through his files—"is not listed here."

Leeth put in an explanation. Sarmon was not a member of the Siva cult; he was merely a friend of Renshell's. Cardona remembered that Leeth had stated that fact in the hotel suite. The whole trail was leading away from Singhar Bund and the Siva cult.

Cardona was silently classing Leeth as an old fool for bringing him here, when Singhar Bund provided a helpful remark.

"I cannot understand why Renshell left us," he declared. "For a while, he followed Siva ardently. He even brought a new student, who has become a true *chela*. I have her card here: her name is Lucille Mayland."

Cardona riveted. His thoughts snapped to an instant connection. He was right, he decided, regarding last night's trouble on Long Island. Welk's falling overboard had nothing to do with the brawl on shore.

Hoodlums had been on their way to Long Island before Welk's accident. There was a reason why they could have picked the dock where the *Wanderer* was stationed. Lucille had been there!

It fitted like a glove. Somebody had gotten rid of Courtney Renshell. To clinch his disappearance, other persons had to be hushed. One was Jack Sarmon, Renshell's close friend. Another could logically be Lucille Mayland.

"The girl was Renshell's fiancée," mused Singhar Bund. "She should know facts concerning him. Miss Mayland was here tonight; but she left immediately after the meeting."

Cardona hadn't seen Lucille. He had been too busy watching Singhar Bund and the yogi. Singhar Bund remarked that a young man had accompanied Lucille to the meeting; but he was a stranger, and Singhar Bund had not inquired his name.

Meanwhile, Cardona had reached for Lucille's card. He read the girl's address. He asked Singhar Bund who else lived there. The Hindu was not certain.

"She lives with her uncle, I believe," said Singhar Bund. "Or perhaps her guardian."

"Her grandfather," corrected Leeth. "His name is Morton Mayland. Sarmon mentioned him. In fact"—Leeth rubbed his chin reflectively—"I believe that Sarmon intended to call at the Mayland residence, to inquire regarding Renshell."

THAT was enough for Cardona. He bundled his false beard and wig; stuffed the disguise into his pocket. Reaching for his hat, he told his companions that he was going directly to the Mayland home.

Phineas Leeth nodded approvingly from his chair; he smiled when Cardona assured him that he would soon hear more about the Renshell matter. Leeth remained in the grotto, while Singhar Bund conducted Cardona out through the deserted temple.

There, Cardona shook hands warmly. He owed thanks to Singhar Bund; also an apology for having mistrusted him. Singhar Bund made light of the matter. He was serious, though, when he presented Cardona with a tiny Siva image.

"Carry this," urged Singhar Bund. "Regard it as a token of my friendship and good will. Whether or not you believe in the power of Siva, this little charm will assure your safety and will bring success to your present venture."

Cardona thrust the little image into his coat pocket. When Joe had left the temple, Singhar Bund stood alone. A glisten came to the Hindu's eyes; his lips parted, to form a contorted smile. Stepping to the giant statue of Siva, Singhar Bund delivered an audible hiss.

The tone was different from the serpent signals that Harry Vincent had heard. After he had hissed, Singhar Bund spoke to the faces of the statue. His words were cryptic, although he uttered them in English:

"All has gone well. The time has come for the one required deed. Let it be done."

Singhar Bund stepped away from the statue. The insidious smile faded from his lips as he opened the brass door to the grotto. Singhar Bund was rejoining his pupil, Phineas Leeth, to discourse on the ways of Siva.

CHAPTER IX
THE SHADOW'S TRAIL

EVER since Harry's departure from the Mayland residence, The Shadow had been investigating the old mansion and the houses that adjoined it. The task had proven an exacting one.

In effecting his first entry, The Shadow had come through a next-door house, hoping to find a route across some connecting roof. He had struck luck in a lower hallway of the adjoining house, before he even reached the stairs.

There, The Shadow's flashlight had shown a panel in the wall, open half an inch. Following it, he had found a passage that led behind the stairs in Mayland's house. That accounted for The Shadow's presence, when Harry came to meet Lucille.

Inspecting Mayland's house, The Shadow had gone everywhere except in the second floor sitting room. That was where Morton Mayland had retired; it was unwise to let the old man know that the premises were being scoured.

Returning to the lower passage, The Shadow went back to the first house; searched it without finding anything of importance. Then, moving along the secret passage, he had made a valuable discovery.

The passage ended in a rough-hewn trapdoor. Beneath was a ladder, that led down into a blocked-off portion of the cellar. The far wall showed a gap in the masonry. The opening led to the farther house in the group of three.

Searching the cellar of the empty house, The Shadow found streaks in the dust outside a white-washed coalbin. Working on the boards, he easily loosened them. There were boxes on the floor of the bin; shifting them, The Shadow uncovered a huge stone fitted in the floor. Its iron ring proved it to be the entrance to some subterranean chamber.

The thick slab was too heavy for one man to lift. The Shadow met that difficulty by a system of leverage. Loose bricks were available; he set them as a fulcrum, then applied a long piece of iron pipe that he found in the cellar.

The slab was budging under The Shadow's prodding effort, when the cloaked worker suddenly ceased his task.

A sharp sound had knifed its echoes into this hidden bin. It was the unmistakable tingle of a telephone bell.

That ringing could come from only one source: Mayland's own house.

The Shadow had seen a telephone in the lower hall. If the old man did not have an extension line upstairs, it would take him a few minutes to answer the call. There was a chance that The Shadow could listen into Mayland's conversation.

The Shadow heard the tingle again, as he emerged from the coalbin. His trip, though, was a long one, even with the guiding beam of his tiny flashlight. He had to travel across one cellar, through the broken wall to Mayland's own house, up the ladder to the passage.

WHEN The Shadow finally reached the panel that opened into Mayland's hallway, he found himself too late. Inching the panel open, he glimpsed Morton Mayland at the front door. The old man was wearing hat and overcoat. He gave the door a hasty slam, an instant after The Shadow spotted him.

Stepping into the hall, The Shadow closed the panel. He followed the same route that Mayland had taken. Edging the front door open, The Shadow spied Mayland beside a street lamp, beckoning toward the apartment building at the corner. Mayland received prompt service. A taxi wheeled up.

The Shadow took advantage of that interval to ease through the front door. Closing it, he descended the steps. He was against the blackness of the brownstone building front when Mayland entered the cab. The Shadow caught the old fellow's hasty order to the cabby.

"Riverbank Apartments," cackled Mayland. "It's on West Eighty-eighth Street. I'll give you the number—"

The cab had started, with Mayland fumbling for the paper on which he had written the number. His destination was evidently one that had been given him over the telephone.

Another taxi detached itself from the corner and rolled up toward the brownstone house. The Shadow expected that. He had a cab of his own, manned by one of his agents—a clever hackie named Moe Shrevnitz—that he had stationed close at hand.

In his orders to Moe, The Shadow had stated that if anyone came to Mayland's or left there, Moe should cruise the street, watching for a signal.

The signal was to be a series of blinks from The Shadow's flashlight. It happened that The Shadow did not give them.

Just as his thumb was about to press the button, The Shadow observed that the cab was not Moe's. It was an extra taxi that had been stationed near the apartment house. For some reason, it had followed the first one, so promptly that Moe had been unable to start.

The strange cab halted squarely in front of Mayland's house. The Shadow could see the driver's face, muffled in the collar of his overcoat. The fellow hunched beside the wheel and waited.

Although this cab was worth investigation, The Shadow could not spare time for it. The cab's arrival on the scene was proof that something special lay behind Mayland's mission. Looking toward the corner, The Shadow saw Moe's cab. It hadn't budged from its station. Moe was smart enough to await The Shadow there.

A quick trip to the corner would enable The Shadow to board Moe's cab. By speedy driving, he could reach the Riverbank Apartments ahead of Mayland. That chance was too good to lose. The Shadow edged from darkness, preparing for a swift glide past the street lamp. He waited a moment, at the sound of footsteps.

A stocky man came out of the darkness; stopped short at Mayland's steps. He looked toward the dim house, then turned toward the cab. That was when The Shadow saw the arrival's face. The newcomer was Joe Cardona.

The ace detective had decided to question the driver of the mystery cab. This was worth observation by The Shadow. He drew closer in the darkness.

"WHO are you waiting for?" The Shadow heard Cardona say. "Anybody from this house?"

The cabby didn't reply until Cardona flashed a badge. Seeing the emblem of authority, the fellow became voluble.

"I ain't waiting for anybody," he growled. "I'm sore, that's what, at the way I was gypped out of a fare! An old gink comes hopping out of this house, see? He gives the high-sign, and I wheel up.

"Then another hack cuts in front of me, and the old geezer takes it. Leaving me here, with nobody! That was just a minute ago—and here I am, still talking to myself."

The cabby had lied regarding the incident; he had also lessened the time interval, for Mayland had been gone fully five minutes. The Shadow sensed that something else was due. It came, when Cardona questioned:

"Where did the old gent go? Got any idea?"

"Have I?" snorted the cab driver. "Didn't he holler it loud enough to wake the neighborhood? He said he wanted to go to the Riverbank Apartments, on Eighty-eighth Street. And besides that—this is a funny one—he was so excited that he gave the apartment number instead of street address. 5 B was what he said."

Cardona yanked open the door of the cab.

"Get going," he told the driver. "To the Riverbank Apartments."

From that conversation, The Shadow had come to prompt conclusions. It was plain that Cardona's driver was hooked up with some curious game. He had arrived here close after the other cab, knowing beforehand where Morton Mayland intended to go. Hence he had told Cardona the address, without having overheard it. Moreover, he had specified an added detail—the apartment number—that Mayland had not mentioned to his own driver.

Just what the game promised was a riddle; but The Shadow saw its likely connection with the past. This was the sort of thing that could be the buildup to a fake accident, like the death of Rodney Welk.

If so, it indicated the coming presence of dacoit murderers at the Riverbank Apartments.

Cardona's cab was gone. The Shadow's flashlight blinked. Moe sped up from the corner; the moment that The Shadow had given him the address, the cabby reported:

"I don't know who sent that second hack here. It shoved into sight just about five minutes before the old guy came out of the house."

THE cab was whipping along an avenue. The Shadow gave Moe another order. The cab halted; Moe hurried into a cigar store to make a telephone call, that took him only two minutes. That was time lost; but it was necessary.

The Shadow had not forgotten that cover-up crews worked with the dacoits. He had ordered Moe to call Burbank, instructing the contact man to

With a snakelike twist, the dacoit whipped the strangle cord toward a more important victim: The Shadow!

send agents to Eighty-eighth Street. If it came to widespread battle, The Shadow could find use for capable reserves.

Moe was back at the wheel; the taxi was bowling northward. A low laugh throbbed from the darkness of the rear seat, as Moe cut in and out of traffic. Cars jammed the avenue ahead; Moe hooked a left turn at the last flicker of the green light. He was cutting through to another avenue, where the going would be faster.

Lost minutes would mean little to The Shadow, by the time this ride was completed. He could

count on Moe to cut down the distance gained by those cabs ahead. The Shadow was confident that he had already overtaken Cardona. He might not catch up with Mayland, but he would be very close, by the time the first cab reached the Riverbank Apartments.

Beneath the folds of his black cloak, The Shadow gripped the cold steel that represented a brace of automatics. His laugh was a tone of whispered prophecy.

Those big guns would again be needed, before tonight's adventure reached its finish.

CHAPTER X
MURDERER'S THRUST

THE Riverbank Apartments, while not on the shores of the Hudson, were close enough to allow for the name. A squatly warehouse flanked the western courtyard of the apartment building.

The top of that warehouse came on a level with the fifth floor of the Riverbank Apartments. To the rear was a row of old houses that fronted on another street. A medley of other buildings chopped the block into a maze of nooks and alleyways.

Morton Mayland was not concerned with the outside scene, when he stopped at the fifth floor door that bore the number "5 B." Raising a scrawny hand, Mayland knocked. A rumbled voice ordered him to enter.

Mayland stepped into a living room where floor lamps formed the only illumination. He closed the door behind him, looked across the room to see a figure seated near the opened windows. A head raised from an easy chair; hands laid a book aside.

An instant later, two men were glaring in mutual recognition. Mayland was the first to cough the other's name:

"Louis Bolingbroke!"

The man in the chair was middle-aged, dark-haired, dark-eyed. His blunt face was a stubborn one; his lips, when they turned downward, showed as sour an expression as Mayland's. Bolingbroke was prompt in his response.

"So it's Morton Mayland!" His rumbly voice carried contempt. "Hounding me again! What brings you here, Mayland? I thought our disputes were settled in the law courts."

Mayland advanced. His fists were clenched; his wrinkled face was tigerish. Those tiny eyes had narrowed; they flashed hate toward Bolingbroke.

"You brought me here," croaked Mayland. "You were not content with your spoils. This hoax was your idea, to gloat over your undeserved victory!"

"Come, Mayland!" rasped Bolingbroke. "This is preposterous!"

Bolingbroke tried to rise. His back gave him a twinge. He was half crippled with lumbago; but Mayland seemed to consider his pain a pretense. As Bolingbroke sagged deep into his chair, Mayland crouched above him.

"Have you forgotten what I promised?" The old man's words came in a hiss. "I warned you, Bolingbroke, that if occasion offered, I would treat you like the rat you are! I told you that these hands of mine"—Mayland extended his scraggly claws—"were itching for your throat!"

Bolingbroke forced himself up from his chair. Fear made him forget pain.

"You didn't really mean that, Mayland—"

"No?" Mayland was disdainful. "You will find out what I really meant, Bolingbroke. I have given you a chance to leave me alone. I have sworn, time and again, that I would not harm you if you stayed from my path. The fault is yours. You have brought this on yourself—"

Mayland completed the words with a quick swoop of his hands. They went for Bolingbroke's throat; the dark-haired man made a clutch to prevent the throttling move. The pair locked in battle.

BOTH fighters were handicapped. Mayland's hate could not make up for his age. Bolingbroke's greater strength was offset by his crippled muscles. Mayland's clutching hands were seeking their mark. To avoid their grip, Bolingbroke rolled from the chair.

The battlers struck a floor lamp; it wobbled, almost fell. There was the clatter of an ash stand. With it, every light in the room was obliterated.

In the darkness, neither Mayland nor Bolingbroke cared about the matter. They were too busy to wonder why the lights had been extinguished. The floor plug that controlled all the lamps was beside an inner doorway, far from the fighters. Yet each thought that the other had caused the darkness.

Other sounds were lost as the strugglers lashed about. Mayland was cackling gleefully at Bolingbroke's shouts for help. The old man was clawing anew for his enemy's throat, when the cries reached a sharp finish.

There was a gurgle from the floor. It was Bolingbroke who gave it. Mayland's laughter shrilled.

Those sounds drowned the sudden clatter of the door. Light from the hallway showed the floor, but did not reach the strugglers. The glow that swept them was the cleaving beam of a tiny flashlight, that spotted an astounding tableau.

Bolingbroke was crumpled on the floor, clutching hopelessly at his neck. Mayland was astride him; but it was not the old man who was responsible for Bolingbroke's torture. The cause lay with another creature, who had secretly entered the room.

Behind Bolingbroke's side-turned head was a Hindu dacoit, whose brown fingers were tightening a strangle cord flung about the invalid's neck!

The dacoit saw the flashlight's beam. A hiss came from his toothy mouth, as he stared toward the opened door. The hiss was answered by a weird laugh: the mockery that only The Shadow could produce.

With a snakelike twist, the dacoit sprang away, whipping the strangle cord from Bolingbroke's neck.

The murderous Hindu hoped for a more important victim; namely, The Shadow. After that, he could return to Bolingbroke.

THE living room was ample for slippery tactics. With amazing speed, the dacoit avoided the flashlight's path. Like a whippet, he lashed through the darkness, driving for The Shadow. The flashlight blinked out as the strangle cord slacked through the air.

The murderer's noose missed The Shadow's neck. Before the dacoit could whisk away, The Shadow gripped him. The twisty Hindu squirmed toward the window, but he could not elude The Shadow's clutch.

Mayland's cackles, Bolingbroke's groans formed an accompaniment to that battle. Wriggling half through the window, the dacoit grabbed the slatted platform of a steel fire escape, gave a jerk that hauled his body through. The Shadow was upon him before he could slip away again.

There, by the rail, The Shadow's gun descended. The dacoit's quick arm movement broke the blow; with the same sweep, it lashed the cord around The Shadow's neck. Before The Shadow's eyes came the apish face. A hiss, more venomous than any serpent's, forced itself between the dacoit's teeth.

The strangler had tricked The Shadow!

The black-cloaked form was sagging, like others that the dacoit had handled. A few more twists of the noose, The Shadow's strength would be gone. The Hindu's fingers were eager with their ugly work; he heard the gurgle from The Shadow's throat.

Then came the counter movement.

Cloaked shoulder hoisted upward; gloved hands lifted the dacoit's knees. With every ounce of his remaining effort, The Shadow fought off his foeman's final move. That heave caught the dacoit unawares. Fingers lost the strangle cord; arms went wide. Grabbing for the fire escape rail, the dacoit shifted in the wrong direction.

Before The Shadow could stay the Hindu, the snakish man was gone across the rail!

There was a crash, three stories below, as the dacoit hit the roof of an extension behind the apartment building. The Shadow took long puffs of air, as he placed the dacoit's strangle cord beneath his cloak.

It had been a close pinch, that fight; and The Shadow needed time to recuperate. He wasn't worried about matters in the living room. Bolingbroke's groans were still audible, and Mayland's chuckles had lost their insane fury. The old man was apparently satisfied, once he had rendered Bolingbroke helpless.

Darkness was utter in the courtyard below, but The Shadow could hear the occasional hisses of the

A hiss forced itself between the dacoit's teeth. The strangler had tricked The Shadow!

dacoit. Light-framed as a monkey, the defeated killer had survived his thirty-foot fall; but he was too crippled to make a prompt getaway. There was still a chance to capture the dacoit. The Shadow arose beside the rail.

AT that instant, the lights in the living room came on again. Turned toward the window, The Shadow had an inward view that showed him the entire scene.

Bolingbroke, flat on the floor; Mayland, crouched beside him; they were not all.

A man had reached in from the next room, to

press the floor plug back in place. He was no Hindu, that intruder; he had the look of a thug whose cap was drawn well over his eyes. His move was the forerunner of the sort that The Shadow had expected—a battle from a cover-up crew, after a dacoit's deed was finished.

The fellow was gone, into that other room, while The Shadow's hands were drawing forth their guns. But The Shadow did not halt his motion. He knew exactly what those lights could mean. Upon quick action with those automatics would depend The Shadow's salvation.

As he whipped the guns into play, The Shadow wheeled about to face across the fire platform's rail. Simultaneously, he was greeted with raucous shouts from the darkness opposite. The edge of the warehouse roof was lined with thuggish marksmen, who could not resist the joy of voicing challenge.

Their pal in the apartment had provided the very chance they wanted. The Shadow was their target, against a background of light.

If ever crooks had gained a full advantage in battle with The Shadow, this crew had found it.

Their cries were a promise of annihilation.

Death to The Shadow!

CHAPTER XI
THE TRIPLE TRAIL

HIS big guns spoke as The Shadow wheeled. Each .45 was aimed at random, although The Shadow chose the roof line as the stretch where bullets could count. He wanted to loose the first shots; he knew they would hurry the enemy's fire.

Revolvers answered. They were hasty. Bullets spattered the wall of the apartment house. The cooler marksmen were aiming for the lighted windows, fingers still on triggers, but they were few. The Shadow evaded them.

His spin did not stop at the full turn. The Shadow was sidestepping as he fired. His swerve carried him along the platform, away from the telltale windows. Two guns barked from the roof just as The Shadow moved. One bullet whistled past The Shadow's shoulder, the other skimmed his ribs.

The wound was stabbing, painful; at the moment, The Shadow did not realize that it was a light one. He flattened in the darkness, determined to continue his plan as long as he proved able. His guns spat again; this time, with results.

The Shadow had an uncanny way of picking gunbursts as his targets. His shots were accurate; howls came from the roof. They were drowned by a new rattle of revolvers. Crooks were shooting for The Shadow, knowing that he could not have traveled far, for the platform of the fire escape provided very little space.

Given a few seconds more, the outnumbering

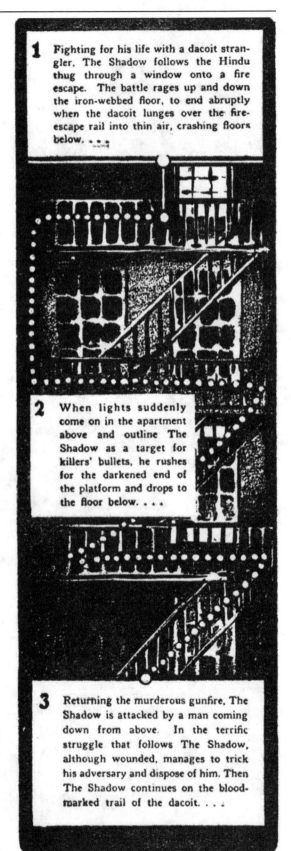

1 Fighting for his life with a dacoit strangler. The Shadow follows the Hindu thug through a window onto a fire escape. The battle rages up and down the iron-webbed floor, to end abruptly when the dacoit lunges over the fire-escape rail into thin air, crashing floors below. . . .

2 When lights suddenly come on in the apartment above and outline The Shadow as a target for killers' bullets, he rushes for the darkened end of the platform and drops to the floor below. . . .

3 Returning the murderous gunfire, The Shadow is attacked by a man coming down from above. In the terrific struggle that follows The Shadow, although wounded, manages to trick his adversary and dispose of him. Then The Shadow continues on the blood-marked trail of the dacoit. . . .

gunmen would have riddled The Shadow with well-placed bullets. It happened that The Shadow had strategy with which they did not reckon. Purposely, The Shadow had chosen what seemed a trap. He had taken to the end of the platform opposite from that of the ladder. The sharpshooters never expected that he would try to reach a spot below.

That was why The Shadow took that course. The moment that he had delivered those shots from prone position, he rolled beneath the rail. Clutching both guns in one hand, he clamped the platform with his other fist and let his body sweep downward. That very motion gave him a sway; as he swung inward, The Shadow relaxed his grip, to plop upon the fourth floor platform.

Bullets pounded the metalwork above. The Shadow let that barrage subside. As sequel, he provided a chilling, mocking laugh. Before the crooks could guess the location of the mirth, The Shadow announced it with bullets.

Shifting back and forth along the rail, The Shadow forgot his wounded side, as he pumped devastation with his guns. Shooting upward, he was picking off the enemy like pigeons on a shooting-gallery rack.

Some were fools enough to fire back. They regretted it. The Shadow always chose as targets the last to shoot at him, as evidenced by his revolver shots. He reached the end of the platform that had a ladder; there were no lighted windows here to betray him. Giving the gunmen a respite, The Shadow descended another story.

THE battle ended more rapidly than The Shadow had expected. There were mobsters in the courtyard below; they began to fire upward, even though The Shadow was protected by the steel platform. They stopped promptly, when police whistles shrilled in the distance.

Other guns began to speak. Crooks were in flight, shouting that the bulls had arrived. Only The Shadow knew the real identity of the new attackers. His agents had arrived. Easing downward, The Shadow continued toward the courtyard.

Almost at the bottom of the fire escape, The Shadow sensed a muffled clatter above him. For the moment, he forgot the dacoit that he wanted to find. This was the man from that other room: the troublemaker who had switched on the lights!

Though ordinary hoodlums had shown ignorance when quizzed by the police, The Shadow knew that every mob required a leader. There were brains among those cover-up squads; and any man smart enough to invade Bolingbroke's apartment, would certainly have intelligence.

That man who followed The Shadow was one who could tell facts regarding recent murders, as readily as any dacoit.

The Shadow waited. His quarry arrived. With a *swish,* the cloaked fighter was upon the fellow, smothering him in the darkness of that lower platform.

The thug had supposed that The Shadow was gone; nevertheless, he was alert—enough so to put up a frenzied struggle, as he hit the platform. Ordinarily, such resistance would have been short-lived. Once The Shadow had the edge in a combat of this sort, an opponent seldom rallied. Tonight, the case was different.

Shifting to gain a complete clutch, The Shadow let his adversary writhe leftward. The Shadow swung in the same direction, jolting hard against the rail. The jounce came squarely on those ribs that had deflected a marksman's bullet.

The hard shock brought immediate agony; instinctively, The Shadow pressed his hand against his side.

The crook caught the rail, came upward. He felt The Shadow's slump, took advantage of it. The conflict underwent a swift reversal; the mobster had the superior position. It was his own luck that made him overeager, plus his ignorance of The Shadow's wounded condition.

Figuring that his advantage was temporary, the crook tried to end matters in a hurry. They were a single flight above the ground, battling close to the hinged steps that hung from the fire escape. The crook shoved The Shadow for the space below.

In those split seconds, The Shadow showed quick strategy. Instead of fighting back, he let himself go. Flung backward to the ladder, he twisted to the right, to land on his unwounded side. He struck the ladder arm first; grabbed hard for a metal step.

It worked as The Shadow calculated. His sudden drop made the crook's forward motion a long one. The fellow couldn't halt himself; he came plunging for The Shadow. But The Shadow wasn't there when the thug landed. The ladder was swinging downward with the cloaked fighter's weight. The crook found emptiness.

Headfirst, the fellow pitched clear over The Shadow, clutching the air as he went. He hit the lower steps, but his momentum was too powerful for him to catch a hold. He finished his plunge with a series of bounces that flattened him in the courtyard.

THE SHADOW changed position slowly, painfully. He was hanging head downward on the steps; he favored his wounded side as he eased around. Whistles were shrilling closer when he reached the ground; the sirens of patrol cars had joined the bedlam. There was not much time to lose.

The Shadow stooped above the silent mobster. Playing his flashlight on a flattish, tough-jawed face, he recognized his assailant. The fellow was

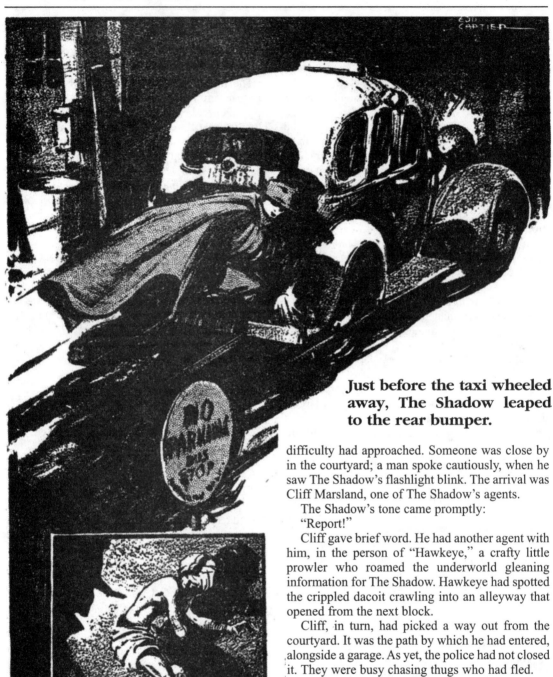

Just before the taxi wheeled away, The Shadow leaped to the rear bumper.

difficulty had approached. Someone was close by in the courtyard; a man spoke cautiously, when he saw The Shadow's flashlight blink. The arrival was Cliff Marsland, one of The Shadow's agents.

The Shadow's tone came promptly:

"Report!"

Cliff gave brief word. He had another agent with him, in the person of "Hawkeye," a crafty little prowler who roamed the underworld gleaning information for The Shadow. Hawkeye had spotted the crippled dacoit crawling into an alleyway that opened from the next block.

Cliff, in turn, had picked a way out from the courtyard. It was the path by which he had entered, alongside a garage. As yet, the police had not closed it. They were busy chasing thugs who had fled.

The Shadow ordered his agents to carry Lucky through that route, leaving it to Cliff to talk to the fellow later. Cliff understood. He and Hawkeye departed with their burden. The Shadow took the more difficult route that led to the dacoit's trail.

He had reached the street when he saw police closing in on the very passage that Cliff had chosen. Pointing an automatic upward, The Shadow fired two shots. That brought the officers in his direction. They saw the gun spurts, but they did not spy the shape that took to a blackened stretch across the street.

"Lucky" Belther, long a lieutenant of notorious racketeers. Lucky had a double reputation. He could frame victims, or put them on the spot—whichever the big shots chose.

Lucky was senseless; that made his removal a problem for The Shadow. But the solution to the

When they arrived at the spot where the shots were fired, The Shadow was gone.

From the alleyway that Hawkeye had mentioned, The Shadow saw his agents lug Lucky past the garage. The patrolmen were too puzzled over the disappearance of the unknown gunner to look in the other direction. His agents clear, The Shadow sought the dacoit's trail.

Blobs of blood furnished the needed route. The dacoit had been badly injured by his long fall. The telltale splotches crossed the next street, entered a space between two buildings on the opposite side. Another block, and The Shadow saw the dacoit himself.

The Hindu was crawling into a taxicab; its number was that of the cab that had brought Mayland to the Riverbank Apartments.

Just before the taxi wheeled away, The Shadow leaped to the rear bumper. Pressed close to the trunk rack, he clung there despite the increased pain from his wounded side.

The cabby chose secluded streets, until he reached an East Side avenue. There, he sped several blocks beneath an elevated, made a turn and stopped on a side street.

The dacoit alighted; he began a huddled sneak into the darkness. The driver saw him depart; never guessed that the Hindu was badly injured. Close to the place he wanted, the dacoit was making a convulsive effort to reach it. The cab pulled away, leaving The Shadow on the street, unseen.

BACK at the Riverbank Apartments, the law had taken over. Joe Cardona was standing in the living room of 5 B, watching a physician revive Louis Bolingbroke. Two policemen held Morton Mayland in charge.

Bolingbroke's eyes opened. Stretched in his easy chair, the blunt-faced man stared toward Mayland. Rearing his head, Bolingbroke panted accusations.

"He tried to murder me!" Bolingbroke pointed to Mayland. "Here in this room! He had his hands on my throat—"

Bolingbroke sank back. Cardona looked at Mayland, who was standing subdued and bewildered. Cardona demanded to know what Mayland had to say for himself. The old man gave an ugly chortle. His eyes flashed new hatred.

"Bah!" uttered Mayland. "I lost my temper, that was all. But when my anger passed, I was satisfied. Bolingbroke hoaxed me into coming here—through Renshell."

"Courtney Renshell?" quizzed Cardona.

Mayland nodded.

"Where's Renshell right now?" demanded Joe. "Did you see him tonight?"

"No," replied Mayland. "The last time I saw Renshell was at my home."

"Then that's where we're going," snapped Cardona, inspired by a sudden hunch. "We'll hold the rest of the questions until we get there. Meanwhile, you're under arrest, on a charge of attempted murder."

In the back of Cardona's mind was his recollection of Mayland's old house, that loomed as gloomy as a silent mausoleum. Cardona had analyzed it as a likely place for murder. He wanted a chance to go inside that mansion, and Mayland's attack on Bolingbroke had provided it.

The triple trail was complete. Lucky Belther was in the hands of The Shadow's agents. The Shadow, himself, had followed the crippled dacoit to a hidden lair. Joe Cardona held Morton Mayland in custody.

Of those trails, two were The Shadow's own. The third, acquired by the law, was one that The Shadow could pick up whenever he might choose.

For the present, The Shadow was most concerned with the Hindu whose course he had pursued.

The Shadow had found a living Serpent of Siva!

CHAPTER XII
CRIME'S PROOF

Two hours produced big results for Joe Cardona. When the ace inspector worked on a case, he kept many men in motion. Once back at Mayland's house, Cardona displayed no hurry in his questioning of the elderly suspect. Joe was awaiting facts from other quarters.

He and his men were in Mayland's upstairs sitting room; frequently, Cardona was called downstairs to the telephone. Each time he made a trip, he left Mayland in the custody of stolid-faced detectives. The hostile looks of those watchdogs worried Mayland.

Meanwhile, Harry and Lucille arrived home from the theater. Cardona met them in the lower hall; checked on the fact that they had attended the meeting of the Siva cult. When Cardona mentioned that he had been there in disguise, Harry remembered the bearded face that he had seen.

To Cardona, however, the events at Bolingbroke's were most important. When he told of all that had happened there, Harry was puzzled, while Lucille showed horror. Cardona wanted them both to remain in the house for a while but he allowed Harry to make a telephone call.

That call was responsible for Cranston's arrival, just at the finish of the two-hour period. The Shadow came in company with the police commissioner, who had come in from the country.

The commissioner, Ralph Weston, had chanced to meet his friend Lamont Cranston, during a chance stop at the Cobalt Club, of which both were members.

As Cranston, The Shadow looked as calm as ever. His appearance was as usual, except for a slight bulge beneath the left side of his tuxedo jacket. The Shadow had found time to have his wound attended.

Cardona was pleased to see Weston and Cranston. The ace was ready to spring a surprise. He buzzed to a detective who was stationed in the downstairs hall. The fellow nodded. Cardona conducted the others up to the sitting room.

Morton Mayland narrowed his beady eyes when Cardona entered. He scarcely noted Lucille and the others. Mayland could tell that Cardona was ready to release a bombshell. He tightened his lips in readiness.

"You've answered a lot of questions, Mr. Mayland," declared Cardona, steadily. "I'm going to repeat a few of them and let you answer them again."

Mayland shrugged. There wasn't much threat in that assertion.

"WHEN did you last see Courtney Renshell?" demanded Cardona.

"A few weeks ago," replied Mayland. "When he called to see Lucille."

"And you next heard from him—"

"When I received this letter." Mayland produced it. "Renshell sent it from Havana."

Cardona brought out some papers from his pocket, compared them with the letter. Mayland smiled dryly.

"You will find," he declared, "that Renshell's signature is bona fide."

Cardona did not doubt the statement. The Shadow saw Joe stroke his finger along the top line of the letter, where the date was typewritten. There was a roughness there that Cardona had detected. The ace laid the letter aside.

"One more question, Mr. Mayland," put in Joe. "You say that you heard from Renshell *since* you received this letter?"

"Certainly," replied Mayland, crisply. "He called me on the telephone this evening. He wanted me to meet him at the Riverbank Apartments, in suite 5 B. So I went there, only to find Bolingbroke."

"Why do you suppose Renshell called you?"

"Probably because Bolingbroke put him up to it."

"But Bolingbroke declares he never heard from Renshell."

"Bah! Bolingbroke is not to be trusted!"

The Shadow was watching Mayland closely. The old man had certainly provided an explanation for a telephone call that he had actually received. It also could account for his hurried departure from the mansion. Nevertheless, the answer did not satisfy Cardona.

"You have tried to establish one fact," Joe told Mayland; "namely, that Renshell has been heard from within the past few weeks. You have a letter to prove he was in Havana a week ago; you declare you heard his voice over the telephone tonight."

Mayland nodded. Cardona beckoned to a detective. The dick brought an object that looked like a large flashlight equipped with an extension cord. Cardona plugged the wire into a floor socket. The device was a portable ultraviolet lamp from the police laboratory.

Cardona flicked the purplish rays on the letter. Under the revealing glare, the dateline showed new features. Like ghostly images, other typewritten words appeared there. They showed a date a year old!

Cardona wheeled to Lucille, with the question:

"Did Renshell take a trip to Havana a year ago?"

"Why, yes!" exclaimed the girl. "I didn't know where he had gone until he wrote to me."

"That's when he sent this letter to Mayland," snapped Cardona. "And you kept it, Mayland"— Joe was concentrating on the old man—"so you could fake it later. You didn't have to forge Renshell's signature. You simply erased one date and put in another, to make the letter appear recent."

Mayland's face was a riddle. His tiny eyes retained their stare; his lips were tighter than before. He gave no answer to Cardona's impeaching statement. Joe added another charge.

"Maybe you did get a telephone call tonight," he asserted, "but it wasn't from Renshell. Listen, Mayland; I've just received a report from Detective Sergeant Markham; I sent him over to Renshell's place. He says a box was shipped from there—a long box, something like a coffin. What do you know about that box?"

Mayland shook his head. He did not specify whether the matter puzzled him, or whether he was totally ignorant of it. Lucille was the person who gave answer.

"That must be the box that Jack Sarmon mentioned!" exclaimed the girl. "He was here—the night before the dory races when he spoke about it!"

"So Sarmon knew about the box?" Cardona had turned to Lucille. "Did he know where it was sent?"

"No. That was a fact he wanted to learn."

"It's one that Markham has found out. That box was shipped to this house!"

A HUSH enveloped the sitting room. Keen eyes watched from the calm face of Cranston; they were noting old Morton Mayland. The accused man was the first to speak. He licked his lips, emitted a cackly laugh, as he declared:

"Search these premises! From top to bottom! See what you can find!"

"We've found something already," retorted Cardona. "That back hallway behind the stairs is a pretty short one, Mayland. One of its panels sounded hollow when I tapped it."

The discovery did not perturb Mayland. He merely chuckled, as he turned to Lucille.

"The old side hallway," recalled Mayland. "Remember how drafty it used to be, Lucille? That is why I had the partition placed there. Of course, those panels would sound hollow."

"Especially the one that opens," jabbed Cardona. "You seem to have had use for that old hallway, Mayland."

Mayland couldn't seem to remember the panel that Cardona mentioned. To jog his memory, the inspector suggested a trip downstairs. When they arrived below, Cardona put detectives to work. They wedged the panel open.

Under the glare of flashlights, the sliding partition looked very crude, for it set a full inch deeper than the other panels. Cardona stepped through the opening, sprayed his flashlight to the left.

"Another panel, into the house next door," remarked Cardona. "You own that building, don't you, Mayland?"

The old man admitted it. Cardona investigated in the opposite direction; he found the trapdoor that led down into the cellar. The group was ready to go in that direction, when another arrival joined them.

This man was Phineas Leeth. Cardona had left word for him at the Ritz Plaza. Leeth listened, gaping, while he heard all that had happened. Then:

"Most amazing, inspector!" expressed Leeth. "Ah! How wise you were to talk with Singhar Bund."

The Hindu's name brought a fierce outburst from Mayland.

"Singhar Bund!" spat the old man. "That faker who duped my niece! He and his Siva cult—bah! I warned you, Lucille, to stay away from there. No one can be trusted who believes in that tommyrot!"

"Sarmon was not a member of the Siva group," objected Leeth, seriously. "He was the one person who was troubled regarding Renshell's disappearance."

"It should have worried me," inserted Lucille, with a cold stare toward old Mayland. "But I was deceived. Not by Singhar Bund, but by my own grandfather!"

Detectives had descended through the trapdoor, to find their way into the next cellar. When they reported, Cardona decided to take everyone to the house next door. They made a roundabout course, using keys that Mayland reluctantly handed over.

Search revealed the empty coalbin, with the steel-ringed slab in the floor. The stone was raised; a ladder was disclosed, leading into a darkened pit.

Cardona descended, followed by the commissioner and Cranston.

Detectives let down an extension cord. The glare of an electric bulb showed a squarish room. In one corner was a long box, nailed tightly shut.

That box bore Mayland's address, painted in scraggly letters.

Cardona told a detective to jimmy the box open. The ace had something else to investigate: a metal door that looked like the mouth of an oven, set in the brick wall. Opening that door, Cardona saw a grating covered with ashes. The space reeked with the odor of burning.

"An incinerator," stated Cardona, "connected with the furnace above. Look, commissioner!"

Cardona was pointing to human bones among the ashes. As he pulled the door wider, something slipped from beneath its hinge. The unwedged object thudded the stone floor. Cardona picked it up.

The object was a wristwatch, badly scorched; but the initials "C. R." were visible upon its back.

"Renshell's," declared Cardona. "He was shipped here in that box. This is where Mayland cremated the body. But why didn't he burn the box, too?"

The top of the box had just been ripped open. Inside lay the gory answer: the dismembered body of another man. Cardona saw a bloody wallet; opened it. He read a name from an identification card.

"Sarmon," said Cardona, soberly. "Chopped up and stowed away, until Mayland could find time to dispose of him the same way. That might have been tonight, if the old man hadn't decided to take a whack at Bolingbroke."

WHEN Cardona left those premises, Morton Mayland went with him. The old man was piteous and huddled, his beady eyes staring, his lips muttering silently. Mayland couldn't seem to understand that he was charged with double murder of the most gruesome sort.

At the Cobalt Club, Police Commissioner Weston tried to forget the hideous sight that he had viewed in the subcellar pit. He thought that Cranston was shaken, too, for his friend was silent and smileless.

Weston would have forgotten that impression, had he followed Cranston later. Leaving the Cobalt Club, the commissioner's friend stepped into his limousine. While the big car rolled eastward, Cranston donned garments of black.

It was the fleeting figure of The Shadow that finally approached a basement entrance in a squalid alley. The Shadow signaled with a low-toned whisper. It was answered by Hawkeye. No one had come to or left this spot within the past hour. Hawkeye, on a relayed order from The Shadow, had been guarding this place.

Sending his agent off duty, The Shadow used a tiny flashlight, while he probed the lock of a rickety door. Entering a dingy room, he found a figure stretched on a thin straw mattress. The scrawny shape was that of the crippled dacoit The Shadow had trailed from Bolingbroke's.

The Serpent was dead. His final spasms had brought him to this rathole where he dwelt. No one connected with the Siva outfit knew of this killer's fate. The Shadow's whispered laugh toned through that dank abode.

Dead, the snakish dacoit could serve The Shadow's plans; better, perhaps, than if the Serpent had remained alive. For tonight, The Shadow had received a full report from Harry Vincent.

The serpent's hiss that Harry had heard close by the Siva statue was a factor upon which The Shadow could base his future measures.

The Shadow had gained insight into the ways of those who followed the commands of Singhar Bund.

CHAPTER XIII
THE OUTER CIRCLE

Two men were seated at a battered table in a squalid room, where the flickery light of a gas jet showed a bottle and glasses placed between them. The air was choked with cigarette smoke, for the windows were tightly shut.

Shades were drawn, also, although outside light trickled past the fringes. Occasionally there came the muffled rumble of an elevated train, as it roared above the Bowery, only a half block away.

The room was the hideaway used by Lucky Belther. The triggerman was entertaining his rescuer, Cliff Marsland.

Lucky's eyes showed admiration between their slitted lids. The thrust of his tough jaw was another proof that he considered Cliff all right. His expression went with the approving words that he growled.

"You're a right guy, Cliff," spoke Lucky. "You yanked me out of a tight spot. There's not many birds could've done it."

Lucky poured himself a large drink; shoved the bottle across to Cliff. In his companion, Lucky saw a man as stolid as himself. Cliff's rugged countenance might have been chiseled from rock. His expression was poker-faced.

Cliff wrapped his fingers around the glass, poured himself a drink. It wasn't more than a swallow, but Lucky didn't guess the fact. Cliff's fingers hid the amount. Raising the glass, Cliff took the contents in one gulp.

"What gets me"—Lucky was bringing up a point that Cliff expected—"is how you showed up when you did. We weren't figuring on having an old home week."

"The coppers were in on it, weren't they?" returned Cliff, coolly. He thumped the bottle in front of Lucky. "So what was screwy about me being there?"

"The bulls were supposed to barge into the picture. That was fixed."

Cliff grinned as though he had heard news. He had another question, that would end Lucky's doubts.

"What about The Shadow?" demanded Cliff. "Did you invite him, too?"

Lucky spat an oath. He rubbed the side of his head, where he had taken a crack against the cement of the courtyard.

"We didn't want The Shadow," he snarled. "How he got into it is something I can't figure. We thought we were ready for him, but—"

"But you weren't," supplied Cliff. "Only I was, until your gorillas queered it."

LUCKY stared; his eyes were blank at first; slowly, they lighted. There was a rumor in the underworld that one tough guy had guts enough to seek a feud with The Shadow. Cliff was said to be that man.

Like others, Lucky had always supposed the story to be hot air, and had dismissed it. But here was Cliff, coolly advancing the claim, and behind it was the fact that Cliff had actually been dogging The Shadow's trail.

Lucky was thinking over events of a few hours ago. He didn't know all about them; and Cliff regarded that as fortunate. Lucky's partial knowledge was just enough to furnish a background for Cliff's bold bluff.

Lucky remembered his fall to the courtyard. He had waked up to find himself in a car driven by Cliff. His rescuer had asked him where to head. Recognizing Cliff, Lucky had told him of this hideout.

After that, Lucky had gone groggy again. When he felt better, he found himself in his own quarters, with Cliff standing by. There had been no sign of The Shadow during that interval. Another fact in Cliff's favor.

"I guess the fireworks did queer it," admitted Lucky. "But how'd you trail The Shadow, Cliff? I didn't know anybody could get away with it."

"The Shadow has stooges, hasn't he?"

Cliff's question brought a prompt nod from Lucky. It had long been conceded that The Shadow must have agents in the underworld, who tipped him off to crime. Lucky shot an eager question:

"You know who the guys are?"

"I'd like to know," replied Cliff, sourly. "The best I could do, though, was mooch in on a phone call that came to a joint on Tenth Avenue. I'd heard

The Shadow was over there; but he was gone when I showed up.

"I got the phone call instead. From some bird who said that Joe Cardona was heading for the Riverbank Apartments. I doped it that The Shadow must have got another tip-off, and was already on the way there. So I went."

Lucky was lighting a crumpled cigarette. His eyes had a glazed look, that wasn't entirely from the drinks that he had taken. He was gathering an idea. After a few moments, he expressed it.

"You've done good for yourself tonight, Cliff," declared Lucky. "You've cut yourself in on a slice of big dough. You know what I was going to do?" Lucky guffawed. "I was going to ask you to scram! Instead, I'm giving you a chance to get in on the racket."

Cliff considered; then shrugged.

"What's in it?" he asked. "A lot of slugs in the belly, like those gorillas of yours got tonight?"

"Not for a guy as smart as you are," replied Lucky. He pulled a watch from his pocket, glanced at it. "Stick around about ten minutes—if you want to be counted in."

Cliff was still dubious. Lucky produced a big bankroll, peeled off a thousand dollars in fifties.

"How's that for dough?" he questioned. "A grand—on the cuff—just for coming in with me."

Cliff took the wad, added it to a roll of his own. He remarked that Lucky was talking his own language. He could be counted in.

THE ten minutes passed. There was a scratchy sound at the door. Lucky motioned for silence; approaching the door, he growled:

"Who is it?"

A voice answered; it came from the keyhole. It uttered two words, hoarsely:

"An Eye!"

Lucky stooped. His own lips came close to the keyhole as he rasped a low answer:

"An Arm!"

The man who entered was a scrawny, pasty-faced fellow, known to Cliff. He was "Gummer" Gilben, an underworld sneak.

Gummer wasn't any too popular in scumland. Everybody knew him, with his baggy trousers, turtleneck sweater, and checkered cap pulled over one ear. Crooks were leery of Gummer, because they thought he was a stool pigeon.

Perhaps Gummer had acted as a stoolie. If so, it was a blind, to keep the police in ignorance of his real work. For the fact that Gummer was in cahoots with Lucky was proof sufficient that the sneak was staging crime.

Gummer wasn't pleased when he saw Cliff. Darty eyes shot a questioning look at Lucky. The flattish-faced crook assured the visitor that Cliff was O.K.; to prove it, Lucky recounted the part that Cliff had played.

It wasn't until after he had poured himself a drink that Gummer made comment.

"What've you told Cliff?" he demanded.

"Not much," resumed Lucky, "but I'm set to spill the works. You know how we stand. You or me—either one—can take in any guy we want."

"I ain't needing nobody in my end of it."

"I wasn't neither, Gummer, until tonight. But my end's got more grief. I may need Cliff again."

Gummer swallowed his drink. He looked Cliff over, as if checking the story that he had heard. His objections faded. He decided that Lucky had the privilege of taking Cliff into it. Lucky lost no time.

"Here's the setup," the triggerman told Cliff. "There's a lot of guys called Eyes—only they don't know it—and Gummer, here, is the bozo who runs them. It's their job to spot certain boobs and see just what they do.

"Then there's another outfit, the Arms. They're clucks, too, that do just what they're told. I run them, see? Only I don't tell them what it's all about. None except you, Cliff."

Cliff gave a short laugh.

"It sounds screwy" was his comment. Then, remembering something: "Except for the dough you handed me. All right. I've followed it so far. The Eyes and the Arms. For what?"

"So the Serpents can croak the stuffed shirts," explained Lucky. "They're another outfit, the Serpents. They do their stuff smooth. The guys they knock off are big-money boys. They do it so neat, everybody thinks it's accidents."

THOUGH Lucky didn't guess it, he was giving Cliff a lot of information that even he, Lucky, did not possess. Cliff had gotten facts regarding the Siva cult from The Shadow. He saw clearly how the whole game copied the symbolism of the Siva statue.

Some genius of evil was using the Siva cult to insidious purpose. Those dacoits were the Serpents who murdered wealthy persons, that their heirs—already members of the cult—could contribute huge funds to Siva. But the Serpents, with all their ability as assassins, could do no more than commit the actual deeds of murdering victims.

Others had to inform when the stage was set, and be on hand to make sure that it stayed that way. They were the Eyes, controlled by Gummer. Still more were needed—strong-arm men who could cover up the flight of the Serpents and throw a false trail to the law. They were the Arms, who took their orders from Lucky.

Considering past deaths, Cliff saw clearly how the outside circle had worked. In the case of Welk, for instance, the Eyes had learned about the cabin cruiser; had seen that the right boxes were aboard.

The Arms had shown up later, bringing a Serpent to contact the one who had hidden aboard the *Wanderer.*

Lucky was right, when he said the Arms had tougher going than the Eyes. Gummer's squad of Eyes—fake taxi drivers and their ilk—were as strong as ever. But battles with The Shadow had thinned the ranks of Lucky's Arms.

Lucky not only needed new recruits; he wanted a capable lieutenant. Cliff was the right man, for he had apparently proven himself in battle with The Shadow. Thus he had come into the outside circle of Eyes and Arms, on an almost equal basis with Lucky.

With Cliff's part established, Lucky and Gummer discussed matters that The Shadow's agent found valuable. Each had a separate hideout; there, they received orders, by telephone, from an unknown source, and made reports, in return. Gummer had already made his report, tonight.

"The Serpent got clear," he told Lucky. "One of the Eyes took him in a taxi. That's why you haven't had a call, asking you what happened to him. I sent the dope through."

When Cliff left, after arranging to return at an appointed hour, Lucky and Gummer were still in conference. They discussed Cliff as soon as he had gone.

"He's the guy I needed," commented Lucky. "He'll be worth his dough. There's a lot of ways I can use him."

"Looks that way to me," agreed Gummer. "Particularly, with this business of him gunning for The Shadow."

"That's what I'm counting on," completed Lucky. "I got a hunch, Gummer, that it won't be long before Cliff meets up with The Shadow."

Lucky was a better prophet than he guessed. At that very moment, Cliff Marsland was on his way to keep an appointment with The Shadow.

CHAPTER XIV
CRIME'S NEW NIGHT

HARRY VINCENT was seated in the lobby of the Hotel Metrolite, glancing over an evening's newspaper. Days had passed since the arrest of Morton Mayland, and Joe Cardona had been busy gathering loose threads in the case.

Like the public, the newspapers had gobbled the evidence that pointed to Mayland's conviction. Even though the old man had not yet come to trial, he was classed as a fiendish murderer whose reign of horror was a monster's work.

Behind those headlines lay hidden, unknown facts; a tribute, if it could be called such, to the evil craft of Singhar Bund. Through subtle measures, the smooth-spoken Hindu had completely diverted suspicion from himself.

The Siva cult had never been a secret organization, although its existence had been known only to a select few. Singhar Bund had always welcomed visitors; had been ready, at any time, to unveil his brass-walled temple to the law. He had chosen Cardona's visit as the proper time to do so.

Then, before Cardona had chance to inquire about the cult's membership, Singhar Bund had sent him scampering upon a gory trail that led to discovery of murder. A path strewn with deaths quite different from the supposed suicides in which the Serpents of Siva specialized.

Morton Mayland had been hoaxed into an attack on Louis Bolingbroke. But for The Shadow, Bolingbroke would have died from a hidden dacoit's cord; the blame to be Mayland's. The death thrust had failed, but it had gone far enough to put Mayland under suspicion.

There was a motive in Mayland's attack on Bolingbroke; that of hatred that had smoldered for years. Next, the finding of Sarmon's body provided a motive in an actual death. Sarmon had been killed because he was searching for Renshell. Bones among ashes, scraps of other clues, indicated the murder of Courtney Renshell.

So far, the law had found no motive to account for Mayland murdering Renshell. That was simply another evidence of craftiness displayed by Singhar Bund. Looking for that motive was keeping Joe Cardona busy. Once the crooked work of the Siva cult was completed, something would certainly come to light, to show why Mayland had wanted Renshell dead.

Meanwhile, the law had totally overlooked the fact that heirs of persons like Rodney Welk were members of the Siva cult. Silence was the main stem of the Siva creed. Those persons were pouring their new wealth into the coffers of Singhar Bund; all the while, they were marching about with placid faces, believing that calm contemplation went with the tiny golden charms they carried.

THE SHADOW knew all that. He had learned that the Siva cult had a member who was a relative of Louis Bolingbroke. If Bolingbroke had died, two desires would have been served for Singhar Bund. One was the framing of old Mayland; the other, the gaining of Bolingbroke's wealth.

Bolingbroke was safe. Singhar Bund could not risk another thrust against him. Even suicide would look bad. But there was no reason why Singhar Bund should not want the deaths of others, whose relations belonged to the Siva cult. New murders were due, to appear as fresh accidents.

So far, The Shadow had made no move against Singhar Bund.

Why?

Harry had gradually found an answer to that question. In the past, murders had been spaced well apart. Going over the schedules of the Siva meetings, The Shadow had learned that one always came before a murder. He could afford to wait until another meeting came.

Meanwhile, The Shadow had gained a double foothold. The Shadow himself was watching the nest where a dead Serpent lay, to learn if the dacoit's death had become known to his comrades. So far, no one had visited that dingy lair, with the exception of Hawkeye, who occasionally relieved The Shadow's vigil.

The Shadow had also learned of the Eyes and Arms. They would be needed in connection with new crime. Cliff was close enough to Lucky Belther to learn when the word was passed. So far, Cliff had gained no inkling of approaching trouble. That suited The Shadow's deduction, that crime would not start until the next meeting of the Siva cult.

Perhaps preparations were underway in moderate fashion, for The Shadow had no tabs on Gummer Gilben and the group of spies called Eyes. But their part was merely preliminary. They did no more than set the stage for crime.

Once word was flashed to the Arms, The Shadow could move despite the Eyes. His task was to beat the Serpents to their goal. Harry was convinced that The Shadow had calculated some method whereby that could be accomplished.

At any rate, the suspense was almost ended. Tonight was the scheduled evening for a meeting of the Siva cult.

Harry was awaiting word regarding that meeting; there was a chance that he would be called upon to attend it, in company with Lucille.

The girl, unhappy over her grandfather's arrest, was living at a friend's apartment. Harry had seen her several times; on each occasion, she had doubted that she would go to the next meeting.

It would be up to Harry to persuade her either to attend the meeting or stay away, according to The Shadow's order.

THE hotel doorman came across the lobby, carrying a bulky package which he placed upon the desk. The name on the package puzzled the clerk. He shook his head; it had been delivered to the wrong hotel. The doorman took the package back to the messenger.

That incident was Harry's cue. He placed his newspaper aside, lighted a cigarette and strolled out to the street. He walked a few paces, saw a parked cab and stepped into it.

The cab was Moe Shrevnitz's. The Shadow sat shrouded in the back seat. The cab moved; as it rolled through neighboring blocks, The Shadow spoke in whispered tones to Harry.

"Remain away from tonight's meeting," came the voice. "Persuade Lucille to do the same."

There was a pause; then a low-pitched, mirthless laugh. The Shadow continued:

"Singhar Bund is attempting a bold policy. He has declared tonight's meeting public. Commissioner Weston will attend, taking his friend Lamont Cranston."

The cab rounded a corner, came to a side door of the hotel. Harry caught last words of instruction. He stepped from the cab. As he closed the door, he would have sworn that the interior was empty.

Yet Harry knew that the cab carried the living presence of The Shadow!

The last instructions had been brief. Harry was to call Lucille; to suggest a theater instead of the cult meeting. She was at the apartment, awaiting word from him. Harry knew that she would be guided by his decision.

Harry smiled at the thought that he and Lucille were temporarily out of the picture. After all, they were practically under the protection of crooks themselves, since both Harry and Lucille carried Siva charms that meant immunity to their bearers. So, for that matter, was Joe Cardona, who had the tiny image that Singhar Bund had given him.

Cardona, it happened, was very useful to crooked affairs, right at present. Without knowing it, he was puffing the smoke screen that covered criminal affairs.

Harry's main thoughts, however, concerned himself and Lucille. Apparently, nothing had occurred to change their status. Even The Shadow regarded them as safe. That satisfied Harry. He did not realize that some chance occurrence might have changed the situation.

There was a message for Harry at the Metrolite desk. It was from Lucille; he was to call her apartment. Had Harry been less confident, he would have analyzed that message; as it was, he merely decided that Lucille was wondering what he intended to do about tonight.

Rather than waste time by going up to his room, Harry chose to make the call from a telephone booth. There were several of them in a quiet corner of the lobby, close to a long exit that led to another street.

Tossing a finished cigarette into a sanded vase, Harry failed to glance toward the darkish exit passage when he passed it.

STOPPING in the first booth, Harry dropped a nickel and dialed Lucille's number. He heard the girl's voice answer; the strain of Lucille's tone gave him his first inkling of danger, but he thought the menace was Lucille's, alone.

"I called you, Harry"—Lucille's voice was striving for its usual calmness—"because I suspected that someone was watching here. I must have been right; for soon after that, the telephone rang. I thought, at first, that it must be you—"

Lucille's voice broke, breathless. Harry spoke encouraging words; he was tense, though he tried not to betray it.

"It was someone else," came Lucille's low whisper. "A voice that I recognized. Harry, that call told me something terribly important. It proved that my grandfather is innocent of murder! Innocent, because—"

A choke came across the wire. Harry heard a suppressed scream; then the heavy *click* of a receiver hook. Lucille's apprehensions were correct. She had been watched; listeners had caught the words that she just uttered!

Something had happened to Lucille, and only Harry knew the fact. The first move would be a call to Burbank. Hastily, Harry slammed the receiver on its hook; shoved his shoulder from the booth, as he dug in his pocket for another nickel.

A padded object thumped the back of Harry's skull. Murmurless, the young man slumped from the telephone booth, into the arms of the husky who had cracked him with the sandbag.

Two hard-faced men stepped sideways from the exit passage; turning their backs to the lobby, they screened all sight of what had happened at the telephone booth.

They and the slugger formed a trio that edged away from the booths, shifting Harry's limp figure ahead of them. Ten seconds later, they were hastening toward the street, carrying their burden.

Crime's new night had begun with the taking of two prisoners. Lucille and Harry were helpless captives, without the knowledge of The Shadow!

CHAPTER XV
THE VOICE OF SIVA

"THE job's all set, Cliff. Here's the lay—"

Lucky Belther broke off his statement as he heard a buzz. It was the muffled telephone bell that was located in his hideout. For a moment, Lucky's thin-slitted eyes glittered a suspicious look.

"The big boy called a while ago," he muttered. "It shouldn't be him again, so soon—"

The buzz was insistent. Lucky went to the telephone; lifting the receiver, he grunted a hello. Tough lips showed a grin of recognition. Lucky nodded toward Cliff; sidemouthed the words:

"The boss, after all!"

A voice was coming over the wire. Cliff could catch no words; merely a *clicky* tone. It didn't fit with the purr that was supposed to be Singhar Bund's. Cliff wondered whether the Hindu was calling with disguised voice, or whether someone else gave orders to Lucky.

It was the first time that Cliff had heard that telephone in use. A while ago, it would have suited him. Right now, it spoiled plans. Lucky had just started to spill important details when the call interrupted. Cliff couldn't stifle the thought that this might change things.

It did. Lucky's face showed a different sort of enthusiasm, when the call was finished.

"The job's all set, Cliff," he declared. "Just like I said. Only, I'm handling it with a crew of Arms. Without you helping me."

"Yeah?" snapped Cliff. "How come?"

"You've got a different job," returned Lucky. "Some dame mixed into things. A couple of Eyes grabbed her; they're taking her to the big shot, wherever he is.

"The moll started to spill some dope to a boyfriend. But the Eyes were wise by that time. So they snagged him; and that's where you come in. You're to take him for a ride."

Cliff's deadpan face showed none of the thoughts that flashed through his mind. Mention of a girl had made him think of Lucille. The fact that a man was in the picture certainly meant Harry. To Cliff was being delegated the duty of putting his own friend on the spot!

"Stick here, Cliff," ordered Lucky, "until I get outside. I got a car there; I'll tell the wheeler where he's to go. I'll leave you a couple of gorillas to help with the rubout. I'll be watching to see you start."

With that, Lucky made a rapid exit. Haste, not mistrust, was the cause; but it put Cliff in a bad jam.

IF Cliff had only learned where he was to go, his task would be easy. Word to The Shadow; delay along the way—Harry would be gone when the murder squad arrived. As it was, the important detail of route was to be in the hands of whoever drove the car.

Cliff had missed out entirely on learning what Lucky's job was to be; but that had dwindled to unimportance. The immediate problem was to save Harry. It took Cliff swift seconds of calculation before he could grab the only answer.

After the murder crew picked up Harry, matters would be in Cliff's charge. He could stall them along, directing the driver where to go. A roundabout route would not arouse suspicion. Cliff could pick a route that would go by a designated place.

Grabbing Lucky's telephone, Cliff dialed Burbank's number. Though he wasn't given to jitters, Cliff found himself telling the contact man the news in a forced, worried voice. Burbank's methodical tone actually pulled Cliff from the doldrums.

The contact man took the report as coolly as a routine announcement. He informed Cliff that

Moe's cab would be at a certain corner, supplying a better location than the one that Cliff suggested. Word, meanwhile, would go to The Shadow. It was up to Cliff to handle the rest.

There was no time for Cliff to think things over, after he had finished the call. By this time, Lucky would be getting suspicious, down there on the street. Cliff slid out through the door; when he reached the sidewalk, he paused to rub the back of his hands across his lips.

That would make Lucky think that Cliff had paused to take a swig from the ever-present bottle. Lucky belonged to that breed of thugs who invariably steeled themselves with a stiff drink. Cliff's adoption of that system would please him.

A touring car was waiting, a short way off. Cliff got in, grunted a greeting to the three men already there.

"Let's go," he told the driver. Then, to allay later chances of suspicion: "Take it easy. We don't want any bulls to stop us and ask questions."

FAR from the tawdry district where Cliff's adventure had started, the Siva cult was going through its ceremonies for the benefit of a curious audience. Beside the three-faced statue with its jeweled eyes, Singhar Bund discoursed on Oriental subjects.

Less than half the persons present were members of the cult. Only one non-member might have been mistaken for a believer in Siva. That lone personage was Lamont Cranston. His face was immobile, his eyes calm.

Yet those eyes had sized the situation. Certain persons were absent; they were the ones who had profited through deaths like that of Rodney Welk. In placing his believers on exhibition, Singhar Bund had wisely found excuses to keep those members away.

Moreover, Singhar Bund was avoiding demonstrations of trickery. He was talking of wonders that had been performed; of others that would be exhibited on later occasions. But with the police commissioner and other skeptics present, Singhar Bund thought it best to confine his activities to a mere lecture.

Finishing his talk, the crafty cult ruler became somewhat bolder. Seeing that listeners were impressed, he motioned toward the alcove that contained the upright casket. Singhar Bund invited all to inspect it.

"A yogi is preparing for that test," he declared. "He must spend a week in fasting, except for a diet of sheep's blood. He is also practicing the necessary breathing exercises needed for this greatest demonstration of *samadhi,* or perfect contemplation.

"At some future time, he will be placed in the confines of that casket; the locks will be shut and sealed. Days later, we shall remove him, alive and unharmed, from a space where no ordinary mortal could breathe safely for a dozen minutes."

The big casket was open. The commissioner looked inside, and was impressed. The interior had a decorative design, like the outside.

Cranston observed that in idle fashion; his eyes also studied the huge hinges that showed when the casket was open.

For a few moments, Singhar Bund seemed suspicious of Cranston's scrutiny. The Hindu suggested that the visitors resume their places, to witness the final ritual. Singhar Bund asked Phineas Leeth if he would lead the procession past the statue of Siva. The droopy-faced man beamed.

"A rare privilege," said Leeth to Weston. "To be the first to salaam Siva is regarded as good omen. Ah, Commissioner, we who believe in Siva find great contentment."

Weston looked to Cranston; as Leeth left them, the commissioner commented that the old man was badly duped. The statement brought a nod from Cranston. His eyes were elsewhere. He was counting the dacoits. All were present, except the one that The Shadow knew to be dead.

These fake yogis had not entered until the end of the meeting; and Singhar Bund had purposely failed to call attention to them. The fact that they were here at all was something that The Shadow understood; for his disguised lips showed traces of a faint smile that Singhar Bund did not observe.

In fact, Singhar Bund was a trifle perplexed when he counted noses for the first time. It was too late, however, for him to investigate the Serpent's absence. He could find out nothing by questioning the other dacoits. Like The Shadow, Singhar Bund knew that the Serpents did not meet outside the temple.

LEETH was back, happy because he had bowed to Siva. Other believers were continuing their slow file to the statue. Commissioner Weston did not look impressed; but Cranston salved Leeth's feelings by the inquiry:

"May others, not as yet believers, approach Siva and do homage?"

"Certainly," returned Leeth. "As soon as the procession has ended. Shall I conduct you there, Mr. Cranston?"

"I would appreciate the favor."

Leeth took Cranston's elbow. They reached Singhar Bund; Leeth announced Cranston as a new convert. Singhar Bund smiled, purred friendly approval. He had noted Cranston several times, and had half believed that this visitor was ripe for admission into the Siva cult.

"You may approach," spoke Singhar Bund, "as soon as the last yogi has passed."

His restraining hand was less pressing than it had been with Harry. There was no need for an iron grip; plushy pressure was sufficient in Cranston's case. That, alone, was sufficient to lull Singhar Bund into security. Cranston was not close enough to hear the hisses of the Serpents as they bowed before Siva.

The Shadow's real purpose was lost to Singhar Bund. It deceived him as effectively as did those mask-like features of Cranston.

When the final Serpent had gone, Singhar Bund urged Cranston forward; then remained to talk to Leeth. That was the great mistake of Singhar Bund. It was his turn to be out of earshot, at a vital moment.

As The Shadow bowed before the statue of Siva, his lips remained motion-

CLYDE BURKE

less as they delivered a hiss. Low-toned, that snakish utterance was a perfect imitation of the sounds that The Shadow had heard the dacoits give. The Shadow was speaking for the missing Serpent.

The Shadow waited, calm in his guise of Cranston. His clever strategy was rewarded. From the bronze lips of the Siva's central head came a response, low-spoken, its words a mingling of English and Hindustani!

The Shadow was hearing the voice of Siva!

CHAPTER XVI
WHERE MURDER LURKED

THE Serpents had withdrawn to obscure corners of the temple when Cranston rejoined Leeth. They were waiting until some of the visitors had withdrawn; but soon they would be on the move. That was something that The Shadow knew.

Singhar Bund politely presented Cranston with a Siva token, remarking upon the virtue that the charm possessed. Commissioner Weston showed

puzzlement to find his friend so gullible. He intended to question Cranston on that score, later.

For the next few minutes, Weston could not shake Leeth. When the commissioner looked around, Cranston was gone. Weston supposed that he had left with some departing visitors. He was right. Stepping from the temple, Weston saw his friend at the bottom of the stairs.

The commissioner hurried to the street. There were not many pedestrians; still, he couldn't see Cranston among them. Weston was still looking back and forth when a wiry young man stepped from a taxi, to give a cheery wave.

"Hello, Commissioner," announced the newcomer. "Remember me—Burke of the *Classic?*"

Weston nodded. He knew Clyde Burke well enough. What he didn't know was that the supposed reporter was actually an agent of The Shadow. Clyde had been sent here by Burbank.

"What about the meeting?" questioned Clyde. "Is it finished?"

"Yes," returned Weston. Then, dryly: "We did not invite reporters."

Clyde ignored the comment.

"Who else was there?" he persisted. "Any prominent persons, beside yourself? Other members of the Cobalt Club?"

"Lamont Cranston was present," replied Weston. "He left, a few minutes ago. I am trying to find him."

Weston was treated to a new surprise—that of a reporter forgetting his assignment. With a mutter that the story wouldn't count for much, Clyde hopped back into the cab and rode away.

One block distant, Clyde dived for the nearest telephone booth.

Something was up, and Clyde knew it. Although Clyde had played a secondary part in recent events, he was well acquainted with their importance. He knew, for instance, what might be due tonight. Chances were that The Shadow could be reached indirectly, through Joe Cardona.

Tonight, the ace inspector was at his desk in headquarters, mulling over the latest clues in connection with the Mayland case. That was why Clyde telephoned Cardona.

The call did not go through. Cardona's line was busy. Worst of all, Clyde could guess the reason. He almost pictured the scene at headquarters.

THERE, Joe Cardona was riveted at a telephone. His swarthy face had lost its usual blandness. Cardona was nodding, gulping responses as he heard the words of a ghostly speaker. Joe Cardona knew those eerie tones.

The Shadow was on the wire!

The mysterious voice finished; the line cut off abruptly. Cardona remained motionless, as though his brain echoed with the news that he had heard. Coming to life, he slammed the receiver and sprang to his feet, He beckoned to a bulky detective sergeant who sat at another desk.

"Let's go, Markham!" snapped Cardona. "We'll need a pair of picked men—good ones—and a squad, besides. I'll tell you all about it while we're on the way."

They were out in the hallway. The telephone bell was tingling again; it was Clyde's call coming through. Cardona hesitated; shook his head.

"He wouldn't be calling again," declared Joe, referring to The Shadow. "Whoever else it is, can't be important."

Soon, Cardona and Markham were riding northward in a police car that carved traffic ahead of it. But they were not the first along that route. Blocks farther north, another car was speeding to the same destination.

When that first car halted, it stopped near a narrow, towering apartment building where the lights of a penthouse formed tiny specks, twenty-odd stories above the street. After that first car parked, a figure glided from it.

The shape was a living one, but too elusive for observing eyes to follow. It blended into darkness; came to a sheltered spot beneath the tall building. The tone of a whispered laugh was captured by a drift of breeze. Then, silence; complete.

Five blocks from the same building, the police car halted. Squad cars pulled up behind it. Cardona gave orders. With Markham and two others, Cardona flagged a taxi. He ordered the driver to go slowly.

Within a few blocks, Cardona noted roving cabs. He saw spots near the big apartment house that looked like lurking places. He had the cab pull up at the apartment house itself, but chose a spot so dark that he and his companions could make a guarded exit.

Telling the cabby what to do, Cardona and his comrades followed the very route that The Shadow had taken.

The cab driver lighted a cigarette. He was about to move ahead, when another taxi pulled alongside. Its driver hailed:

"Hello, hackie! Anything wrong?"

"Just lighting a smoke," replied Cardona's cabby. "Then I'm pulling into the feed line up ahead."

The second cab's motor stalled. Its driver was making sure that the other taxi was moving into the feed line. That part of the street was lighted. The cab showed empty when it arrived there. The roving cabby drove away.

THE doorway that Cardona found led to a service elevator. No one was aboard it. The group stepped into the car and rode to the top floor. There, Cardona told one of his men:

"Take the elevator down to the bottom. Then come up the stairs. It's a long climb, but it's going to be worth it. Stick outside the tower door."

That door was locked from the inside. Cardona opened it; stationed the second dick there. With Markham following, Joe opened an opposite door. He whispered for silence as they stepped into the hallway of the penthouse.

Markham gaped at the magnificence that surrounded them. There was a living room thick with heavy Oriental rugs; its walls were adorned with Italian tapestries that must have cost a fortune. The furniture was of the finest mahogany that Markham had ever seen.

One doorway opened into a library, where rows of vellum-bound books lined the shelves. On the other side was the entrance to the bedrooms. Straight ahead, a door opened to a terrace that was tiled with marble, a tinkling fountain in its center.

Cardona had already told Markham what this place represented. The penthouse was the New York residence of Cuyler Selwood, Midwest motor magnate. Its lavish furnishings were trivial, compared with those of his Michigan palace.

Selwood was in New York at present; usually, his penthouse was manned by a retinue of servants. Tonight, the place was curiously silent. Its tomblike hush was disconcerting, even to Cardona. Though he represented the law, Joe would ordinarily have stopped on the threshold.

Right now, he was buoyed to a special duty by memory of that voice from the telephone. Cardona liked to play hunches; but it was more than a hunch, that call.

When The Shadow paved the path, Cardona had never known it to be a false one.

The ace stole across the thick-napped rug, with the detective sergeant at his heels. They reached the terrace, where new splendor greeted them.

The parapets surrounded an Italian garden, transplanted from some Roman villa. There were benches beneath flowering arches. Beyond the central fountain stood a group statue in marble, formed of carved mermaids and dolphins, raised above a mirrored pool.

Two huge vases in the nearer corners of the garden were the hiding spots that The Shadow had ordered. Cardona sent Markham to one; he was about to take the other station, when he heard a voice within the penthouse. Cardona peered through the crack of a partly opened door, to observe the speaker.

The man had come from the library. He was portly, baldish; wearing a rumpled smoking jacket. His pudgy fingers drew a cigar from lips that were topped by a close-clipped mustache.

"Raymond!" bawled the portly man. "Why don't you answer? Craig—where are you?"

The man was Selwood; his face was purplish with anger, because the servants did not answer. He turned toward the roof; paused as he heard a telephone bell tingle.

"Hello!" Selwood was savage; then his tone became sarcastic. "So it's you, Eleanor. My favorite niece, because you are the only one I have... No, I'm not angry with you. I'm just annoyed by what you told me this afternoon...

"You must give up that foolishness. Spending money on that flimflam Hindu stuff is ridiculous! I knew something had come over you. I could tell it by the way you kept a moony smirk on your face…"

SELWOOD paused. His face showed a grimace. He pressed one hand to his heart; tried to speak over the telephone. It was half a minute before he found words. Then:

"No, no, Eleanor," he said. "I'm all right. I overexerted myself, shouting for the servants... I remember now, that Raymond had to go for that prescription of mine. Yes, and Craig has probably made his evening trip to the kennels, to look after the wolfhounds...

"Yes, the doctor was here this afternoon. Told me to go easy. Said I'd get over this morbid complex of mine. Only sometimes, Eleanor—you're not the only one who has heard me say it—I find that life tires me, in spite of all my wealth."

Whatever the niece replied, it must have been sympathetic, for Cardona could see a slight smile spread on Selwood's lips. The millionaire placed the telephone on its stand; removed his hand from his chest. He puffed at his cigar, as he came slowly toward the door where Cardona watched.

Joe was out of sight when Selwood entered the garden. He saw the portly man pace slowly past the fountain, then approach the side of the roof where he had the best view of the city's lights. The life

that the glow offered seemed to soothe Selwood. His puffs on the cigar became more contented.

A figure writhed from the penthouse door. Neither Cardona nor Markham saw it, for both were watching Selwood. The thing crouched low as it crept along a pathway, like a human snake. Another serpentine figure came silently from the penthouse; took the same writhing course along the path where overhanging vines hid the marble's whiteness.

There was a rustle from a window of the penthouse. Cardona looked up through the vines beside him. He couldn't trace the figure that twisted along the parapet, anymore than he could have spotted a python in a jungle. But the sound told that danger was due; when it was suddenly repeated, Cardona waited no longer.

Fully alert, he spotted the first creatures that had crawled to the garden; for they were in back of Selwood, at a place where the blackness ended. Cardona saw brownish faces with leering, monkeyish teeth. He heard the whistle of a sibilant signal.

Cardona answered that hiss with a shout to Markham. Joe was bounding out from cover; and the brawny detective sergeant followed him. With all their speed, they were too late. Cardona saw a brown man rise, whip a thin cord about Selwood's neck.

The millionaire went backward with a gurgle, into a mass of brownish arms that rose like viper heads, ready to hoist him from the parapet when his struggle ceased. They were working faster than Cardona could pull his revolver from his pocket.

The scene was a horrible nightmare, that needed some jolt to break its spell. The needed break came—more chilling, more fearful than the sight of Siva's living Serpents. And it came from a place least expected.

From the statuary group beyond the fountain pealed the   avenger.

That tone was the eerie laugh of The Shadow!

CHAPTER XVII
BLACK FLIGHT

THE Serpents of Siva whirled at The Shadow's challenge. They needed mere seconds to dispose of Selwood; but they knew that seconds were not enough. Nor could they resist an answer to the cloaked foeman whose identity they knew.

Selwood flattened inside the parapet, the torturing cord gone from his thick neck. The scrawny Serpents lashed out into fanwise formation, to attack The Shadow. The speed with which they found cover was amazing.

So, too, was the answer of The Shadow's guns. Muzzles spat flame from above the clustered statuary. Bullets sizzled the fringes of the quick-chosen hiding spots, huddling the dacoits in their cover.

Once that gunfire ended, the stranglers would have had their chance anew, provided that The Shadow had been the only foe who menaced them. But The Shadow was counting on a pair of capable reserves, in Cardona and Markham.

They could see where The Shadow's bullets spattered the marble. The shots told them where the dacoits crouched. Though the snakish killers had wriggled from the sight of the headquarters men, they had not gained shelter from a rear attack. Cardona and Markham blasted bullets into the vines that The Shadow's gunfire indicated.

One Serpent shrieked, came diving toward the fountain, clipped by a slug from Cardona's Police Positive. The others gave up their lurking tactics. They bounded from cover, sweeping out their strangle cords as they sped for Cardona and Markham. Murderers by instinct, the dacoits had a skill at self-preservation. They were taking the best course for it.

One brownish devil reached Cardona; another was making for Markham. They wanted to speed nooses around the necks of their antagonists; twist them, helpless, as shields against The Shadow's fire. With their rapid advance, the strokes could have been accomplished against any marksman, other than The Shadow.

Even his aim could not drop the dacoits as they sped for their prey; but The Shadow sent his shots when they reached their objectives.

There was a timely instant, when the first Serpent locked with Cardona. Joe's arms went wide as the noose coiled above his shoulders; but before the dacoit could twist behind Cardona, The Shadow fired.

The dacoit spilled, twisting like a crippled reptile. Before Cardona could pounce upon the writhing Serpent, there was a burst from The Shadow's other gun. A clipping bullet literally slashed a dacoit from Markham's floundering grasp, just as the detective sergeant was losing the momentary grip that he had gained.

The last dacoit was loping through the penthouse. He was safe from The Shadow's fire; he thought that his fellow Serpents had disposed of Cardona and Markham. That was why the creature did not zigzag, nor look behind him.

The dacoit's mistake was his final one. Cardona and Markham were at the doorway leading from the terrace before the Serpent reached the passage to the elevator. The pair unloaded a barrage. Their bullets rolled the dacoit to the floor. Looking about, they saw that The Shadow's targets had ceased their writhing.

Serpents of Siva had been wiped into oblivion; and with the triumph, Joe Cardona had found crime's answer.

"I know where that bunch came from," snapped Joe, to Markham. "They belong to Singhar Bund— the Hindu that runs the Siva racket—"

A CLANG from the elevator interrupted. Into the penthouse came a flood of fresh fighters, headed by Lucky Belther. Cardona and Markham were ducking behind furniture when the Arms began their fire; but they couldn't stand a chance against those odds. They needed The Shadow as badly as before; and their cloaked ally supported them.

Lucky and his crew forgot the open path to the terrace, to deal with Cardona and Markham. Hardly had crooks aimed toward corners, before The Shadow's laugh reached them from the garden doorway. They wheeled, to see the cloaked shape silhouetted against the marble background.

They heard The Shadow speak again—with bullets.

Beaten to the first shots, mobsters sprawled. Those who fired, peppered wide of The Shadow, for they had no time for accuracy with their diverted aim.

Cardona and Markham supplied shots from their barricades. Hard upon that rapid fire came the flanking attack of the two detectives, posted at the top of the stairs.

One crook survived that scorching test. Lucky Belther again proved that his nickname was deserved; this time, without requiring aid.

He made a lone dash for the elevator; The Shadow triggered a bullet after him, but the shot was necessarily high. Cardona and Markham had sprung out to the middle of the room, forcing The Shadow's change of fire.

Lucky sprang between the two detectives. When their guns spurted in his direction, the sliding door of the elevator received the bullets. Lucky was away, in flight.

The Shadow followed, taking the long stairway to the street; the delay did not disturb him, for he knew what was due below. The roar of battle was audible before he reached the ground.

Lucky had joined a reserve crew, only to find them harried by Cardona's squad. The police were closing a cordon, to hem in the crooks.

There was battle through that neighborhood. Police patrol cars had cut in to deal with roving taxicabs, manned by Eyes who sought to relieve the hard-pressed Arms. The thugs were faring badly. They were heavily outnumbered; and the police knew where to look for them.

The Shadow had business elsewhere. He started for the spot where he had parked his car; his laugh pealed a strident challenge that brought fire from gunmen who were battling a batch of police.

From the statuary group beyond the fountain pealed the weird mirth of a hidden avanger. That tone was the eerie laugh of The Shadow.

Gunners couldn't find The Shadow. He jabbed timely shots that dropped a pair of them. The officers did the rest. The Shadow let them handle the scattered hoodlums. His path was clear.

Hand on the knob of the coupé's door, The Shadow sidestepped as a man flung up beside him. Recklessly, the fellow didn't care what happened, provided he reached The Shadow. Had he been a foeman, a sledged gun would have felled him. In the dark, he ran that risk. It happened that The Shadow's gun did not swing.

The approach told him that this was no hoodlum. Shoving out an arm, The Shadow blocked the panting arrival; half pushed him into the car. It was Clyde Burke, guided by The Shadow's laugh to the spot where his chief was stationed.

Clyde had gone to headquarters. He'd heard what was up. He was here, as fast as he could make it, to tell The Shadow what had happened to Harry. Clyde had inserted a call to Burbank, at the nearest telephone. Word was in from Moe Shrevnitz, telling where Cliff had taken Harry.

THE coupé was off, whipping for an avenue. It wheeled a corner, into the path of a big sedan. As brakes screeched, The Shadow clung too tightly to the wheel to roll himself from view. There were mobsters in that sedan—fleeing Arms of Siva—with Lucky among them.

The Shadow did not wait for battle. He swung the coupé clear; was away when crooks began their fire. A taxi shot into sight. Staring from its window was Gummer Gilben. He had Eyes with him. Like the Arms, they were bent on flight.

The Shadow had chosen a route that he had mentioned to Joe Cardona: a lone, twisty course that was to be left open by the police cordon. Crooks would never have found it for themselves. But it became theirs, thanks to The Shadow.

The Shadow was in flight!

So crooks thought; and they saw opportunity. They wanted to quit this neighborhood; and they liked battle, when the odds were their own. Outnumbering The Shadow, emboldened by the false belief that he feared them, thugs took up the trail.

For that half dozen who pursued The Shadow, a full two score had been left for capture by the law. But neither Lucky nor Gummer minded that. The small fry could take the rap. It would be victory, after all, if Lucky and Gummer could bag The Shadow.

Police had been told that a coupé should be passed unmolested. That ruling did not apply to a heavy sedan and a wildcat taxicab. Squad cars took up the chase, hoping to catch The Shadow's pursuers.

Clinging to the opened window of the coupé, Clyde heard the gritted laugh that rasped from The Shadow's hidden lips. Clyde understood. The Shadow was passing up an opportunity.

He could lose those pursuers in a maze of streets, and leave them to the law. That, however, would mean delay. Not a second could be lost in reaching Harry.

Moreover, The Shadow was increasing the odds that lay against him. Unless he outdistanced the mobsters behind, they would be on deck when the goal was reached.

There was a chance that the squad cars might stick close. That would help, if it occurred. But the chase was spreading, with the crooks doing better than the police. Had Clyde been at the wheel, he would not have shoved that accelerator to the floor; for he could see the consequences far ahead.

The Shadow saw them, as well as Clyde; but he gave the coupé every ounce of gas. Cross streets whisked by so rapidly that Clyde could scarcely count them. Ahead, Clyde saw the big red neon sign that topped an old hotel. That was where the route turned right, to the vicinity of Hell's Kitchen, where Cliff Marsland had finally completed his tour with Harry Vincent and the thugs who were waiting for him to be bumped off.

Like a thing of doom, the light was looming closer, bringing the moment when The Shadow would again be forced to stage a dangerous rescue.

Again, Clyde heard The Shadow's laugh; its whisper a prophecy of battle, that might prove The Shadow's last.

CHAPTER XVIII
CHANGED COURSES

THE alleyway was silent, except for a low-growled voice that gave continued threats:

"Not talking, huh? We've got a way to squeeze it out of mugs like you! How'd you like some heat—real heat?"

The tone was Cliff's; the threatened man was Harry. There were other listeners, though, who were irked by the delay.

"Let him have it, Cliff!"

The suggestion came from the man at the wheel of the death car; and gorillas added their approval. Cliff gave them answer.

"I'm making this lug blab," he announced. "Get it? Or don't you?"

"Lucky didn't say to make him squawk," returned an objector. "He didn't say to stall, either, getting here."

Cliff snorted his contempt—not for Lucky, but for the speaker.

"Lucky left it to me," he told the crew. "Where to bring the guy, and how to handle him. How do you know what Lucky told me?"

"Because he told us." The driver bulged over from the front seat, poked a gun toward Harry's ribs. "And if you ain't croaking the guy, we are!"

There was a slight thud in the darkness, as Cliff's automatic gave a downward drop against the fellow's gun hand. The driver withdrew his fist, with a snarl.

"There's one thing Lucky didn't tell you," snapped Cliff. "He didn't say who this guy was, did he?"

Growls responded in the negative.

"You're right, he didn't," added Cliff, "because he didn't know. So I'll put you wise." He was ready with his final argument. "This guy is a stooge that's working for The Shadow! That's why I want him to talk."

The argument brought delay. Cliff's effort to quiz Harry brought approval. Gorillas were muttering among themselves. If Cliff was right, he was playing a good bet. Those mutters kept on, while Cliff resumed his probe of Harry.

In his turn, Harry said nothing. Talk wouldn't help Cliff's stall. Cliff had been doing well enough without it.

While he growled at Harry, Cliff was conscious of the mutters of the thugs with him. They didn't quite suit him. A few words struck Cliff as sour. He sensed their import. One thug had whispered the impression that maybe Cliff knew too much about The Shadow. The setup sounded phony.

Pretending not to hear, Cliff reached beside him. He found the knob of the door; covered its squeak by raising his tone. His hand came back to his left hip; crossing beneath his right elbow, it shoved a spare gun against Harry's fingers.

Cliff's grip found Harry's forearm. Cliff jerked leftward; snatched Harry toward the door. Adding to the plunge, Harry went sprawling to the curb, as Cliff shouted:

"All right! Give it!"

SHOVING half out from the door, Cliff supplied

the first shots, over Harry's head. Gleefully, the driver leaned from his own window, jabbed his gun toward Harry's rolling form.

Cliff sledged another gun-blow for the driver; but this was no gentle knuckle rap.

The automatic thudded the driver's skull, with a wallop that slumped the fellow deep beneath the wheel.

Right after that, Cliff was locked with two tough fighters, both to his right. One was jabbing a gun from the front seat; the other had a grip around Cliff's neck. It was a tussle that left Cliff very little chance, after the next thirty seconds. In taking out the driver, he had given the other pair the odds.

The door by the driver's seat yanked open. The slugged crook rolled inert to the curb. Harry came shoving through, to side with Cliff. He pitched on the front-seat gorilla. It was timely aid, but it brought a bad break.

Cliff, too, was occupied with that same fighter. The thug in the rear was twisted, with his gun hand high. He managed to squirm by Cliff; thwacked a cross-blow to Harry's head. Cliff stopped it partially, but not enough.

All was grim in that darkness. The next instant the situation was revealed, by a glare that swathed in from the mouth of the alley. Blinding light showed Harry, wavering above the wheel. It spotted Cliff, rolling for the open side door, with glittering revolver barrels shoving toward him.

Crooks hesitated, in the brilliance of those flooding headlights. A big gun spoke ahead of theirs. Bullets from an automatic whistled through the open sides of the touring car, as a coupé rocketed alongside.

The light was gone; in its place came a fierce laugh, from a fighter whose right hand laid a gun across his left elbow. Still gripping the coupé's wheel, The Shadow pumped new shots into the touring car.

Gunmen had forgotten Cliff and Harry. They were turning to battle The Shadow. That move didn't help them. The Shadow's shots came first, put them out of the fray for good.

The Shadow shoved Clyde from the right side of the coupé; gave him the quick order:

"Get that car started! Bring Marsland and Vincent along! Keep beside me!"

The coupé was moving ahead when Clyde reached the touring car. Cliff piled into the machine when Clyde told him. Shoving Harry to the right, Clyde grabbed the wheel. The starter grated. The car was moving when two others wheeled into the alley.

Jouncing through the alley, the touring car and the coupé were open targets for Lucky and Gummer; but of the two machines, they wanted the coupé. They saw a body by the curb, but did not recognize it. They thought the dead man to be Harry.

As they sized it, The Shadow was trying to finish Cliff and his three gorillas, for they saw and heard the bursts of a gun. Side by side, the pursuers closed upon the coupé; they saw its door swing wide; their bullets began to drill.

The touring car kept onward, but the coupe careened. It took the curb and crashed a building wall. They were alongside, Lucky's car first, then Gummer's, when one of their band gave a raucous shout and pointed.

Up ahead, the touring car was swinging from the alley into the glow of the street lamp. Rising from the open car's step, they saw The Shadow. Doors were open on the right; two forms came sprawling lifelessly from within the car. The Shadow shoved into the rear seat. The doors slammed shut.

HOW the game had changed, Lucky and Gummer couldn't guess; but they weren't ready to call it quits. The Shadow was still in flight.

Motors roared, beginning a new pursuit. Once through the alley, they caught the touring car's trail; and they followed it, unmolested.

The crooks had shaken off the squad car, through sheer speed. Sirens told that the police were heading for a scene of finished battle: that alley where no living fighters remained, where chance for a trail was ended.

Of four available drivers, himself included, The Shadow had placed the least expert at the wheel. Clyde was doing a good job, but he couldn't get the distance that he needed to outpace the crooks, even though The Shadow guided him.

As the race continued, it became apparent that The Shadow did not want to end the pursuit. Between his steady instructions to Clyde, he told his agents what came next. They listened, almost rapt, as they heard The Shadow's plan.

Picking his streets, The Shadow gave word for a final spurt, to be followed by a sharp turn to the right. Accomplished, Clyde gave the brakes within a hundred feet. Agents sprang from the car and dived for a doorway to which The Shadow pointed.

They were inside when The Shadow opened fire back toward the corner. Mobster guns answered a few seconds later. By that time, The Shadow had joined his own followers. Through the door, The Shadow ordered it clamped shut.

They were in a little courtyard between two buildings, with thugs banging at the barring door. The Shadow picked a window, smashed its glass with a gun butt. The window came up; the four climbed through.

This was the interior of an antique shop, closed for the night. Evidently The Shadow had been in the place before. Uncannily, he picked a corner and ordered Cliff and Harry to shove aside a big chest of drawers.

Once the chest was clear, the agents saw a

locked door. The Shadow finished the lock with a single bullet. They went through to a passage beyond. The corridor was leading them in the direction of an alley that Clyde had noticed, when he stopped the car.

The Shadow halted by a cobwebbed door. Again, he blasted a lock. The four emerged into a space that formed an air shaft. There was a window opposite. The Shadow smashed it in, took an inward dive through it before his agents could follow.

There was a scuffle within a room. When the three agents reached the scene, they saw The Shadow rising from above the figure of a bearded Hindu, whose turban had rolled to the floor. The Shadow had knocked the guard senseless.

It was Harry who realized where they were. This was the floor below the Siva temple! It was split up into secret rooms and routes, as Harry had supposed.

The Shadow had not been idle, during those times that he had let Hawkeye relieve him. He had been gaining a considerable knowledge of these premises, through secret search.

THE SHADOW took keys from the Hindu's sash. He found the one that unlocked a steel door in the far wall of the room. Stepping into a tiny cell, he emerged with a prisoner. The captive was Lucille Mayland, bound and gagged.

While Harry and Cliff cut the cords that held Lucille, The Shadow was speaking to the girl in whispered tones. Lucille's eyes showed flashes of mingled understanding and amazement. When she was free, The Shadow pointed to another door.

The agents were to take Lucille through there; out by the alleyway. Other moves were to follow; but not until the police arrived. They would be here soon, headed by Joe Cardona. Meanwhile, the path was clear. Lucky and Gummer and their mobs would not molest the getaway.

Proof of that was already coming from the air shaft. Mobsters had reached the last door that The Shadow had broken. The Shadow was remaining, to lure them on another trail. He waited in a passage just beyond the door through which the agents carried Lucille.

Lucky was the first thug through the window. He saw the flattened Hindu. The sight puzzled him, until Gummer arrived.

"Cripes!" voiced Gummer. "This is the joint where we brought the moll! Lamp that, Lucky"— he pointed to the vacant cell—"it's where we shoved her!"

"Yeah?" demanded Lucky. "Then where's she got to?"

"The Shadow's snagged her," snarled Gummer, "and he's taken her out the other way. Unless he's pulled another fast one. Maybe this guy can tell us."

The "guy" was the Hindu, who was showing signs of life. They brought him to his feet. He shook his head. He couldn't understand the questions that were asked him, let alone answer them.

Gummer opened the far door, gave a sudden shout. The rest joined him, as he dropped back. Gummer was pointing to a passage that ended in a solid wall.

"The Shadow!" he gulped. "I seen him there!"

Lucky believed where others doubted. He jogged the Hindu's shoulder; pointed to the dead-end passage. The bearded man reached to the wall, pressed a hidden switch. A panel slid upward.

Framed on that threshold stood The Shadow. Guns stowed away, he stood with folded arms. From his lips came a new, mirthful challenge, that echoed its defiance to the startled horde of blinking crooks!

CHAPTER XIX
THE FINAL TRAP

LONG-HELD though The Shadow's position seemed to the enemies who viewed it, his stand was no more than momentary. Before a gun could be lifted against him, The Shadow wheeled. With sweeping stride, he appeared to vanish upward.

Where he had been, thugs saw the background of a metal stairway. They headed for it, with Lucky leading the chase. Tailing the gun crew came the bearded Hindu, his wits recovered. That guardian of the lower cell was babbling words that no one understood.

The stairway surrounded a squarish wall, that was far larger than any pillar. The Shadow was a turn ahead of the men who followed him. Lucky caught no more than a glimpse of a swishing robe at every corner.

A doorway was closing at the stair top. Lucky flung himself against it, then yanked the knob. The door opened; Lucky went through. He saw a corridor, a door to the right. It was a large, wide portal, and Lucky was sure The Shadow had gone through it.

What alarmed the crook was the blatant sounds he heard, from somewhere outside. He thought that he caught the shrill of police whistles. Stopping near the doorway, he looked toward a flight of stairs. The sounds came louder, up that broad stairway.

Gummer arrived, to recognize the sounds. He swung to Lucky, in alarm:

"The bulls!"

Lucky nodded, glowering. It was the cops, all right; and there was no use in going back. That downstairs maze would only prove a trap. Lucky looked toward the open doorway; saw brass portals hanging on huge hinges. Turning to the crew, he pointed at the doorway.

"The Shadow's in there!" spat Lucky. "Come on—let's get him!"

This time, the hoodlums went first, for Lucky knew what might be due, and so did Gummer. Guns ripped from the instant the first thug entered. Bringing up the rear, the mobleaders stopped just inside the doorway.

For the first time, they viewed the temple of Siva.

Bullets were pounding those brass-faced walls. Crooks were dropping, with smoking guns in their fists. The Shadow had taken the alcove on the right. He was firing from cover.

Three fresh fighters made a dash across the floor. They were after a bead on The Shadow's vantage spot; but he had left it. He was following their course; cutting in, he flung himself into the trio, milling with his guns.

Footsteps were pounding on the outside stairs. Lucky grabbed a big door; Gummer took the other. They hurried the barriers shut. The bearded Hindu, babbling distractedly, did the only deed that remained to him. He dropped a big bar into place, to clamp the doors shut.

Lucky turned, expecting to witness The Shadow's finish. Instead, he saw the black-cloaked fighter dodging past the Siva statue, to the left. There was a door open to the right of the statue; from it peered the alarmed face of Singhar Bund.

The cult leader saw no more than gun smoke. He slammed his own door, blocking all entrance to his grotto.

"GET The Shadow!"

Lucky bawled the order. Half of his crew had floundered. The rest were diving for the side alcoves. The cry rallied a few to action; but The Shadow had the antidote for the poison they wanted to deal.

As Lucky and two others gained the angle they needed, The Shadow was away again, spinning deep into the alcove at the left of the statue.

Though momentarily out of range, he had put himself in a spot he could not leave. It was Gummer who recognized it; he reached the Siva statue, thrust a revolver past a bronze arm that held a trident. The Shadow saw the pointing muzzle. He fired; Gummer ducked back.

Lucky and the rest made a sudden attack. The Shadow met them point-blank with a fire of three swift shots. With a back step, he grabbed the door of the big metal casket that stood just behind him. Taking that last refuge, he hauled the door shut.

Lucky reached the casket. Panting, he grabbed the padlocks, snapped them into place. As he finished with the last, he sagged. Gummer reached him; heard his dying cough. Lucky had dared too much, in that last sortie against The Shadow.

There was ominous silence beyond the big brass doors that Lucky and Gummer had closed. Gummer spun about, snapped to the crooks about him:

"Why ain't the bulls ramming? They ought to be trying to get in here. Say"—he turned to the bearded Hindu—"ain't there another way out of this joint?"

The Hindu was gesticulating, trying to explain something. It didn't register with Gummer. He nudged his thumb toward the casket in the alcove.

"Lucky boxed The Shadow," he told the Hindu. "You savvy that, don't you? He's as good as croaked, The Shadow is—but so are we, unless you get us out of here before—"

Gummer was predicting trouble from the brass doors. It came before his sentence was completed. A dull explosion quivered the building. Gummer went staggering against the Siva statue. Reeling to his feet, he looked toward the doors.

Smoke was filtering through shattered brass. Joe Cardona had remembered those barriers. He had come equipped to demolish them, if Singhar Bund tried to block the police. What went for Singhar Bund, went double for the mobsters who had invaded the Siva temple.

Police were pouring through. Gummer rose to meet them with bullets, along with the remainder of the gang, who now accepted him as leader. They charged into a barrage from police revolvers. Gummer staggered, fell as he turned toward the Siva statue.

Some of the thugs had been gunned down with him; others were surrendering to the law. But the only man that Gummer saw, was the bearded Hindu.

He had gone berserk when the police crashed through. His hand was loosening from a knife handle. Like Gummer, he was through.

WITH dying motions, the Hindu pointed to the Siva statue. He moved his lips; used a hand to cup his ear. Pointing again, he lowered his fingers to touch his lips. His meaning at last was plain.

The dying Hindu wanted Gummer to perform a last task: to speak to the Siva statue. Perhaps it was Gummer's own distorted mental condition that made him understand. Furthermore, he forgot his own plight, in his urge to do the Hindu's bidding.

Gummer began to crawl toward the statue. He toppled; planked his weight forward and clutched the bronze knees with his hands. Raising himself, despite the pain that caught him, Gummer choked the words:

"It's Gummer! I'm through—like Lucky. We got—we got The Shadow. He's through—The Shadow —"

Fingers slipping from the bronze, Gummer curled in a heap. His glazed eyes turned upward, toward a face they could not see.

Joe Cardona was stooping above the dead crook, wondering what quirk had caused Gummer to utter those last words.

Because of the big brass doors, Cardona had heard no sound of the battle in the temple. The thick barriers had cut off all communication. There was nothing to show that The Shadow had been here; not even the batch of mobsters upon the floor.

Cardona supposed that some of those hoodlums had been flattened by the explosion. In the smoke, the police had depended upon sheer force of numbers to riddle the opposition. The fact that so many defenders had taken bullets did not surprise Cardona. He credited his squad with having performed exceptional marksmanship.

Nor did Cardona note the oddly satisfied expression on the faces of wounded prisoners who were filing outward. They were keeping mum; but they couldn't completely control their elation over The Shadow's finish. If the police didn't yank him from that coffin in a hurry, The Shadow would be dead for sure.

The police didn't know that The Shadow was in there! Even Cardona, the No. 1 detective, hadn't wised to it. The defeated mobbies didn't intend to tell him.

Cardona was concerned with the door that led to Singhar Bund's grotto. He was about to order another charge of explosive, when the door cautiously opened. Cardona sprang toward it, covered the crack with a revolver point. The door swung wide.

There stood Singhar Bund. He was wearing a tuxedo instead of robe; but he still had on his turban. His hands were lifted slightly; his lips wore a forced smile.

"So it is you, inspector!" Singhar Bund tried to look pleased. "I heard the explosion. I am grateful. You have rescued me from a desperate situation."

"We'll see about that," returned Cardona. "Who else is in that grotto?"

"A few of my *chelas*. I was consulting the crystal. It clouded, just before the trouble began. I remained calm; later, the crystal cleared, and—"

"And you stuck your nose out? That bunk is through, Singhar Bund. I'm arresting you, for murder!"

Singhar Bund stared, a horrified innocence forced to his face. From the room came others, who had attended the earlier meeting; among them was Phineas Leeth.

"You folks can go home," Cardona told them. "I'll take care of this faker."

"But I need witnesses!" protested Singhar Bund. "Those who can testify that I was here all evening."

Cardona agreed that those who wished could stay. A few of the less nervous cult members remained; Leeth was among them. The rest had gone, when Commissioner Weston arrived to congratulate Cardona on his work.

Those congratulations brought a stolid smile from the ace inspector. Cardona was thinking of The Shadow's part. Joe's one hope was that he could return the favor to The Shadow. Sometime,

perhaps, The Shadow would be in a plight where Cardona could really aid him.

While he considered that improbable prospect, Inspector Joe Cardona was staring at the padlocked casket wherein The Shadow had been entombed by men of crime!

CHAPTER XX
SYMBOLS OF SIVA

SINGHAR BUND stood with folded arms before the statue of Siva. His smile had gone; for he had heard a deeper accusation than he thought would come.

Singhar Bund was ready to shift blame for the deaths of Renshell and Sarmon; evidence still pinned them on Morton Mayland. But the names that Cardona mentioned made the suave Hindu quiver.

"And then Welk," completed Cardona. "He was the last of those fake accident victims. But you went after Bolingbroke, and, tonight, you made a stab at Selwood.

"Those dacoits needed to get Selwood worst of all, because he knew that his niece was goofy about this cockeyed cult of yours. That finishes you, Singhar Bund."

The Hindu shifted. He saw Commissioner Weston was as firm-faced as Cardona. With them were two detectives, ready to clamp the bracelets on Singhar Bund. Of the members who composed the Siva cult, all were gone, with one exception.

Phineas Leeth was present. He looked crushed. His eyes had reflected horror, as they viewed the twitchy face of the man whom he had once upheld.

Licking his dried lips, Singhar Bund tried to find some answer. Words did not come. He could not dispute that list that Cardona held: the one with the names of victims whose wealth had filled the coffers of Siva.

Where the list had come from, Singhar Bund could not guess. Cardona knew, but did not mention it. The list was from The Shadow.

Cardona had found it back at headquarters. The statement had borne The Shadow's signature when Cardona first read it; but that had faded, afterward. The incriminating facts, typewritten to the finest detail, had remained.

There was a knock against one of the shattered brass doors. Cardona turned, to see Lucille Mayland. Singhar Bund showed new worry when the girl entered. Lucille no longer had that self-sufficient air that went with the followers of Siva.

Coolly, Lucille told the story of her abduction; how she had been held a prisoner in a cell room below the temple. When she had finished, she looked past Singhar Bund. She was studying the statue, when she declared:

"Siva has many arms—"

Lucille paused. Cardona supplied the rest.

"Lucky Belther and his outfit," said Joe. "They were called the Arms. The strong-arm boys."

"And many eyes—"

"Gummer Gilben and his crew. We finished the lot of them."

Lucille studied the gruesome necklace that girded the throat of Siva.

"We know about that, too," stated Cardona. "The Serpents were a bunch of dacoits. They're finished. But the skulls were victims. They pin the goods on Singhar Bund."

LUCILLE still eyed the statue. She was remembering words that The Shadow had spoken. Not knowing the girl's thoughts, Cardona took another channel.

"We'll clear your grandfather," he told Lucille. "It's plain enough that he was the goat for this Siva stuff. Singhar Bund had to have a fall guy."

Lucille's eyes were still fixed upon the placid faces of the giant Siva. In emotionless tone, she stated another fact:

"Siva has three heads—"

Cardona looked at the statue, then at Weston. He started to say something; the commissioner intervened.

"The girl's right!" snapped Weston, always intrigued by the unusual. "There are three heads on the statue, inspector. The symbolism should certainly apply."

Dumfoundment held Cardona; then came the inevitable hunch. With a quick turn, Cardona looked at Singhar Bund, saw the alarm that the Hindu registered. Another half turn, Cardona spied another face that was trying to control itself. With a long stride, Cardona reached Phineas Leeth.

"You're in it!" snapped Cardona. "Sure, you're in it! Passing yourself as Sap No. 1, to lead on the suckers. Who started me on the phony trail, anyway? You did!

"That's why you called me up to the Ritz Plaza, to ask me what I knew about Hindus. You were worried, weren't you? And when I went out to get my whiskers, you called Singhar Bund, to tell him I'd be at the meeting. That's how he knew who I was."

Leeth was protesting, wildly. Cardona laughed him down. Joe was pleased because The Shadow had left him something to find out for himself, even though The Shadow had previously divined it.

"This racket needed dough to get started," snorted Cardona. "Not just a little; but a lot. That makes you the angel, Leeth; and Singhar Bund is the front. Only there's one more guy"—Joe was thinking hard, but finding no answer—"one more: the real brain!"

"I can name him," declared Lucille. "Gladly, too, because his connection with these crimes is strongest proof of my grandfather's innocence.

Tonight, when I suspected I was watched, someone called me on the telephone.

"I recognized his voice; and he knew it. That is why I was taken prisoner. But I am free; and I can name the man whose voice I heard. Courtney Renshell—the third and central Head of Siva!"

ALL eyes were on Lucille. Ears heard a muffled sound that they scarcely noted, until it finished with a sudden clang. The stroke came from the Siva statue.

Turning, they saw uptilted sheets of bronze. The platform fronting the huge idol had lifted apart on hinges.

In the space stood a sallow, dark-haired man whose face blazed fury. His eyes were as vicious as those of the departed Serpents. The hiss from his lips was more snakish than their signal call. The revolvers in Renshell's fists were trained to cover all members of the group except Phineas Leeth and Singhar Bund.

Arms were stretched. Weston and Cardona glowered their chagrin. The dicks looked sullen, especially when Leeth and Singhar Bund helped themselves to the revolvers that the detectives carried.

Lucille's eyes remained steady. The girl felt no terror.

Oddly, she had expected Renshell to appear from some secret place. The square walls of the lower floor were explained. The metal stairway girded the secret room wherein Renshell had lodged after his disappearance.

"For once," sneered Renshell, "I can waste words. My methods, it appears, were learned by someone who calls himself 'The Shadow.' Since we have not heard from him, in person, I shall divulge the facts he learned.

"His process was so simple that I did not foresee it. He merely went on the assumption that Morton Mayland was innocent. Because of that, he suspected the letter with the changed date—the main evidence against Mayland.

"I wrote that letter, giving it a former date. I erased the false date myself; in its place I inscribed the correct one. That was for your benefit, Inspector Cardona. I supposed that you would test the letter with ultraviolet light.

"The bones and ashes of a dissecting room corpse, along with my wristwatch, were sufficient evidence to prove my demise. Of course, the box that I shipped to Mayland's was valuable. But the murder of Sarmon—done by my Serpents, in Mayland's own home—was best of all."

UNDERSTANDING of many things gripped Joe Cardona. It was Renshell, familiar with Mayland's premises, who had fixed the passages, by having them cut in from the empty houses.

Renshell, too, had known of Mayland's feud with Bolingbroke. Renshell had called Mayland, exactly as the old man said, to hoax him to Bolingbroke's apartment. There, again, The Shadow, convinced of Mayland's innocence, had taken the old man's testimony as proof that Renshell still lived.

Renshell had come back to his favorite theme, upon which he gloated.

"The Shadow!" he exclaimed, with lips that expressed disdain. "He was clever—very clever— particularly tonight, when he spoke for one of my Serpents. I learned that, when Singhar Bund told me that only four had come here. I, unfortunately, had given orders to five, through the loudspeaker in the Siva statue.

"Words spoken to Siva always reach my ears. That is why I know that all of you are doomed. Because only one person could save you; and he no longer lives. Somewhere, along tonight's trail, my Arms and Eyes disposed of The Shadow!"

There was a grating sound, as scarcely noted as the *clang* that had announced Renshell's appearance. It came from the alcove to the left of the Siva statue. Singhar Bund happened to be on that side; chance turned the Hindu's gaze to the upright casket.

The sarcophagus had opened. Not from the padlocked side, but at the hinged edge. From the outswung door was stepping a shape in black.

Singhar Bund tried to gulp a warning; he was too stupefied to turn his gun toward The Shadow.

"The fake casket"—Singhar Bund was pumping words mechanically—"with the fake hinges, rigged so the yogi could come out! The air holes—to let him breathe—he could hear through those! He heard everything—"

There was no need for Singhar Bund to spout the identity of the person who had heard. The Shadow declared it, as he took a long stride from the alcove. With one automatic covering Singhar Bund, he thrust the other straight for Courtney Renshell.

WITH a quick drop, Renshell went below the tilted platform edge, hoping that the brass square would serve him as a shield. The Shadow made a sidestep toward the alcove, then an evasive shift in the opposite direction.

Tricked, Renshell fired wide. He was keeping his guns close to shelter. Before he could aim anew, The Shadow was at an outer angle. Automatics spoke, their targets Renshell's gun arms. With those blasts came the blast of a revolver.

Flinging caution aside, Joe Cardona had whipped out the revolver that crooks had not bothered to take from him. Joe was doing his best to return The Shadow's favor. It helped his aim.

As Renshell's arms flopped from the slugs that clipped them, the mastercrook sprawled dead. Cardona's bullet had reached the schemer's heart.

Singhar Bund was aiming during that action. So was Phineas Leeth. But their belated efforts were hopeless. Chiming with the blasts delivered by The Shadow and Cardona, two other guns produced a staccato from the shattered brass gates.

Harry and Cliff had accompanied Lucille to the temple. They had held Renshell covered from the moment of his appearance. When The Shadow took on Renshell, his agents cared for Leeth and Singhar Bund. Both were sprawled wounded on the floor, their pilfered revolvers unfired.

Echoes were prolonged within that room of brass, as The Shadow left those lesser murderers to the law. Crossing the alcoved temple, the black-cloaked avenger reached the open gates. His laugh quivered, to add new echoes that threw back resonance from every wall.

When Lucille looked, The Shadow was gone. Weston and Cardona, too, were staring, amazed at the swiftness of their rescuer's departure. All eyes were startled, except those jeweled optics of the Siva statue, that shone—a dozen of them—with flashing brilliance.

The faces of the maligned image held their downcast gaze. They seemed to beam with satisfaction upon the sprawled form of Courtney Renshell. He, the real master of the Siva Serpents, had paid his price for murder.

Only the power of The Shadow had solved the riddle of the killer who dwelt beneath the image of Siva. The Shadow's strategy had brought that murderer to light.

THE END

Coming in THE SHADOW Volume 13:
TWO OF THE DARK AVENGER'S STRANGEST ADVENTURES—
A torturous Aztec punishment results in the creation of
SIX MEN OF EVIL
plus Lamont and Margo enter a lost world of prehistoric terror as they meet
THE DEVIL MONSTERS

Spotlight on The Shadow:
THE DARK MASTER OF MAGIC
by Anthony Tollin

In the winter of 1930, Street and Smith executives decided to take advantage of the burgeoning popularity of their mysterious radio narrator and build a characterization to suit the voice—a crime-fighting sleuth who would be featured in a magazine of his own. The assignment went to magician-turned-journalist Walter B. Gibson, who brought along his lifelong love of prestidigitation:

> By 1930, I was doing Thurston scripts for a proposed radio show, again with fiction in the ascendant, but the project was postponed when Thurston signed a year's contract for a children's radio show. Having a year to spare, I took up mystery writing on my own and developed a character called The Shadow, whose fictional adventures, appearing in a magazine of the same title, were to keep me considerably occupied for nearly twenty years, during which period I turned out 282 Shadow novels under the pen name of Maxwell Grant.

The 33-year-old wordsmith was an authority on stage magic, having already authored more than two dozen volumes on sleight of hand, astrology and ancient mysteries, including ghostwritten books for such legendary magicians as Harry Houdini, Howard Thurston and Harry Blackstone. Gibson would use his vast magical knowledge to bring radio's phantom narrator to literary life: "By combining Houdini's penchant for escapes with the hypnotic power of Tibetan mystics, plus the knowledge shared by Thurston and Blackstone in the creation of illusions, such a character would have unlimited scope when confronted with surprise situations, yet all could be brought within the range of creditability."

In the pages of *The Shadow Magazine,* Gibson would reveal secrets of Hindu fakirs and famous stage illusionists, as he had previously done in magic books and syndicated features.

> My backlog of magical experience was helpful in creating both situations and devices for The Shadow, who frequently vanished from the midst of attacking crooks or arrived suddenly from nowhere to wreak vengeance on evildoers. He also specialized in quick changes, discarding his black cloak and slouch hat to assume the role of Lamont Cranston, a debonair clubman, or to appear in some other guise that suited his immediate need.

Following Houdini's death on October 31, 1926 (now National Magic Day), his widow turned over the escape artist's private notebooks to Gibson, who in 1930 authored the definitive book on the legendary magician's secrets, *Houdini's Escapes.*

HOUDINI
276 WEST 113TH STREET
NEW YORK. N. Y.
February 9th, 1926.

Mr. Walter B. Gibson,
Concord Hall,
Phila. Pa.

Dear Gibson:-

     This is to inform you that you are to be one of the officials on the investigation for the test or tests that may take place at the Chestnut Street Opera House, Wednesday, February 10th, where the Christian Spiritual Union will endeavor to prove to the public that intercommunication with the dead is a reality.

Enclosed you will find copy of the challenge.

Sincerely yours,

Houdini

Walter Gibson was introduced to Sir Arthur Conan Doyle (left) by their mutual friend Harry Houdini (right). Gibson sometimes assisted Houdini, an active debunker of fake spiritualists, in his ghostbusting activities and later incorporated the experiences into Shadow novels like *The Ghost Makers*.

The Shadow's wall-climbing was inspired by the turn-of-the-century "Walking Upside Down" illusion pictured in Walter Gibson's 1920s newspaper feature.

In his Shadow novels, Gibson frequently called upon the secrets he had gleaned from Houdini's personal notebooks and memoranda. While Houdini achieved his greatest fame as an escape artist, he'd begun his career as a traditional magician, and his act consisted of both escapes and elaborate magic illusions. He revived his famous "Metamorphosis" trunk trick on June 2, 1922 at a Society of American Magicians banquet, assisted by Sir Arthur Conan Doyle. "Houdini gave a perfectly amazing performance," Sherlock Holmes' creator recalled, "in which having been packed into a bag and the bag into a trunk, corded up and locked, he was out again after only a few seconds' concealment in a tent, while in his place his wife was found, equally bound, bagged and boxed, with my dresscoat on which I had put upon him before I tied his hands behind him. Houdini is the greatest conjurer in the world and this is his greatest trick."

Houdini eventually introduced his ghostwriter to Conan Doyle. "He, at the time, was great friends with Houdini because, while they were in opposite camps,

he knew that Houdini was sincere in his disbelief of spiritualism. So they batted it back and forth and, of course, Doyle was always trying to convert Houdini." While visiting with Conan Doyle that weekend, Walter discovered that the British author was already familiar with Gibson's syndicated features on spiritualism and ancient mysteries.

As developed by Gibson, The Shadow inherited Sherlock Holmes' deductive abilities along with Houdini's prowess as an escape artist and ghost-buster. Walter performed on the same stage with Houdini in 1923, and also assisted his friend in investigations debunking phony spiritualists. His work with Houdini unmasking fake mediums inspired Shadow novels like *The Ghost Makers,* just as Houdini's torturous escape techniques would bring a sense of reality to pulp thrillers like *Green Eyes.*

"When The Shadow required gadgets, I took pains to make them valid," Gibson explained. "I patterned his escapes from traps on those found in Houdini's own notes. The Shadow was skilled in climbing cliffs or buildings in the fashion of a human fly; but when he encountered a wall too sheer and smooth to allow finger grips or toeholds, I supplied him with a set of suction cups, like those used in 'Walking Upside Down' beneath the dome of a theater, as described in my old syndicate article."

Gibson had written: "Before 1900 acrobats were performing as human flies, using rubber suckers to walk upside down on ceilings. They were real human flies.

"The cups work on a simple scientific principle. A concave disk of soft rubber is attached to the bottom of each of the performer's shoes, and the edges of the disks moistened.

The Shadow's "Devil's Whisper" was an important defensive weapon.

"Each time the foot is pressed against the surface of the ceiling, a vacuum is created, so that the air is ejected from within the concave disk, and the edges stick tightly, preventing the air from returning when the foot pressure is relaxed."

A secret pocket concealed in The Shadow's black cloak contained a dangerous stage magician's chemical compound that had recently fallen out of favor.

When The Shadow was trapped under the looming gun muzzles of gloating, trigger-happy crooks, he managed to stay his execution momentarily by raising his ungloved hands with palms wide open. A thrust of his right hand, with a snap of its thumb and fingers—and a loud blast, accompanied by a vivid flash and a puff of smoke, wiped the leers from their evil faces. Blinded, the staggered would-be assassins recoiled, with their puny guns popping harmlessly upward, while The Shadow, whipping a brace of .45 automatics from beneath his cloak, slugged his way through his stupefied foemen, turning himself from victim into victor.

Whenever The Shadow staged that caper, I would supply a footnote (signed by Maxwell Grant) stating that The Shadow used two highly potent chemical substances to produce the blast—so potent, in fact, that to reveal their composition might prove disastrous. Today there are Shadow "buffs" who hark back to those days before they were born and wonder why such an impossibility was thrust upon them under the head of scientific fact. It may surprise them to learn that this startling effect was listed by magic dealers under the title of the "Devil's Whisper" and was guaranteed to wake up any audience when a magician walked on stage and snapped his fingers to prove that he was there.

It went off the market after a Chicago magic dealer demonstrated it for a customer, using several times the recommended amount. He lost his hand in the blast, which knocked both men unconscious. People arriving on the scene found the office so badly damaged that they thought a time bomb had exploded there. So the description in the Shadow novels was by no means fanciful and the warning footnote, with its refusal to divulge the secret formula, was significant indeed.

While The Shadow utilized many elements of stage magic in his battles against evil, in one instance the process was reversed and a Shadow vanish moved from a Gibson novel onto the stage:

…I stationed The Shadow in a stack of huge truck tires outside of a garage. By thrusting his automatic muzzles between the tires, he drove off a horde of gunmen whose own shots failed to penetrate his improvised pillbox. When finally sure that he was out of ammunition, the gunners charged en masse and snatched away the tires from the top of the stack to the bottom, only to find that The Shadow again was gone.

I sent that story on to Blackstone the magician, along with some appropriate suggestions. Before the season was over, Blackstone was presenting a stage illusion in which a girl crawled into a rack of tires, only to vanish when the tires were rolled away and formed into an upright stack, from which she reappeared. Blackstone continued to perform the tire illusion as an outstanding feature of his show throughout his career as America's foremost magician.

The "Tire Trick" pioneered by The Shadow was not only a fixture of the original Blackstone show, but was resurrected decades later by Blackstone, Jr., in his elaborate Broadway revival of stage magic.

The Shadow knows … the hidden secrets of the world's greatest magicians! •

Harry Blackstone's famous "Tire Trick" vanish (left) was suggested by his friend Walter Gibson, and inspired by a shadowy getaway in *The Lone Tiger* (right).

HOUDINI'S SHADOWY SUCCESSOR

The Shadow's mastery of escape was an inheritance from Houdini, bequeathed by the famed escape artist through his private notebooks and memoranda to his biographer Walter Gibson, who in turn entrusted the secrets to the Dark Avenger.

Nowhere is this legacy better showcased than in this excerpt from Walter Gibson's fifteenth Shadow novel Green Eyes, *in which the Master of Darkness establishes himself as Houdini's heir. And who but a close friend and confidant of Houdini could have so dramatically related the torturous pain and exhaustion routinely confronted by the world's greatest escapist in many of his famous escapes?*

As an instrument of agony, the Chinese torture rack was one of the strangest and most formidable devices in all the world. It brought slower pain than did the infernal creations of the Middle Ages, but its work was sure.

Ling Soo had spoken the truth when he had praised this Oriental contrivance; but he had been in error when he had said that escape was impossible. Some years before, one man had managed to extricate himself from its toils. The American, Houdini, had allowed himself to be fastened in a Chinese torture rack and had worked his way free after long and strenuous efforts.

There had been only one Houdini—a master of his art. Strong and powerful, he had used his amazing ingenuity to its utmost in that escape. Now The Shadow, weakened from his terrible fall into the hold of the ship, was confronted by the same problem that had taxed the skill of Houdini.

With The Shadow, it meant life or death. Unless his mighty mind could divine the only possible way of overcoming the hold of this machine, unless his weary muscles could respond to the efforts that were demanded, The Shadow would perish!

Time, too, was short. The Shadow, with wired ropes about his wrists, had been restrained while unconscious. He had gained no opportunity to fight against the bonds when they had been placed upon him.

His arms were already wearied from the strain which they had undergone. For he had dangled long before his consciousness had returned to him!

There he hung. His fingers could not reach the knots upon his wrists. They were more than a foot below the crossbeam of the rack. It was humanly impossible to move upward. Nor could his feet avail him, for they barely touched the floor!

Buried alive in the hollow of the deep-set Chinese junk, The Shadow faced the most terrible situation in his long career.

Free, he could struggle against odds that were seemingly unconquerable. Bound with ordinary restraints, he could fight his way free. But he was now in the grasp of the powerful device that was the greatest machination ever designed by a subtle, Oriental mind!

Could The Shadow meet this formidable test— the one that Houdini alone had undergone successfully?

His motionless, hanging body, with its still shadow stretched across the floor, betokened complete helplessness. The longer that it remained in that position, the more The Shadow's strength would dwindle. That was the most sinister factor of this horrible Chinese torture rack.

At last, The Shadow moved. In the silence of that room, broken only by a soft lapping of tiny waves against the wooden sides of the *Pung-Shoon,* the hands of The Shadow clutched above his head. Futilely at first, they finally succeeded in gripping the rope that led to the beam above.

But the fingers, alone, could afford no aid. Although they worked with supernormal strength, they did not raise the body a fraction of an inch.

The fingers did not seek that impossible task. They were twisting at the rope. The dangling form began to sway. The toes added to the sidewise motion. Grazing the floor, they added to the swing.

The action was prolonged and tedious. The fingers, gripping, worked from above. The feet raised slightly from the floor each time the body moved gently to one side. As it went in the opposite direction, the feet, stretched toes downward, added an impetus.

Inch by inch, the motion increased. Each swing was longer, now. Fingers and toes, working together and using every possible effort, were increasing the momentum.

Tedious though it seemed, The Shadow was gaining what he desired.

His body was swinging like a living pendulum!

Harry Houdini

What was the purpose of this amazing action?

It could not strain the stout rope. That was too firmly fastened. Ling Soo had left naught to chance. Seemingly, The Shadow was expending tremendous effort—all in vain!

Yet the pendulum swing kept on, while the grotesque shadow on the floor followed back and forth beneath the glow of the single lantern.

Wider—longer were the swings. Off to the right, The Shadow's foot almost touched the upright post on that side. Back went the swing; the left foot just touched the other post.

The wild swings still increased. Then came the final one, that served The Shadow's purpose.

The right foot, stretching to its utmost, went barely past the upright post. The extended toes were just beyond that spot. With uncanny skill, the tip of the foot caught the post and stopped the swing.

The body did not return across the floor between the posts. Instead, the foot made the utmost of its momentary hold. It squirmed and worked until the ankle was beyond the post. Then, with the body moving upward, the knee made its grip. The left leg had joined in the work now.

Inch by inch, The Shadow's lower limbs were climbing to the top of the upright post!

The objective was reached. The Shadow rested. His body, doubled, was beneath the crossbeam. His knees gripping near the joint of the upright post, were taking the strain from those tired wrists and arms.

Now The Shadow writhed in superhuman effort. Difficult though his first action had been, the present task was stupendous.

Twice he failed; but on the third time, with a mighty lunge, he urged his body to the top of the crossbeam. Poised there, balanced on the beam, his body was relieved of all burden. His hands, coming up with him, were pressed against his tired form.

One obstacle yet remained—those tightly knotted ropes, with wire bindings.

How could The Shadow work against them? His hands were helpless. His muscles were tired to the utmost. The straining wrists seemed scarcely capable of further action. Their strength was gone.

With elbows gripping the sides of the upright beam, The Shadow steadied his body. His head bent forward. His lips were against those binding ropes. With his teeth, The Shadow attacked the knots!

He did not strive to undo the twisted bits of wire. The cord, with its knots, was the real force that held the wrists so tightly clamped together. Each tug that The Shadow made—each grip that his teeth supplied—served to weaken the strong knots.

They loosened gradually. The wires kept them from coming further undone. But now the wrists were aiding. The rest that they had received had afforded them new strength.

They spread and pressed, forcing the wires to the sides of the knots. The knots tightened; but the wrists had gained a slack!

Again, the teeth worked while the wrists rested. Once more the knots were slowly loosened. Then came the sharp tug of the straining wrists. The slack increased; but the binding wires now held with a tighter grip.

The wrists moved backward and forward. The ropes chafed them raw. They twisted and turned until finally they rested side by side, with a hand upon each forearm.

The Shadow's legs were holding him now. Each time he tugged with his arms, his form nearly toppled from its perch. At last, when strength seemed gone, the amazing man rested for a moment; then gave a final, mighty pull, his bound arms traveling in opposite directions.

The right arm came free! Its wrist was out of the bond!

But the sudden release had thrown The Shadow's body to one side—toward the front of the torture rack. His knees lost their hold. The right hand clutched for the crossbeam too late. With his left wrist still tangled in the loop, The Shadow plunged toward the floor.

It was the left hand, seizing the crossbeam as it passed, that broke the fall. Momentarily, The Shadow hung poised; then his fingers slipped away.

The cord came taut as the left arm fell; the wrist, now held only by a large, loose loop, wrenched free. The Shadow caught himself as he landed on his right side.

He lay there, a strange figure in the guise of Foy. His face was streaked with blood. His wrists were raw. His lips were bleeding from contact with the binding wires. His strength seemed gone, as he breathed heavily and did not seek to move.

The Shadow had accomplished the seemingly impossible! He had escaped from the Chinese torture rack! He had duplicated the feat of the great Houdini, under the most difficult of all conditions! •

THE MAGIGALS MYSTERY

A complete novel from the private annals of The Shadow as told to **Maxwell Grant**

CHAPTER I
THE CRYSTAL SKULL

WHEN Lamont Cranston entered the lobby of the Hotel Harbison, he found it filled with Magigals. They were of many shapes and sizes, they all wore big badges with red ribbons that said "Magigals" in gold letters, and they were holding the most unusual convention in the history of Chicago.

The Magigals are a society of women magicians with chapters all over the country. They had picked Chicago for their convention because it was centrally located and the attendance had exceeded all expectations. Although this was only the opening day, the convention was already rated as a huge success, except by a lineup of dour-faced hotel guests who were checking out as fast as more Magigals arrived.

Because of the unexpected turnout, the Magigals had not been able to find enough hotel rooms for all their extra delegates. Being magicians, they had tackled that problem in a characteristic way. Staid

guests of the Hotel Harbison had been disturbed by loud raps on their doors. Upon opening their doors, they had been terrified by collapsing skeletons that floundered across the thresholds, only to rise, bow, and dance away.

The electric lights were also acting temperamental. The doors in the Harbison had special locks that put out the room lights when the key was turned from the outside by a departing guest. The Magigals had found some way to get at this device, because rooms were suddenly going black while the guests were still inside. That wasn't all; everytime an outraged guest fumbled in the dark for a telephone, a lighted electric light bulb floated in through the transom, circled the room and floated out again.

Lights weren't all that were floating around the Hotel Harbison, however. Doves were flying up and down the corridors, rabbits were hopping in and out of elevators, and everytime a beleaguered guest answered a ringing telephone, he heard ducks quacking across the wire. It was easier for one

guest to check out than try to have five hundred Magigals thrown out, so guests were checking out, one by one.

Lamont Cranston heard them exchanging tales of woe as he passed the line of people leaving the hotel. Of course, the Magigals were being very nice about it. They were parading all along the line, showing their victims card tricks, cutting ribbons and restoring them, shaking silk handkerchiefs and making them change color. But invariably, they would reach into a victim's inside pocket and bring out a string of sausages, a cabbage, or even a live alligator. After that, nobody minded much about leaving the Hotel Harbison.

At the message desk in the spacious lobby, Cranston gave his name and inquired for any telegrams. There were none, so he left word that he would be waiting in the lobby. Then Cranston elbowed his way through a group of Magigals who were offering to burn his necktie and restore it, along with a few odd miracles such as making his cuff links disappear or transporting his watch into the center of a loaf of bread. With a suave smile, Cranston dismissed these entreaties and continued over to the newsstand.

There, newspaper headlines marked a weakness in the Magigals Convention. Such a gathering should have gained notice on the front page, but it hadn't. The headlines were devoted to more shocking news. Chicago was experiencing a suicide wave, tallying eight cases in a mere three days. In ratio to the city's population, this was small, but considering the type of suicides, it was unprecedented.

These were not suicides of the type brought on by poverty, despondency, or any of the usual contributory causes. Every suicide was a man of means, reputedly in good health. Nor were they suicides of the prosaic gas-pipe variety. Instead, the victims went in for the spectacular. One man had deliberately wheeled a hired automobile in front of a streamlined flyer, Milwaukee-bound. Another had flavored a mint julep with a powdery poison and tossed off the drink in one of Chicago's most exclusive bars. A third had rammed a speedboat head-on into one of the massive intake cribs of the Chicago water system, a tower-shaped structure rearing from the waters of Lake Michigan, two miles off shore.

Most startling of all was the man who had risen with the curtain in the Civic Opera House, finishing his trip with a plunge to the stage in the presence of two thousand witnesses. Considering that the stage of the opera house was thirteen stories high, it was not remarkable that the man failed to survive the fall.

All the victims were from out of town. They came from such cities as Dubuque, Zanesville, Tampa, Spokane, and Wichita, all of which had practically nothing in common. They were registered at fine hotels or visiting at swanky apartments. All had come to Chicago on business or for a good time. None of them had gone broke, for money had been found in their pockets as well as bankbooks in their suitcases. Yet all had climaxed their Chicago stay by seeking death in some spectacular manner.

The psychiatrists had the answer, according to a newspaper which Cranston picked up and began to read. It was a form of autosuggestion, each suicide copying the example of another. If traced back, the case histories of these individuals would show that all had psychopathic trends. Such a suicide epidemic could grow into a form of mass hysteria. It behooved the public at large to remain calm.

The Chicago police were taking this theory seriously. Plainclothes men were stationed in all public meeting places to discourage suicide attempts. This applied to the Harbison lobby where the Magigals were in conclave and Cranston was hearing grumbles from the regular guests on that score.

According to the regulars who had isolated themselves by the newsstand, it would be very jolly if the Magigals caught the mass hysteria and made front page news by eliminating themselves, their magic and all, in one wholesale suicide pact.

"Look at those dizzy dames," one man was saying. "They're mobbing that poor soul who runs the perfume counter. Only they aren't buying perfume, they're probably showing him card tricks and getting ready to pull a pet skunk out of the back of his coat collar."

Cranston looked toward the perfume counter and observed a cluster of Magigals. But if they were hounding the dapper clerk behind the counter, it wasn't by dint of card tricks. On the contrary, they seemed to be pleading with him, but his only response was a continued head shake.

Sauntering over, Cranston watched from the fringe of a dozen Magigals and saw that the clerk was ready to capitulate.

"All right, girls," the dapper clerk was saying wearily. "I'll show you the crystal skull. It's been on display for a week, though, so why couldn't you come around to see it earlier?"

"Because the convention didn't begin until today," piped a stylish Magigal, "and we didn't hear about the skull until we arrived."

"This is a magical convention," put in another. "That's why we're all interested in the crystal skull and it's all the more reason why you ought to keep it on display."

"It's been sold, I tell you," the clerk pleaded. "I was just packing it for delivery."

That brought a series of sallies from the Magigals.

"Sold? For how much?"

"Who bought it and why?"

"Maybe we'll give you a better offer!"

Spreading his hands helplessly, the clerk looked around for moral support. He saw Cranston and was encouraged by the latter's calm demeanor. Lamont Cranston was a man who never became excited. His features, which seemed cast from a fixed mold, were immobile, except when his thin lips betrayed a suggestion of a smile which in itself was cryptic. His eyes, though steady, had a friendly mildness on occasions such as this. The perfume clerk, much beflustered by the congregated Magigals, felt that he could depend upon Cranston as an ally.

Relieved, the clerk glanced away and saw another man on the border of the circling Magigals. This chap, too, was handsome, but in a silkier way than Cranston. Indeed, he was over-handsome and his pose of confidence could well have been defined as conceit. From his wavy hair down to the pointed mustache above his indulgently smiling lips, he showed suavity in every facial line. He was dawdling with a cigarette in a long amber holder and the light laugh that he delivered caused the Magigals to glance in his direction.

Immediately, half the Magigals forgot the crystal skull and began to buzz among themselves.

"That's John Halifax! He must have flown in from Hollywood!"

"They said he might be here for the convention, but we thought it was only a press stunt!"

"Somebody claimed he was working in pictures —"

"That was only talk. He's really planning to go out with his big show. They say he intends to carry ten tons of illusions and twenty girls."

"Maybe he will hire some of us! I'd rather be with the Halifax show than play kiddie dates around department stores."

The attention showered upon Halifax was helpful to the perfume clerk. It gave him a chance to exhibit the crystal skull while some of the excitement was diverted elsewhere. Opening a large package behind the counter, the clerk brought out the crystal skull and set it on display.

The crystal skull was quite a remarkable device.

It was life size, assuming that the term "life" could be applied to a skull. It was made entirely of a transparent substance resembling glass, rendering the skull both unbreakable and light in weight. One indication of this was the skull's articulated jaw. It was hinged to the skull proper, yet with no trace of the joining. If of glass, the jaw would necessarily have been molded and, therefore, become an immovable part of the skull itself. This jaw, however, wagged up and down, as the clerk brought the skull toward the counter.

The clerk was not handling the skull itself. He was lifting a square base, like a small platform a foot square and three or four inches thick, on which the skull was fixed. The skull's mounting consisted of oversized vertebrae, transparent like the skull. The base, too, was of that same clear substance, with four small legs at the corners, so that when the square platform was placed upon the counter, it stood completely isolated.

Set deep in the hollow eye sockets of the skull were two huge rhinestones that glittered with the brilliancy of diamonds. Otherwise, the skull was undecorated, though the platform was ornamented with circular lines that formed an intriguing criss-cross, like engraved filigree, or lacework. The brilliants gave the skull a certain semblance of life, enabling it to stare directly back at any human eyes which might focus upon it.

Such eyes were meeting the skull's right now.

The human eyes belonged to a Magigal whose badge proclaimed her hometown as Seattle. She was an intriguing girl, so intriguing that Cranston found himself spending more time on her than on the skull. Her oval face was finely formed, its features accentuated in a setting of black hair which parted in the center and fell to the girl's shoulders. She looked pale, but that was due partly to the darkness of her jet-black hair. The slightness of her makeup could also have accounted for her pallid appearance, but Cranston attributed it largely to the girl's intensity.

For the girl's nerves seemed taut, her whole interest riveted upon the eyes of the skull. Her lips, so drawn that their color seemed that of a wilted rose, were moving, were delivering a singsong undertone. Cranston was close enough to catch the girl's words.

"Listen, skull," the girl was saying. "Listen and remember. My name is Verity Joyce. I came from Seattle to Chicago. I am staying at the Hotel Harbison and am attending the Magigals Convention."

As Verity concluded her monotone, the skull began to nod as though understanding all that the girl had said. Yet the skull, of crystalline construction, seemingly lacked all capability of containing any hidden mechanism. The same applied to the platform on which the skull was resting.

As the skull's nod ended, Verity proceeded.

"Speak, skull," the girl urged. "Tell me all you know. Repeat whatever you have heard."

The skull swiveled from side to side in a slow but decisive head shake. Verity watched and waited, with pursed lips and puzzled frown; then, disappointed, the girl turned away. The clerk, prowling restlessly behind the counter, decided that it was time to end the demonstration.

"It's a crazy thing, that skull," the clerk said, speaking to Cranston, who was now standing alone. "You say things to it and it nods or shakes its head, only the answers don't make sense. You hold some fingers in front of its eyes though, and it always counts them right."

By way of evidence, the clerk held three fingers beyond the skull's eyes and the skull obliged by clicking its jaws three times. Lifting the platform, skull and all, the clerk put it down beneath the counter.

"Back you go into your box, Bosco," said the clerk. "You're safe now. I'm putting you where the Magigals won't get you."

Even before this, the Magigals had lost all enthusiasm for the skull; in fact, Verity Joyce alone had remained to test the mysterious contraption. The other Magigals had concentrated on John Halifax and were bombarding the suave young man with questions and demands for autographs. Halifax was giving them a standard Hollywood smile as he scrawled his signature and the only girl he really noticed was Verity Joyce.

Discounting the fact that Verity was probably as attractive as any Magigal in the group, Halifax's interest in the raven-haired girl was probably due to the fact that she was giving him no notice. Verity's thoughts were elsewhere and her solemn expression showed it. But whether she was brooding over the comparatively poor showing of the crystal skull, or simply trying to outsmart the other Magigals in their play for Halifax, was something of a question.

As for Lamont Cranston, he no longer had time to analyze either form of skullduggery. A bellboy was parading the Harbison lobby waving a telegram and calling for Mr. Cranston. Leaving the perfume counter, Cranston acknowledged the call and tore open the telegram. It was the very sort of telegram that he had expected, but it promised Cranston results sooner than he had anticipated.

Thrusting the telegram into his pocket, Cranston started for a phone booth, impervious to the milling Magigals about him. They and their curious convention could go their way, along with John Halifax, Verity Joyce and the puzzling if not amazing crystal skull which some ingenious mechanic had evidently fashioned to serve as an advertising device.

Lamont Cranston had gained a mission in Chicago, a mission that he had hoped to find. From now on he would be investigating the strange suicide wave that had swept the lakeshore city. Already Cranston held a theory regarding that singular epidemic; now he was to put it to the test.

The question in Cranston's mind was this: Whether or not the chain of so-called suicides was a veil for something known as murder. From Cranston's immobile lips came a weird, whispered laugh, so uncanny that it might well have crept from the jaws of the crystal skull he had so recently viewed. That mirth proclaimed Cranston's adequacy for the test he was to undertake. It was the laugh of the world's most celebrated crime-hunter: The Shadow.

CHAPTER II
DEATH GOES BERSERK

TELEPHONES were ringing right and left around Inspector Rick Smedley. Never in his years of experience on the Chicago police had Rick encountered anything so hectic as this. Half a dozen assistants were busy answering the calls, but they couldn't keep up with them. More help would be needed, but by then Inspector Smedley would be a madman.

Big, bluff, brawny and with a face as purple as Lake Michigan under one of its sweetest summer sunsets, Rick Smedley didn't look like a man who ever had a weak moment. But he'd had one when he'd agreed to use his office as a clearing house for phone calls relating to the suicide wave. That had been the day before yesterday; by now, the deluge was overwhelming, yet Rick was inclined to believe it a mere trickle, compared with what was still to come.

At least Rick had finally promised himself some relief. Originally, he had intended to answer each call personally. Later, he'd left that to assistants who weeded out the calls and passed the more important on to Rick. Now, the inspector had decided that even the most intelligent calls could be handled by subordinates, his capacity being solely that of a director. But it still wasn't the answer. What Rick had to do was get away from all this for a while and he intended to do just that.

Cling-a-ling-a-linggggggg—

Six phones were jangling at once. From the jargon of answers that his men gave, Inspector Smedley could gather what was coming over the wire. Some crank was sitting with a gun pressed to his head, asking the police to wait and hear the shot. Another caller was asking if bay rum were a poison, having just seen a bearded man purchase a bottle in a drugstore. Somebody was saying that a pet dog had just jumped off the end of a Lake Michigan pier, indicating that animals were succumbing to the suicide mania. Out of all this, one of Smedley's men was waving a telephone at Rick himself.

"It's for you, Inspector. It's Lester Tyburn."

"Lester Tyburn?" echoed Smedley. "You mean somebody says he's Lester Tyburn, the soap manufacturer?"

"That's right."

"Tell him to smother himself in his own suds," advised Smedley. "We can't discriminate where suicide is concerned. Anyway, Tyburn will find it cheaper to leave his money to his wife than keep on paying her all that alimony."

Smedley's man gave a weary smile.

"It's really Tyburn, Inspector. He isn't talking about committing suicide. He wants to find some way to prevent it."

"That's a help," decided Smedley. "Give me the phone."

Over the phone, Smedley heard a man's crisp voice announcing himself as Lester Tyburn. Then, after Smedley stated his own identity, Tyburn proceeded:

"I'd like to see you, Inspector. It's only a small favor, but most important to me. I'm worried about the way people are committing suicide in conspicuous places."

"You're worried?" demanded Smedley. "What do you think I am and everybody else in Chicago?"

"That's just my point," declared Tyburn. "You must take preventative measures, Inspector."

"If you don't read the papers," snapped Smedley, "why don't you listen to the radio? We've posted men in every el station, theater, hotel lobby, department store, museum, taproom and children's playground. What else do you ask?"

"You should be checking on all special events," argued Tyburn. "I read the newspapers and so do these suicides or they wouldn't know there was a suicide wave. But we're wasting time, Inspector. If you can come and see me, I might give you a suggestion that will prove a useful weapon to you. How soon could you make it?"

That last line was a welcome punch line to Smedley's tired ears.

"Right now!" rejoined the inspector. "Where can I see you?"

"At my apartment in the Armistead Arms," replied Tyburn. "It's quarter of nine and you can easily make it in fifteen minutes. May I expect you at nine o'clock?"

"Nine on the dot, if not sooner."

As soon as Smedley hung up, a new sound greeted him. It was the clicking of a teletype, and from across the office, a detective was giving Smedley a hurried beckon. Going to the Teletype machine, the inspector read the message that was coming through.

NEW YORK. OFFCL GX33. TO INSPEC. SMEDLEY CHI. POLICE. REQUEST CONFIDENTIAL INFO RE SUICIDE WAVE PREVENTION METHODS AND POSSIBLE CRIME CONNECTION. EXPECT PERSONAL CONTACT L. CRANSTON TO RECEIVE SAME IMMEDIATE. R. WESTON COMM. POLICE. N. Y. REPLY OFFCL W32QX5.

Snatching the tape from the Teletype machine, Inspector Smedley broke into a tirade.

"We've had enough crackpot local calls," Smedley stormed, "without having the New York police go goofy on us. What's this stuff about a possible crime connection? And who is this Cranston the New York commissioner has authorized to contact us?"

An answer came from one of the helpers who was holding a telephone.

"Call for you, Inspector. Mr. Cranston at the Hotel Harbison. Sounds like there's been a suicide there."

Snatching up the telephone, Smedley heard only bedlam over the wire. He shouted a "Hello" and a calm voice spoke out of the confusion.

"Hello, Inspector Smedley." The tone was Cranston's. "No trouble here at the Harbison. Nothing but a Magigals convention. Did you receive a wire from Commissioner Weston in New York?"

"I did," returned Smedley, "and what does he mean by these suicides having a possible crime connection?"

"That was my suggestion," Cranston replied. "It occurred to me that what looks like suicide often turns out to be murder."

"And you think the Chicago police might be covering up murder?"

"I think you could possibly be unaware of it."

From anyone other than such a quiet-toned speaker, such a suggestion would have elicited a verbal blast from Inspector Smedley. But there was something authentic in that calm voice, a note that offered a solution to the confusion that reigned in Smedley's own mind. Remembering his appointment with Lester Tyburn, another man of status who held opinions pertaining to the suicide wave, Rick Smedley decided that he could lose nothing by bringing Cranston into the interview. Indeed, for the first time in forty-eight hours, Rick let his bluff face relax into a smile at the thought of letting a couple of amateur sherlocks have their say.

"You have something, Mr. Cranston," decided Rick, politely. "I'll tell you what to do. Get in a cab and go to the Armistead Arms. It's right across the river from the Hotel Harbison. Ask for Mr. Lester Tyburn and tell him I sent you. I'll meet you there in about fifteen minutes."

Ringing telephones remained unanswered while the members of Smedley's staff stared in profound amazement. Never had they dreamed that the tempestuous inspector could adopt such an appeasing mood. But they were disillusioned the moment that Rick hung up.

"Answer those telephones!" howled Rick. "If any more yaps bother you, cut them off! Give me paper and a pencil and let me at that Teletype! I'll send that stuffed shirt of a New York commissioner a message that will bum up the tape at the other end!"

What Rick Smedley sent was printable only on a police teletype. It took three minutes for Rick to get the message off and he paced the office five minutes more, waiting for a reply. When it came, it was couched in terms that made Rick's message sound like something out of *Emily Post's Book of Etiquette*. Rick thought he had gone the limit in telling the New York police to mind their own business, but Commissioner Weston had topped him and in anything but stuffed shirt style. Translated, Weston had suggested that the whole Chicago force jump into the Chicago River, Lake Michigan being far too good for them.

In two minutes, Rick Smedley consigned Manhattan Island to an unnamed destination and advised Weston to take the voyage with it. Sending that across the Teletype, Rick departed to keep his appointment with Lester Tyburn, meanwhile framing choice statements as a greeting for Lamont Cranston.

Having lost more than ten minutes of the

scheduled fifteen that he had allotted for the trip to the Armistead Arms, Rick Smedley tried to make up time by having the chauffeur of the police car siren his way through traffic. But time-saving methods failed when the car neared the Chicago River, which Rick, like Cranston, had to cross to reach the Armistead Arms.

A bridge across the narrow river was rising to allow a ship to pass through. Along the river other such bridges were rising in succession, lifting in hinged fashion from the shore ends. Fuming, Smedley glared through the windshield of the car until his arm was grabbed by the police chauffeur beside him.

"Look, Inspector!"

Out of a small group of pedestrians who were halted by the rising bridge sprang a man who was screaming wildly as he flung aside his hat and the coat which other men were gripping to restrain him. Onto the rising bridge he dashed, up its inclining walk, which increased its slope so steadily that frantic followers lost their footing when they tried to overtake him. But the lone man, inspired by frenzy and the speed he had picked up in his early dash, managed to reach the towering end of the hoisted bridge. There, high above the crowd, he gave a crazy twist and plunged to the river in a headlong dive.

By then, Inspector Smedley was out of the police car and dashing through the throng. Passing men who were sliding down from the tilted walk, Rick reached the river just as a wheezy tugboat came sloshing beneath the upraised bridge. The skipper of the craft had seen the madman's dive; bells were clanging to put the tug's engine in reverse and its squealy whistle was shrilling an alarm. Members of the crew were peeling off their jerseys and diving overboard in a hurried effort to find the crazed man who had made the suicidal plunge.

Along the shore, other witnesses were trying to point out the spot where the man had disappeared. From the river, small boats were coming to the scene. Flashlights, automobile headlights, finally searchlights, played along the murky waters of the river, but all in vain. The members of the tugboat crew were climbing on board their craft again, shaking their heads, and pointing out where they thought the man had gone under, but there was no sign of the victim.

Police were arriving to aid the search. They were questioning witnesses and examining the hat and coat that the man had thrown away. The tugboat was waved on through, so that the bridge could be lowered. The police were watching the river in case the body reappeared; after that, they would begin to drag for the victim, the customary procedure.

Joining the police, Rick Smedley showed his inspector's badge, asked to see the contents of the coat. No papers of any consequence were in the pockets; merely a pack of cigarettes and some matches which bore an advertisement for the Chicago and Eastern Illinois Railroad. The matches might prove a clue to the man's identity; Smedley returned them to one of the officers and looked at the hat.

The hat label showed it had been purchased in a Chicago store and it was a new hat. It bore the initials W. B. But Smedley wasn't in a mood to pursue this investigation further. He was off duty, he had an appointment, and besides, he was sick of the suicide business. Leaving the police to continue with their routine, Smedley returned to his car, told the chauffeur to drive him on to the Armistead Arms. They crossed the river, reached their destination, and Smedley went up to Tyburn's apartment.

There, Lester Tyburn, a tall, rugged-faced man with grizzled hair, greeted Rick Smedley and introduced him to Lamont Cranston, the other man Smedley wanted to meet. Judging from a pair of empty drinking glasses, Cranston had arrived about the time that Smedley himself was expected, a half hour ago. With a gruff comment, "I guess I need it," Smedley accepted a drink that Tyburn offered him.

Then, wheeling to Cranston, whose manner was as calm as his voice on the telephone had indicated, Rick Smedley declared brusquely:

"If you're wondering why I'm late, I'll tell you. I've been watching the suicide wave at firsthand. If you want to know if there are any new cases, the answer is yes. I know, because I saw the latest one happen. So don't tell me it's murder. We haven't been having murders in Chicago and won't be, unless somebody asks for it."

From Smedley's mood it seemed that Lamont Cranston might be that "somebody," so Cranston merely smiled and did not ask for details. Those would come later, of that he was sure. Gesturing to Tyburn, who apparently hadn't grasped the point at issue, Cranston spoke in calming tone to Smedley.

"Mr. Tyburn has a problem, Inspector," said Cranston. "He was telling me about it and I'm sure that you can help him. Why not let him state it, while you sit down and relax?"

Inspector Rick Smedley decided that this was the best advice he had been given in all of three days.

CHAPTER III
CROSSED PATHS

LESTER TYBURN came directly to the point. He was impatient to get at it, so impatient that he kept glancing at his wrist watch, which registered approximately nine fifteen.

"Briefly, it's this, Inspector," declared Tyburn.

"There's no telling where suicide will strike next, but we can be pretty sure that the men who intend it will go out of their way to make a public show of it. Maybe they steel their nerves that way."

Rick Smedley nodded. He had just witnessed a case that supported Tyburn's opinion, which in turn was based upon the manner of the previous suicides.

"Here's something, then, that might attract them," continued Tyburn. He picked up the society page of the Sunday paper, spread it in front of Smedley. "My wife is giving a big charity affair up at Longwood, our North Shore estate. It's listed as one of the big social events of the year, but it won't be difficult for anyone to get into it. I don't want crazy people diving into lily ponds or impaling themselves on picket fences. But they're likely to be, if this suicide wave continues."

"Your place is twenty miles north," objected Smedley, looking up from the newspaper. "That puts it outside of our jurisdiction."

"All the more reason to worry," returned Tyburn. "The way you are clamping down on suicides, some of these fanatics may figure that a trip up the lake would be a healthy way to start out to die."

"But you have a local police force at Longwood."

"About enough to count on the fingers of one hand. They'll be on duty. Of course I have Regan— he's a private detective—and some hired men on the estate. But I want something resembling official protection."

Rick Smedley shook his head.

"If I come there," stated Rick, "it won't be official."

Tyburn promptly took Rick's words as a promise. "You'll come, then," said Tyburn. "That will be excellent. You have relieved my mind, Inspector. In fact, you have relieved it so far, that I shall allow the charity event to proceed. I was about to order it canceled, the entertainment, bazaar, everything, rather than run the risk of some unfortunate incident. As it now stands, should some fanatic go berserk during the lawn party, you would be there, to prevent a suicide attempt."

The idea appealed to Smedley and he was nodding that he thought as much, until he recalled his own experience of fifteen minutes earlier, when he had proven quite inept at halting a suicide in the Chicago River. Nevertheless, that case had only sharpened Rick's desire to crack the suicide wave in what might be termed its budding stages.

"You've laid out my future pattern, Mr. Tyburn," declared Smedley, tapping the newspaper. "I'll have men covering all these society events, including weddings. That's where the cranks will show up next."

"Then you'll positively be at Longwood, the night of the lawn party," said Tyburn, stepping to an alcove to pick up a telephone. "Please excuse me while I phone the estate and tell the caretakers that the party will be held as scheduled."

While Tyburn was telling the switchboard to get the Longwood number, Smedley scanned the soap-king's sumptuous apartment. The living room where Smedley and Cranston were seated represented only a small portion of the place, but it was probably typical of the rest. Spacious, yet well-filled with furniture, its rental probably approached a thousand dollars monthly, while the expensive furnishings, which included magnificent tapestries and drapes, represented a small fortune in themselves.

Conspicuous upon an ornate side table was a large gold picture frame; in it, the colored portrait of a beautiful blonde with dreamy eyes who looked like a "cover" girl. Cranston noticed Smedley eye the portrait and deliver a slight knowing nod. That blonde's picture had been in the news fairly frequently, for she was Gail Tyburn, wife of the millionaire.

Tyburn saw Smedley studying the portrait and, briefly, Tyburn's gray-mottled eyebrows bristled into a frown. Then, getting an answer to his phone call, Tyburn began booming in an authoritative tone that demanded all attention, including Smedley's.

Tyburn was talking to somebody named Webster, who from the conversation turned out to be the gatekeeper at the Longwood estate. Next, Tyburn asked for Morse, the gardener, who promptly came on the telephone. Finally, with a narrowed glance across the room toward Gail's picture, Tyburn asked where Chaffin was. Chaffin was right there at the other end of the line and so Tyburn asked that he be put on. The questions that Tyburn put to Chaffin were quite pointed. He wanted to know whether Mrs. Tyburn had been using the big car and if not, why not. Apparently, Chaffin was very prompt with his answers, for Tyburn ended the call a few minutes later. Pacing across the room he halted abruptly at the table where Gail's portrait stood. He looked from the picture to his visitors. Then:

"There's no secret about it," declared Tyburn, in a testy tone. "My wife and I have been separated for the past few months and whether it's to be temporary or permanent depends on her. Or you might say that it depends on Regan, the private detective. I've hired him to check on Gail."

Smedley accepted this with a bluff nod, as though such things were bound to happen. Cranston's reaction was entirely impassive. This encouraged Tyburn to give further details.

"I told Gail she could have the Longwood place for herself," said Tyburn, his voice becoming confidential, "but she hasn't been out there in weeks. You just heard me talking with Webster, the gate-keeper and Morse, the gardener. They're in charge of what is practically an empty house. That's all right; it's Gail's privilege to stay in town.

"But Chaffin, the chauffeur, is out there, too. His only job is to drive my wife's car and he tells me he's been idle for a week. Yet Gail has been seen constantly around Chicago—read some of those society columns if you don't believe me—and how she's been getting about without a car is a mystery. Unless"—Tyburn threw strong emphasis on the word—"unless Regan comes up with a solution."

Rick Smedley was busy with pencil and note-book, his purpose partly to divert Tyburn from unloading his matrimonial problems.

"Webster—Morse—Chaffin," jotted Rick. "All out at Longwood. They'll be there the night of the party, too?"

"There and at your service," replied Tyburn. "That will include Chaffin, because even if my wife decides to use her own car for a change, the lawn party is her idea, so she'll be there and have the car handy. You can depend on Gail showing up at anyplace where she's in the limelight."

The phone rang as Tyburn finished. The grizzled man answered the call, spoke in short, choppy phrases and hung up. Turning to Smedley, Tyburn said:

"That was Hagathorn, so you'd better add his name to the list. Skip Hagathorn, we call him. He pilots my cabin cruiser. I've been trying to reach him at Holland, Michigan, across the lake, where he took the boat for an overhauling. Skip will be at the party and you'll find him useful. Like the others, he knows the grounds at Longwood and will help you check on any suspicious characters that may show up there."

It was close to nine thirty and Tyburn had cov-ered all the needed details. Deciding that he had better return to headquarters, Smedley invited Cranston to join him and the two left together. As soon as they were in the police car, Smedley gave Cranston a sharp glance and remarked:

"That shows how this suicide stuff is getting on people's nerves. Tyburn hasn't caught the mania himself, but he's imagining that everybody else has. From the way he insisted on my coming to Longwood, you'd think he was sure that something was going to happen out there."

"Perhaps Tyburn has come to my own conclu-sion," rejoined Cranston, "namely that murder, not suicide, is the answer to these deaths. I can't imag-ine a better setting for a murder than a millionaire's estate after dark, particularly with a lot of strangers on the premises. It would be very embarrassing, too, on a night when the millionaire and his wife were meeting for the first time in months, possibly for a reconciliation."

Smedley answered that with a snort, which he followed by giving a sweeping gesture from the car. They were crossing the Chicago River, which the police had started to drag.

"Would you call this murder?" Rick demanded. "I saw the crazy guy jump, myself. There wasn't a chance for anybody to get at him or even near him. We'll find the body by morning and you can come around and have a look at it. If you still think it's murder, try and convince me. Then we can work back from there."

The police car pulled up beside the Hotel Harbison and Cranston took it that this was Smedley's way of saying good night. Affably, Cranston left the car and went into the hotel, while Smedley kept on to headquarters.

It took somebody as efficient as The Shadow to get a room in the Hotel Harbison, considering how thoroughly the Magigals had taken over that estab-lishment. However, Cranston had already maneu-vered it and when he reached his room, he prompt-ly took a black cloak and slouch hat from a secret compartment in one of his suitcases. Then he went down by the fire tower, to reach the back passage leading behind the shops that lined the hotel lobby.

There, clad in the black garments, Cranston became a mysterious gliding figure that no chance passer would have noticed. He was The Shadow, master of blackness, bound upon a quest. Finding the rear door of the perfume shop, Cranston opened it with a pointed, probing pick and entered a small storeroom, closing the door so softly behind him that not the slightest sound occurred. With a tiny flashlight, The Shadow picked out the box he wanted, the one that contained the crystal skull. It had a baggage check attached and was marked "For Delivery" but it bore no name. The shape of the box itself was more important than the label, for it was the only one of the right form to contain the crystal skull.

As The Shadow stooped to open the well-tied box, footsteps sounded at the front door of the storeroom. Whipping back into the darkness, The Shadow became part of the general background as the door swung open and two bellboys entered. One was holding a baggage check; the other pointed to the box with the crystal skull. They tallied the two checks and nodded.

"This is the box," one said. "Bring it along. That dizzy dame is in an awful hurry."

"Yeah," said the other, "and she was pulling a five dollar bill from her pocketbook. Let's get back before she finds anything smaller."

The bellboys took the box that The Shadow had hoped to examine. Hardly had they left by the

The Shadow watched the two bellboys. One held a baggage check; the other pointed to the box with the crystal skull. "This must be it," he said. "We'd better scram. That dame was in a hurry to get this."

front, before The Shadow made his exit by the back way. Taking off cloak and hat, he was carrying them over his arm when he skirted the lobby, just as bellboys reached the street door with their burden. There they were met by a trim, well-dressed woman who gave them a five dollar bill as they put the box into a waiting cab.

By the hotel lights, The Shadow, now in the guise of Lamont Cranston, recognized the lady who had called to get the crystal skull. He recognized her from a photograph that he had seen at the Armistead Arms. The woman was Gail Tyburn.

Even before the cab pulled away, Cranston was looking for other observers and saw one. A squatty man in a tan coat with a brown felt hat was lighting a cigar over by the hotel wall and making a bad job of it because he was trying to watch the woman at the same time. As Gail's cab started, the squatty man

cut out to the street, hoping to flag a cab for himself. As for Cranston, he took a shorter way to pick
up Gail's trail. Traffic at the next street turned right
and the red light hadn't yet changed. This gave
Cranston time to stroll rapidly back through the
lobby and down a side passage to another door that
fronted on the other street, where he was sure a cab
would be parked, as that street had a hack stand.

Gail's cab came along just as Cranston reached
the side door, but there the trail ended without need
for Cranston to take a cab of his own. Gail's cab
halted and was met by a brawny but handsome
man, who scooped out the box the moment that the
cab door opened. Waving the cab along, he tossed
a departing kiss to the lady in the rear seat. He
turned, entered the hotel carrying the box, and
wearing his perpetual smile, the smile that
belonged to John Halifax.

Halifax had hardly got inside the hotel before
the squatty man with the tan coat came hurrying
around the corner and stopped. There were a couple of cabs handy, but they could do him no good
now. The cab containing Gail Tyburn was gone.

Going into the hotel, Cranston saw Halifax
entering one of the elevators that flanked this side
of the lobby. Stopping at the desk, Cranston asked
for Halifax's room number. The room was 1412, on
the same floor as Cranston's.

Only a few minutes later, the transom of Room
1412 inched inwards, silently. A keen eye,
obscured by the blackness of a slouch hat above it,
peered into the room where Halifax was taking the
final cords from the precious box. At least The
Shadow was here to see what Halifax did with the
crystal skull, which was the next best alternative to
The Shadow inspecting it on his own.

Halifax was eager as the package came wide
open. Then, a low mutter escaped him. Instead of
the crystal skull, the package contained bottles of
cheap perfume, that went sliding helter-skelter on
the bed where Halifax had opened the package.

The watching eye vanished; the transom inched
shut. A whispered laugh trailed softly from the corner of the corridor, marking The Shadow's departure. When the cloaked figure reappeared again, it
was at the rear door of the perfume shop.

Studying the lock closely under the direct glare
of his tiny but powerful flashlight, The Shadow
now detected scratches on the metal. His pick
hadn't made those scratches; his job had been too
neat for that. The marks meant that someone had
picked the lock earlier, someone who had taken the
crystal skull and filled its box with perfume bottles
to give it the necessary weight.

Removing hat and cloak, The Shadow strolled
out through the lobby as Lamont Cranston and lin-
gered beside a phone booth where a squatty man in

a tan coat and brown hat was making a phone call.
Cranston caught the man's name as he gave it over
the phone and wasn't at all surprised to hear it.

"Hello," the squatty man was saying, "Yeah, this
is Regan... Yeah, I spotted your wife, Mr.
Tyburn...Right after I gave you that routine call at
just nine thirty... No, nobody was with her, but she
picked up a big package and took it along... Not in
a car, she went in a cab that she had waiting... No,
nobody was with her... Yeah, I'll find out all I can."

There was a lot that Regan wasn't going to find
out, particularly that Gail Tyburn had made off with
the wrong package, or more specifically the wrong
contents. The question now was who had taken the
crystal skull and Lamont Cranston could readily
recall a person who had taken special interest in that
skull at the very time when Halifax, too, had seen it.

Going over to the desk, Cranston stopped at a
window marked "Magigal Convention
Registration" and inquired for Miss Verity Joyce of
Seattle. The registration clerk made a thorough
check of the list.

"There is no Miss Joyce stopping at the Hotel
Harbison," the clerk said. "In fact, I can't even find
the name on the registration list. There must be
some mistake, sir."

There wasn't any mistake, though Lamont
Cranston didn't say so. The whole thing obviously
had been well planned in advance and it bore the
elements of mystery that appealed to Cranston's
other self, The Shadow.

Lester Tyburn, the harried millionaire; his wife
Gail, the blond gadabout; John Halifax, the heart
crusher who let ladies do his skull shopping for
him—All three dropped somewhat into insignifi-
cance when compared with a black-haired beauty
with soulful eyes whose name might not even be
Verity Joyce and whose skill at picking locks rated
close to The Shadow's own.

A slight smile showed on Cranston's lips as he
thought of two sleuths named Smedley and Regan
and wondered what they would think of all this. Yet
there was something grim about Cranston's smile.

If murder lay behind Chicago's suicide wave,
Cranston was now sure that the crystal skull had
some connection with it and that the disappearance
of that particular piece of evidence might prove the
forerunner of further crime.

CHAPTER IV
MAGIC SPELLS MURDER

AT ten o'clock the next morning, Lamont
Cranston received a phone call from Inspector
Smedley. Rick announced that the body of the
bridge suicide had been found and that water-
soaked papers in a wallet had identified him as
William Brett of Evansville, Indiana.

The wallet also contained a parcel check bearing the name of the Dearborn Station. Smedley had gone to the depot and claimed a suitcase which proved by its contents to be Brett's. At present, Smedley was tabulating the articles from the case and would be quite pleased to have Cranston come over and help him, if only it would put an end to the unrequested Teletype messages from his New York friend, Police Commissioner Weston.

Cranston went promptly to police headquarters and found Smedley at a table where Brett's belongings were on display. They consisted of wearing apparel, some magazines, cigarettes, writing paper and a pack of playing cards. To these, Smedley had added Brett's hat and coat, plus the pack of cigarettes and the match pack that had been found in the coat pocket.

"It's obvious," declared Smedley, "that Brett was on his way back to Evansville when the suicide bug got him. Now we've got to find out where he was stopping in Chicago, who he saw while he was here. Probably he was in town a couple of days at least, in order to catch the suicide fever.

"He may have said something to somebody that would have given an indication of the trend his mind was taking."

"Hardly, Inspector," said Cranston, "unless he confided in the clerk at the store where he bought this new hat. I doubt that Brett arrived in Chicago before yesterday afternoon. He must have left the suitcase at the Dearborn Station when he got off the train."

Smedley gave a heavy frown as an invitation for Cranston to clarify his deduction with a bill of particulars.

"This match pack covers that situation," stated Cranston, opening the pack to show it half filled with matches. "It bears an advertisement of the Chicago and Eastern Illinois Railway and is the sort of pack that Brett would have picked up in a club car on that line. The C. and E.I. is the only road that comes in from Evansville and if Brett had been in Chicago much longer than an afternoon, he would have used up all the matches in his only pack. You'll find that Brett came to Chicago only yesterday."

Out of the jangle of phones that persisted in Smedley's office came a call for the inspector. Answering it, Rick found himself talking to Evansville. The data that Rick was getting corresponded with Cranston's statement.

"Yes, this is Inspector Smedley," Rick was saying. "Facts on William Brett... Yes, I'm ready... Came to Chicago yesterday, you say... Wasn't sure about staying over... Said he might come back on the sleeper... Would wire family as to intentions... Prosperous hardware manufacturer... No indica-tions of mental depression... Simply a routine business trip... Made them occasionally—"

"Ask about Brett's medals," suggested Cranston, catching Smedley's eye. "Find out if he ever tried for an Olympic team."

Thinking that Cranston was playing some sort of hunch, Smedley put questions along that line and finally hung up the receiver savagely.

"What kind of steer were you giving me?" Rick asked Cranston. "This Brett wasn't ever an athlete. His age is fifty-six and he only took up golf five years ago. He even gave up bowling duckpins because he thought it too strenuous."

"I wanted to know if Brett happened to be a swimmer," explained Cranston. "Experienced swimmers don't usually try suicide by jumping into water. But at that, they've underrated Brett down in Evansville. He must have been something of an athlete."

"And who gave you that idea?"

"You did, Inspector, from your description of Brett's death plunge. You said he shook loose some men who tried to hold him back and went up that rising bridge like a monkey while the people who tried to chase him all came sliding down."

Smedley's bluff face took on one of its purplish tinges. Then:

"The guy was berserk," gruffed Rick. "I've seen plenty of cases where people like that outdid themselves. Still"—Rick's face sober in the manner of a judge's—"you put a fair question and it warrants a fitting answer. It's over at the morgue, the answer: Brett's body. Do you want to see it?"

"Not right now," replied Cranston. "I don't doubt it's Brett's body. I'm simply questioning whether it was Brett who jumped off the bridge."

"You mean maybe somebody else jumped?"

"Exactly."

"Then what became of the fellow who did jump?"

"He could have climbed on board the tug with the crew that dived off to look for Brett."

Smedley began a speculative frown that turned into a disparaging glower.

"That would mean the whole thing was a plant," Rick argued. "We saw a guy jump and we found a body. If the fellow that jumped was picked up, the body must have been dumped by the same bunch that covered for the jumper."

"Which means the tugboat crew," put in Cranston. "How far from the bridge was the body found?"

"Pretty far," admitted Smedley. "In the direction that the tug was coming from, too. But there wasn't anything hooked to it. In fact, the body was floating when they finally found it."

"I've heard of bodies being weighted with salt," remarked Cranston. "Enough of it, inside the clothes, will sink the body and hold it until the salt melts."

"But the Chicago River isn't salt water," reminded Smedley. "The brine would have left stains, so salt is out. Guess again, Mr. Cranston."

"Very well. My guess is sugar."

Rick began another of his glowers, then gave an indulgent laugh.

"We'll look into it," Rick promised. "I've got to admit you're on the ball, Mr. Cranston. But there still isn't any connection between this case and those other suicides. Look at the stuff in Brett's suitcase. According to your theory, it wouldn't have been touched if he'd left it at the Dearborn Station, coming into town. Yet what do you see that's out of the ordinary?"

Cranston found one thing among Brett's belongings that might be an answer to Smedley's query, namely the pack of playing cards. Opening the pack, Cranston studied the cards rather intently, even counting them to make sure the pack was complete.

"Prewar manufacture," defined Cranston. "Standard design, but obsolete. Yet this pack has been very little used. Brett may have had it for years."

As he spoke, Cranston was holding the cards to the light, studying them from every angle.

"Maybe Brett played solitaire," suggested Smedley. "That would be enough to make anybody want to jump off a bridge."

"He might have performed card tricks," remarked Cranston, spreading the pack. "Take a card, Inspector. Hold it right in front of your eyes and concentrate upon it."

Cranston shifted his position while Smedley was taking the card, but, otherwise, there was nothing unusual in his action. Looking at the card, Smedley gave a nod.

"All right. I'm looking at it. Want me to tell you what it is?"

"That won't be necessary," returned Cranston. "I can tell you that the card is the six of hearts."

"Say!" Rick's tone was startled. "Do you mean this pack is marked and you've spotted the system at one try? Maybe Brett was a card sharp, on the side."

"Hardly, with this pack," said Cranston. "It isn't marked. It's more unusual than a marked deck. In fact, it is practically unique. Turn toward that strong sunlight, Inspector, and look at the back of the card."

Doing exactly as Cranston told him, Smedley delivered another and more profound exclamation.

"Why, the whole card becomes transparent!" Rick grabbed for another card, gave it a similar test. "Against the light, the faces show right through. I didn't know they made cards like this!"

"They don't" was Cranston's verdict. "I never saw a pack exactly like this. It would be useless at a gambling table, but it's perfect for card tricks, particularly with people spread out around a room. I am sure we can class William Brett as an amateur magician of sorts."

"What do you mean of sorts?"

"He can't belong to the usual run, or he would have a lot of the gadgets they sell around magic shops. Instead, he shows up with a trick that a professional magician would envy. What about some of those other suicides, Inspector? Did you find any packs of cards on them or anything in the same line?"

Rick Smedley went to a special file cabinet and brought out boxes labeled with the names of previous victims. Looking through the effects of Jerome Alton, from Dubuque, Cranston found a cigarette case and opened it. Studying it intently, he finally closed the case and scrutinized it from the outside.

"That case was empty when we found it," stated Smedley, referring to a record sheet. "There were no cigarettes found among Alton's belongings."

"Alton didn't need to carry them," said Cranston. "Not while he owned this case. Have a cigarette, Inspector."

Opening the case, Cranston extended it to Smedley who found himself taking a cigarette. Rick's eyes opened wide; he stared sharply at Cranston, who merely smiled and snapped the case shut.

"A cigarette for you," remarked Cranston, "and one for me."

Opening the case again, Cranston removed a cigarette for himself. Then he was snapping the case, opening it, and with each action a cigarette appeared within. Completely baffled, Rick Smedley sat back and shook his head.

"What goes on?" demanded Rick. "Where do those cigarettes come from? If it isn't magic, I'd say that case was a pocket cigarette factory!"

"As good a definition as any," returned Cranston. "I've caught the secret of it; now let's get a look at the mechanism."

With the delicacy of a watchmaker, Cranston patiently probed the cigarette case until it came apart in two sections, revealing its secret. The ends of the cigarette case were thick and formed hollow compartments containing flaky tobacco, tightly packed. Between the outside of the case and an inner lining was a pleated sheet of very thin paper. The closing of the case flipped a strip of metal that released sufficient tobacco into an approaching segment of paper, with a rotary action. The rolling of the cigarette was completed as the case opened, the metal strip going into place again.

"Very neat" was Cranston's verdict. "It works from either end, according to how you turn the cigarette case. That gives it double capacity. It should work about a dozen times before needing a refill."

Rick Smedley began pawing through file boxes to find more oddities. He had luck with every attempt, though in each case it was Cranston who identified the tricky objects.

One suicide victim, Lloyd Stelton, from Zanesville, had carried a lot of Chinese coins. Rick had regarded these as trivial souvenirs until Cranston tested one by ringing it, weighing it, spinning it, and finally tasting it. Then, filling a drinking cup with water, Cranston dropped the Chinese coin into the cup. In about six seconds, the coin dissolved until nothing was left of it.

"We'll have one of these analyzed," said Cranston. "I'll need some of the others, Inspector. Now let's have a look at those two pencils which belonged to Ward Bronson, of Tampa. They look quite ordinary, but they aren't a standard make. It's odd that one should be green, the other red."

It was indeed odd, as Cranston demonstrated after he finally probed the secret of the pencils. When Cranston held the red pencil in his right hand, and the green in his left, and rubbed one lightly across the other, a strange thing happened. The green pencil turned out to be in Cranston's right hand, while his left now held the red. Repeating the transposition a few times, Cranston handed the pencils to Smedley, but Rick, more baffled than ever, couldn't begin to fathom their secret.

Among the effects of George Krugg, of Spokane, Cranston found a matchbox that was very wonderful. When you opened it, you drew out a lighted match; at least, that was the way Cranston did it. But when Rick Smedley tried it, his match wasn't lighted; in fact, it wouldn't light at all when Rick tried to strike it on the box.

Cranston's experiments and the resultant discoveries occupied a considerable length of time. He would have liked to have continued with other articles that were filed under the names of further suicide victims, but Cranston felt that his point was proven and he was anxious to put his findings to a more practical test. Briefly, Cranston summed it all up for Smedley's benefit.

"Every one of these tricks is unique," Cranston told Rick. "I doubt that the magical fraternity at large has even heard of them. That would indicate some connection between the men who owned them, each the possessor of some mysterious device which, so far as we can guess, was his exclusive and individual property. Do you follow me?"

"Follow you!" retorted Rick. "I'm far enough ahead to figure that any bunch as nuts as this crowd would have gone in for a suicide pact. You've made sense where the suicide wave is concerned, but you're still a long way from murder."

"If I could uncover some outside influence," continued Cranston, quite unruffled, "some focal point, let us say, that concerns these victims and their tricks, I believe that you would agree it was worthy of investigation."

"Of course I'd agree."

"And if it were strong enough to indicate a murder motive—"

"You're jumping the question, Mr. Cranston. I'd have to find evidence of murder."

"In every case?"

"No, I'll grant you a point there. If you link up the lot and I find evidence in two cases or more, I'll agree that the motive could point entirely to murder. But you'll have to chase all over the country, to all the towns these victims came from, before you'll establish what you want."

Cranston shook his head.

"Not necessarily," he said. "The victims all died in Chicago; therefore the reason may be right here. But you'll have to let me borrow all these gadgets, so that I can make the rounds."

"Make the rounds?" echoed Smedley. "What rounds?"

"The rounds of the places where magicians meet," replied Cranston. "Chicago has several such places. My term 'rounds' is particularly appropriate, because the first place I intend to visit is called the Magicians' Round Table. I would like to see what happens there when I deliver a few minor miracles."

Rick Smedley was quite agreeable. He gestured for Cranston to take whatever tricks he wanted and depart upon his self-appointed mission. Pocketing the various articles, Cranston rose and Rick politely escorted him to the door. There, Cranston inserted a reminder.

"I'll check for clues from these tricks," Cranston told Smedley, "but, meanwhile, Inspector, I'm counting upon you to go back over the details of these suicides and see what new evidence you can find, pointing to something more serious than suicide."

"Leave it to me," assured Smedley, with one of his indulgent laughs. "You handle the magic, Mr. Cranston, and I'll take care of the murder."

CHAPTER V
AROUND THE ROUND TABLE

THE MAGICIANS' ROUND TABLE had begun its daily session when Lamont Cranston arrived.

A Chicago institution for more than twenty years, the Round Table had undergone some gradual changes during that period. Originally a daily luncheon club where magical hobbyists hobnobbed with visiting professionals, this informal group now went into all-afternoon sessions. Its gathering place was Drake's Restaurant and there the magicians occupied their own corner, not at a round table, which they had long since outgrown, but at a series of regular restaurant tables set together like a banquet table to which extensions could be added as needed.

Lamont Cranston was already passingly acquainted with some of the Chicago magic fans. Recognized by a few he knew, Cranston was given an immediate welcome. Taking his place at a table, he was introduced to the men nearest him with the promise that he would meet more before the session ended. Introductions were gradual around the Round Table, because the various clusters were so busy discussing diverse phases of magic.

None of the Magigals was present. They were holding their own luncheon and afternoon business session behind locked doors at the Hotel Harbison. Nevertheless, the Magigals Convention had swelled the Round Table attendance, because of the out-of-towners who had come to be present at a big show which the Magigals had scheduled for the general public, male magicians included.

Cranston was learning about all this from a chap on his right named Chick Schoke, who was one of the Round Table regulars and knew everybody, local or out of town.

"That's Dorny Dornfield at the end of the table," identified Chick. "He was one of the founders of this outfit. He's an emcee as well as a magician and he stars at all the magical conventions. He's talking to Monk Watson, the most versatile character in magic. The fellow with them is Larry Arcuri; he's in from New York, where he organized a get-together group patterned after this one, which now meets daily at the Hotel Dixie.

"The energetic chap across the way is Doc Tarbell, who prepared a whole correspondence course in magic and now goes on lecture tours. Two places to the right is Milbourne Christopher who did magic in the front lines when he was a G.I. and has written up his own experiences along with those of other magicians. Between them is Theo Bamberg who toured the world under the professional name of Okito. He's giving them a whole hatful of tricks and anecdotes.

"That boisterous group at the other end are more serious than they look. They're all editors of magical magazines: Al Plough of the *Linking Ring,* Walt Gibson of *Conjurors',* Mel Melson of *Tops* and Bill Sachs, who handles the magic column in the *Billboard.* They're expecting John Mulholland of the *Sphinx;* but Gerry Larsen, who edits the *Genii* won't be around because she's one of the *Magigals.* In fact, she started that organization.

"Right over there is Rufus Steele, who probably knows more about gambling devices than anybody since Erdnase, who wrote a book on the subject and then mysteriously disappeared right here in Chicago. He's talking with Johnny Platt and Dai Vernon, who is a past master at card technique. Speaking of cards, if you have a pack handy, I'll show you a neat ace trick."

This was exactly what Cranston had wanted, though he hadn't said so. Producing the pack that he had gotten at Smedley's office, he handed it to Schoke, who immediately demonstrated a very nifty trick in which two pairs of aces, placed back to back, red and black respectively, changed their positions in some unaccountable fashion.

Demonstrations of magic, oddly enough, were purely secondary proceedings at the Round Table; in fact, anything in the way of strictly ordinary trickery was almost taboo. This was where connoisseurs of the art gathered and they preferred to discuss the lore and intricacies of magic to watching stereotyped performances. However, anything subtle, deft or novel was always appreciated. Aware of this, Cranston was ready when the pack was returned to him. Immediately he went into an impromptu act.

Asking that the pack be shuffled, Cranston brought out a Hotel Harbison memo pad, tore two slips of paper from it and passed each to persons across the table, handing pencils along with them. He had someone spread the pack so that the men with the pencils could each take a card at random. The cards taken, each person, at Cranston's request, wrote the name of his chosen card on a slip and folded it.

Next, Cranston had each man pass his card to the other, so that each would know the other's choice. Thereby, he learned the faces of the cards, seeing them through the backs, against the light. With a fountain pen, Cranston wrote two names on other paper slips, tossed them across the table. When the papers were opened, the names that Cranston had written proved identical with those that the card choosers had written in pencil.

Neatly done, that trick, but Cranston followed it with another startling number. Taking back the pencils, he called attention to the fact that one was red, the other green. Rubbing one across the other, Cranston caused them to change places from hand to hand, while the Round Table habitués left their places to cluster closer about the source of this baffling mystery.

Tossing the pencils for examination, Cranston opened the cigarette case that he had borrowed from Smedley. Showing it empty, he closed it and produced a cigarette within. Asking someone to take the cigarette, Cranston closed the case and produced another, then another, and another. This went on until a dozen men were holding cigarettes, for Cranston had remembered to refill the amazing cigarette case while on his way to the Round Table.

To top it all, Cranston began furnishing lights for those cigarettes by drawing lighted matches from what looked like a perfectly ordinary matchbox and proved to be just such when he tossed the box on the table so that others could try the trick without success. That ended the most amazing display of impromptu mysteries that the Round Table had ever witnessed.

There were at least thirty people at the Round Table and Cranston was studying their faces without finding the one he wanted to see. The handsome countenance of John Halifax was missing from the throng. So Cranston decided to bide his time a while, in case the Hollywood mystic arrived and heard echoes of the chatter that was going on about the impromptu miracles.

From across the table, Rufus Steele handed Cranston his pack of cards. Steele, the expert, had given the pack a few deft riffles to see if little dots danced back and forth across the backs, this being the sure way of detecting a marked pack. This pack, however, stood the test.

Now the magic editors were politely monopolizing Cranston to learn if he would furnish any of his tricks for the pages of their magazines. No one had seen any of those tricks before, which was exactly what Cranston wanted to know.

A waitress came to the table saying there was a phone call for Mr. Cranston. Taking his props with him, Cranston went to the telephone, learned that the call was from police headquarters and that Inspector Smedley wanted him to come to the Hotel Royal at once. Important though it sounded, this urgent call would have spoiled Cranston's day, if he hadn't found two men waiting for him as he left the telephone.

The pair consisted of Rufus Steele, the man who knew cards so thoroughly, and Milbourne Christopher who specialized in magical research.

"If that pack of yours is the only thing it can be," declared Steele, "it's something that certain manufacturers have tried to produce for years, without luck."

"In America, yes," agreed Christopher, "but I have seen European packs that met those specifications."

Quite aware of what both speakers meant, Cranston gave a mild display of interest.

"I've heard of one man who might have had such a pack," said Steele. "They called him Professor Marsh."

"Professor Sedley Marsh," elaborated Christopher. "I've crossed his trail, too, but this is the first time I ever linked him with card work. Those other specialties were typical of Marsh."

"In that case," suggested Cranston, "you might tell me something about Professor Marsh."

Briefly, the story was this:

The annals of modern magic held many names to conjure with: Charlier, Erdnase, Joseffy, Jordan, Malini, Ansbach. These were men whose careers, at least in part, had been as mysterious as their methods and creations. Some had passed along their secrets, sometimes at great prices, or occasionally to chosen pupils who were sworn to preserve such secrecy as in the days when magic had been a heritage from master to apprentice.

One man belonging in this ultra category was Professor Sedley Marsh. That name, however, was not to be found in any record whatever. Reputedly, Marsh was as elusive as his methods. Only one word could define him; that word was "untraceable." In fact, Marsh could have been charged off as a myth, but for one rumor that persisted; namely, that Marsh had confided his methods in certain trusted pupils who were sworn to absolute secrecy both as to the tricks and their source.

None of this favored group were amateur magicians nor members of magical organizations. They were all wealthy men whom Marsh had personally approached, stirred their interest with his wizardry and finally had sold them on the idea of buying some of his exclusives at fabulous prices. Only rarely someone who might be a Marsh pupil had performed one or more of these exclusives in the presence of magicians. Doubtless, this was in accord with some agreement set by Marsh himself.

Rumor went that Marsh had promised an amazing legacy to his unknown pupils: that secrets and devices which he was guarding until death would be theirs after his demise. When that time came, the pupils could identify themselves, each to the other, by their knowledge of Marsh Magic. Wild though this rumor might be, it gained credence by the fact that Marsh's pupils were as secretive as their master, all apparently holding back their own pet feats of wizardry until some appointed time when they would need them.

Cranston listened to this quite impassively as though analyzing every statement. The whole story told, he gave an obliging nod, said good-bye and left. That was the perfect departure, the sort that a bona fide Marsh pupil would have made. This was important, too, because from the suppositions that he had heard regarding such people, Cranston could have vouched for their existence. They were represented by the alleged suicide victims whose tricks Cranston had displayed.

Murder, not suicide, was behind those Chicago deaths. Of that, Cranston was now certain; the next step was to prove it to the satisfaction of Inspector Rick Smedley. Preliminary to that, Cranston was trying to prove it to his own satisfaction; perhaps too much so.

Logically, the man behind murder would be a Marsh pupil, too. His purpose, judging from his wholesale measures to date, must be to eliminate all others of the clan. Since all were secretive as to their identity, the killer must have found some way to uncover them. From indications already at hand, this would depend on the victims. They would have to declare themselves.

Unwitting victims could do just that by performing their pet tricks in public and thus identifying themselves as Marsh men. Granted that they avoided the company of other magicians, such a rule might no longer apply if something important were at stake, such as Marsh's legacy. Nor might it apply at all to the potential murderer who sought to ferret out Marsh's pupils. Hunters often belonged to a different brood than the hunted. Assuming that a mastermind was playing every angle, he might be watching all places where magicians gathered on the chance that a man equipped with Marsh methods should appear there and be in a mood to display his marvels.

That explained why Lament Cranston had gone to the Round Table in the first place, though at that time, his theory had been more general than specific. Now the theory had become a substantial thing, provided that the speculations which Cranston had just heard regarding Professor Marsh had any substance to them. At least, it encouraged Cranston to play the game further.

Cranston played it by strolling through Chicago's central area, the Loop, in a manner calculated to encourage followers. He delayed his course by picking the wrong time to cross streets, then altering his route according to the traffic lights. This was a system that would force awkward moves on the part of anyone who had taken up his trail. But by the time Cranston reached the Hotel Royal, this policy had brought him no results.

Inspector Smedley, the perfect portrait of impatience, was waiting in the lobby when Cranston reached the Royal. His greeting was on the sarcastic side.

"I hope you've had a good time with those tricks," declared Smedley. "Did anyone try to murder you?"

"Sorry," replied Cranston. "Nobody tried."

"Did you feel any urge to commit suicide?"

"None at all."

"Then come up to the fifteenth floor," invited Rick, "and I'll show you the apartment of a man who not only felt the suicide urge but followed it. He hasn't any tricks in his suitcase and there's no way anyone could have got into his place to murder him."

Unquestionably, Rick Smedley was in a gloating mood at having successfully spiked the theory built by Lamont Cranston.

CHAPTER VI
MURDER PLAYS WARY

THE latest victim was named Edward Fleer. He came from New London, Connecticut, and his body looked about the size of a beetle, when Smedley pointed it out to Cranston from the courtyard window of Suite 1420 in the Hotel Royal. Fleer was lying on the roof of a one-story extension, twelve floors below. One from fourteen subtracted to twelve at the Hotel Royal, because it had no thirteenth floor, not wanting to shy away superstitious guests.

The kitchen occupied the low extension and the cooks and kitchen help had heard Fleer's body thump when it landed, so the report of this new suicide had come quite promptly to the police. Fleer had been wearing a dressing gown when he jumped and no personal effects had been found on his body, which would shortly be removed to the morgue.

Smedley conducted Cranston about the hotel suite, which was large enough to be called an apartment, except that it had only one entrance. The large living room had windows fronting toward the lake, looking across some intervening buildings, one a warehouse, while the bedroom, from which Fleer had plunged, had windows only on the courtyard. The hotel was eighteen stories high and Smedley pointed out that for anyone to fly in and out at such a level, expressly to toss Fleer from a window, would be just about too unlikely to be considered in anything more intelligent than idiotic circles.

"That door was really locked," added Rick, pointing to a heavy door that had been smashed loose at the hinges. "The regular bolt and the chain bolt were both thrown. We had to bash the door down. But take a look at Fleer's effects. If you can find any tricks in the lot, I'll eat them and I won't ask for mayonnaise."

While Cranston was looking over an array of rather ordinary articles, Smedley phoned headquarters and found that a call was waiting from Longwood. Smedley had the call put through and soon was talking with Lester Tyburn. At mention of Tyburn's name, Cranston listened intently on the chance that Gail might enter the conversation. Smedley's replies were too brief to get much from them, but Rick elaborated, after finishing his chat with Tyburn.

"Tyburn was calling from police headquarters," informed Rick. "The Longwood police headquarters, I mean. I talked to the chief and they're counting on me to be at that clambake that Mrs. Tyburn intends to throw. After all, Tyburn owns the premises, so his wife can't very well object."

"Has Mrs. Tyburn been out there today?" asked Cranston.

"No sign of her," replied Rick. "Tyburn just came from the place and was talking to the three men who work there, the same ones he phoned last night, including Mrs. Tyburn's chauffeur. They haven't even heard from her."

"And when is Tyburn coming into town?"

"Right away. His cabin cruiser is waiting at the Longwood dock. That fellow Skip Hagathorn brought it over from Michigan. Tyburn says it will take him an hour or more to come into Chicago, as the motor has new pistons and he doesn't want to push it too hard. But how are you making out with Fleer's stuff?"

"There's nothing special in the suitcase," conceded Cranston. "But what about these articles on the dresser?"

He gestured to a watch and a ring lying near it. The watch was of a standard make, the ring simply a heavy signet bearing the initials E.F., which logically identified it as Fleer's.

"The watch was on the dresser," stated Rick. "The ring was on the washstand in the bathroom. Fleer evidently had left it there while he was washing his hands."

"And the watch was stopped when you found it?"

"No. It was running when I found it." Rick took a look at the watch and stroked his chin. "That's funny. It stopped just ten minutes ago, when I went downstairs to wait for you. I guess it was just about run down."

Picking up the watch, Cranston began to wind it, halting after a few turns of the stem.

"It was just about fully wound, Inspector."

Picking up the watch, Rick shook it. The watch started, but as Rick replaced it on the table, it stopped again. More puzzled than ever, Rick looked at Cranston, who asked:

"Did you ever swallow a signet ring?"

"No," gruffed Rick. "Why?"

Cranston picked up Fleer's ring and put it on. He brought his hand over to a bunch of keys that were lying on the far side of the dresser. The keys made a sudden jump in the air and hit the ring with a clang.

"A magnetic ring," defined Cranston. "Composed of one of those new alloys that absorb magnetic power most phenomenally and retain it. Nobody would suspect that a simple ring could be so magnetic. Let's see what might go with it."

There was a box of golf balls in a dresser drawer. When Cranston opened it, three golf balls came up with his hand, hanging there like a daisy chain.

"Metal cores," declared Cranston. "I won't let you eat them, Rick, because I want to take them along with the ring. They'll go well with those other tricks. Now will you think in terms of murder?"

"Not right yet," returned Rick. "You've linked this case with the others, but it still could be suicide. This is even a wilder theory than the one you had about Brett's death, last night. Well, you've found your trick, so keep it and let's go."

As they left the Hotel Royal, Cranston suggested that they walk by the lakeside. Rick obliged and as they passed the hotel, Cranston pointed upward.

"Painters at work," remarked Cranston. "A pretty daring job, hanging down from that roof on a scaffold. Working their way from the top down. So far, they've only reached the sixteenth floor."

Rick stared upward, his mouth saying things that his voice didn't utter. Suddenly he found words:

"They could have done it!"

"But they probably didn't," said Cranston. "When you check, Inspector, you will find that those painters were out to lunch at the time Fleer began a one-way trip from his bedroom window. That left the scaffold very handy for another crew that wanted it. All they needed was to dress like painters, let themselves down to Fleer's living room window, enter and gang up on him. Naturally, they'd have pitched him into the courtyard. They needed time to get up to the roof again, on the other side of the building. Maybe they threw that extra chain bolt, Inspector, just to make it harder for you."

"I'll see you later," returned Smedley. "I'm going back to the hotel and see what I can uncover there. You stick to the magic angle. I'll get whatever I can on murder."

Soon after that, Cranston put in a call to a man named Burbank, who served as The Shadow's contact to certain agents long in his service. Cranston had brought his own investigating squad to Chicago for special duty of the sort that had developed.

So far, all reports were negative.

A neatly handled inquiry at the Harbison perfume counter had proved that the clerk knew no more than he claimed and the same applied to the proprietor. The crystal skull had been delivered there a week before, bearing the label of a wholesale jewelry firm in New York and accompanied by a card which stated "For Display." The stub of a package check had also come with the skull and a printed sheet announced that a representative would call for the display unit on a date that was filled in with a rubber stamp.

Perfumers had been testing the value of displays in recent months, handling them in routine fashion. So the crystal skull had been accepted on its own merit and the Harbison perfumer hadn't bothered to contact the New York wholesaler.

Instructing Burbank to check the New York end, Cranston also detailed data concerning Professor Marsh. This was to be followed through, but meanwhile, Cranston wanted any facts on John Halifax, Gail Tyburn and Verity Joyce.

Halifax and Gail were easy. They'd been lunching that day with friends at a very swanky café and it would probably be mentioned by a Chicago columnist who was also present. They had gone their separate ways afterward. But as for Verity Joyce, nothing had been learned concerning her.

That left Cranston to his own devices, which wasn't a hard assignment considering that he had a pocketful of them.

That evening, Lamont Cranston dined at the Pump Room in the Ambassador East. There, recognizing a few acquaintances from the Round Table, he soon found himself in their company and next they were joined by Bert Allerton, presiding genius of the Pump Room. Allerton was a professional magician, one of the most unusual in the business. In a mild, almost benign fashion, he would chat with guests while a flower mysteriously left his buttonhole and traveled over to his opposite lapel, only to return to its starting point. Reaching beneath the dinner table, he brought out a bird cage that he found there and asked Cranston to hold it. Before Cranston could take it, the bird cage vanished in a sudden style that would have done credit to The Shadow.

Those were only a few of Allerton's wonders. He had a whole galaxy of close-up marvels. But while he performed them, he admitted that he wouldn't be averse to seeing a few things which he had unfortunately missed by being unable to attend the Round Table that day.

Cranston did the business with the cigarette case and followed it with the lighted matches from the box. Then, as an encore, he handed out a Chinese coin, let someone place it beneath a napkin and drop it in a glass of water. With a wave of his hands, Cranston suggested that the glass be uncovered and the water poured out. This was done, leaving everyone quite amazed to find the coin vanished. Napkin and glass were subjected to thorough inspection; never had either left the hands of the spectators. That was the really baffling part of it.

If anyone had been at the Pump Room watching for something strictly unusual, this would have been it. On that account, when Cranston left he insisted on going in a cab alone. He picked up a package that he had checked and in the cab, he opened it. The contents proved to be the black garb of The Shadow, complete to a brace of guns. Cranston had purposely mixed his directions to the cabby so that retracing his route would be necessary. This was in case something resembling a suicide squad happened to be on his trail. Only they weren't.

Cranston's next stop was in Cicero at a rendezvous inhabited by a most capable gentleman named Johnny Paul. From behind the bar, Johnny performed some very unusual marvels and in plenty. One of his best was an unfathomable stunt of causing a genuine ice cube to vanish when he tossed it from his right hand and land in a glass that he was holding in his left, with the top covered so that the cube couldn't possibly arrive there, except that it did.

Johnny Paul liked to watch tricks as well as do them and he was quite intrigued when Cranston produced a cigarette from an empty case. Before Cranston could supply a lighted match from his matchbox, Johnny drew one lighted from his pocket, a clever bit of business that Professor Marsh must have missed. So Cranston passed up the matchbox and brought out the golf balls.

No golf balls ever before behaved like those.

Cranston made them move back and forth across the table at the mere snap of his fingers. They rolled in circles around drinking glasses. When Cranston inverted a glass over a golf ball and snapped his fingers above the glass, the ball jumped up inside it. Most surprising of all was Cranston's three ball balance where he held a golf ball in his right hand, two others set upon it, with his left hand ready to catch the balls if they dropped—which they didn't.

In testing the merits of the wonderful ring, Cranston had discovered that its magnetic field was sufficient to control three balls thus balanced, holding them to the balance point as with an invisible glue. People were so busy watching the golf balls that they never got around to noticing the signet ring. Hence no one wondered how the initials E.F. fitted with the name Lamont Cranston.

When Cranston left, Johnny Paul was entertaining the customers with his version of the famous Cups and Balls, a demonstration so remarkable that it captured attention even after Cranston's near miracles. People were so intrigued at watching little rubber balls pass to, fro and through solid metal cups that Cranston was able to slip away unnoticed.

Unnoticed, that was, except by any person who might have been watching him purposely, intending to stalk him down as one of the marked pupils of Professor Sedley Marsh. Again, however, Cranston was due for disappointment. Once more The Shadow, riding unseen in the gloomy interior of a taxicab, Cranston found the trip back to Chicago definitely monotonous.

The monotony ended at Matt Schulien's.

This was a restaurant on Halsted Street, run by the Schulien Brothers. Matt, portly and genial, made a specialty of serving magic to the customers. He could do card tricks by the hour and he performed them at an actual round table, a big one, while the crowd gathered all about.

Matt was at work when Cranston arrived. Noticing a few magical faces in the throng, Cranston was recognized in turn and soon found a place. Buzzes reached Matt regarding Cranston's wizardry and soon the two were introduced. Following that introduction Cranston did the Chinese coin trick and again scored a hit with it. Then they were back to cards again. After Matt uncannily restored a card that a spectator had torn to pieces, Cranston suggested that they do a two pack trick. This brought the Marsh-made pack into the game and very soon Cranston was naming anybody's card as soon as it was taken.

When Cranston left the restaurant an hour later, he employed his Shadow tactics again. He was hoping that a car would overtake his cab, that faces would peer into the cab only to find it apparently empty. After that, things would happen to The Shadow's liking. But nothing did happen. The cab arrived serenely at the Hotel Harbison and it was Lamont Cranston who alighted, a package under his arm.

Up in his room, Cranston switched immediately to The Shadow's garb, then eased himself out the window and along a ledge which was anything but wide. Entering a darkened room, he moved out to the corridor and merged with a gloomy stretch of the hallway that was made to order for his black garb. Even a keen-eyed interloper could have blundered right into The Shadow, without noticing him there.

For half an hour, The Shadow played this one-man game of hide-and-seek to no avail. Nothing happening, he returned to his room, became Cranston again and decided to call it a night. What he'd established tonight was all on the negative side. It fitted, though, with the story that the pupils of Professor Marsh abhorred the company of all other magicians. Whoever was hounding them, simply wasn't looking for victims in the places that Cranston had visited.

There was a chance that stories might reach the man behind murder, stories of a wealthy New Yorker named Lamont Cranston who was performing Marsh magic everywhere he went. This was Cranston's only hope of dividends for the time that he had invested.

Against these was the possibility that there wasn't a Professor Marsh; that perhaps there never had been. It could be just a name, coined as a gag, to explain the origin of tricks that couldn't be traced. In that case, nobody was committing a chain of well-planned murders in Chicago. People were just succumbing to a suicide wave, the way Inspector Smedley figured it and the epidemic was spreading most rapidly among persons with the quirked minds of amateur tricksters.

Such dour thoughts disturbed Lamont Cranston as he stared from his window at the city lights. Never before had he advertised himself as target for murder without getting prompt results. That this should happen in Chicago of all cities was discouraging, indeed.

Yes, life had its disappointments. It was becoming too safe for Lamont Cranston and that applied equally to The Shadow.

CHAPTER VII
EAST COMES WEST

THE next day, Chicago was serene. The suicide wave was over, ended as suddenly as it had begun. By mid-afternoon, not a single suicide had been reported during the past twenty-four hours. This was highly encouraging from the statistical standpoint.

On a national basis, suicide cases annually struck a ratio of one to ten thousand, or one case to every million of population. With a population of some three and a half million, Chicago's quota should, therefore, have averaged one suicide a day. This, of course, included the more prosaic cases as well as the spectacular kind that had been making headlines lately.

Hence Chicago was now back to better than normal and everybody was breathing more easily, particularly Inspector Rick Smedley. Also, Rick was breathing easily because he was enjoying the pleasant air of Lake Michigan. He was visiting Lester Tyburn on the latter's elegant cabin cruiser the *Cerberus,* which was moored off Navy Pier. Lamont Cranston was also visiting on board the craft and they were chatting pleasantly with Tyburn, while Skip Hagathorn, pilot of the *Cerberus,* was serving drinks from the cruiser's galley.

Skip was a limber, tawny-faced chap, who looked as though he enjoyed outdoor life. As a direct contrast, a squatty man with a tan coat and a brown hat was perched uncomfortably in a deck chair, his moonface looking yearningly toward land. This was Regan, the private detective assigned to Gail Tyburn. Regan was waiting for Tyburn to read his latest report, which consisted of a dozen thin paper pages, typed single space.

"I'm glad the suicide wave is over," Tyburn was telling Smedley. "That is, I hope it's over. Frankly, I feel you deserve the credit, the way you've had the police keep watching all the places where some frustrated character might just decide to put himself out in a big way."

"This last case wasn't like that," reminded Smedley, glumly. "Fleer didn't kill himself in front of a crowd. I only wish he had."

The glance that Rick gave Cranston was expressive. It meant that Rick hadn't got very far with the clue of the lunching painters at the Hotel Royal. Then, snapping from his low mood, Rick continued:

"We're getting results, though, Mr. Tyburn. What's more we're going to stay right with it. Compliments help, especially when they come from people like yourself."

Tyburn bowed an acknowledgment. Then:

"Tell me, Smedley," he asked. "When do you go off duty today?"

"At seven o'clock this evening."

"Too late," said Tyburn. "I want to get this cruiser up to Longwood before dark. But here's a suggestion, Smedley: Why don't you drive up there? You could make it by eight o'clock. I never take more than an hour, even with traffic. It's only about twenty-five miles."

"You mean to your estate in Longwood?"

"No, no. You wouldn't be able to find the place without an Indian guide. I mean the police headquarters. I'll get over there at eight and be waiting for you. Then we can make the arrangements for the Fiesta Night or whatever Gail intends to call that oversized society picnic. From what you've just told me, how your vigilance has halted this suicide craze, I'm more anxious than ever to have your services."

Rick agreed to be in Longwood at eight that evening. Therewith, Regan found a chance to get in a few words.

"If you'll read my report, Mr. Tyburn," said the private op, in a gruff, impatient tone, "I'll go back on duty. You're paying me to find out facts. I want to earn my money."

"You're earning it," conceded Tyburn, "but don't expect me to read all this drivel. Why, if Gail stops for a milk shake, you have to specify whether she ordered chocolate or vanilla. You even worry about the kind of flowers she wears."

"That's all important," argued Regan. "Suppose I lose her somewhere? I go into a drugstore or a flower shop and ask if a lady was just in there. They remember milk shakes or flowers better than they do faces. Besides, when it comes to cocktails, those details are more important. Maybe you won't believe it, but about half the dames around the ritzy bars are always letting some guy switch them to some different brand of drink. That's how you know when they've been switching boyfriends."

Interested, Tyburn thumbed through the report.

"Alexanders and more Alexanders," remarked Tyburn. "That's all Gail drinks. I suppose that an Alexander is Halifax's favorite drink."

"That's right," acknowledged Regan, "except when he takes brandy-and-soda. Then it's always Martell's brandy. You'll find it in my reports."

Tyburn gave an indulgent smile.

"Very well, Regan. You know your business;

stick to it. But why be in a hurry to go ashore? Your report says that Gail is meeting Halifax at the Mirror Grill at five thirty. Your work won't begin until then."

Regan had tilted his head and was listening uneasily to the lap of waves against the cruiser. A breeze was spanking up the lake and a slight roll of the ship was becoming more noticeable.

"I might run across one of them earlier," argued Regan. "Frankly, I'm trying to check on Halifax in his spare time. It may be important."

"Very well," decided Tyburn. "Skip will take you ashore."

Hagathorn beckoned Regan to a little outboard tender that was hitched to the *Cerberus*. Remembering something, Regan pulled a big manila envelope from his pocket, began opening it to show the contents to Tyburn.

"Here are the exhibits," explained Regan. "They go with the report. Things I picked up during my investigation."

"You mean theater programs, wilted flowers, hatchecks, match packs, cocktail menus, and all that sort of truck, I suppose." Tyburn gave a depreciating laugh. "Your reports tell everything, Regan. Why waste time collecting rubbish?"

"But I've given you memo sheets with phone numbers—"

"All mentioned in your reports."

"But when I find envelopes or letters in some person's handwriting—"

"Look, Regan," interrupted Tyburn. "I'm not criticizing your work. On the contrary, I am commending it. From now on"—Tyburn's tone was very patient—"be as meticulous as you want; in fact, more so than ever. Only try to classify these exhibits as you call them according to their importance. Understand?"

Regan nodded.

"And when you phone me," added Tyburn, "don't pour out everything in one blue streak. Be brief and if there's anything that particularly interests me, I'll ask for details. The rest can go in your reports; but even in that case, give me a condensation. The remainder can be supplementary, purely for the record. If it means more work to do it that way, I'll pay for the overtime."

Tyburn dismissed Regan with a wave and Skip helped the private detective into the tender. Then the outboard was whizzing shoreward and Regan, hanging onto his hat, was bobbing like a jack-in-the-box at the bow. They could see him waving frantically to Skip, who simply responded by veering the tender into the wake of speedboats that were roaring along the lakefront. In fact the speedboats got into the game themselves as if they had been loitering around, just for the fun of tormenting

Regan. They whizzed across the tender's path so that Skip could get the benefit of sudden waves, which he took in expert style. After what amounted to a pretzel-shaped tour, the tender finally dropped Regan off at the pier.

"I guess Regan annoys Skip, too," Tyburn was saying. "I'll tell Skip, though, to stop his fooling when he takes you two ashore. Regan is a good man, but a fool. If that silly wife of mine sails off to Reno on account of a Grade B movie actor, I just want the facts, that's all. I won't fight a divorce, but I will fight alimony. I'm not in the soap business to buy swimming pools for Halifax.

"Regan has found out all my lawyers will need, but I can't fire the fellow because he's done an honest job and I may need him again. Gail and Halifax are palsy-walsy; that's beyond dispute. If Gail takes it seriously enough to start a divorce move, I'll have my lawyers throw a scare into Halifax. He'll drop Gail like the hot potato she is, and she'll come running home."

Rick Smedley inserted a dry opinion. "Maybe they've figured you to be a Foxy Grandpa," suggested Rick. "They might be playing house right now, without you knowing it."

"The only house Gail has," reminded Tyburn, "is the place out at Longwood. That's why I'm paying three men to stay there on a twenty-four hour basis: Morse, Webster and Chaffin. Of course, Chaffin is on call when Gail needs the car, but she hasn't called him. Skip Hagathorn has full charge of this ship so that Gail can't decide on a Great Lakes cruise with John Halifax as a stowaway. All Gail can do is stay in town and run up hotel bills, at hotels where I have credit."

"You've covered it well," agreed Cranston, "from your side, Tyburn. But what about Halifax?"

"He stays with friends," replied Tyburn. "With one friend until he wears out his welcome, then he sponges on another. Regan has a list of all of them. The only way he's getting by, is by borrowing Gail's pin money. He hasn't a chance of establishing a Chicago residence of his own. He doesn't have a shekel to rub against a ducat."

Finishing his harangue with a laugh of real amusement, Tyburn took time out to chide Skip, who had just returned.

"Lay off the porpoise stunts, Skip," ordered Tyburn. "You're captain of a cabin cruiser, remember? Bring us another round of drinks; then you can take my friends ashore and we'll put off for Longwood."

It was when Cranston and Smedley were leaving that Tyburn added the final note to his conversation.

"My problems may only be trivial," admitted Tyburn, "but they concern two people who may think otherwise. One or the other may feel frustrated, or even persecuted. Those are complexes which psychiatrists have linked with the recent suicide wave." With that, Tyburn looked directly at Smedley and added, "You may realize now, inspector, why I feel it's important for you to handle the Longwood proposition."

Ashore, Cranston accompanied Smedley to headquarters, where Rick checked over recent reports. Nobody had yet checked the name of the tug that had been passing through the Chicago River at the time of Brett's jump, nor had any witnesses testified to the presence of strange painters at the Hotel Royal. Fleer's alleged jump had taken place when the regular painters were at lunch; that much had been established, nothing more.

"Not much in the murder line," decided Smedley. "How are you making out with magic, Mr. Cranston?"

"It's a bit barren, too," admitted Cranston. "I haven't met up with anyone I really wanted to fool. I'll phone you when you get back from Longwood, Inspector."

Stopping by at the Round Table, which was just breaking up for the afternoon, Cranston shook hands with the few magicians he found there and remarked that he had forgotten to sign the guest book of the day before. While doing that, he looked over the names of the other guests, on the chance that a few strangers had dropped in after his departure and heard about his tricks. There was one name Cranston was looking for but didn't expect to find. He didn't find it. That name was John Halifax.

In fact, John Halifax hadn't been seen at any magical rendezvous the day before. That, however, didn't mean that Halifax was hard to find. Knowing the right place to go, Cranston went there: the Mirror Grill.

A brand-new nightspot in Chicago, the Mirror Grill lived up to its name. It was enclosed completely by mirrors, which gave the guests the privilege of seeing themselves as others saw them, which in most instances meant double. There, Cranston ran into immediate luck. John Halifax and Gail Tyburn were at a large table with half a dozen other people, among them a man Cranston knew. Chancing by, Cranston was recognized, invited to join the group and was promptly introduced all around.

The Mirror Grill was well filled, which seemed rather surprising for this hour, until Cranston learned that it was featuring an innovation, a Cocktail Hour Show. An orchestra began to appear on a mirror-backed platform and immediately the voice of Gail Tyburn became peevishly evident above the buzz of general conversation.

"But I tell you, Johnny," Gail was protesting, "I don't want to see this show."

Halifax tilted his head to make his fixed smile look indulgent.

"It's only a short show, pretty."

"Johnny!" Gail's eyes flashed. "I told you not to call me things like that, at least not—"

Gail caught herself before adding "in public" to her statement. Halifax by then was covering his own slip.

"I said that it was only a pretty short show," Halifax declared. "Now tell us why you don't want to see it. Is it because there is a magician in the show, or is it because there is a magician in the show?"

"Both!" snapped Gail, seeing no humor in Halifax's query. "You know how I hate magic—"

"Except when I perform it," inserted Halifax. Then, to the rest of the group he added, "Gail appreciates talent, that's all. You can't blame her. She wants the best."

Snapping his fingers for a waiter, Halifax ordered Gail another Alexander. That was enough for Gail; she was the sort who wouldn't take orders, even indirectly. Impetuously, Gail came to her feet while Halifax, rising slowly, showed her a printed program that was standing like a little easel on the table.

"But you've never seen this magician," began Halifax. "He's a Chinese wizard, named Chung Loo."

"I don't care what he is!" stormed Gail. "I'm not going to watch him, nor do I intend to see those Magigals perform tonight. Magigals! They must be a fine-looking lot! How could they wear evening gowns and do their magic without sleeves? I'm leaving, Mr. Halifax, and when you get this magic off your mind, you can look me up."

Gail was tearing up the program as she strode away. Following her, Halifax turned to call back to the group, above the rising music of the orchestra.

"I'll be back in time to catch Chung Loo's act. There's no use in letting Gail go away mad."

By the time she reached the door, Gail had torn the program into pieces and was throwing them away. Cranston saw a chunky man stoop forward from a table near the door to gather up the pieces. The man was Regan; he was pocketing this new "exhibit" as Halifax hurried by to overtake Gail outside. Then, in a sidling manner which he evidently felt a private detective should use, Regan also hurried out.

Remarking that he had friends at another table, Cranston followed. When he reached a foyer filled with potted palms and little side doorways, he saw Gail through an outer door, getting into a cab. Regan was standing in the entrance, hand on hip, apparently looking for Halifax. But Cranston, knowing that Halifax intended to return, was no longer concerned with The Smile, not for the present.

A girl had captured Cranston's eye, a girl who was hurrying in through the entrance, right past Regan, who didn't even notice her, not knowing who she was. The girl's face formed a perfect oval; her features, though finely formed, were pale, perhaps through worry. Again, it could have been the background of flowing black hair that produced that pallor by contrast.

The girl was Verity Joyce.

Cranston lost himself among the palms while Verity hurried by into the Mirror Grill. A few moments later, Cranston followed her. Scarcely had Cranston seen Verity settle at a corner table, before the orchestra hit a discordant Oriental beat and every light in the Mirror Grill and the outside foyer was extinguished.

Then, a single spot of light thrust itself upon the stage and probed there, searchingly. The orchestra hit a strange jangle, replete with bells. Drums beat as the light moved; suddenly, a weird face appeared in the glow. Cymbals crashed, the whole stage lighted and there stood a bowing Chinese in a Mandarin robe, surrounded by a curious array of Oriental paraphernalia, with tapestries and screens as a background, covering the mirrored walls.

Such was Chung Loo's introduction to his public and they liked it. The whole thing was bizarre and authentic. Something from the East had been transported to the West as though the magician himself had arrived at the rub of an Aladdin's lamp.

All eyes but Cranston's were fixed on that brilliant stage. His eyes were looking for Verity Joyce but could not find her. Even the eyes of The Shadow could not penetrate the complete darkness that persisted everywhere save on the stage itself.

Lamont Cranston decided to watch Chung Loo.

CHAPTER VIII
AMONG THE MAGIGALS

CHUNG LOO was worth watching.

His act was a series of dazzling surprises, all in Chinese style. From a curious table shaped like a dragon's head with flashing eyes, Chung Loo picked up a pair of bowls, showed them empty and handed them to a girl in Chinese costume.

Spreading his hands in air, Chung Loo caught fistfuls of rice, flung the grains clattering into a bowl until it was filled. Snatching the bowls, he poured the rice from one into the other, clapped the mouths of the bowls together. Whipping the bowls apart, Chung Loo showed that the rice had turned to water, which he poured from bowl to bowl. Again he inverted one bowl upon the other, turned them horizontally and swung them apart, mouths upward.

Each bowl was now filled with fire, its flames flaring fiercely as high as Chung Loo's shoulders.

As the audience gasped, Chung Loo tossed the fire bowls in midair where they turned to huge bouquets of flowers, which the magician caught and flung to his assistant. There was only one slip; the girl nearly muffed the flowers but the audience hardly noticed this. Chung Loo saw it, gave his assistant a glare as he went into his next trick.

This was the instantaneous transformation of several silk handkerchiefs into a huge banner bearing a silver dragon. Chung Loo threw the banner to the girl who nearly tangled herself in it, but by then, Chung Loo was picking up three taborets and tossing the ornamental stools in the air, where he handled them like a juggler. This was a stunt, indeed, juggling three articles of furniture and Chung Loo prolonged it because of the applause, which was fortunate, for the girl was slow in coming on again. She was bringing three large cloths, of the style called foulards. As the girl arrived, Chung Loo neatly finished his juggling by planting the taborets one, two, three in a row.

Then, whipping the cloths one by one, Chung Loo spread each above a taboret; snatching the cloths away, he revealed stacks of fish bowls three feet high. Not content with this, the magician met the girl halfway across the stage, where she was tardily returning with the dragon cloth. Somersaulting toward the audience, Chung Loo came up to his feet, flinging the cloth to display a fish bowl two feet wide that he had captured from nowhere during his acrobatic stunt.

From then on, Chung Loo was like a whirling dervish with his rapid-fire act. He transformed fishbowls to birdcages, produced a lighted lamp on a tray. He planted a pane of glass on a bowl filled with goldfish, inverted another bowl on the glass, turned both over and caused the fish to drop through the glass sheet, water and all.

Most amazing were the magic butterflies, which Chung Loo tore deftly and swiftly from sheets of colored paper. They became alive, flitted through hoops and finally circled over the audience. By then, the spectators were convinced that Chung Loo could do about everything except vanish in a cloud of smoke, so the wizard proved that he could do that, too. Impatiently grabbing a large cloth from the slow-moving girl, Chung Loo flung it over him with a wave of his arms. There was a great burst of flame, a cloud of smoke, and as it cleared, the girl was bowing ceremoniously toward the spot where Chung Loo had been. Then, as the smoke thinned away, the girl hesitantly turned, spread a large fan and waved it as she pointed above the heads of the audience.

Every stage light went off. In the utter blackness, tiny points of light appeared, like multitudes of fireflies which for aught anyone knew, might be the reincarnation of Chung Loo. There were gasps, awed exclamations, finally the clapping of hands. The fireflies danced fantastically, changed colors in kaleidoscopic style, then suddenly vanished in little puffs of flame. That was all. It was enough.

On came the lights of the Mirror Grill, showing a blinking, gaping audience that the wizardry of the vanished Chung Loo had thoroughly captivated.

Three things had definitely impressed Lamont Cranston and he was weighing them now. Those three were the opening bowl routine, the goldfish through the glass sheet, and finally the fantastic fireflies. They had points of novelty that some of the other tricks missed; all in all, a distinct touch of the incredible.

And the incredible, where Lamont Cranston was concerned, had begun to link with the name of Professor Marsh.

Mere thought of that name snapped Cranston from his reverie. He turned to look for Verity Joyce. For once, the usually alert Mr. Cranston was too late. During those entrancing minutes when all had been blackness except for the alluring sparkle of the varicolored fireflies, the girl with the black hair and soulful face had slipped from the Mirror Room.

Glancing about, Cranston saw John Halifax. The Smile was over by a wall, an ideal place, since a mirrored panel gave his reflection and thus produced two images for the world to admire. But vanity wasn't the cause of Halifax being there. In the darkness that had persisted throughout Chung Loo's act, Halifax, trying to regain his table, could only have found his way along the wall. Now that he could see the table, he was working his way there, to resume his seat beside the empty chair that Gail Tyburn had left.

Cranston wangled his way to the same objective and sat down with the group in time to hear Halifax answer queries regarding his authoritative opinion of Chung Loo's act.

"Middling" was Halifax's easy-toned comment. "Or perhaps I should say middling to muddling. Good magic, but Chung Loo outraced his assistant. That wasn't her fault, it was his for hiring her. If he knows his business, he'll get a new girl. Then, if I see the act again, I might give it a better appraisal. The tricks look new, but that's because they're old and, therefore, you haven't ever seen them."

Cranston didn't agree with Halifax's last remark, but he didn't dispute the point. It was the stock answer that many professionals would give rather than admit there were tricks of their trade they didn't know.

"Well, my good people," said Halifax, rising from his chair. "I have an important engagement in the near soon. The Magigals are holding sway and I must be there. After all, they represent at least a portion of my public."

With that, Halifax sauntered from the Mirror Grill, past a group of people who had entered after the lights came on. Among the group was Regan, who gave Halifax a steady, but puzzled stare, the last part evidenced by the way the private dick scratched his head. Then, abruptly, Regan clamped his brown hat on his head and started on Halifax's trail.

People were talking about staying for Chung Loo's next show, but it turned out that it wasn't scheduled until ten o'clock. As the group broke up, Cranston went with them. He was realizing that he hadn't anything to do until ten, if then. Inspector Smedley was due at Longwood to meet Lester Tyburn at eight o'clock; if Rick stayed there an hour, he wouldn't be leaving until nine and, therefore, wouldn't be back until ten. But there would be

Chung Loo was like a whirling dervish and the audience went mad about him. Suddenly, he grabbed a large cloth from the girl and flung it over him with a wild wave of his arms. There was a cloud of smoke and as it cleared the girl was bowing toard where Chung Loo had been.

nothing that Cranston could learn from Rick's preliminary visit to the Longwood police headquarters.

Lamont Cranston decided to see the Magigals' show.

Decorum was the keynote at the Hotel Harbison when Cranston arrived there. No pranking tonight among the Magigals; instead they were prinking to look their very best. Since the organization was unique, it had decided to make the show the same. The bill had several scheduled acts, but between them, surprise numbers were slated. In fact, any Magigal was privileged to do from three to five minutes if she could convince the committee that her work was sufficiently good to grace this show.

Also, there were to be two intermissions and during these informal groups were to gather around tables at which all comers, guests included, could toss impromptu trickery.

The first act was under way when Cranston arrived. He watched Magigals perform all sorts of magic from sleights to illusions. Then came the intermission and the informalities began. Mooching around, taking copious notes, was the indefatigable Regan. He was particularly interested in a table where John Halifax was showing some very expert card deals.

So was Lamont Cranston.

There was a special reason on Cranston's part. Out of the crowd of Magigals who had swarmed about Halifax, like flowers enfolding a bee, had come the mystery face that Cranston wanted to see again.

Verity Joyce.

The girl's face had color, now; her eyes were sharp, with a vivid sparkle. She was peering over Halifax's shoulder, but wasn't watching his sleights. Instead, Verity was scanning the crowd, apparently looking for someone else.

Perhaps she was expecting a crystal skull to come popping out of nowhere.

At any rate, she was a trifle disappointed, for her gaze began to droop. She wasn't noticing Regan, apparently didn't know him, though he had elbowed close to Halifax in order to jot down everything The Smile was doing.

Finished with his card work, Halifax gave a broad gesture of his arms, practically took a bow as he smiled his way backward. Somebody else was due to follow, so Cranston eased into Halifax's place. Cranston did just three tricks for the Magigals, the cigarette case, the lighted matches from box, and the dissolving coin. It was just a case of playing policy, a going through of the motions. Having worked these Marsh effects at so many other places without the result he wanted, Cranston merely felt that the Magigals at least were entitled to witness them.

There wasn't time for anymore, much though the Magigals were amazed by Cranston's miracles.

The intermission was over, so Cranston gathered up his props, elbowed Regan out of the way, almost knocking the pencil from the detective's hand. Cranston noticed that Halifax was standing with folded arms, impressed at least by the tricks that he had just seen. But Verity Joyce, though she had been watching a few moments before, had slipped away again.

She was getting very adept at that, Verity was. Leaving Cranston at loose ends, everytime. This time, he had nothing to do but watch the first specialty act on the second part of the bill. Indifference left Cranston when he saw the girl who walked on as one of the surprises. She was a real surprise from Cranston's standpoint:

Verity Joyce!

A soft laugh came from Cranston's lips. What he had taken for a disappearance on Verity's part was merely a matter of her getting ready for an act she was to do. Then the act began and with it, Cranston's interest reached intensity.

The girl could do astounding magic. Into a transparent plastic bag, Verity thrust her hand, showed it back and front, then closed it. Opening her hand, the girl revealed an egg, which she removed and placed in a glass. Back into the bag went her hand; the result, another egg. This continued until Verity had produced half a dozen eggs.

Next, over all six glasses, Verity placed circular sheets of paper. Catching two cigarettes from the air, one with each hand, she passed them above the glasses. Instantly, the paper cylinders disappeared in a quick flash of flame. Five of the six glasses were empty; in the sixth were all the eggs, forming a zigzag stack up to the very top of the glass and even above it.

That was all.

It was enough for Cranston. The enthusiastic spectators knew they were applauding good magic, but they couldn't have named the particular brand. Cranston could, for he recognized the touch that made it different.

Verity Joyce, the mysterious Magigal, had done two tricks that bore the exclusive and inventive touch of Professor Marsh. Of this Cranston was certain, for his own performance of such had given him a definite insight as to the basic phases of Marsh magic. Putting the rule in reverse, Verity could have recognized the origin of Cranston's tricks. Important though that point might be, it was secondary to another prospect.

If death threatened Cranston as a possessor of genuine Marsh secrets, Verity would also be venturing along that same trail which led to what was so far called suicide.

The optimistic note was that no death thrusts had come Cranston's way; therefore, Verity might not be in danger. But Cranston was inclined to be pessimistic. He still felt that bad luck or wrong timing could be the reason why he had been ignored. There was still a chance that he could be spotted, perhaps right here. Since the same applied to Verity, Cranston decided to watch the girl, making sure that this time she did not slip away.

Moving away, Cranston looked for Halifax; saw the handsome Hollywood wizard watching the show. Not knowing that he was being watched, Halifax had relaxed his smile into one of genuine interest at Verity's performance. The credit that Halifax had refused to give Chung Loo vocally, he was extending silently to Verity.

In a phone booth at the side of the room, Regan was making a call, reading from his notes as he glanced from the booth. Cranston saw him there, observed that the detective was watching Halifax. It was now about nine thirty, the usual time for Regan to report to Tyburn. The phone booths were in an alcove, hence Regan had a good observation spot where he wouldn't ordinarily be noticed. In his hand, Regan was holding a notebook, from which he was reading, leaving Tyburn the privilege of questioning him on any specific points.

As he answered queries that doubtless came from Tyburn, Regan kept watching Halifax and also tilted his head to look toward the stage, because Halifax was looking at the show. Thus, in a sense, Tyburn was getting Halifax's observations at second hand through Regan. But all that ended as Cranston, strolling past the alcove, reached the exit from the improvised platform which formed a stage.

Halifax, watching a full stage act which was following Verity's turn, had suddenly tired of the show and had started elsewhere. Of all places, Halifax was heading straight for the alcove where the phone booths were located. Cranston could no longer see Regan, but he correctly pictured the fellow's reactions. As Halifax neared the alcove, Regan came out, head bowed while he lighted a cigarette so that Halifax would not see his face, while with his other hand, Regan was stuffing notes into his pocket.

This room was actually a banquet hall converted to an auditorium with built-up platform and folding chairs. Hence Cranston wasn't sure that Verity would leave by the particular stage exit that he had chosen, for there might be another on the opposite side. So Cranston went backstage, where several Magigals were bustling about, getting their acts ready.

Moving around behind the backdrop, Cranston saw Verity Joyce in the other wing. The girl was talking on a backstage telephone, just finishing the call when Cranston spied her. Hurriedly, Verity came behind the backdrop, heading directly toward Cranston who promptly disappeared. He didn't

need The Shadow's regalia to accomplish this. All Cranston did was grip the edge of the backdrop and roll himself within it. Verity went past and as her footsteps faded, Cranston unfolded himself from the curtain to take up the trail.

That trail led directly to the street, where the doorman bowed Verity into a cab as it pulled up. There was another cab behind and Cranston not only hailed it, but was on board by the time Verity's cab pulled away. Telling the driver that he had a friend in the other cab who was guiding him to his destination, Cranston stayed right on Verity's trail. In methodical fashion, he looked back toward the doorway of the Hotel Harbison and saw Regan pounding along the street, waving his arms at the doorman.

It was another of those quaint situations that fitted Regan so aptly. Apparently, he'd seen Halifax take a cab and had rushed up to the corner to find one for himself. By then, Verity and Cranston in turn had come from the hotel and taken cabs; now, Regan was rushing back too late, with papers flapping from his overstuffed pockets, only to find that he was still left at the post.

Luck favored Regan, however, for as Cranston looked back, he saw the doorman flag another cab and gesture the gumshoe into it. Next, Regan's cab was trailing Cranston's, which Regan might just have been dumb enough to mistake for the cab that Halifax had taken.

Things at least were on the move, though all this might prove a blind trail. Regan's call had been a routine report to Tyburn; of that, Cranston was certain, though he could check it later. As for Halifax, whatever the purpose of his phone call, he had made it after witnessing two persons—Lamont Cranston and Verity Joyce—perform magic of the type identified with Professor Marsh. That in itself might produce immediate results.

The final factor was Verity Joyce herself. Had she planned to perform her magic before she saw Cranston do his? Had she purposely done those Marsh tricks so that Cranston could witness them? Why had she been talking to someone on the telephone immediately afterward? Did she know that Halifax had left the show before she came from backstage? Was she hoping that someone would pick up her trail, and if so, whom?

Lamont Cranston answered his own barrage of questions with a softly whispered laugh, the sort of mirth that usually preceded the advent of The Shadow into the business that was to come.

CHAPTER IX
THE LAST BET

VERITY'S trail led right back to the Mirror Grill.

That wasn't too pleasing to Cranston, who felt that he was playing his last bet in the game of making himself a target for murder. Nevertheless, he kept on the trail.

So did Regan.

At first, Regan's cab dogged Cranston's as persistently as Cranston's driver kept tagging the cab in which Verity rode. Later, Regan's cab turned off somewhere, but by the time the others neared the Mirror Grill, it shot into sight again. Then the cabs were halting in succession, dropping off their passengers.

Nobody seemed interested in anybody else. Verity was heading directly into the Mirror Grill itself. Cranston was following in leisurely fashion, as if merely a chance arrival. Regan was ignoring Verity entirely and overlooking Cranston. Cagily, the private detective was trying to spot someone else, doubtless Halifax. He was just stubborn enough, Regan, to suppose that Halifax had pulled out in one of those two cabs just ahead of his own. But Cranston was dismissing Regan from present consideration.

Verity Joyce demanded full attention.

So Cranston thought, until he entered the Mirror Grill. There he saw another lady who looked as though she needed attention and wasn't getting it. A blonde with an upsweep hairdo topped by a hat that looked like a pint-sized snowplow taking a banked curve on a roller coaster. She was the subject of Tyburn's one-woman photo gallery, the same dreamy-eyed charmer who had been monopolizing John Halifax, Gail Tyburn.

Maybe Gail had got over her cocktail hour pout. Perhaps she'd decided it was time for him to be forgiven; or for her to be. Whatever the case, she had returned to the scene of their last rendezvous and she was looking for somebody. Probably Halifax.

Cranston decided to let Gail look while he watched Verity, who was a quicker hand at slipping out of sight. Verity wasn't at a table near the doorway, as she had been at cocktail time. Instead, she had found a seat at a very poor table, to one side of the mirrored room, a place that nobody else wanted because a pillar with big mirrors blocked the view of the stage. Before Cranston could wonder too much why Verity had taken that location, he learned the reason.

Thinking herself unobserved, the dark-haired girl reached for the nearest wall mirror, pressed it inward like a panel and slipped right through from sight.

A nice disappearance and done with mirrors, too. For that, Verity deserved a blue Magigal badge instead of just a red one. Perhaps Cranston would rate an honorary membership if he did the same trick. Smiling at the thought, he worked his way around the tables, took the vacant seat, picked the

moment when the orchestra began to arrive, and pressed the mirror just as Verity had.

The panel wasn't bolted from the other side. It gave quite freely and Cranston stepped through, letting it hinge shut behind him. He was in a passage that led behind the wall, simply a short route that obviously went backstage. Following along it, Cranston came to the stage itself, paused where steps turned to go up, and listened to voices that he heard above.

Verity Joyce was speaking to a man who spoke in short-clipped sentences. Moving to a closer vantage point, Cranston saw that the man was Chung Loo.

"And since your phone call interested me," Verity was saying, "I came here. You say you can use me in the act. Why?"

"Because of egg trick," replied Chung Loo. "Very good."

"How do you know it's good?" demanded Verity. "I didn't see you there. Anyway, you called me right after my turn."

"Luck, maybe," said Chung Loo. "I ask Magigals: Tell me, who does what tricks tonight. When I hear Miss Joyce, egg trick, I decide to call you."

"I don't intend to sell the egg trick—"

"I don't buy anyway. I know plenty tricks already."

"Then what do you want?"

"An assistant. Good one. Anybody handle eggs, sure to be good. I tell Magigals I want assistant bad. I don't mean bad assistant. Good assistant."

Verity was nodding; she paused to study Chung Loo closely. From longer range, Cranston could fairly well analyze Verity's impressions. Chung Loo looked the part of a magician, the sort who was wrapped closely in the art. His face was cryptic; only his mouth was expressive. The little mustachios that drooped to the sides of his chin gave his features a demoniac touch, but that fitted the magical character he strove to represent. Apart from the fact that he, too, was a specialist in Marsh magic, Chung Loo looked sincere and substantial.

Moreover, Chung Loo did need an assistant badly. Having seen the show, Verity knew it. Still, she wanted to probe a trifle further.

"You told the Magigals you had an opening for an assistant?"

Chung Loo bowed acknowledgment.

"But why didn't they announce it?" queried Verity. "Half those Magigals would like to go with a show."

"Committee lady say same," returned Chung Loo, blandly. "But she say no use to announce. They all want to go with Halifax."

"They can all go to Halifax," said Verity, "if that's the way they feel. Every picture I ever saw of

Halifax was framed thick with girls. What chance would just one have?"

Chung Loo merely shrugged.

"You take job, lady?"

"I'll take it," agreed Verity. "How soon?"

"Beginning next show," replied Chung Loo. "You watch this one back here. You see enough to be better than girl I have now. She say she quit, anyway."

Drumbeats were coming from the orchestra. It was almost time for Chung Loo to start his act. Moving back along the passage, Cranston went through the mirror and found a better seat than the one at the special table. Lights blinked; the show was on.

Only once during Chung Loo's act did the lights go up enough for Cranston to spot other people about him. That was when Chung Loo was juggling the three taborets. During that spell, Cranston spied Gail at a table, Regan at another. Then things went dark and stayed that way until the finish of the firefly number. Gail and Regan were still there; Verity would probably be coming out soon. So Cranston strolled out through the foyer, carrying a small portfolio under his arm. It would do just as well to wait outside. Then he could check on people as they came along.

When Cranston stepped to the sidewalk, he stepped into adventure. The Mirror Grill was near a corner and hardly had Cranston appeared beside the curb, before a big truck rumbled around the corner. It was swerving fast, but looked as though it were going to hit the sidewalk near where Cranston stood.

Cranston did the natural thing. He made a quick dart in the other direction, so the truck would pass him. Then, in one quick flash, he saw that the truck had a trailer, a big one. The truck was under control, but the trailer wasn't. It was making a wide sideswipe, about to climb the curb at the very spot where Cranston expected to find a zone of safety.

With an amazing twist, Cranston came about, grabbed for the truck and caught a hanging chain with one hand. The wrench on his arm was terrific, but the chain snatched Cranston up and out of disaster's path. Hitting the curb with its wheels, the trailer not only toppled; it snapped its hitch. As Cranston swung from the chain like a trapeze jumper, he saw a few tons of trailer smack the sidewalk in conclusive style, covering about every inch of area where Cranston would have been.

Landing in the street a hundred feet ahead, Cranston saw the truck take the next corner, its driver totally unconcerned by the loss of such a minor item as a trailer. There was a taxicab parked across the way, its driver sitting petrified. In three bounds, Cranston was inside the cab, speaking persuasively to the driver.

"Let's go, chum," suggested Cranston. "We'll say

we didn't see it happen. If anybody was mashed under that go-cart, we can't help them. Why stick around and waste time being witnesses?"

The cabby caught the idea and started. But there wasn't any copyright on Cranston's notion. A car parked further down the street was doing the same thing and a few other cabs began showing skittish tendencies, as though wanting passengers as an excuse to get away from this particular scene.

Cranston's cab rounded a few corners at his suggestion. The car that followed did the same. Farther back, Cranston could see other lights turning a corner. All Cranston did was sit back and relax with a whispered laugh.

He could afford that laugh, being no longer Cranston.

On the cab seat, Cranston's portfolio was lying wide open and empty. He was now wearing a black cloak and hat, while he stowed a brace of heavy automatics in special holsters meant for them. The portfolio came last; Cranston simply spread it and placed it around his body, beneath the black cloak. Until then, he could still have regarded himself as Cranston; fully girded, equipped for the action he had so long awaited, he was The Shadow.

None of this was noticed by the driver of The Shadow's cab. The hackie was pretty much perturbed, talking to his passenger spasmodically in reference to the recent trailer crash. Meanwhile, in Cranston's tone, The Shadow was inserting directions to the driver.

"Cheez, if that trailer hadda swung the other way!" the driver was saying. "It woulda clipped this buggy for sure!"

"Speaking of turns," came Cranston's tone, "take the next corner to the left."

"Whatta smashup that woulda been," continued the cabby. "More'n a smashup. It woulda been a mash-up, with me the mash."

"Next corner, right."

"Flatter'n a pancake, that's what this hack would be right now if that trailer hadda hit it."

"Take another right at the next corner."

"And the way that truck kept right on going! The goon that was driving it acted like nothing had happened!"

"Another right turn," Cranston's voice ordered quietly. "Take it a little faster."

As the cabby complied, he became a trifle argumentative.

"Hey, mister." The cabby darted a glance back to the rear seat. "Not to be too inquisitive, but who's driving this cab? I don't mind you telling me when to turn and where, but how I'm to do it is my business, see?"

The cabby was looking for his passenger but couldn't locate him in the back seat. He heard the voice, though, that replied, more imperturbably than ever:

"Very well, driver. Take the next street right and drive as slowly as you like. Just don't block traffic, that's all."

"Next right," began the cabby. "Here goes—hey!" He was darting longer looks into the rear seat now. "What's the idea? We're going in a circle. And what's this stuff about not blocking traffic?"

Still unable to locate the mysterious passenger who spoke in the quiet tone, the cab driver tried to clinch his final argument by looking back through the rear window. He didn't like that crack about not blocking traffic in a street where there probably wasn't any.

But the cabby changed his mind as he heard the shriek of brakes, saw a rakish car take the corner behind him on practically two wheels and follow with a sudden spurt. He remembered now, the cabby, that he'd seen lights turning corners in his mirror and he recalled that rakish car as it outlined itself in the glow of a corner streetlight.

It was one of the cars that had been parked across from the Mirror Grill before the trailer crash. The cabby had been studying its long, low lines, figuring it to be an old buggy, but a fast one. The kind of car that made him think of the old hijacking days in Chicago, except that it was a lot newer than the cars used then. Nevertheless, that reminder was sufficient.

The cabby knew now why his passenger had wanted him to drive in circles. The man in the back seat had been wanting to learn if they were being tailed.

They were.

That, too, was enough. The cabby gave his hack the gun. It launched forward like a diver from a springboard. If he couldn't beat pursuers on the turns, he'd try it on the straightaway. Poor judgment, for the long-lined car was probably much faster than the cab, but it was exactly what The Shadow wanted, at least for the present.

Subtly, The Shadow had suggested danger to the cabby and the man had taken the hint. That proved the cabby was desperate; now he'd do whatever The Shadow told him. All during his driving about Chicago, The Shadow had pictured a situation such as this, hence he had long ago resolved what his course would be. He had even been studying the cab drivers, their impulses and responses, so that if he happened to get a skittish specimen, he could plan accordingly.

Three blocks more before another turn; that was The Shadow's plan, on the theory it would bluff the pursuing car. But before the cab reached the next corner, The Shadow changed his strategy. From around a corner, just two blocks ahead, came a big truck that identified itself the moment it hove into sight. It was riding light and carefree, having dropped plenty of weight in the form of a trailer.

It was the death-truck, back in the game again!

The way the truck veered, its short squatty build, were the features that identified it. That truck, bound on murder once, would logically be sticking to its task. It was coming head-on toward The Shadow's racing cab and the driver of the truck could see the pursuing car which proved that the cab must contain Lamont Cranston, the man slated for quick death.

The Shadow had made a last bet to make himself murder's target and it was paying off in the form of a daily double!

CHAPTER X
ALONG THE LAKEFRONT

"TURN left."

It was the whispered voice of The Shadow that gave the command; no longer the quiet tone of Cranston.

The effect on the cab driver was electric. He, too, had recognized the truck; knew that he was boxed between it and the pursuing car. He hadn't an idea that he was near a corner; for all he knew, he might be aiming straight for the wall of a building when he made that swerve. But the command of The Shadow's voice was all-compelling. The cabby swung the cab.

Tires screeching, the cab threatened to topple as its right wheels grazed the far curb of an intersecting street. It was like the mad swing that the truck had made when it flung the loosened trailer at Cranston. So sudden was the cab's change of direction that the pursuing car overshot the mark and had to haul back. Further down the street, however, the driver of the approaching truck saw the cab's veer in time to swing into a crossstreet a block away.

That did not perturb The Shadow; quite the opposite. His whispered laugh came as an encouragement to the harried cab driver. The cab had gained enough leeway to shake the car that was chasing it. The truck, though a fast one, couldn't overtake the cab if it made another turn left.

This was a time when The Shadow laughed too soon.

He repeated the order, "Turn left" as the cab reached the next corner. The cabby started to obey, braked the car, and yanked it into reverse. The street into which he tried to turn was blocked off for repairs. Beyond a barrier with red lights lay a great gaping stretch, totally devoid of paving. The trip would have come to a sudden end right there, had the cabby attempted to navigate that gap.

Now they were racing along the same street that

they had tried to leave. The car behind them had gained, not lost by the cab's delay. The next cross street was topped by an elevated structure and the pursuing car was cutting over to the cab's left, hoping either to get abreast of it, or to ram it when it tried to take another turn to the left.

The Shadow's next command took care of that: "Turn right."

The cabby did it on two wheels, those on the left. Daring though his swerve was, it rated as trivial, compared to The Shadow's own maneuver. The door on the left flung open and The Shadow launched outward with it. As he went, he caught the handle of the front door beside the cabby and yanked it open, too.

Startled, the driver could only clutch the steering wheel to hold himself in place as the door flew wide beside him. He couldn't watch what was happening, for he was completing the cab's swing into the street where the elevated railway ran. Nor did the men in the car behind see what happened, for The Shadow and the flying doors were out of their sight.

First, The Shadow grazed an elevated pillar. What prevented him from really bashing it, was his quick grab at the cab's front door. However, that was not his only purpose in pulling the front door wide. Performing an amazing twirl on the running board of the cab, handling the two doors as an acrobat would twist between a pair of gymnasium rings, The Shadow literally wrenched himself from the rear of the cab into the front, just as the cab hit the straight stretch down the street beneath the elevated.

In a trice, The Shadow had turned himself from a passenger into a driver.

As the cab righted itself, the doors came slamming shut and The Shadow also flung himself in the same direction, jouncing the cabby out from beneath the wheel. An instant later, The Shadow himself was handling the helm and in an unprecedented style. The pursuing car was right behind him, cutting over to the left, while the truck, which had been gaining all the time, had swung into this street from the next corner and was taking the wrong side of the street, to meet the cab head-on.

Neat business, this, the swift car boxing the cab so that the truck could bash it. Except that The Shadow didn't give it time to work the trick. He swerved the cab to the left, just beyond an elevated pillar, to get there ahead of the rakish car. The truck saw the maneuver, swung promptly across the street to meet the cab on that side.

Again, The Shadow was guessing a jump ahead. Instead of continuing that swerve to the left, he whipped the cab to the right. He simply snaked himself out of the trap, leaving the other car to meet the truck point-blank, if it were so inclined.

The car didn't take the bait. It came after the cab, and the truck, about a hundred feet ahead, angled itself across the street to close a new and fatal box. But The Shadow was still giving the cab an undulating course. Whipping around an el pillar, he cut left, all the way across the street, zigzagging right past the truck before its driver could counter the maneuver.

Even then The Shadow's neat tactics had not ended. He came right again, around another pillar, clear over to the proper side of the street, where he swung in back of the fast moving car that had been trying to overtake him. The driver of that car and his companions were still looking for the cab, because the truck in passing had obscured it. They expected to see it loping on the left, but it wasn't there. Before they could guess that it had pulled behind them, the car passed the next corner. There, The Shadow simply turned to the right and took another street.

It had been in and out, around and between the el posts, a mad flirt with death that left the cabby sitting numbed beside The Shadow, glad that his amazing passenger had taken over the wheel. This, however, was not the end of the danger trail. Somehow, the cab seemed to have lost its speed. The car behind was resuming the chase.

There was a reason for this. The Shadow had not forgotten his original purpose, not even after that wild experience beneath the elevated. He wanted followers to keep along his trail, so that he could trick them. His only problem now was the safety of the cab driver and The Shadow had a way to settle that.

Aiming straight for Michigan Boulevard, The Shadow crossed that lakeside thoroughfare and spurted the cab into Grant Park, which formed the central link in Chicago's chain of lakefront parks. There, he made a sudden turn to the left, threw his weight against the cabby on his right and pulled the handle of the door on that side. The Shadow gunned the cab as the door went wide.

Out went the cabby with the flying door. Lacking The Shadow's acrobatic ability, the cabby couldn't find anything to grab except some flowers of a huge bush that flanked the corner and found a bristly but happy landing place. The Shadow's parting laugh ended with the slam of the door as it slapped back into place. Then the cab was gone and before the dumbfounded cabby could find wits enough to crawl from his nest, the pursuing car had swung past also, without noticing the reclining figure in the bush.

Up ahead, the cab was coming to a halt. The rakish car hauled up beside it, dropping two men, one of whom approached the cab in crouching style from the near side, while the other circled it to cover the opposite doors. In through the windows, they suddenly shoved guns and flashlights.

All they found was an empty cab. The Shadow had already filtered from the vehicle in his own shadowy fashion.

The men were puzzled, but they didn't stand around and advertise the fact. Instead, they extinguished their flashlights, dodged back to their car and started away. To all intents, they might have been police in a prowl car, taking a look into an abandoned taxicab. They had good reason to be cautious, for other cars were coming along this driveway and a double blockade would cause too much notice, particularly if a real police car showed upon the scene.

Nevertheless, these unknowns weren't giving up their hunt.

Somewhere further down the driveway, they pulled off the road and extinguished the lights of the car. They probably thought that the cab driver, and perhaps his passenger, had ducked for cover of the bushes and would return to the cab now that the way looked clear. In fact, the car had pulled far enough along to fool anybody who might be hiding in the shrubbery.

That didn't apply to The Shadow.

The cloaked investigator was already on the rove, preparing to turn the hunters into the hunted. His keen ears sensing the cessation of the car's motor, The Shadow was able to locate it fairly accurately in the dark. He had moved somewhat ahead, playing the hunch that the other men would do the same with their car. The hunch was paying off.

Indeed, The Shadow had reached the crux of this expedition, perhaps of his whole investigation in Chicago. The very method of this compact gang fitted with his theory, the same theory which he had thrown at Inspector Rick Smedley as an argument that murder, not suicide, was the thing to be investigated.

The list of strange deaths all savored of strongarm tactics, with William Brett and Edward Fleer, the cases which The Shadow had personally studied as Cranston, representing two illustrations of that point. In those cases, too, The Shadow had figured the handiwork of an extra man, or even a crew, whose purpose was to pave the way to murder and do the cover-up work.

Somebody must have done the jump from the bridge into the Chicago River, while the others were operating on the tugboat, after knocking off Brett and dumping his body. Similarly, unless someone had checked on Fleer, or even rigged the business of the scaffold, the trick of the substitute painters would not have been possible.

That man of daredevil quality had been in the game again tonight, for only such a hand could have launched a huge trailer as a lethal weapon with Cranston as its target. The bunch in the waiting car in this case had resembled cover-uppers until the deed of murder had been passed along to them. Now they were stalking Cranston as they had gone after Fleer, Brett and previous victims.

There were differences, however. They didn't have their reckless companion handy; at least, not yet. He had been left somewhere back along the line with his truck. This was a time, though, when they wouldn't ordinarily need him. The plan to dispose of Cranston was anything but subtle; it was brutal, as witness the business with the trailer.

An accidental death would be better than a faked suicide, for it wouldn't be linked with the other cases. Besides, Cranston was too full of life and magic to be the sort who would do away with himself. He might become morbid, but not until after the Magigals had finished their convention and the killers couldn't wait that long. They couldn't wait because their boss wouldn't let them, whoever that boss might be. Even now The Shadow was speculating on the identity of the mind behind the game of death and he had a variety of guesses, which included women along with men.

The way to settle the present party and gain a direct lead to lead direct to the source. That was to take out the murder crew one by one. This was exactly what The Shadow intended to do and even if he only managed to bag the first of three prospects, his task would be accomplished. One would unquestionably be a lead to all and, therefore, to the whole game.

From close to where he gauged the car was parked, The Shadow caught the blink of guarded flashlights, which gradually diverged, then disappeared. They were prowling separately, the three men from the car, which was made to The Shadow's order. Not that he ordinarily minded handling three killers at a clip; there were times when he preferred it. On this occasion, however, The Shadow did not want to produce a situation wherein he might have to deal them their own medicine. A captured killer would be better than a dead one, because he could be made to talk.

There were creeping sounds along the grass and among the shrubs. The prowlers were skirting The Shadow instead of finding him, partly because of his own shifting tactics, which went unheard. They were looking for Cranston and a taxi driver, not The Shadow; that was where the creeping men were making a grave mistake.

They would converge again as they neared the empty cab, tightening their circle slowly, surely. They'd pause though before they came too close to each other, so they could listen for sounds ahead and learn if anyone had tried to sneak back to the cab. Now The Shadow was gliding along the rim of the imaginary circle, just outside it, ready to decide which killer he should overpower first. One of the three was almost sure to lag; he would be the logical choice.

The creepers were slackening sooner than The Shadow expected. The reason was that other cars had stopped briefly along the driveway, then gone on again. Apparently, the abandoned cab was exciting some curiosity. This might work even more to The Shadow's advantage. It could mean that the murder crew would postpone their hunt. Their game was to do away with Cranston in such a way that his death would look like the work of typical park prowlers engaged in a standard holdup. It wouldn't do for the whole crew to come bounding up on a victim in sight of witnesses. If they decided to give up this present job, they would retreat, bringing themselves back into The Shadow's own bailiwick.

The Shadow waited, on that very chance.

Suddenly, a flashlight blinked, not from along the three-man circle, but from a darkened space across the driveway. Immediately, the creeping men flashed signals of their own. The result brought a quick finish to The Shadow's well-formed plan. Instead of a slow retreat, the three promptly began to draw together and start a rapid sideward departure along the line of the driveway.

The Shadow took immediate bearings on his present position. Off obliquely to the right, he could see the great white shape of the Chicago Natural History Museum, its marble mass looming in ghostly fashion in the darkness. Beyond it the skyline of Chicago was etched against the night, revealed by the city's own illumination. The Shadow was facing inward from the lake; therefore, he knew that the crooks were heading northward.

Going in that direction, The Shadow spotted dim figures cutting across his path. They weren't going back to their car, those three, they were heading for the causeway leading to Northern Island, where the Planetarium occupied the northeast corner. Just as they had tried to box The Shadow earlier, so were they boxing themselves now.

All that The Shadow had to do was follow, catch up with the trio after they became careless, which they would, now that they had given up their hunt for Cranston. He might not even have to nab them one by one; a quick surprise when they least suspected it, might result in the bagging of all three.

A whispered laugh that vanished in the sigh of the lake breeze was The Shadow's prophecy of trouble for those three. It wasn't a bad prediction, but he might have included himself along with it.

Surprises might be due for anyone, even The Shadow.

CHAPTER XI
THE STARS RULE ALL

THE esplanade approaching the Planetarium was divided by a series of twelve pools, all in a long line, with a ledge along the sides. Those pools represented the signs of the zodiac, whose symbols since ancient times have been regarded as a ruling agency in the affairs of mankind.

In its turn, the esplanade was flanked by separated hedgerows, while straight ahead, the Planetarium loomed like a mighty cheesebox topped with a squatty turret that supported a huge dome. It was along this route that three men were hurrying, keeping well apart as if they did not know each other and showing preference for the darkish shelter of the hedges.

There were other people walking along the esplanade, but they were few and far between. Comparatively speaking, the concourse was deserted except for the three men and the cloaked figure that was on their trail. If he had personally conjured up this situation, The Shadow couldn't have had it more to order.

In the darkness, the three men fitted the term of nondescript. They differed somewhat in gait and size, but they were all wearing dark clothes. As for The Shadow, he couldn't even be seen, let alone described. Gaining ground along beside a hedge, The Shadow was represented only by a fleeting patch of black, his own shadow gliding against the white paving of the esplanade.

There was only one thing certain about those three men up ahead, and that was their own uncertainty. They had evidenced it previously, now they were to show the trait again. Just as The Shadow was silently overtaking the last man of the lot, the fellow broke into a rapid jog. Simultaneously, the middle man halted in his tracks. The man up front wheeled about and came hurrying back toward the others.

They couldn't have suspected that The Shadow was close upon them; certainly not all three. The only man who might have guessed it was the one who had suddenly sprung forward almost from The Shadow's grasp. But he hadn't given any signal, not even a blink of his flashlight, so his action could not account for those of the men ahead.

That was why The Shadow decided to play the role of a one-man cleanup squad. Whipping his brace of automatics from beneath his cloak, he flung himself directly upon the trio as they came together. With his drive, he delivered an uncanny laugh, which carried a chill that even the winter lake winds had never matched when they raked this esplanade.

A bit sporting of The Shadow, to announce him-

The Shadow decided to play the role of a one-man clean-up squad. He flung himself directly upon the men, laughing softly as he did so. Instead of a warning, The Shadow's sardonic laugh was a threat and more. It had thrown shivers into hardened killers in the past and it did the same on this occasion.

self so lustily, but the three men didn't take it in that light. Instead of a warning, The Shadow's sardonic laugh was a threat and more. It had thrown shivers into hardened killers in the past and it did the same on this occasion. Instead of uniting The Shadow's three foemen, it threw them into confusion. It was each man for himself and no two thought alike.

One fellow fumbled for a gun, while backing in his tracks. A second turned to dive for a safety that didn't exist. The third made a wild spring in the direction of the laugh, hoping to grab The Shadow bare-handed and hold him until the others helped.

It was a perfect setup for The Shadow.

Slashing crosswise with a black gloved fist, The Shadow reeled the man who was springing at him. It was powerful, that backhand blow, for in his fist, The Shadow carried the added weight of an automatic. With a twist, The Shadow hooked the staggered man under the arm, pitching him bodily upon the fellow who was trying to draw a gun. As the pair flattened, The Shadow was spinning away to overtake the coward who had started to run.

That task was ridiculously easy.

True to type, the man had tried to dive for a hiding place. The nearest was the hedge, so he had ploughed right into it, tangling himself worse than the cabby whom The Shadow had helpfully pitched into a bush, back along the distant driveway. Cloaking one automatic, The Shadow used his free hand to haul the fugitive from the hedge with a terrific roundabout sweep that should have added him to the pair already piled upon the paving. With that The Shadow could have subdued the three as easily as one.

It was the fourth man who made the trouble.

The Shadow hadn't counted him at all, but he was to prove the most formidable of the lot. He came vaulting over the hedge, swinging a weapon ahead of him. That weapon was a flashlight which the fellow had been blinking as a signal to the others that this was to be their meeting spot. The Shadow hadn't seen the flashes, for they were half-smothered by the hedge.

Full force, the flashlight found The Shadow's head as he hoisted his gun hand to ward away the blow. He warded too late, but he bobbed his head at the same time, which deflected the flashlight as it landed. The Shadow's slouch hat also took some of the brunt, but if the flashlight had been heavier, the blow would have stunned The Shadow.

As it was, the flashlight barrel cracked apart, scattering the batteries. Staggered by the blow, The Shadow lost his grip on the man he had started to fling. Coming around blindly, he grappled with the fellow who had sprung across the hedge and tried to lay home a gunstroke in retaliation for the blow from the flashlight.

The Shadow's adversary whipped out a revolver in time to meet the sledging automatic. The guns clanked and the pair wheeled apart, to drive in for another clash. By then, the men The Shadow had first flattened were on their feet and grabbing him from in back. Twisting out of their clutch, The Shadow wheeled them into the path of the big man, who halted his gun swing just in time to avoid knocking out one of his companions.

From then on it was a whirling fray, in which The Shadow, though half-groggy, proved his prowess at dealing with men of crime. His twists were sudden, often in reverse, the sort that made it impossible to hold him. Never, though, did he wheel away. Always he came in for further combat, so rapidly that no one could bring a gun into play. Always, The Shadow was using one man as a shield against the others, generally disappearing from behind such a human buffer to come in at an angle upon another fighter.

With it, The Shadow had an uncanny faculty for spotting a revolver's glint. His reach was so long that he invariably could whack another weapon or the hand that held it with his own automatic. All during the brief, twisty fray, The Shadow was car-

rying his adversaries out into the open so they couldn't box him up against the hedge.

The finish occurred at the center of the esplanade, not far from the Planetarium itself. There, one man managed a quick aim at The Shadow, but before he could pull his revolver trigger, The Shadow's automatic came whipping straight up to meet the fellow's gun hand and carry clear up to his chin.

There was a howl as the revolver scaled from the man's hand, a splash as he took a flying back dive into one of the zodiac pools. Coming full around, The Shadow grappled with another enemy whose revolver stabbed wildly twice as he and The Shadow climbed the ledge beside another pool. Twisting free, The Shadow tripped this fellow into the water, thus temporarily eliminating two foemen.

There were two others, one the big man. As The Shadow sprang for them, the other fled for the hedge. Alone, the big man grappled madly with The Shadow. Meanwhile the first pair were clambering from the pools, drenching the paving with their dripping clothes, as they, too, took to flight. Here was The Shadow's chance to make a capture, the biggest man of the lot. But as The Shadow twisted to drive a solid stroke with his automatic, he slipped on the wet paving and lost his grip.

The big man dashed for the hedge and cleared it before The Shadow could prop up an elbow and overtake him with a shot. Coming to his feet, The Shadow started in pursuit among the hedges and finally came into the clear. Though he had used a flashlight along the hedgerows, The Shadow hadn't found a sign of the four.

Only the lake lay in this direction, so The Shadow doubled back along the trail. He saw figures beyond the hedges, moving into the entrance of the Planetarium, but they were too distant to be identified. Nevertheless, there was a chance that the scattered thugs were taking refuge in the building, perhaps individually, so The Shadow headed there. Inside the entrance, he saw that a show was about to start in the Planetarium room. One of the attendants was about to close the door.

Whipping off his cloak and hat, The Shadow packed them in the self-folding portfolio, along with his gloves and automatics. As Lamont Cranston, he reached the Planetarium room just in time for the show. The lights were already dimming when this last customer joined the audience.

Like some monstrous Martian creature, the huge projection instrument towered above the circles of chairs which held the scattered spectators. Taking a seat, Cranston looked over the audience, hoping to identify certain unworthy members before they recognized him. In the dim chamber, that was difficult, yet the advantage was Cranston's. He was sure that the two with the soaked clothes hadn't entered; the other pair, if present, would be huddling in their chairs to avoid notice.

Picking out such prospects, Cranston changed his seat a few times to get a closer look at them, always approaching from in back. At close range, none of them appeared to be the men he wanted, and by then the chamber was too dark to continue the hunt. The lecturer was speaking, calling attention to the horizon of the great domed room. There, the fading light showed a representation of Chicago's skyline, so realistically proportioned that the walls of the room could have vanished, placing the audience outdoors.

Except that this was Chicago's skyline of some hours ago, when dusk was settling over the city. Gradually, the silhouetted buildings were wiped out, indicating that night had fallen. That night would pass in terms of minutes rather than hours, here in the Planetarium, until artificial dawn would again bring the skyline into a gradually increasing light.

Stars were studding the sky, as represented by the great dome. Leaning back in his chair, Cranston smiled to himself. This was, indeed, an interesting sequel to the battle that he had waged as The Shadow. It was getting back to nature in a safe way. Nice to look at the starry heavens above Chicago, here indoors. Better than out of doors, where anything might happen, particularly in Grant Park.

The stars were moving on their speeded up routine. Cranston's head was swimming slightly, too, from the effects of that jarring flashlight blow. He'd forgotten it in the heat of the fray, but perhaps it accounted for a few oversights. The battle could be marked as a victory for The Shadow, but it had fallen below his own exacting specifications. At least one member of that murderous tribe should have been bagged as a trophy. Lamont Cranston felt more than slightly disappointed in The Shadow.

That made it The Shadow's turn to be disappointed in Lamont Cranston and the turn was coming very soon.

There was a slight stir behind Cranston's chair, as though someone had taken a seat there. Then, as Cranston raised his head slightly, something cold and round planted itself squarely in the back of his neck. Above the lecturer's droning spiel, Cranston heard a firm contralto tone announce:

"Stay right where you are. The slightest move may be your last."

Cranston stayed motionless. But the voice hadn't admonished him not to think. How this had happened was a puzzle that didn't link with the crooks that Cranston was hunting. The voice was unquestionably a woman's; how long she intended to keep Cranston at this gunpoint was the next question.

That question needed an answer and Cranston decided to provide it. He could hear another stir in the row behind him, indicating that someone else was creeping into the invisible scene. Perhaps the voice had been faked; if so, Cranston might be really on the spot. It would be folly, though, for anyone to fire a shot. The lecturer's talk, the buzz of the star projector, wouldn't be enough to cover the report of a gun.

Cranston moved his neck, almost less than slightly. Gradually, he was easing the pressure there, getting his shoulder and one hand around. Then he twisted, carrying his neck clear and thrusting his hand not for the gun, but for the wrist above it. Cranston heard a sharp gasp, a woman's gasp with a twinge more of surprise than terror. That came as he caught the wrist and shoved it high. Then, with his other hand, Cranston made a snatch for the gun, but too late.

The gun was gone and in the darkness, Cranston's fingers brushed a man's hand, the very hand that had tugged away the gun a split-second ahead of his grasp!

Launching over the back of his chair, Cranston grabbed for the man who had snatched the gun. Cranston wanted that gun and he found it, but not the way he wanted. Unless he wanted it in the worst way. The result certainly fitted that specification.

Down out of the blackness came the gun, swung full force by the hand that had taken it. It found a head that no longer wore a slouch hat and found it squarely. As Cranston took the blow, the whole great room about him seemed to light with a sudden burst of shooting stars that shamed the pitiful show that the projector was etching on the interior of the dome.

Lamont Cranston saw the light, nothing more. Sliding down between the rows of chairs he flattened upon his portfolio as it struck the floor ahead of him. Night was still moving at its geared-up pace and the lecturer was announcing the approach of dawn in those artificial heavens; but Lamont Cranston neither heard nor saw.

The Shadow was noted for moving swifter than the night. This was a place where night moved swifter than The Shadow. Either that, or this just wasn't The Shadow's night.

CHAPTER XII
REGAN REPORTS

SHOOTING stars were throbbing into mighty sunbursts and with them, Lamont Cranston could feel his head swell, then contract, time and again all in monotonous rhythm. Then, through his aching brain, came a slow recollection of what had happened.

Cranston opened his eyes. He saw the silhouette of Chicago's skyline creeping back to life again, in a light like a dim dawn. Cranston was lying with his head propped on an arm and the portion of the skyline that he saw was so set that it seemed to be within a frame.

There was something wrong with that painted picture. It wasn't illuminating fast enough. Time might be passing slowly to Cranston's numbed senses and hazy vision, but he still could gauge it somewhat by his head throbs. Painfully, he counted ten of them, but the light showed no increase.

If something had gone wrong with the Planetarium show, it was all the better. For now Cranston was remembering what had happened in the midst of it, as well as he could remember. Something had come out of somewhere, probably the constellation of Orion the warrior, and had clouted Cranston properly. Now he recalled what it was that hit him, the butt end of a gun.

Cranston could vaguely recollect the stroke as he stared at the dim panorama which represented dawn. Whoever gave the blow must have lost the gun with it, for it had been practically flung at Cranston's head. Just a wild chance in the darkness, but it was no longer dark here. If Cranston could find that gun, or his own portfolio which contained a brace of automatics!

Half rising, Cranston began to paw around on the chance of finding the missing gun, if missing it were. Realizing that some other person might be planning a similar search, Cranston raised his head wearily. Between himself and skylined light he saw a huddled man slouched in a chair at the next lower level. Something in the fellow's crouch indicated that he might be planning a surge as soon as the light increased sufficiently. So Cranston decided not to concede that chance.

With a lunge, Cranston reached the huddled man and tried to clamp him in the chair thinking that like all the seats in the auditorium, it would be fixed solidly to the floor. Instead, it was loose. Cranston bowled it over, man and all. They hit the floor together, came up against a wall. By then, the other man was roused and grappling, while Cranston's senses swam anew. Then they were at grips by the frame through which the skyline showed and a breeze, whipping Cranston's face, brought back his scattered wits as he looked at the man with whom he struggled.

That man was Regan, the private detective.

This wasn't the planetarium chamber with its circles of seats. It was Cranston's own room at the Hotel Harbison. That skyline and the dawn that etched it weren't artificial; they were real. What Cranston had been looking at was actually Chicago.

Relaxing, Cranston let Regan get his breath. Turning on a table lamp, Cranston set the chair upright, then went over and sat down on the bed, which was where he had been lying when he came back to his senses. Now it was Regan's turn.

"Whew!" expressed Regan, as he sat down in the chair. "You sure came back fast. I should have figured maybe you'd be surprised to find yourself back here."

"I wasn't, precisely," rejoined Cranston. "I thought I was finding myself back over in the Adler Planetarium. I take it that you helped me out of there."

"Lugged is the word for it," said Regan. "You were lying there like something had really hit you. They were going to call for an ambulance, until I showed them my credentials and said I'd be responsible."

"Whom do you mean by *they?*"

"The professors or whatever they are that run that shooting star gallery. I told them I'd met you out on Tyburn's cruiser, that you'd been having dizzy spells and the doctor had said you ought to take a lake trip. They listened."

That brought a smile from Cranston. Regan, of all people to be recommending lake cruises, after the way he'd balked at a speedboat ride with Skip Hagathorn.

"I found your briefcase and brought it along." Regan gestured to the bureau and Cranston saw the portfolio lying there. "And then," added Regan, "I took a look under those seats, while the professors were carrying you out to a cab. I found your gun."

Reaching into his pocket, Regan brought out an automatic that looked to be of .32 caliber and tossed it on the bed where it clattered slightly as it landed. He asked cagily, "Yours?"

Cranston nodded, watching Regan from beneath lowered brows. He was convinced now that Regan hadn't opened the portfolio, which would, indeed, have been difficult as it had a very tricky catch. Therefore, the detective couldn't know that Cranston was The Shadow. By claiming the loose gun to be his own, Cranston was diverting Regan's thoughts from the portfolio, which he probably thought contained nothing more than papers pertinent to the suicide cases that Cranston had been studying with Smedley.

"Kind of risky toting a rod around," observed Regan. "They're fussy about that, even here in Chicago."

Cranston said nothing. He had picked up the gun and was beginning to study it.

"Of course, knowing Inspector Smedley like you do," continued Regan, with a shrug, "it shouldn't matter much. Of course, he likes to handle things his own way and didn't like the New

York commissioner butting in on it. Maybe Smedley would like to get that out of his hair."

"Tell me, Regan," asked Cranston, suddenly, "aren't you working exclusively for Lester Tyburn?"

"Why, yes." Regan hesitated. "Well, not exactly on an exclusive basis."

"But you were covering a job for him last night—"

"Of course. Why are you asking?"

"Just to learn what you are after," retorted Cranston. "If this is a shakedown, Regan, forget it. You're a wrong guy and you picked up a wrong gun. You can see for yourself that this trigger is jammed so the gun won't fire even though it's loaded."

By way of illustration, Cranston was approaching Regan with the gun, tugging at the trigger. The muzzle was pointed straight at Regan's stomach and the dick was waving his hands excitedly as he came to his feet, kicking over the chair behind him.

"Take that thing away!" cried Regan. "Forget what I said. I'm not asking for anything. Take it away!"

"Don't worry," assured Cranston. "This gun won't pitch any slugs your way."

"I'll work with you!" screeched Regan. "I'll tell you my business without asking yours. Only lay off that trigger!"

Regan was in the corner now and Cranston, his face showing surprise, had finally managed to release the jammed trigger. He gave it a tug and Regan sagged in the corner with a howl, only to sit there staring at what he saw.

The automatic had gone off, but not in orthodox fashion. Nothing had left the muzzle; instead a section of the barrel had popped up on a spring, just above the handle. Poked in sight were half a dozen cigarettes, standing upright.

"Have one, Regan," suggested Cranston, proffering the dummy gun. "Haven't you seen these before? They're novelty cigarette cases, sold at magic shops and such places. This one doesn't happen to be mine. Somebody slugged me with it and dropped it. I'd like to find out who did it and why."

Cranston could have answered his own question in part, but he wanted to hear what Regan had to say. He knew that some woman had been using the gun to bluff him; that when he grabbed for it, a man who was working closer in the darkness had snatched it first and used it as a bludgeon. It was fortunate that the gun wasn't a real one for it would have been much heavier than this. Maybe Cranston would have slept through the real dawn as well as the artificial one, in that case.

"There's only two people who might have been carrying it," declared Regan. "Halifax or the Joyce dame."

Cranston's eyebrows raised as though asking Regan to give the particulars of his deduction.

"You ought to know," gruffed Regan. "You were over there at the Mirror Grill, too."

"I remember being at the Planetarium," rejoined Cranston, with a smile. "I'm asking who else was there."

"All right."

With a resigned shrug, Regan set his chair upright again and sat down. Then he went into his spiel.

"I was over watching the Magigals, see?" Regan began. "I'm tailing Halifax for a change. It's as good as shadowing Gail Tyburn anyway, because what the old man wants to know is how often his frau gets together with her smiling boyfriend.

"I call up Tyburn and report to him. He's with Rick Smedley having a conference with the local coppers out at Longwood. I'm reporting like he asked, giving it brief, except when he wants certain particulars. I'm just winding up when this Halifax comes to make a phone call, so I duck outside and wait, see?

"Next, Halifax shows outside, grabs a cab and says to get to the Mirror Grill and hurry. That being the place where he left Gail Tyburn, I figured she'd be back there, and she was. Only Halifax wasn't. That's the part that gets me. Maybe he thought that I was tailing him and told the cabby outside the Harbison to take him to the Mirror Grill as a blind. He could have changed the address after he got in the cab."

As he concluded, Regan gave Cranston a very sharp look. Probably Regan either knew or suspected that Cranston had been both at the Harbison and the Mirror Grill. Still, he might have seen him at only one of those places or perhaps not at all. In any case, it was Cranston's purpose to keep Regan talking, so he followed that policy.

"So you saw Gail Tyburn," stated Cranston. "Then she should be the woman in the case. But who is this Joyce girl you mentioned? How does she enter?"

"She was on the bill at the Magigal show," explained Regan. "It was right after her act that Halifax left. Maybe he could have been phoning her. I've got to check downstairs here and find out if there's a backstage telephone in the ballroom. Anyway, she headed for the Mirror Grill, too."

"You saw her leave the Harbison?"

"There were a couple of cabs that pulled out before I could grab one. I saw a dame going into the Mirror Grill right after I got there, but didn't notice her close enough to be sure who she was. I was too busy trying to spot Halifax. Then, when I got inside the place, I saw Gail Tyburn. She was looking for Halifax, too, I guess. Only he wasn't around."

"And you didn't see this Joyce girl?"

"Not a sign of her, at least not then."

"What did you say her first name was?"

"I didn't say," replied Regan, cagily. "I know what it is, though, because it was on the bill at the Magigals. Her first name is Verity and she does tricks with eggs."

Cranston nodded, as though tricks were of only slight consequence in his life. Then he said to Regan, "Go on."

Regan went on.

"Just then a Chinese magic act gets started," said Regan. "At the Mirror Grill, I mean. Some guy called Chung Loo was working there and his act wound up with a blackout. Then on came the lights and I'm getting a look at Gail Tyburn, but no sign of Mr. John Q. Halifax. Then who goes sailing out of the place all of a sudden but the Joyce dame. She must have been in there all along."

"So you followed her?"

"Sure. By then I was putting one and one together and getting three. Halifax ditches Gail and winds up at the Magigal show. There he sees this Verity Joyce and it's a cinch she saw him, too. On account of she was around when Halifax was doing card tricks—"

As Regan cut off suddenly, Cranston gave a slight laugh. Regan's first answer was a shrug. Then:

"Yeah, I saw you doing tricks there, too," Regan admitted. "So maybe I'm not telling you too much that you don't know."

"I'm interested in what happened at the Mirror Grill," said Cranston, calmly, "so let's have it."

"If you were there, I didn't see you," declared Regan, defensively, "but I've already told you I was trying to spot Halifax. Anyway, right after the show, this Verity Joyce goes piling out like she's trying to catch up with somebody. See?"

Cranston saw and nodded.

"That's the first time I spotted her," continued Regan. "It looked like Halifax had somehow got word to Verity to meet him some other place, since Gail was around. So I came outside, too. There's a trailer piled up on the sidewalk; been an accident, I guess. But there's a cab pulling out across the street and a car starting right after it."

"And where was Verity?"

"Getting into another cab. She joined right up with the caravan, so I did the same. When I looked behind, another cab was starting. It was coming along, too."

"Did any more follow?"

"They might have. Only it was a coincidence, maybe. After all, it was show-break at the Mirror Grill and that is when a lot of people yell for cabs."

"Naturally. Go on, Regan."

"Well, the first cab and the car got out of sight somewhere, but finally, I spot another cab, the one with Verity in it, I think, and I notice it's picked up the same two cars, one of them a cab. We were all heading out of the Loop by that time, over across Michigan Boulevard. Next thing, we're in Grant Park and there's a cab hauled up beside the driveway, but the car that was chasing it has disappeared. All I could do was follow Verity's cab and it was hers all right, because I saw her get out of it. So I did the same."

"And there were other cabs behind you?"

"One that stopped somewhere. Who was in it, I don't know."

"It couldn't have been Halifax?"

"If he'd come from the Mirror Grill, yes," decided Regan. "But I've told you I didn't see him around there. Maybe he went out in that first cab. Still, he could have been at the Planetarium and waiting there. Maybe you can guess. You were over there."

Regan put the final statement bluntly. Cranston gave him a calm reply.

"I like planetariums," stated Cranston, "or perhaps I should term them planetaria. I had been to the Fels Planetarium in Philadelphia, the Hayden in New York. I felt that a visit to Chicago would be wasted unless I visited the Adler Planetarium. Now that I have seen all three, I feel that I have achieved something. Life should never be too mundane. It is inspiring to travel among the celestial spheres and view the heavens in their orbits."

The language brought puzzled blinks from Regan. Then the detective came back to his theme.

"There was a fight going on along the esplanade," said Regan. "A bunch of guys were in it and somebody knocked a couple of them into those pools."

"The zodiac pools?" queried Cranston, quite interested. "You wouldn't know which ones?"

"One guy got clouted into Virgo," informed Regan, referring to some notes that he pulled from his pocket, "and the other landed in Libra. Then they all beat it and I chased after them."

"Where did they go?"

"Over toward the lake. Since they couldn't have gone any further, I figured they'd ducked back into the Planetarium. So that's where I went. I got there just as the show was starting, if you want to call it a show."

"I didn't see much of it," conceded Cranston, rubbing the part of his head that still ached. "You'll have to tell me the rest, Regan."

"When the lights came on," said Regan, "they showed dawn"—he gestured toward the window, where the Chicago skyscrapers were now plainly visible in the rosy light—"and it looked just like it does now. I'm right inside the door, see, casing the whole joint. I'm looking for guys to come out, particularly a couple that need dry suits.

"Only who comes out but John Halifax with that big smile of his. How he kept his teeth grinning after watching that bum show is more than I can figure. Then who else comes along but Verity Joyce, with that worried pan of hers. It wasn't just an expression; she was really worried. They weren't together. In fact, they didn't notice each other. Maybe, though, they were just acting like they were each there alone.

"If they'd figured on meeting up though, they couldn't have picked a better spot than that Planetarium, for more than a lot of reasons." Regan paused with a wise nod. Then: "But I'm still wondering what happened to that bunch that was fighting outside. I figure maybe some of them are hiding in among the seats. So I start looking around and I come across you. I call the professors and you know the rest."

Regan relaxed, his story finished. The room was now bathed in strong daylight. Dawn had come more slowly here than in the Planetarium, but Regan's report had unquestionably been more entertaining than the windup of the Planetarium lecture.

Rising, Lamont Cranston went over and turned off the table lamp. Regan's attitude became quizzical.

"All right, Mr. Cranston," suggested Regan. "It's your say. What comes next?"

"Next," replied Cranston in his most casual tone, "we go down to the breakfast room and order ham and eggs. Remind me, Regan, to tell the waitress that I like my eggs over easy."

CHAPTER XIII
MURDER MUST OUT

DURING breakfast, Cranston hoped to get more information out of Regan, so he went at the proposition systematically but tactfully. Cranston's way was to speculate at first, bringing up questions indirectly. He chose a good subject for a starter: Verity Joyce.

"I remember the Joyce girl," said Cranston. "A very neat number. I mean her magic, of course. Just why did those egg tricks particularly intrigue you, Regan?"

"They didn't," replied Regan. "I just wasn't missing anything, that was all. It's the way I work, like I told Mr. Tyburn. I always see that people get their money's worth."

"Even when you offer to sell back guns?"

"Let's forget that, Mr. Cranston. You've got to admit that I wasn't passing up anything out at the Planetarium, or I wouldn't have found you lying there. Let's forget the egg tricks, too, and talk about the dame."

"You have her address?"

"No, but I wouldn't mind getting it."

"How about asking Halifax for it?"

"A good idea." Regan rubbed his chin. "I'm not exactly chummy with Halifax, though. I wish you'd ask Halifax for me."

"So you can make a date with Verity Joyce?"

"I wish I could," returned Regan, glumly. "Anything to get her away from Halifax. Don't think I'm a fellow who is always trying to snag a few extra bucks, just because I thought it would be worth something to you, bringing you back from the Planetarium and picking up the loose gun I thought was yours. If I do favors on a cash basis, it's because I deserve a little extra. There's plenty of times I have to hand over dough for favors done to me."

Cranston was thinking ahead on that one.

"You mean you'd pay the Joyce girl to drop Halifax," said Cranston with a nod. "Naturally, you would, since you want to keep Tyburn as a customer. He won't need your services any longer if he learns that Halifax has dropped Gail and is taking up with Verity."

"That's right," admitted Regan. "It proves I'm honest. The only way Tyburn could find out, would be through me. I'll put it through on my report if it turns out to be a fact. Everything goes on my report if it belongs there. But if I offer somebody like the Joyce dame a free trip to Bermuda and she takes it, that's my own business."

Perhaps it was. At any rate, Cranston was impressed by the way Regan balanced his own code of ethics. Switching the subject, Cranston remarked:

"Odd, the way that mob disappeared near the Planetarium. If I didn't have your word for it, Regan, I could hardly believe it ever happened."

"It happened all right."

"They couldn't very well have doubled back. Dodging you would be pretty difficult, Regan."

Regan swelled at the compliment, never guessing what was in Cranston's mind. Cranston's logic was this: As The Shadow, he, too, had pursued the four men off beyond the Planetarium. For all four to escape The Shadow would have been highly artful on their part, since he had covered most avenues of escape. The only way they could have eluded The Shadow was to cut back between him and the Planetarium itself.

In the course of events, Cranston hadn't seen Regan at all. He was taking Regan's own claim of having been on the spot, for it tallied satisfactorily. It was natural that Regan hadn't seen The Shadow. The question was: Why hadn't The Shadow seen Regan?

The answer was obvious.

Regan must have been coming toward the lake

by the one route that The Shadow had been forced to neglect, along which four men of murder would have had to double back. Regan couldn't possibly have missed all four, or putting it the other way, all four couldn't have missed Regan. The fact that Regan was around to tell the tale was proof that he hadn't been anywhere near the thugs when they finally escaped. They would have taken him as an enemy and it would have been short shrift for Regan.

Of course, Regan didn't know all that. He was simply accepting his own over-valuation as a sleuth when he decided:

"There's only one place they could have gone. They must have ducked into the lake. Two of them were wet anyway, so why should they care? And if they didn't care, why should the others? That made them all wet." Regan chuckled. "That's a good one, huh? All wet!"

"I believe you have it, Regan," asserted Cranston. "Of course, you intend to include this in your report to Tyburn."

"I put everything in my reports," bragged Regan. "I don't even miss a trick." He laughed again, but not as heartily. "I sprang that gag on Tyburn himself last night, when I was phoning him at nine thirty. I didn't miss a trick, get it? I mean the tricks that I was watching at the Magigals show. I noted them all down and all I had to do was read them off. I've still got my notes here"—Regan flipped the papers that were sticking from his coat pockets—"and as soon as I get over to my office, I'll start typing them out."

Another voice promptly intervened. "Better get over to your office soon then, Regan," it said. "You've got a lot to do. So have I, but I won't be needing you."

The voice belonged to Inspector Smedley, who had strolled into the Harbison breakfast room. Regan gave Rick an affable nod, gulped what was left of his coffee, mouthed a "So long" to Cranston, and was on his way.

"Little ears have big pitchers," said Rick to Cranston, "and by that I mean Regan. He'd like to work along with me, but I don't believe in the pot and the kettle washing each other. If he heard me say that the suicide wave is really over, he'd go around taking some of the credit for it."

"He might," agreed Cranston, "considering that you were out of town last night and couldn't have been doing much to stop it."

"I wasn't away all night," returned Rick. "But I'll admit I was gone most of the evening. That place at Longwood took some looking over."

"You were out at Tyburn's estate? I thought you were only going to the Longwood police headquarters."

"That was the original idea," said Rick, snapping his fingers for a cup of coffee. "But when I saw what Tyburn was up against, I decided he and I would have to plan things right."

"You mean the Longwood force is inadequate?"

"Totally. Their headquarters needs a new roof, their squad car is about the speed of a Model T, they're carrying guns that were left over from the Spanish War, and their badges look like giveaway prizes at a firemen's carnival. That covers the Longwood police in a thumb-nose sketch."

Smiling at Rick's summary, Cranston asked:

"They don't mind your taking charge at Tyburn's place?"

"Mind?" echoed Rick. "They'd have elected me chief if I'd wanted the job. They couldn't begin to handle it." Rick took a look from the counter where they were seated, then said, "Let's go over to that corner table. It has a tablecloth and I can draw you a diagram."

They went to the table and Rick drew the diagram. It took up most of the tablecloth because Tyburn's estate was a big one.

"The place is just in from the lake," explained Rick. "This is a barbwire fence running along the front road. Here's the gate, way down here, with a house where the three hired hands stay, except when they're out working on the grounds. Webster, the gatekeeper, Morse, the gardener, Chaffin, the chauffeur."

"Mrs. Tyburn's chauffeur," nodded Cranston. "He was out there?"

"He was," replied Rick. "Why do you ask?"

"Because I saw Gail Tyburn and John Halifax wasn't with her. She left him and said maybe she'd see him later, maybe not. I thought that would be one time when she would want her car."

"She didn't phone for it while I was there. In fact, she hasn't used the car since Tyburn brought the subject up."

"What time were you there, Inspector?"

Rick calculated.

"I left at seven prompt," he stated. "Traffic was light and I made it in just about forty-five minutes driving pretty fast. Tyburn was at the police headquarters, but he took me right over to the place. Thought I ought to see the estate before it got too dark. I got a general look at the premises and met the three hired hands. It was getting dark by then, so we went back to the Longwood headquarters."

"At what time was that?"

"Eight twenty. We got to the headquarters at exactly half past and the ride took just ten minutes. Tyburn was clocking it, so we would know how long it would take the local force to get there, in case they were ever needed. We stalled there until nine o'clock. That's when I got a line on the inadequacy, as you politely term it, of the Longwood police."

"Then you came back to the city?"

"No. Tyburn wanted me to see the mansion. We drove back to the estate. Webster had locked the gates for the night, but we rang and he showed up and let us in. We scared up Morse and Chaffin. They brought flashlights and lamps, so they could take us into the big house."

"The electricity is cut off?"

"Sure. Mrs. Tyburn is supposed to pay the bills out of her household allowance. So she disconnected the electricity, the gas, even the telephones. Downstairs, the furniture is all covered over, in the reception rooms and such. On the second floor, some of the rooms are locked, on the top floor, all of them. No heat, no nothing. Gail Tyburn needs all her spare pennies so that Smile-face Halifax can catch money out of the air."

"You mean that's Tyburn's opinion."

"It's everybody's, except maybe yours. One swallow doesn't make a drink, Cranston, and just because you saw Gail Tyburn doing the town alone for once, doesn't mean that Halifax isn't her steady. You might catch her sometime with her hair down, but that would be unusual, too. Generally, she wouldn't be seen without Halifax anymore than she would without a permanent."

Cranston nodded to show that he accepted Rick's opinion. The inspector made more markings on the cloth.

Then:

"Here's the house," said Rick, "set way back. Out front is the lawn, trees set all around it. Over here is the Oriental garden, with pools and a stream that runs under bridges and then goes out of bounds to the lake. That's about all, except that Gail regards the house as hers and has all the keys. Webster keeps one to the back door, probably in case of fire. With all the shrubbery, trees and whatnot, it will take good covering, that lawn picnic will, to make sure that nobody goes sneaking off somewhere to commit suicide in pleasant surroundings."

"Tyburn still thinks that may happen?"

"He thinks anything may happen and I don't blame him. Anyway, to conclude my story, we looked the place over from about nine ten until half past. Then we heard the phone ringing from out at the gatehouse, where there's a phone still connected and paid for personally by Tyburn."

"That must have been Regan, phoning his routine report."

"It was. Tyburn went and talked to him. Then, having no drinks in the house, Tyburn suggested that he and I drive out to a roadhouse. I said good enough. I needed a drink after being in that clammy mausoleum that Gail Tyburn refuses to call home.

We stayed at the roadhouse about an hour, then drove back to the place and said good night to the boys. After that, I drove back to the city."

"Tyburn didn't come in with you?"

"No. He was staying on his cruiser. Skip Hagathorn was around; at the police station when I got there. He dropped back while we were going through the mansion. He was waiting to pick up Tyburn at the time we said good night."

Rick was studying Cranston, waiting for a query. When none came, Rick decided to answer what was probably in Cranston's mind.

"There's no way any of this could have a bearing on Gail Tyburn," assured Rick. "Tyburn strictly avoids any criticism of his wife in front of the servants, so that puts them in a neutral class. If she came out there, they'd know it, so that's why she never shows up. She wouldn't want to be without Halifax and the hired hands would recognize him. They'd be too apt to talk. So if you want to know where Gail Tyburn went last night, I can tell you one place she didn't go. That place was home."

Getting up from the table, Rick suggested that they go over to headquarters and arrange for the official announcement that the suicide wave was finished. Rick made the suggestion with a slight touch of sarcasm which he probably hoped that Cranston would take back to New York, for the benefit of Commissioner Weston.

"You're welcome to stay around, of course," Rick told Cranston as they neared headquarters. "I know you wouldn't want to miss the picnic out at Longwood. They'll have everything from a maypole to dancing on the green. Only there won't be any suicides, not while I'm around. The epidemic is over, anyway."

Rick changed that opinion the moment he entered his office. There, people were busy at telephones again and communications were rattling over the Teletype. Some long-faced assistants met the inspector and handed him a report that had just come in. Rick crumpled the sheet angrily, chucked it into a basket.

"It's begun again," groaned Rick to Cranston. "Another suicide, just found this morning. An antique dealer on the North Side, named Paul Corland. The madness has started all over."

"Perhaps not," observed Cranston. "You can still say that Chicago is free from suicide."

"And how?"

"By calling it murder, right from scratch. This case will probably prove the point. Murder beginning with the first of those cases that we analyzed and ending with this one, we can hope." Cranston's voice was smooth, even.

"Murder will out," declared Rick, "and in this case it is out, which puts us right back on the suicide trail. I've read the report, Cranston, but you haven't. Come along and you'll see what suicide looks like, with no room for argument."

As they left, Lamont Cranston found the remnants of his headache throbbing those words that Rick Smedley had spoken: "Murder will out." Of that, Cranston was certain and he was willing to apply it to the death of Paul Corland, sight unseen.

If murderers had gained their way last night, Lamont Cranston himself would have been a victim. His hunch was that the killers had not been idle earlier. Should that hunch be right, Lamont Cranston was on his way to another scene of murder.

CHAPTER XIV
CRIMES ANSWER

THEY rode up Michigan Avenue to Lake Shore Drive with Rick Smedley, in the style of the veteran police inspector, maintaining a cryptic attitude regarding Corland's death. Lamont Cranston expected this, for he had met with many officers of Smedley's type. Their way of looking smart was simply to play dumb, letting people form their own conclusions.

Not that Rick Smedley remained silent. To the contrary. He appeared interested in the passing sights, giving the impression that the only reason Chicago had begun to tick this early in the morning was because Rick Smedley was on hand to supervise it. How Chicago managed to function on days when Rick slept late, was something the inspector didn't care to suggest.

From the flow of Michigan Avenue traffic, Rick took a careful look to see if the famous old Chicago Water Tower was still standing after its eighty years of existence. He leaned forward to study the Palmolive Building to make sure it still had its beacon tower. When the car reached Lake Shore Drive, Rick carefully checked the greensward of Lincoln Park on the chance that mad dogs might be running loose there and he took a good look at the lagoon in case any dead ducks were floating on it.

About the only thing that Rick didn't watch was the traffic, because that wasn't his department. Cars were charging into Chicago like the famous Light Brigade, with violations to the left of them, violations to the right of them, but Rick was watching the spaces of Lake Michigan, where speedboats were zooming along the shore.

"Those babies are the tickets," Rick told Cranston, referring to the speedboats. "Even an old plugger can do better than thirty and you can step up a real job to better than sixty. I saw a lot of them kicking around out at Longwood. They start off smooth and easy, then all of a sudden they pick up and zoom off like a shot. I'd rather have one of those jobs than a cabin cruiser like Tyburn's. Those things can really run rings around a cruiser."

The car turned left, away from the lake, picked a diagonal street for a few blocks, made a left oblique and finally pulled up in a back alley at what looked like a delivery entrance. Alighting, Rick badged his way through a few uniformed police who were guarding the place and Cranston went with him. They came into the back of the antique shop belonging to Paul Corland. There Rick introduced Cranston to a precinct detective and the checkup began.

There wasn't much to check, however. The case was open and shut in more ways than one. The back door was open, but that was because the police had broken it down, smashing the bolt and setting off the burglar alarm. A big back room was filled with old and beaten-down furniture that went under the misnomer of antiques. Apparently, it was Corland's rule to pick out items from that reserve and place them in the front shop, where they looked better, because there was less junk with which to compare them.

Reached by a connecting door, which was made of steel and slid open, the front shop proved quite attractive, as it contained many pieces of fine pottery, Oriental carvings, ornate metalware, music boxes and cabinets of all sizes from huge mahogany chests down to ivory jewel cases.

The connecting door, too, had been bolted, and from the front side. The police had given it the torch, setting off another alarm. All this, however, was preferable to cracking through the front, where locked bars crisscrossed the show windows and the heavy street door was triple locked and wired with the inevitable alarm system.

There was an office in one corner, but its door wasn't locked. To lock it would have been unnecessary as the little room was windowless, merely a partitioned corner of the front shop. Corland's safe was in that office. It was a formidable contrivance which an expert was at present trying to open.

Considering that the shop was barred and bolted both front and back, there had to be an exit by which Corland could have left. There was such a door, in the sidewall of the shop. It was steel, too, and locked from the other side. The police had worked through it, then found that they'd gone to a lot of unnecessary trouble. Beyond the steel door was a small apartment, where Corland had lived when in Chicago and also where he had died, last night.

The steel door connecting from apartment into shop not only was wired to the anti-burglar system; it had a time lock on the apartment side, hence Corland didn't have to carry a key to it. This was a not uncommon notion. It meant that if burglars attempted to persuade Corland to unlock his shop and let them in, he couldn't oblige, not even at gunpoint. The shop just couldn't be opened until nine in the morning, even if Corland wanted and the burglary alarm was ingeniously set to the time-lock on the all-important door.

The police could have saved themselves a lot of bashing if they'd waited until nine o'clock. Trouble was, they didn't know that Corland had an apartment with this private way out. At least they'd accomplished one thing; they had kept the apartment intact. As it stood, it formed something of a sealed room problem, taken in reverse. The police might as well have cracked through a solid wall, as come by the route that they had used.

However, there wasn't any problem. The apartment consisted of bedroom, bath and kitchenette. The bedroom could have been classed more as a living room with a sleeping alcove, which Corland didn't use because the room had a daybed. The windows were metal-framed, solidly locked from the inside. The door of the apartment, on the far side of the living room, was the only exit except the steel door into the shop. The door on the far side had a lock of the usual spring latch type, but it was further equipped with a chain bolt, which was in place.

Thus Corland had been safely ensconced at home the night before, with nothing to molest him other than his own worries and the lengths to which they might prod him.

Corland must have been tormented by severe mental prods. He had gone to the sleeping alcove, which had a solidly locked skylight overhead. To the metal bar which clamped the skylight shut, the antique dealer had attached a silk cord, taken from one of a pair of drapes that masked the steel door to the shop. He had looped the other end of the cord around his neck and had hung himself. His body had been dangling there in the alcove when the police found it. Now, cut down, it was awaiting the trip to the morgue.

Inspector Smedley began checking on the circumstances leading to this rather prompt discovery of a suicide. Though Corland had hung himself the night before, it was not yet time for his shop to open this morning. Ordinarily, that would have been the time for people to wonder where Corland was.

Last night, Corland had closed shop at exactly eight thirty, bowing a few late customers out. He was a stickler for details, always closing exactly on the dot. Particularly so, last night, because Corland had been expecting a phone call at nine o'clock, in his apartment. It had to do with some insurance matters, as he was leaving for Mexico in the morning.

The insurance man had phoned; no answer. He'd even come around to the apartment, knocked awhile, then gone around the neighborhood to some stores and bars that Corland patronized. The proprietors of those places had expected to see Corland, too, this being his last night in town.

Corland had been scheduled for a dawn flight on a plane leaving for Mexico. He hadn't shown up at the airport and that was when his friends had begun to worry about him. None of these friends was very close to Corland; they were mostly persons who had come to know him through business transactions. Corland was well liked, but kept much to himself, seldom confiding in anyone.

In Corland's writing desk, in the apartment, were postcards, and on the desk a portable typewriter. It was Corland's practice to send out typed cards relating to antiques. One of his customers had received such a card in the early mail today. It described some antiques and priced them. At the finish, Corland had typed a final line:

"If I am dead when you receive this card, show it to my attorney."

Naturally, upon receiving such an ominous statement, the customer had phoned police headquarters, adding one more reason why the law should lose no time in finding out what had happened to Paul Corland.

There was an old alarm clock lying on the writing desk. Its time was set at quarter of nine, but it wasn't running. The alarm was set for four thirty, which would have awakened Corland so he could get to the airport. But neither the time nor the alarm had been wound. Obviously, Corland had seen no use in winding the clock when he had suddenly decided to take a trip that would carry him further than Mexico.

The final evidence came from neighbors whose second floor window opened just over Corland's skylight. They had heard thumping sounds outside their window at quarter of nine last night, or thereabouts. Looking out, they'd seen an outline of someone beneath the skylight, apparently trying to pound it open. Then the person had given up the task. Obviously, it had been Corland, fixing his suicide cord. These witnesses had thought nothing more about the matter, not even being acquainted with Corland. After the police came around and began to question the neighborhood, the people next door had told their brief but significant story.

Cranston learned all this as Smedley checked the report. Then Rick opened the apartment door and they went out through a passage to the back alley. That checked, Rick started to return indoors when Cranston asked:

"How far is it to the lake, inspector?"

"About three minutes' drive," replied Smedley,

"if you came straight over. What's on your mind? Do you think Corland considered jumping in Lake Michigan or do you figure that the noise from those speedboats drove him to suicide?"

The distant buzz of the speedboats could be heard while Rick spoke. They used the lake as a broad boulevard, day and night, those whizzing craft. So Rick had a right to feel that his query had a bit of humor in it. What made him really laugh, though, was Cranston's answer.

"Neither," said Cranston. "I'm not thinking about suicide. I deal in terms of murder."

Rick laughed and let it go at that.

They went through the apartment into the antique shop and there Cranston began to look at some of the odd objects. Among them, he found a very old drinking horn, tipped it upside down and shook it.

"Looking for a drink?" laughed Rick. "Corland wouldn't have kept any in that. He had a few bottles up in his kitchenette."

For answer, Cranston tipped the horn again and to Rick's amazement, liquid flowed out, filling a glass which Cranston had placed below.

"Corland's mind apparently ran to tricks, too," observed Cranston. "Like the minds of Fleer, Brett, and the others."

Rick became a trifle ruffled.

"That's an antique," he said, referring to the drinking horn. "These other fellows had new gadgets."

"Like this," suggested Cranston, picking up a square box made of chromium plated metal. "Very modern, I would say, but it has an ancient inscription engraved upon it."

Rick saw the inscription, but couldn't read it, as it was engraved in queer characters. Leaning toward the box, Cranston spoke two words:

"Open sesame."

To Rick's amazement, the lid of the box opened slowly and mysteriously. While Rick was staring to see if Cranston had pressed some secret spring, Cranston said, "Close sesame." The lid of the box went shut in the same slow, mechanical style.

"How did you dope that out?" asked Rick.

"From the inscription," replied Cranston. "It's in Arabic. It says this is the box of Ali Baba and that the magic words will make it open and close."

"How did you know what the words were?"

"From reading the *Arabian Nights.*"

"The only knights I ever read about," said Rick, "were King Arthur's. That box must have a gadget. See if you can find it."

Cranston found it, a little disk set in the top, with tiny holes so that a voice would reach the disc and cause it to vibrate, thus starting a clockwork mechanism that opened and closed the top. Testing the box again, he found that a simple pronunciation of the letter "S" would operate the box both ways.

"Other words beside 'sesame' would do," declared Cranston, "but that is the most appropriate word. I think we're on the right trail, inspector. This box reminds me of the crystal skull."

"The which?"

"I should have mentioned it before," replied Cranston, in a regretful tone. "The crystal skull was on display at the Hotel Harbison when the Magigals came to town. When you said 'Listen, skull,' it listened. When you said 'Speak, skull,' it was probably supposed to speak, only it didn't."

"Where is the skull now?"

"Somebody bought it. Either John Halifax or Gail Tyburn, I think, but I don't think either of them has it."

"Always getting back to those two," snorted Rick. "You've been talking too much to Regan. That's his department, so let him have it. Come into the apartment and we'll finish checking on this suicide case."

They went into the apartment. Corland's body had been removed. Ceremoniously, Rick gestured about the place and reconstructed the final scene in Corland's life.

"The door was locked with the chain bolt on," declared Rick. "Corland had come in from mailing some postcards. He may have picked up this book and started to read it."

Rick picked up a book that was lying by the daybed. It was a copy of *Hamlet,* with a ribbon marking a page. Rick opened at the ribbon and gave a snort.

"Shakespeare," said Rick. "A scene about some gravediggers. That may have given Corland morbid ideas." Rick closed the book, tossed it back onto the table. "Anyway, Corland decided to hang himself. See that big chest?" Rick pointed to the object in question. "You can tell that it was in the alcove, by the lack of dust on the floor there. Corland pulled it out after he'd fixed the rope. Do you follow?"

"I'm ahead of you," returned Cranston. "Why didn't he just leave the chest there and stand on it when he hung himself?"

"Because he couldn't kick it out from under him," explained Rick, patiently. "Look over there, under the writing table. See that little red footstool? That's what he used to stand on, it's right in line with the alcove. In fact, it's the only thing he could have used."

The thing that Rick termed a footstool was a Chinese taboret, one of several antiques that were in the apartment. Cranston went over, picked it up. His eyes became reflective as he weighed the taboret.

"That's how Corland did it," decided Rick, "and I suppose you'll still be telling me it's murder."

"It definitely was murder," came Cranston's calm-toned verdict. "Corland did not take his own life. He was overpowered, choked, and strung up in the alcove to make his death appear a suicide. I can prove it."

Rick gave another snort. "How?"

For answer, Cranston set the red taboret in the direct center of the alcove, then gestured to Rick.

"Suppose you were Corland," suggested Cranston. "He was about your build, Rick, though probably considerably heavier. Anyway, your reach would be about the same. I'd like to see just how Corland would have reached for that cord and tied it about his neck. Would you show me your idea of it?"

"Sure thing," returned Rick. "It must have been a cinch."

It couldn't have been a cinch for Corland. Rick Smedley found that out before he even went through the motions of preparing himself for an imaginary hanging. Rick lifted one foot, placed it on the taboret, brought his other foot up to join it. The moment the taboret received Rick's full weight, it collapsed in a mass of flying splinters, amid which Rick Smedley floundered to the floor—and hard.

"In order to have kicked away that taboret," said Cranston, calmly, "Paul Corland would have had to stand on it first. You've just proved that he couldn't have stood on it, Rick, and that wipes out your theory of suicide."

Before Rick could nod while picking himself up from the floor, Cranston added the positive verdict:

"Paul Corland was murdered."

CHAPTER XV
THE SHADOW'S PLAN

WITH murder proven, the next thing was to track it to its source and Inspector Rick Smedley was only too anxious to begin. Appreciating Rick's new mood, Lamont Cranston promptly provided leads. The first was the big chest that stood near the alcove.

"You were correct regarding this chest," declared Cranston. "It must have been there in the alcove. Why not put it back there before we analyze this case further?"

Taking the suggestion, Rick started to lift the chest only to find that he couldn't budge it. The chest was made of teakwood and felt as heavy as iron. Cranston took the other end; together, he and Rick hoisted the chest back where it belonged.

"Two points the murderers overlooked," stated Cranston. "Not only was the taboret too frail to support Corland's weight, the chest was too heavy for him to move alone."

"Right enough," agreed Rick. "But how do you explain this?"

From his pocket, Rick took the postcard that one of Corland's customers had received that morning, with the final statement that in the event of his death, the card should be shown to his lawyer as proof of an intended sale of antiques.

"Take a close look," said Rick, handing the card to Cranston, "and you will see that all the typing was done on the same machine. That's it, right over there." Rick pointed to the typewriter on the writing desk. "I know, because I've already compared the type."

Cranston gave the card a close scrutiny. Then:

"Check the last sentence," he said. "You'll see that the line is slightly off register and slanted a trifle, too. Microscopic examination will make it evident that it was added later. The killers must have found this card already typed and signed. There was enough space to add a death statement above Corland's signature."

Studying the card, Rick decided that Cranston was right.

"A smart job," conceded Rick, "but not smart enough. This is evidence we can use against the murderers when we find them. You've proved, too, that there must be more than one killer, because it took at least two men to move that chest. One of them must have banged the skylight purposely to attract attention and make the people next door think it was Corland. But why?"

"That's easily answered," informed Cranston. "They wanted to establish the time of Corland's supposed suicide. They even set the old alarm clock at quarter of nine." Picking up the clock, Cranston wound it a few turns, then shook it without result. "Do you know, Rick, this clock is practically an antique itself. They must have found it in the closet. It probably hasn't run for years. It certainly won't run now."

Rick rubbed his chin, puzzled.

"I've heard of faking the time of someone's death," Rick said, "but this is the other way about. Suicide or murder, the time was all the same. Corland must have been bumped about a quarter of nine, just as we originally figured. If the killers were here at that time, why should they be advertising it?"

"Probably to support an alibi," said Cranston.

"But if they were here," argued Rick, "how could they have an alibi?"

Judging by Cranston's distant gaze, he might have answered that question, but he didn't. Actually, Cranston was comparing the strong-arm murder of Paul Corland with another attempt that had failed. He was thinking of the death attack on himself, which had been a running affair starting at the Mirror Grill and ending near the Adler Planetarium.

Chung Loo started his act at the Mirror Grill shortly before ten o'clock, ending about ten minutes after the hour. The chase, with its rapid culmination on the esplanade, had occupied some twenty minutes, bringing the time to half past ten. That, like the time of Corland's murder, would need to be an alibi period, where the killers were concerned.

"Skip the alibi," suggested Rick, getting no reply from Cranston. "How did the murderers get out of here? That's more important. In fact, the whole case hinges on it."

Methodically, Cranston went to the door of the apartment, opened it and stepped outside. Closing the door to a slight crack, he slid his fingers through and tried to manipulate the chain bolt. It didn't work, because Cranston's fingers pressed the crack too wide. Cranston withdrew his fingers, when they returned, they held a long nail file. Manipulating the file deftly with his fingertips, Cranston engaged a link of the chain, raised the bolt and neatly flipped it so that it caught in the socket.

Through the slight crack, Cranston told Smedley:

"It would be much easier, Rick, with one of those flexible metal rulers. A little practice and anyone could do it."

Rick unbolted the door and came out.

"Let's get back to headquarters," said Rick. "I'm going to try and tie this case in with those other murders. I called them suicides once, but I've changed my mind about it now. Only we'll let it ride along as a suicide wave for the present."

At headquarters, Rick had amassed a great deal of data regarding the earlier victims, all based on reports from their respective hometowns. Following the clues that Cranston had gained, Rick had learned one thing at least; there were people who recalled that each of the victims had occasionally done a few remarkable impromptu tricks. They had claimed, too, that they had learned their magic from a master at the art.

"If we're getting someplace," declared Rick, "I'd say it was no place. Unless"—he eyed Cranston hopefully—"unless you can tell me who this master could be."

"I've heard tell of a Professor Marsh," returned Cranston. "Sedley Marsh was the full name. According to rumor, he may be dead. If he is, he could have left his remaining secrets to his pupils."

Rick wrote down the name Sedley Marsh.

"But I still think you have two better leads," continued Cranston. "The tugboat and the painters. If you can find some similar lead connected with the earlier murders, go after it."

"I will," promised Rick, "but this thing kind of gets me. If Marsh died here in Chicago, this is where the bunch would come to collect whatever he promised them. Maybe they thought it was first come, first served. Instead, it looks like he who laughs last, laughs longest."

Leaving headquarters, Cranston went back to his hotel and contacted Burbank. There were still no details on Professor Marsh. Apparently, he had kept the secret of his death as completely as those which he had sold to his pupils while he was alive. And therein, Cranston saw an answer.

In all the reports that Smedley had received, there was nothing to show in the way of correspondence between the victims and their unnamed tutor. That stood as proof that Marsh must either have given all his instructions verbally, or that anything he had ever written had been destroyed, probably by agreement.

It followed, therefore, that Marsh had either managed to call his pupils individually before he died; or failing that, had seen to it that letters reached them telling them to come to Chicago. They would logically have destroyed such letters if that had been the understanding, or such instructions came in letters themselves. Their method of identification, Cranston was already sure, was through the tricks they performed. They would have had no suspicion that murder awaited them in Chicago.

Yet there must be more to it, some formality or system, whereby Marsh's pupils were to get together. That answer could lie only in the crystal skull and it might be known now to the person who had acquired that trophy. In all likelihood, that person was Verity Joyce.

Another point impressed Cranston. The murder of Paul Corland, though Cranston had cracked it, was every bit as ingenious as any of the others, perhaps more so. It was one case wherein suicide had been faked to the absolute limit. This wasn't because it was the latest in the list. With the police classing all the murders as suicides, the killers could have afforded to become careless. Yet the plans, in Corland's death, had been very thorough.

There was only one answer. Corland must have been suspicious. He had better opportunity to gain suspicion, since he was living in Chicago while the other victims were from out of town. The proof of the theory lay in the fact that Corland had planned to leave Chicago. He alone was willing to pass up the legacy from Professor Marsh, unquestionably because he valued his life more.

Behind murder lay a sharp, keen mind, the mind of a man who knew that Corland might have left some clue. That was why the murder crew had been told to set the suicide stage with meticulous detail. Their mistake was that they had overdone it.

Where had that crew been in the time between Corland's death and the thrust at Cranston?

The mental question brought a whispered laugh from the lips of the man most concerned, Cranston himself. It was an echo of a laugh belonging to The Shadow, that mysterious investigator who was supposed to know all, and would, before long. From approximately quarter of nine until nearly quarter past ten, an hour and a half, killers had been off duty. That time element was important, too.

Yet the immediate lead was still Verity Joyce, provided she could again be found. That might be rather easy, around cocktail time this afternoon. Meanwhile, Lamont Cranston saw no reason to be idle. Picking up the telephone, he called Regan's office and received a prompt answer.

Regan was glad to hear from Cranston. He wanted to know what had happened with Rick Smedley.

"Routine stuff," said Cranston. "Just another crack-brained suicide. Speaking of routine, I suppose you're geared to it as usual. What's the latest on John Halifax and Gail Tyburn?"

"All lovey-dovey," replied Regan. "They're lunching together at a new place on State Street called the Anchorage."

"How did you find that out?" Cranston questioned. "Did you capture one of Halifax's carrier pigeons in flight?"

"Simpler than that," returned Regan. "Old Tyburn cut off all Gail's credit. The only place she could get it on her own would have to be a new one. So I called the Anchorage to learn if she had a luncheon reservation. They said yes."

"Better check on them," said Cranston, "and keep watch for any peculiar characters with your other eye."

It was one o'clock when Gail and Halifax met at the Anchorage. The only person resembling a suspicious character was an old gentleman named Isaac Twambley, who sat at an adjacent table. He was a withery sort and very hard of hearing, because when a waiter told him he was wanted on the telephone, the news had to be practically shouted into old Twambley's ear.

Regan, seated around beyond a pillar, wished that he could have taken Twambley's vantage spot but Regan couldn't afford to be seen by Gail and Halifax. When Twambley came back to his table, the loving couple gave him a brief glance and continued with a low-toned conversation.

"Don't worry about that venerable character," said Halifax, referring to Twambley. "He's as deaf as the post that Regan is hiding behind."

"That stupid Regan!" exclaimed Gail. "How long will Lester keep up this silly business of having me watched by a common private detective?"

"As long as I'm in town, I suppose," returned Halifax. "Perhaps we'd better not be seen together so often."

"You've said that before," pouted Gail, "and I don't like it. Not while all those Magigals are in town."

"Their convention ended today, Gail, and that makes it more difficult. Being a magician, I had a reason to be around Chicago while the convention was in session."

"That stupid convention!"

"That's just where you're mistaken, sweet. You should have played along with it. If you pretended to be interested in watching magicians work, you could see me whenever you want."

Gail's dreamy face brightened as if she had gained a wonderful idea.

"Why, of course!" she exclaimed. "How silly I was not to stay at the Mirror Grill yesterday."

"I couldn't tell you then, beautiful," continued Halifax, "because there were too many people around. But why don't you go back there today? Ask to see Chung Loo. Tell him you know me and that he's as wonderful as I am."

"But he isn't!"

"I mean as a magician. Actually, he does some very neat tricks. I wonder where he got them."

"I really wouldn't know."

"I know you wouldn't, but you might find out. Why don't you engage Chung Loo for that lawn party tomorrow night?"

"But I thought—"

"You thought that I intended to appear there," interposed Halifax, with a smile, "but you know, dear, that I can't. It would be too obvious."

"But Chung Loo is working at the Mirror Grill."

"He's only filling in for two days. He'll be free tomorrow. Get him out to Longwood and give Regan something to worry about. He'll come there expecting to see me."

Gail laughed at that and so did Halifax. With another bright look, Gail added:

"It will worry Lester, too. That's the part I like. He will be looking everywhere else for you. Maybe, though, you could be there."

Slowly, Halifax was shaking his head.

"But if you aren't there," Gail persisted, "I can't give you the—"

Gail caught herself as Halifax put his fingers to his lips. He must have guessed what she was going to say, because he started the gesture from the moment Gail began to speak.

They had finished lunch and now Halifax was glancing at his watch. Mentioning something about an appointment, he suggested that they leave. As they neared the door, Halifax looked for Regan, saw the detective easing out of sight. Halifax gave a nod which meant for Gail to go ahead. She did and Regan tagged along, in what he thought was an unnoticed style.

Giving Regan a head start, Halifax went out to the street and there found a convenient store window that attracted his attention. Keeping a watch on the door of the Anchorage, Halifax saw old Twambley come out, hobbling on a cane. As the old man turned in the other direction, Halifax gave a short laugh.

There was a good reason why Halifax had cut Gail's statement short, back in the restaurant. He was quite sure that the old man was a plant, probably some stooge of Regan's. If so, what he had heard didn't matter. It wasn't anything that Regan didn't know or couldn't have figured out.

Halifax was half right.

Old Twambley had heard everything, but he wasn't working for Regan. As he hobbled around the corner, Twambley delivered a slight laugh of his own. It was identical with the whispered laugh that Cranston sometimes gave, an echo of The Shadow's.

What little The Shadow had learned was helpful, more perhaps than John Halifax supposed. It meant, for one thing, that The Shadow's task would be easier around cocktail time at the Mirror Grill. Until then, The Shadow expected no further developments.

A development came, however, when The Shadow, again guised as Cranston, was about to leave his room at the Harbison, later that afternoon. Answering a phone call, he found Rick Smedley on the wire.

"Something that may interest you, Cranston," the inspector said. "I've been going over Corland's mailing list. I found a name on it that may mean something."

"Mine, I suppose," returned Cranston. "I buy antiques and I suppose that nearly every dealer has me listed. They have a way of finding out each other's customers, you know."

"No, not your name," laughed Rick. "Gail Tyburn's. She had an account there and she's on a list that looks like active customers. Maybe it was Corland who sold her that crystal skull. I've called the perfume shop that displayed it and they're mystified themselves about where it came from and what happened to it."

"You're going to question Gail Tyburn?"

"Not until after the party tomorrow night. I'll see you then, Cranston."

That was all, but it was enough. Better news than Cranston had expected from Inspector Smedley, especially the part that Rick was postponing the matter of the crystal skull. The Shadow already had a plan that might involve the crystal skull.

The Shadow's plan was set for this very afternoon.

CHAPTER XVI
SECRET OF THE SKULL

CHUNG LOO, the Chinese wizard, not only could speak English, he could read it. He preferred Chinese newspapers, but there was also a copy of a Chicago journal lying on his dressing table. Verity Joyce noticed this when she stopped in the dressing room to tell Chung Loo that she was ready. Glancing at the newspaper, she was somewhat horrified to learn that the suicide wave had begun again, the newest victim a man named Paul Corland.

Hearing a footstep, Verity turned to see Chung Loo. For a moment the girl was horrified by the demoniac expression on his face, then, as a bland smile spread upon his lips, the girl decided it was all a matter of makeup. He had to play the devil-man, Chung Loo, to do a proper show. His smile itself was intriguing, involving his lips only, never bringing even a wrinkle to the remainder of his face.

Chung Loo's smile must have signified approval, for he was studying Verity's own make-up. Wearing a Chinese costume, the girl looked the complete part. She had fixed her face with saffron greasepaint, sharpened her eyebrows with a jet-black pencil. Her lips were perfect in their ruddy contrast, while her hair now formed a tight topknot under her tiny hat.

"Very good," approved Chung Loo. "How long did it take?"

"Nearly an hour," replied Verity.

"Too long." Chung Loo came over to the dressing table, picked up the Chicago newspaper and looked for something underneath it. "You must cut it to half an hour at most. That is about the usual time. Of course, for myself"—Chung Loo smiled again as he dropped the newspaper in a wastebasket—"I take only a few minutes. Being Chinese, I am practically playing a straight part."

A bell was ringing the five-minute call, so they went on stage. Verity noticed that Chung Loo kept watching her nervously. He couldn't be blamed, perhaps, considering that she was a new assistant, but Verity felt it should be the other way about. At least, that was the impression she tried to give Chung Loo.

This was the cocktail show, but the audience was a large one. It started in its usual strident style and as the act progressed, Verity found no trouble in keeping pace with Chung Loo. But that wasn't all to Verity's credit. Chung Loo, it seemed, was slower than usual, fumbling at times. When the lights came on after the firefly illusion, Verity was happy that it was over.

A waiter had come back with a message for Chung

Loo, stating that a Mrs. Tyburn would like to speak with him. Verity heard the name, tightened her lips, and went into her dressing room. It was Verity now who was nervous with haste as she changed from her Chinese clothes and hurriedly took off the makeup that had taken so long to put on.

Then, finding her way out from backstage, Verity left the Mirror Grill wearing strictly American clothes and trying to look like anybody but Chung Loo's assistant. Spotting the lights of a cab, Verity hailed it, gave the driver an address and was on her way.

The cab threaded a course to the West Side and there Verity alighted at a presentable rooming house. Indoors, she went up to a second floor room and shouted until a sleepy-looking man appeared. Verity gestured to some large suitcases that were already packed, took a dollar bill from her purse and said:

"I'm leaving, George. I've already paid Mrs. Blake. She probably told you. I'll send my forwarding address later."

George nodded, picked up the bags. "There's a box in the closet," added Verity. "I want to leave it here. Mrs. Blake said I could put it in Locker D."

"It's there already," informed George. "I took it down an hour ago. I'll give you the key unless you want Mrs. Blake to mail it. Shall I get you a cab, Miss Joyce?"

Verity nodded and followed George downstairs. It was then that darkness stirred in the second floor hall, a shadowy blackness that had followed Verity upstairs. In fact, that shape, for such it was, had come by cab all the way from the Mirror Grill. Now, however, the trail was to be broken.

As Verity went out through the front door, the shape that had followed her turned at the bottom of the stairs and moved back along the ground floor hall. Now visible, had anyone been present to observe it, the figure was that of a being cloaked in black, who moved with silent tread. Having tracked Verity to her lodging, hearing mention of a box that might contain the crystal skull, The Shadow intended to inspect the trophy that somehow was looming larger than ever before in affairs of murder.

In the cellar, The Shadow found Locker D in a remote corner. The padlock gave him practically no trouble and he opened a slat door into the locker, which consisted of two stone walls and an adjoining partition to Locker C. There were some old trunks against the wall; on one of them stood a large square wooden box, bearing the name of Verity Joyce.

Pulling the cord of an overhead light, The Shadow no longer needed his flashlight while he pried open the box and discovered the crystal skull, platform and all. Setting the thing up on its box, The Shadow went to the slat door and listened.

From outside, he heard the faint rumble of a departing taxicab. Therewith, The Shadow concentrated entirely upon the skull.

It was a fascinating contrivance, this crystal skull with the glittering rhinestone eyes that shone like mammoth diamonds. The Shadow studied it from all angles, looking down through the transparent base that had the crisscrossed circular lines as its only decorations. Then, under the glare of the large overhead bulb, The Shadow began to test the skull.

When The Shadow passed his black-gloved hand before the skull's eyes, the transparent head turned from right to left. When he asked it questions, the skull nodded or shook its head. Sometimes it clicked its jaws as if counting numbers. In all, the demonstration was most effective, yet not exactly amazing.

Those rhinestone eyes unquestionably concealed the mechanism, which was the equivalent of a photoelectric cell. Perhaps the skull's inventor—in all probability Professor Marsh—had planned to develop the skull into something that would exhibit more intelligence. But when The Shadow thought in terms of the Ali Baba box that he had tested back at Corland's, he decided that even now the skull might show something more remarkable than it had so far.

Remembering how Verity had addressed the skull, The Shadow tried the same system. In sibilant tone, he said:

"Listen, skull."

The skull nodded. "Speak, skull," continued The Shadow. "Tell me all you know. Repeat whatever you have heard."

The skull wagged its head.

That was the part that had balked Verity. Apparently, the girl was following a system that only partly worked. This was the thing that The Shadow had come to test and until today, he could not have tried the idea that was in his mind. Again, The Shadow was thinking in terms of Corland's and a book that Smedley had picked up from the table beside Corland's daybed.

That book was a copy of *Hamlet;* it was marked at the gravedigger's scene. That scene involved a skull and the skull had a name. The Shadow spoke that name now, as he addressed the crystal skull.

"Speak, Yorick."

The jaws of the skull opened and a voice spoke. It stated:

"Listen, skull. Listen and remember. My name is Jerome Alton, from Dubuque. I shall be at the opera house this evening, wearing a light-gray coat and carrying a gold-headed cane. If I do not hear from you, I shall speak to you again tomorrow—"

A pause. A different voice came from the skull:

"Listen, skull, and remember. I am Lloyd Stelton

from Zanesville. I am stopping at the Lakeview Hotel, and can be reached there at any hour—"

"Listen, skull," a third voice said. "Remember what I say. I am Ward Bronson. I come from Tampa. You will find me at the Hawthorne Club, where I have a guest card—"

Next came two more voices, giving names that to The Shadow seemed singularly familiar, though he had never heard them. They were those of William Brett and Edward Fleer. Another pause, then a voice announced:

"Listen, skull. I am Paul Corland. I live here in Chicago and you will find me listed in the phone book—" A pause followed, then came Corland's voice anew, speaking in low but sharp command: "Speak, Yorick! Tell me all that you have heard!"

It fitted perfectly. Corland not only knew how to record a statement to the listening skull; he had used the key name "Yorick" to obtain an answer in the form of everything that the others had said. To add a final check, The Shadow listened closely while the skull continued. From the opened jaws came the voice of Verity Joyce, low, serious, stating her name after the opening words of "Listen, skull!" Then came the words with which Verity had failed to make the skull talk.

"Speak, skull, tell me all you know—"

Verity's voice kept on, but The Shadow wasn't listening to it. Another sound had attracted his attention, a noise behind him. It was the slight scraping of the slat door, the sudden click of the padlock. Wheeling about, The Shadow whipped an automatic from beneath his cloak as he swung clear of the skull with the moving jaws that was completing Verity's statement.

A revolver blazed two shots, straight for the spot where The Shadow had been. Instead of The Shadow, the bullets found the crystal skull, cracked it and broke it loose from the platform which supported it. Then the gun muzzle was gone, to find other slats through which to poke, that its owner might aim again at The Shadow.

And for once, The Shadow was at the huge disadvantage which he usually thrust upon his foemen. Here in the locker, the light was bright, fully revealing The Shadow, despite his black garb. But the man in the cellar, with darkness as his background, was invisible beyond the slat door!

All that could betray The Shadow's opponent was his gun muzzle, but he no longer intended to shove it into view. As The Shadow made a sudden skid across the locker, his arm sweeping against the flat, thick platform that had supported the skull, the murderous revolver stabbed between a pair of slats, just too late to clip the cloaked fighter.

The Shadow was literally trapped. His dodging tactics could only prolong the impossible battle.

His enemy had all the cellar to rove, giving him opportunity even to reload, clear of The Shadow's range. Realizing this, The Shadow took a different course, but a mad one.

With a whirl, The Shadow flung himself hard against the slat door on the chance that he could crash it with a single jolt. The barrier gave a few inches, that was all. The man beyond it gave no mercy. As the black form of The Shadow blocked the light, the hidden marksman fired three shots point-blank between the slats, choosing The Shadow's heart as the target.

Jolted backward with the first shot, The Shadow flung one arm upward. As the second bullet jarred him further, his hand swung its automatic at the hanging light. With the third burst from the merciless revolver, the light crashed. In the blackness, there was a tumbling, thudding sound, The Shadow's sprawl.

Then silence.

Half a minute ticked by.

Then came a grating laugh. The man of murder had reloaded. But he didn't use a flashlight; he wasn't taking chances that The Shadow, dying, might still manage to return a shot. Instead, this canny enemy raked the floor with six bullets, firing each from between a different pair of slats, confident that one or more of the slugs would be added to the quota that The Shadow had already accepted.

Silence, then departing footsteps. The closing of an outer door. Silence again.

A whispered laugh stirred the blackness of what should have been a dead man's cell. A tiny flashlight gleamed as The Shadow warily climbed from in back of a trunk that was a few feet from the wall. Reaching the slat door, he shoved an automatic through and whacked the padlock, breaking it. His avenue of escape was open, should the frustrated murderer return.

This would have amazed the man who had fired those point-blank bullets. The Shadow hadn't been behind the trunk when the first three shots were fired. He could have toppled there purposely, after knocking out the light, thus nullifying the bullets that were delivered later. But it was incredible that he should have survived the flaying he had taken from the triple blast.

There was an explanation, however, and The Shadow's probing flashlight uncovered it.

On the floor lay the foot-square block of transparent plastic forming the platform that had supported the crystal skull. It was cracked now, but its four-inch thickness had served The Shadow well. In his twist toward the slatted door, The Shadow had scooped up the square slab as a shield. Unseen against the slats, that square of tough material had taken the bullets intended for The Shadow's heart.

The impact of the slugs had jolted The Shadow and so had the back dive with which he had cleared the trunk after his swinging gun had smashed the hanging light. But the bullets themselves had never reached him and in addition they had solved a most interesting problem.

Cracked by the shots, the plastic square showed itself to be of three-ply construction. Its edge had been broken, showing the interior. From between two square layers, The Shadow pulled out the core of the plastic platform, in the shape of a round disk. That disk was scored with circular lines, hidden by the ornamental tracings on the platform top.

The disk was a transparent phonograph record. Above it, a thin, flat arm held a tiny needle. The whole thing connected with a transparent mechanism, also of some special plastic, that had operated down through the neck of the crystal skull. This was indeed, a remarkable invention, an invisible recording device, with automatic playback, housed in a transparent container!

Both delicate and intricate, the machine could be geared to operate by the vibratory tones of different words. The little box at Corland's had worked both ways from the sibilance of the word "Sesame," but this device was twofold. "Listen, skull!" was the combination that made the thing record.

"Speak, Yorick!" put the playback into operation.

The transparent disk, preserved between the cracked layers of steel-tough plastic, would serve The Shadow as future evidence against the murderers whose victims could still speak for themselves. But The Shadow did not have to play it now, to recall the salient differences of the various speakers.

All the victims had been content with asking the skull to listen—with one exception. Paul Corland had added:

"Speak, Yorick!" to learn if the skull would answer, which it had. Verity Joyce had talked to the skull and tried to make it answer, but without result, as "Speak, skull" had not been the key.

Apparently, no one else had even tried to make the skull talk. That problem still bothered The Shadow as he tucked the disk beneath his cloak and padlocked the slat door of the locker where a murderer believed that a cloaked victim was lying dead. The shots had not been heard in the remote corner of this house, for all was as calm as ever when The Shadow reached the street.

Finding a corner cab with a sleepy driver, The Shadow stepped into it and gave a downtown address in Cranston's voice. During the trip, The Shadow switched to his guise of Cranston. His destination proved to be a music shop. His portfolio under his arm, he entered, asked to hear some of the latest records, and was ushered into a sound-proof room where he was given a supply.

The first record that Cranston played was the plastic disk from the platform of the crystal skull. It came much more clearly than from the jaws of the skull. So clearly that Cranston could hear an interpolation that had not been audible when he played the record before.

Between the statements of each speaker, The Shadow heard a low, ominous whisper giving the key words: "Speak, Yorick!" None followed the speech of Verity Joyce, however. She had been the last person either to confide in the skull or to question it.

Low, forced in tone, the telltale whisper proved only that someone acquainted with the riddle of the skull had made the most of it to learn the name of each successive victim and where that person could be reached. Who that person was still remained the pressing problem. To find him, would be to find a murderer.

Tonight, that murderer had found The Shadow. Of that there was no question. It would be The Shadow's business to make sure that the next meeting was the other way around.

CHAPTER XVII
DISASTER AHEAD

THAT night, Lamont Cranston vanished from Chicago. It was not until noon the next day that he reappeared; then, the place where he arrived was Smedley's office. The brawny, bluff-faced inspector was glad to see Cranston, but at the same time registered indignation because his visitor hadn't shown up earlier.

"I've been calling the Harbison all morning," stormed Rick. "They said you hadn't checked out, but they didn't know where you were. I was thinking you'd gone back to New York, right when this case was getting hot!"

Lamont Cranston smiled, but slightly. Rick Smedley didn't know how hot it really had got. However, for the present, Cranston preferred to be a listener.

"There's a tinge of suspicion in every one of those cases we called suicide," declared Rick. "But I can't lay a finger on any of them. One man hired an automobile and got struck on the Milwaukee tracks; another went to a bar, where he'd never been before; a third for some reason went out in a speedboat and cracked up."

As Rick paused, Cranston shrugged. "Wrecking a speedboat wouldn't be too difficult," he said. "I was trying one out last night. They're tricky."

"With John Halifax?" queried Rick, with a bluff stare.

"No," replied Cranston. "Why did you ask?"

"I'll come to that later," returned Rick. "So you took a speedboat trip last night."

"Yes, up to Milwaukee," said Cranston. "Like you said, you have the whole lake for a boulevard. But when they're doing sixty, they're sensitive to every little ripple. There's not many you can let go that fast, even if they can do it."

"At night," agreed Rick, "it would be tougher."

"No, the moonlight was perfect," argued Cranston, "and the lake was very calm. I clocked it to Longwood, for a sample. Twenty minutes flat."

"But Longwood is more than twenty miles—"

"By road, yes, but under twenty by the lake route. I stopped in Longwood, by the way, to see how well that police force functioned."

"How well did they?"

"Not at all. There wasn't even an officer in headquarters. They must have all gone out to eat. They ought to turn the police duty over to those men who work on Tyburn's estate. They really patrol those grounds."

Rick gave a wise smile.

"That's what I ordered them to do," he said. "I want them to be in practice for tonight. You didn't stop and ask for Tyburn, did you?"

"No."

"You wouldn't have found him. He was out in his cruiser. He needed to get away from some new worries. You'll find out what they are, when we go over to his apartment. Now, let's get back to those murders. We've located the tugboat. She was the *Bluebird,* ready to be junked. She was moved to another berth, but who did it, we don't know. You're right about the painters, too. We found extra sets of suits, stuffed in a furnace. Somebody had tried to burn them in a hurry, but it didn't work.

"All this proves something, though"—Rick was thrumming the desk with his knuckles as he spoke. "It proves that whoever is mastering these murders has a small mob, practically on call. By the way"—Rick's eyes narrowed—"what time did you come back down the lake?"

"At about dawn."

"It must have been nice," observed Rick. "Seeing the Chicago skyline brighten is a very pretty sight. Even in the Planetarium, if you're awake to watch it."

Cranston gave a mild look of surprise.

"I found out that you were there," continued Rick. "What happened?"

"Somebody sledged me with this," replied Cranston, tossing the dummy cigarette gun on the desk. "As to who it was, your guess is as good as mine, perhaps better."

"Why were you over at the Planetarium?"

"Because it was the one public place you had forgotten," replied Cranston. "I thought it might be a good spot for a murder, so I thought I'd have a look at it before suggesting that you keep it covered."

"It's covered now," said Rick, "but it should have been before. We might have spotted a car that was abandoned in Grant Park. We found it there, yesterday. It had been stolen from a used car lot and who do you suppose had been looking for it, wanting maybe to buy it?"

"That's easy. John Halifax. He's noted for wanting to buy anything," replied Cranston. "Cars, airplanes, trucks. Once he even wanted to buy a combination Pullman and baggage car to travel his show."

"You're right about the trucks," agreed Rick. "There was a job with a trailer that was wrecked just before things happened over in Grant Park. Halifax had been pricing that, too. It was taken from a garage where he had gone to see it."

"Halifax might be interested in speedboats too," suggested Cranston, "but I don't think he'd go for antiques."

"We've already checked the speedboats," said Rick, "and you're right. That was what I intended to tell you. But antiques aren't in Halifax's department. Gail Tyburn goes for those."

"Would either be interested in phonograph records?"

"I haven't checked. Why do you ask?"

"I thought," said Cranston, "that you might listen to this one."

From his portfolio, Cranston produced the transparent record. Much intrigued, Smedley decided to play it immediately on an office machine. When the record began its listing of murder victims in their own voices, with the whispered words "Speak, Yorick!" coming after each, Rick was very much agog.

"Where did you pick up this thing, Cranston?"

"I was looking for a girl named Verity Joyce," stated Cranston. "Today, I found that she'd checked out of her boardinghouse. She'd left a box in a cellar locker, so I found a chance to go down there. Somebody had been doing target practice at the box, through the slats of the locker door. The crystal skull was in the box and it was knocked all apart and so was the platform on which the skull stood. This disk had slid out of the platform and I could just reach it through the slats. So I brought it along."

"That whisper," muttered Rick. "It might be anybody's, even a woman's. Where did the girl live? I'll send a squad car there, right away."

"I wouldn't," said Cranston. "I'd have the place watched, but at a reasonable distance. If anybody comes to pick up what's left of the skull, that would be the time to pick them up with it."

Rick nodded that Cranston was right.

"Nor would I mention it to anyone," added Cranston, "until after tonight. Something may be brewing out at Longwood."

"You're right," agreed Rick. "There's a magician billed to do a show there and Gail Tyburn won't look at anybody but the Great Halifax. It's her party, so draw your own conclusions. I'm counting on you to be there, because you're marked as somebody who knows those Marsh tricks. Maybe that's why you were slugged at the Planetarium, so you'd better watch yourself out at Longwood. About this Verity Joyce"—Rick rubbed his chin—"does she do any of that Marsh magic?"

"I would say yes," replied Cranston, "after watching her at the Magigal show."

"No wonder she ducked out," decided Rick, "but there's still another angle. Somebody could be doing those tricks as a come-on to the suckers. By suckers, I mean victims, or potential victims, who didn't register their names on this record you found. That leaves a big question mark around Verity Joyce or anybody else that's strutting that Marsh stuff. Come on, let's go to Tyburn's."

Cranston could have added a few facts if Smedley had paved the way, but he was just as glad not to. Rick had analyzed matters rather well, regarding the murder crew; but Cranston, as The Shadow, had carried the situation further. Last night, he'd drawn fire from the master's hand, in person. The reason was that the crew hadn't been needed, just to pick up a box that Verity Joyce was leaving in a cellar. By being first on the scene, The Shadow had forced a murder attempt from someone who had until then left such work to others.

The intruder in the cellar could have been almost anyone, even Verity herself, if she'd decided to double back on the chance of trapping someone who sought the crystal skull. The main point, however, was that the master hand in this game was quite ready to do murder personally when helpers were not available.

AT the Armistead Arms, Cranston and Smedley saw Regan snooping around outside. The reason was explained when they reached Tyburn's apartment. Gail Tyburn was visiting her husband and they had evidently reached a heated state of argument when the visitors arrived.

"So you're Inspector Smedley," stormed Gail. "Very kind of you to come out this evening and see that no one gets murdered during my lawn party."

"Suicide is the word, Mrs. Tyburn," returned Rick. "We just don't want the wave to spread."

"That's what Lester tells me," said Gail. "So call it suicide if you wish. But since the estate will be under complete protection, perhaps you can convince Lester that he should let me wear some of my jewels, particularly my diamond necklace."

"You have an excellent replica," interrupted Tyburn. "Why not wear it, Gail, as you always do?"

"Because there are people who would know the difference," retorted Gail. "This is my party and the necklace is still mine or is it?"

"Until we settle our personal affairs, it is yours," decided Tyburn. "Still, that is no reason why something worth fifty thousand dollars should be put in jeopardy."

"If you don't trust Inspector Smedley to protect a necklace," argued Gail, "how much good can he be at preventing murder or suicide?"

Tyburn couldn't answer that one.

"Very well," he said, "I shall bring along the diamond necklace. You may wear it, under my protest."

Gail smiled sweetly as though her whole married life had been a career of riding over Tyburn's protests. Turning to Smedley and Cranston, Gail said:

"I have my car today. Could I drop you gentlemen anywhere?"

"Yes," replied Cranston promptly. "You can take us over to Navy Pier. We want to try out a speedboat John Halifax once planned to buy."

It was a neat thrust, for it made Gail ill at ease. Flustered, she tried to pretend that she'd never heard of Halifax. Tyburn promptly picked up the theme.

"I'll phone Skip Hagathorn," said Tyburn, "and have him meet you there. He might give you an opinion on the boat. Afterward, we can go to Longwood in my cruiser."

"Or my car," put in Gail. "I prefer Chaffin as a chauffeur to Hagathorn as a skipper."

"Anything for an argument," said Tyburn, wearily. "Good-bye, Gail. I'll see you later."

Cranston and Smedley went out with Gail and stepped into her luxurious car, which was piloted by Chaffin, a sleek, polite chap. This amazed Regan who stood dumbfounded as the limousine drove away; then decided to go into the Armistead Arms and deliver a package of reports and exhibits to Lester Tyburn.

When the big car reached Navy Pier, Skip Hagathorn was there. So was the speedboat, with the man who had brought it from its mooring. Skip volunteered to go along with Cranston and Smedley while they tried out the craft.

"Too bad you didn't bring Regan," Skip laughed. "We'd give him a real thrill. But don't expect too much from this plugger"—he spoke from the side of his mouth, behind his hand—"because it's too cheap a buy, or Halifax wouldn't have looked at it. That's why I said we'd test it out ourselves. I want to see if the motor has been doped."

Rick took the wheel with Cranston beside him, while Skip sat in back. As they spurted away, Skip tilted his head to catch the motor's thrumm. Finally, he tapped Rick's shoulder and said:

"Open it up."

Giving the gun, Rick found that the boat responded well. Bow high, it was roaring into the forties. Above the noise, Skip shouted into Rick's ear:

"Go left around that breakwater, but watch for anything coming from the right."

Rick banked the speedboat to the left. He was swinging it at top speed, when another shout came from Skip:

"Look out!"

Even as he shouted, Skip was diving overboard, but Cranston was acting still faster. He'd been looking left, not right, and he saw the hazard too, a moored barge squarely in the speedboat's path. With a fling that matched Skip's, Cranston took Rick with him and they hit the water with the barge a full hundred feet away.

That would have been a lot of leeway in an ordinary crash, but in this case it was slightly more than scant. Instead of merely crashing, the speedboat exploded with a terrific blast as it struck the barge and the whole center of the barge disappeared with it.

The bow of the speedboat had been filled with a high explosive, converting it into a veritable warhead. Anyone who had stayed with it until the last moment would have gone to oblivion along with the vanished craft!

CHAPTER XVIII
CHINESE MAGIC

THAT narrow squeak from absolute disaster was a more than gentle reminder to Lamont Cranston that Chicago wasn't a very safe place for him to show himself. After he had hauled Inspector Smedley ashore with a sidearm rescue stroke, Cranston went to find some dry clothes and promptly did another disappearance, leaving Rick to handle the tag ends.

Cranston reappeared in time to ride out to Longwood with Smedley in Gail Tyburn's car. Chaffin proved to be an excellent chauffeur, while Gail made chatty company. It was dusk when they rode through the big gates of Tyburn's estate, where two rugged men, Webster, the gatekeeper, and Morse, the gardener, were posted like two big watchdogs, checking on all comers.

"That trip was safe enough," avowed Rick, when he and Cranston had alighted to stroll the great lawn. "I figured it would be. Halifax wouldn't have planted an infernal machine in his girlfriend's car."

"If Gail is still his girlfriend," returned Cranston. "He's a great switcher, you know. I suppose our ride proves that Halifax still loves Gail or wants to pretend so. Or maybe Chaffin is just safer to ride with than Skip Hagathorn."

"I wouldn't say so. It was my fault that we almost hit that barge. When Skip said to go left around the breakwater, he meant go around the left end of it and look to the right, which would be natural. But we were already going toward the right end, so I turned left around it instead. What's more, I looked the wrong way. Skip explained my mistake, afterward."

Cranston was watching the guests arrive and spread about the lawn. There were tables where bottles of soda and spring water cost a dollar and a half, while ice was a dollar for a small cardboard bucket. Guests brought their own liquor, for Longwood was a dry town. There were small tents and pavilions where roulette and dice wheels were in operation and the proceeds of the games, like those of the refreshments, were all going to charity.

Among the guests, Cranston saw a considerable sprinkling of men who looked like Chicago plainclothes men. There were others, a trifle on the sportier side, who were obviously private detectives, assisting Regan, who was all about the place. Neither Lester Tyburn nor Inspector Smedley intended to take any chances on crime rearing its ugly head.

"I've put a general flyer out for Halifax," Smedley told Cranston. "There's only one place he won't be picked up and that's here. I just want to make sure he shows, that's all. I'm not making any accusations until after I've tracked down his gang, but that won't take long. Whenever Halifax starts out with a show, he hires back a lot of his old help and those are the guys I'm looking for. I got lists of them from some theatrical agents who used to send expense money to bring them on. If any have been in Chicago lately, they will be the boys I want."

THE guests were walking in from the gate, a few hundred yards away, as all cars except those bound on special business, had to be parked outside. A cluster of people were very interested in two new arrivals who wore Chinese costumes and were bowing as they walked along. One was Chung Loo, the other Verity Joyce, in her Chinese makeup. Either Verity didn't want to be recognized, or she thought that there would be no dressing room facilities at Longwood. However, that had all been arranged. Meeting the two foreign-looking arrivals, Gail Tyburn escorted them into the big mansion, where the ground floor rooms had been made ready for the party.

Lester Tyburn arrived with Skip Hagathorn. They had come up from Chicago in the cabin cruiser.

Sending Skip to join Chaffin and help tend the gate, Tyburn suggested a stroll in the Oriental garden, which lay just past a special stage that had been erected in one corner of the lawn.

By then, dusk had settled. Caterers were beginning to serve refreshments at long tables on the lawn. Lights were glowing in many colors from wires strung among the trees, forming an effect as brilliant as the firefly illusion performed by Chung Loo. Here, however, in the garden, Chinese lanterns were the theme. They cast a mellow glow in the canal that ran beneath a quaintly curved bridge near a miniature golden pagoda. Looking along the canal, Cranston could see the curve where it joined a stream that flowed between deep banks, out beneath the barbwire fence that barred the outer world.

"I've brought the necklace," Tyburn told Smedley and Cranston. He held the necklace into the light and its diamonds magnified the dull reflection into a thousand sparkles. "Gail was right, a replica would be recognized in these surroundings. After all, I bought it for her to wear on suitable occasions and I suppose this is one of them. But I only want her to wear it until after the show, so I'll speak to her about it then. When the guests begin drinking and playing those games heavy— well, that's when anything may happen."

"I'll be around," promised Rick, "and my men will be ready."

"Halifax isn't going to show," added Tyburn. "Gail just told me she hired a Chinese magician instead. That means Halifax won't be here—"

"Who says John Halifax won't be here?" came a cheery interruption. "Wherever there is magic, there you will find John Halifax."

It was Halifax in person, smart in white evening clothes. At sight of Halifax's gleaming smile, Tyburn remembered the diamond necklace and hastily pocketed it, but left an end in sight. Shaking hands with Cranston, whom he had met, Halifax looked at Rick Smedley as though wondering who he might be.

Cranston introduced the Chicago inspector.

"Nice to know you, Inspector," said Halifax. "I may be needing you if my luck gives out. Do you know, I was thinking of buying a car and a truck. When I went around yesterday, the car had been stolen and the truck was wrecked with its trailer. Tonight, I heard that a speedboat blew up, the very one that I intended to buy.

"If things like that happen after I buy anything, I'll look you up, Inspector. Right now, I'll leave you"—he gestured over toward the portable stage—"because the show is about to start. I want to see this Chinese, Chung something-or-other, and wish him luck."

The stage lights had been turned on; the orchestra was tuning up. Halifax went around behind the stage, while Tyburn hurriedly found Gail and gave her the necklace. By then, Cranston and Smedley had joined the audience. All this happened in some three or four minutes. Then the show began.

Chung Loo had changed his routine tonight. He was working more deliberately, interspersing his novelties with standard Chinese magic. In fact, he was holding back some of his best stunts for the finish, such as his juggling feats. More bland than ever, he relaxed occasionally to put mimicry into the broad smile that graced his lips alone. Verity, looking one hundred percent Chinese, was assisting Chung Loo very gracefully.

Near the end of his act, Chung Loo introduced a very special number. He brought on a huge brass pistol, definitely a Chinese model, and asked for the loan of something valuable. Gail Tyburn, playing queen bee in the front row, promptly arose, detached her necklace and dangled it in the footlights where everyone could get the full effect of its dazzle. Taking the necklace, Chung Loo poured it into the gun muzzle, added some powder and wadding, then pointed the gun at a toy pagoda that Verity was holding above her head.

The gun boomed, the pagoda dropped open. Inside was another, then a third. When the final pagoda was opened, Chung Loo reached into it and brought out the necklace, which he returned to Gail with a profound bow, while the audience applauded. Taking both the gun and the little pagodas, Verity toddled off the stage.

"Say, that was something!" said Rick to Cranston. "It looked about impossible. I've seen a lot of stalling with tricks like that, but not with this one, there wasn't."

Cranston didn't reply. He was no longer around. Skirting the audience, Cranston was going toward the car where he had left his portfolio. There, totally unnoticed, he changed to the black garb of The Shadow. Chung Loo was doing some artful jugglery, cutting an apple in the air with a tossed knife, while Verity stood by. But even if the audience hadn't been watching Chung Loo, they would not have seen The Shadow. He was doing an amazing glide across a lighted stretch beside some trees, his form seemingly no more than the wavering shadow cast by the gently swaying boughs. Noiselessly ascending some steps, The Shadow found a curtained booth that proved to be an improvised dressing room used by Verity Joyce.

There, beside the mirror of a dressing table, lay the diamond necklace. It could have been a duplicate, of course, because even Chung Loo, the Chinese wizard, couldn't actually have made one thing be in two places simultaneously. But The

Shadow, from his own knowledge of ways magical, felt positive that this was not the duplicate. Near it lay the brass pistol, and the real necklace had actually gone into that gun.

Picking up the necklace, The Shadow raised it to the light, watching the mirror to note how effectively the sparkle was reflected. That look into the mirror proved fortunate. There, The Shadow saw more than the necklace. Beyond his own reflection, he saw that of Verity Joyce, in her Chinese garb and makeup, hand raised and holding the sharp knife that Chung Loo had just used in his juggling trick.

The point of the knife was poised just above The Shadow's shoulders, ready for a downward stab!

Death could have followed The Shadow's slightest move, so strained was Verity's pose. Slight moves, however, were not part of The Shadow's system in circumstances such as this. Without an instant's hesitation, he whirled full about, speeding a clamping fist to Verity's wrist before the girl could do no more than recoil. If she'd intended to turn that back step into a driving thrust, she never had the chance.

Out from the light of the dressing room, down the steps and to the darkness behind the backdrop of the stage, The Shadow carried Verity as she struggled. Already he had taken away the knife and now had it entangled with the necklace. He was also stifling any cries that Verity might have given, but now, away from interference, he was willing to let the girl talk.

Verity's gasp came defiantly:

"You... you murderer!"

The Shadow whispered a laugh that was anything but murderous. Nevertheless, Verity held to her opinion.

"I saw you over by the Planetarium," she said. "I know you must be working with Cranston. You were around at the Hotel Harbison, too, after I took the crystal skull that Cranston wanted. You may even be Cranston, though perhaps you're not. Anyway, I saw the tricks he performed, my uncle's tricks!"

The Shadow's tone came sibilant:

"Your uncle, then, was Professor Sedley Marsh."

"You know it as well as I do," retorted Verity. "Why else would you suppose that I was performing some tricks of his?"

"Perhaps Cranston was performing them for the same reason."

"You mean to contact my uncle's pupils?"

"That was his reason."

Even in the gloom, The Shadow could see furrows beneath the makeup on Verity's forehead. Then the girl said:

"But before my uncle died, in a Canadian sanitarium, he sent me a letter, like the others."

"And the letters said—"

"Nothing. They were merely empty envelopes. That was the agreement. But they were mailed from here in Chicago."

"And that meant—"

"That all were to come here. They were to find the crystal skull and speak to it, telling who they were and how they could be reached."

"And the skull was supposed to speak to you—"

"Yes." Verity was still responding to The Shadow's phrases, as they came in a compelling monotone. "But something must have gone wrong. The skull would not speak. So all I could do was try to find someone who knew what had happened."

"Someone like Chung Loo—"

"Yes. I trusted him instead of Cranston. Both were doing my uncle's magic, but Chung Loo contacted me. I felt that one might be a friend, the other a killer. Perhaps both were friends or maybe from what you tell me, I had twisted them about. But when I saw you in the dressing room, just now, taking the necklace—"

"You thought that I must be an enemy. This, however, happens to be the real necklace."

"I know. Chung Loo told me he was to keep it. That made me trust him all the more, because he didn't have to tell me. He said it was all arranged and I began to think that soon he would confide in me on other matters. I'll tell you more, whatever I learn later. But now"—Verity turned a troubled glance toward the stage—"you must let me return. Chung Loo will need me as soon as he finishes his juggling."

Releasing Verity, The Shadow kept the necklace. As the girl went up the steps to the stage, The Shadow sidled around toward the front. From a shaded spot, half protected by a tree, he saw Chung Loo reaching the finale of his juggling routine. The Chinese wizard had scooped up three taborets and was starting to toss them in the air.

Then came an interruption. Up from the audience bounded Rick Smedley, pulling a revolver as he came.

"Stop this show!" the inspector was shouting. "Stop it, in the name of the law! I want you for murder, Chung Loo!"

CHAPTER XIX
TRAILS REVERSED

WITH a great bound, Chung Loo sprang to the far side of the stage and over the footlights to the ground. Rick Smedley was shooting at the fleeing Chinese wizard, but the flying taborets acted like a moving target in a shooting gallery. Rick's bullets caught them in midair, splintering them in telltale fashion.

Rick had recognized those taborets as duplicates

of the frail stool that he had broken at Corland's. There was enough of the unusual in Chung Loo's magic to link it with the fabled methods of Professor Marsh. And now, to support the sudden theory that Rick had formed, namely that Chung Loo was the spider in a web of crime, Lester Tyburn was leaping to the other corner of the stage, waving a necklace that didn't glitter as it should, while he shouted to the audience:

"This necklace! It's false! Chung Loo has stolen the real one. Capture him while I see if I can find the other one."

Tyburn ducked away, on his side of the stage, as though fearful that Chung Loo might return some of Smedley's shots, which would have put Tyburn directly in line. Chung Loo, however, was not pausing in flight. Skirting the lawn, where Chicago detectives and private dicks were weeding themselves from spectators who were listed in the Social Register, Chung Loo sped for the intricate paths of the Oriental garden. At least a dozen pursuers immediately formed a cordon to surround him, while others threaded after Chung Loo through the maze.

The Shadow was among those who reached the garden, where the subdued lights of the Chinese lanterns aided his gliding progress. All along, The Shadow could hear shouts from here and there, as Chung Loo appeared suddenly from some new quarter. Unfortunately, The Shadow was blocked off by a huge ornamental Chinese gate at the time the climax came.

On one of the humped bridges, Chung Loo ran squarely into Regan; turned and darted the other way again, as the squatty operative shouted:

"Stop him if you can, but don't worry if he gets away! I can tell you all about him. He's—"

Darting down the bridge as he shouted, Regan was stopped short by a blast that sounded like a miniature of the motorboat explosion. It came, though, in the form of a gunshot, with all the volume of an ancient blunderbuss. Regan caved face forward on the bridge; as he rolled down it, the weapon itself was flung beside him. It was the brass pistol that Chung Loo had used in the necklace act.

Chung Loo, himself, was dodging away from the shrubbery at the end of the bridge. Springing for him was Tyburn, who grabbed him but lost his grip on the magician's silk robe. Stumbling, Tyburn sprawled headlong across the path of Rick Smedley, who was cutting in from another direction. Chung Loo, darting off at another angle, skirted a lily pond while his two pursuers were getting to their feet. Then, as men headed toward him from the other direction, Chung Loo sprang off through an ornamental Chinese archway.

The Shadow was coming around beside the gate.

He saw three men converging on the archway, with Smedley and Tyburn coming through from the other side. In the midst of it all, Chung Loo was gone. There was a clump of shrubbery near, but it was less than waist high and men were cutting in between the bushes without encountering the missing Chinese.

It was as if Chung Loo had dissolved into nothing. They gathered around, Tyburn, Smedley and the others, to shake their heads in baffled fashion. Among the arrivals was Halifax, staring about as puzzled as the rest. Deciding that he should be with them, The Shadow took off his cloak and hat, bundled them inconspicuously under one arm and joined the group.

They were going back to look at Regan's body. One full charge from that huge Chinese gun had been enough. Regan was dead, killed instantly. Rick Smedley picked up the pistol as evidence against Chung Loo and shouted for men to keep searching the garden until they trapped the missing Chinese. The others, meanwhile—Cranston, Smedley and Halifax—started back across the humped bridge to the great lawn.

There they found Gail Tyburn, in the midst of a circle of sympathetic guests. But Lester Tyburn saw no point in humoring his wife.

"Fifty thousand dollars, that necklace cost," stormed Tyburn, "and you hand it over to a Chinese magician who gives you a phony instead."

"But it was my necklace," protested Gail. "I had a right—"

"Your necklace!" interrupted Tyburn. "It was bought with my money, wasn't it? This is worse than when you ordered all those antiques that you never even looked at."

"We've argued about that before," protested Gail. "I told you I know nothing about those antiques. They came while I was away."

"They were ordered in your name and they are still up in the attic."

"You never received any bills for the antiques. If you had, you certainly would have shown them to me."

"I'll get the bills, eventually," said Tyburn, in a resigned tone. "I always do. Perhaps in this case, you bought that junk with some of the money I've been giving you."

"You mean my so-called allowance?" demanded Gail. "It isn't enough to buy false whiskers for that comic opera detective that you've hired to keep annoying me—"

"Don't speak of Regan that way," interrupted Tyburn, his face going solemn. "He's lying over there in the garden dead, poor fellow. All because he was doing his duty, Gail, trying to regain your stolen necklace."

Gail began to sob and Halifax promptly played the big-brother act so she could rest her head on his shoulder. They started to walk away and Cranston could hear Gail's choky words:

"If he hadn't chided me... about those antiques! I... I don't know a thing about them. They were sent here and I said to let them come and take them away again, only they didn't. But they haven't cost Lester a cent—"

Soothingly, Halifax was urging Gail to tell him all about it, right from the beginning.

Meanwhile, Rick Smedley had arrived to talk to Tyburn. This gave Cranston a chance to step up to the stage and find something lying by the footlights. He turned, displaying a sparkling object which had actually come from his own pocket.

"Here's the necklace, Tyburn," called Cranston. "How it landed here, I couldn't say, but it looks like the genuine one."

When Lester Tyburn hurried over, Cranston handed him the necklace so that he could show it to Rick Smedley. That gave Cranston his chance to go around the stage, switch back to his guise of The Shadow and find Verity Joyce. The girl was in the improvised dressing room, hurriedly taking off her Chinese makeup.

"What's happened?" asked Verity anxiously. "They didn't catch up with Chung Loo?"

"They will soon," replied The Shadow, grimly, "or something pretty close to it."

A shout came from out front and The Shadow wheeled to peer through the curtains. He saw a man running from the garden, carrying a Chinese robe, a wig, and an object that looked like a deflated mask. Other searchers were following, all shouting the news.

"We found these under a bayberry bush!"

"The outfit Chung Loo was wearing, mask and all."

"The mask is a regular false face, with the mouth missing. The mustaches hid the joint!"

"That's why Chung Loo could smile and make his face look real."

"He's a fake, but one thing is certain, he's a magician."

"Find the Chinese girl who worked with him!"

"That's an idea. She can tell us all about him. Anyway she was his accomplice!"

Even before those final words were spoken, The Shadow knew that they were coming. He was back in the dressing room, giving Verity a hand at getting off her Chinese robe, which was as tight fitting as an evening gown. Footsteps were pounding upon the stage as Verity scrambled into her own dress; then, while she was still tangled in its folds, The Shadow literally whirled her to the space behind the stage and down the steps. Getting Verity

into the Tyburn limousine, The Shadow left her there, bundled his cloak and hat beneath a bumperette and strolled back as Cranston to the scene of the excitement.

Rick Smedley was pumping questions at Lester Tyburn.

"Remember what Regan shouted just before Chung Loo shot him? Something he could tell us about Chung Loo? Didn't Regan mention anything about it to you?"

"Regan mentioned a lot of things," replied Tyburn, patiently, "but most of them meant nothing. You will recall how I told him not to bother with so much detail. I have his report here, though. I always file them, even though I don't read them."

Pulling out a sheaf of onionskin paper, Tyburn began thumbing through its pages. Suddenly, he stopped.

"This is odd," said Tyburn. "Twice, when Regan was trailing Halifax, there was a complete break in the trail. He says check back to the phone call from John Halifax to Verity Joyce." Tyburn thumbed the pages. "Now jump ahead to Chung Loo—"

Pausing as he reached the proper page, Tyburn lifted his gray-streaked eyebrows.

"This explains it, inspector," said Tyburn, in a surprised tone. "There wasn't any Chung Loo. That we know. But Regan says that whenever Halifax's trail ended, Chung Loo's began. He got back stage, found a combination wig and mask, a zipper robe, all fixed for a quick change. John Halifax and Chung Loo are one and the same!"

Rick Smedley had figured that already. Somebody must have played Chung Loo and whoever did must have been a magician. That accounted for Halifax being here, as well as his willingness to let this fancy, high-priced date go to Chung Loo. Now all Rick had to do was find Halifax.

That wasn't easy. When Rick looked over to where Halifax had been sympathizing with Gail, he saw the blond Mrs. Tyburn standing alone beneath a weeping willow tree. Out in the driveway, a caterer's truck suddenly roared off down the driveway and, as it flashed past, Rick recognized Halifax at the wheel. Rick shouted madly, but not loudly enough. His voice couldn't be heard out at the gate, where that truck would certainly be allowed to pass.

"Get other cars!" bawled Rick. "Go after him! We'll send out a general alarm and cover every road for miles around. We won't let that guy get away!"

There was a brief flurry of new excitement as some detectives came from back stage bringing Verity's Chinese attire, but Rick Smedley was too busy with the Halifax matter to give attention to this lesser discovery. Cranston, however, saw well enough ahead to know that Verity Joyce would soon be in the fugitive class along with John Halifax. Strolling over to the big car, Cranston saw Chaffin nearby and beckoned for the sleek chauffeur to take the wheel.

"Mrs. Tyburn said we could use the car," explained Cranston, calmly. "You can bring it back shortly."

Chaffin drove them out through the gate and Cranston explained things to Verity as they rode along.

"Halifax will be back," assured Cranston. "To begin with, he can't get far away. Again, he has plenty at stake here."

"You mean Mrs. Tyburn's diamond necklace."

"More than that. He's after a lead to your uncle's legacy and I'm sure he thinks he can find it at the mansion."

"Then we must come back here, too!"

"Exactly," said Cranston with a nod. They were past the gates now, riding down a back road. "I'll take you back, now that we're beginning to understand each other."

Cranston might have mentioned that The Shadow had been the person who arranged that understanding, but he left it to Verity to form that conclusion for herself. They swung a corner, passing the caterer's truck, ditched beside the road and Cranston gave a slight laugh, quite unlike The Shadow's.

"The police will think that Halifax picked up another car," remarked Cranston. "But we can count on Johnny to outguess them. It doesn't matter, since he won't be outguessing us."

Cranston stopped the car near the half dozen buildings that formed the center of Longwood; told Chaffin he could return to the Tyburn estate. Stepping behind the limousine before it pulled away, Cranston reclaimed cloak and hat from beneath the bumperette without letting Verity see him do it. Keeping the bundle on the far side, Cranston conducted Verity down a rustic path to a small boathouse. There they stepped into a rowboat and Cranston poked the bundle into the bow.

To Verity's surprise, Cranston rowed away from the lake, back inland toward the Tyburn estate. They came to a huge barbwire fence, but Verity noticed that the banks of the stream cut deep beneath it; in fact, the fence was a few feet above their heads as they drifted under. Then, with muffled oars, Cranston worked the boat into a canal that proved to be the one in Tyburn's Oriental garden.

They could hear men patrolling the road outside the picket fence. Rick Smedley had called for the state police to take over that job. But inside the grounds, all was quiet and unwatched. Whether John Halifax had returned by the water route, or slipped through the gate while pursuers were crowding out through it, Verity couldn't guess, but she was sure that Halifax was smart enough to work it either way.

Softly, Cranston told Verity to steal toward the mansion, that he would attend to the boat. Following orders, Verity found a figure awaiting her there, against the whiteness of the mansion's pillars. Cranston had made a rapid shortcut to the mansion without Verity realizing it. The waiting figure was that of The Shadow.

The big front door was open, as it had been at the time of the party. Using a flashlight guardedly, The Shadow conducted Verity to the second floor. There they found an unlocked door, with a stairway to the third. At the top, another short flight, again unbarred, took them to the attic that Lester Tyburn had mentioned.

The attic was filled with partly opened boxes and among them, a man in shirt sleeves was working busily. The attic had no windows, so he had been free to turn on some electric lights. They were in operation, because Gail Tyburn had arranged for electricity to illuminate the grounds for the lawn party.

It wasn't difficult to recognize the man who was working at the boxes, even though he was out of character. The face that the arrivals saw still wore its never-failing smile.

The Shadow was right when he said that John Halifax would return. Those boxes that he was unpacking contained the very things that would bring him. One glance at the objects that Halifax had unpacked told that these were the fabled treasures left by Verity's uncle, Professor Sedley Marsh!

CHAPTER XX
CRIME'S LAST STROKE

AMONG the items already uncovered by Halifax, were curious looking lamps, strangely shaped fish bowls, cages, frames and even a few cabinets, built tall and upright, mounted on platforms. They were the stupendous ideas of yesteryear, magical creations that had never been shown to the public and which, therefore, could still produce a sensation.

Doubtless, Professor Marsh had been impressed by such magic masters of the past as Kellar, Thurston and Raymond, the great American magicians of their day. Therefore, his mind had turned to stage illusions as well as smaller devices. There were many of the last-named items, however. Halifax was at present studying a carved hand that rested on a board, while beside him were miniature figures, one a Hindu holding a flute, another a Mediaeval archer gripping a crossbow, with a quiver of arrows at his side.

Both as Chung Loo and himself, John Halifax preferred stage work to close-up magic, thus he was totally wrapped in the prizes which he had uncovered. It would take something equally mysterious to jolt Halifax from his present mood, so The Shadow provided it: a low, sinister laugh that rose to a whispery crescendo, bringing ghoulish shivers echoing from the attic's rafters.

Halifax raised his face, smile and all. His right hand went toward where his coat pocket would be, if Halifax had still been wearing his coat. Then, seeing that The Shadow had drawn an automatic, trained full upon him, Halifax simply folded his arms and retained his smile.

One thing that put Halifax at ease was sight of Verity Joyce. Almost ignoring The Shadow, the smiling magician bowed to the girl and said:

"I am glad you are here. These are your uncle's properties. I wanted you to claim them."

A whisper from The Shadow signaled that Verity was to question Halifax on that score.

"You were one of my uncle's pupils?" queried Verity.

"No," replied Halifax. "His pupils never took up magic professionally. In fact, they seldom associated with magicians at all. So I wouldn't be their type."

"How did you find out about them?"

"Through rumor, inquiry, and finally, luck."

"What sort of luck?"

Halifax studied Verity narrowly, then let his gaze flicker toward The Shadow. Meeting a pair of burning eyes, Halifax came right to the point.

"Everybody who tried to check on Professor Marsh thought in terms of small magic only," declared Halifax. "I decided that anyone so inventive as Sedley Marsh must have had big ideas, too. So I looked for persons who might have bigger stuff that looked like Marsh magic. I found such a man here in Chicago, an antique dealer named Paul Corland."

Halifax paused to note the effect on the listeners. Verity remained poker-faced; The Shadow's eyes still retained their cryptic burn.

"Corland had some unusual apparatus that he claimed was real Chinese," continued Halifax. "I knew otherwise but did not say so. When Corland finally sold me those items, I was sure that I had acquired some bona fide Marsh magic. One day I visited Corland and found him repairing a crystal skull in his shop. The skull couldn't be Chinese, so I was sure about my Marsh theory.

"I stayed around Chicago, hoping to find Professor Marsh. I figured that his pupils wouldn't want the larger apparatus. Corland looked like the exception, but he had lost his interest. Meanwhile, I had met Gail Tyburn. In fact, she looked me up in Hollywood. She had learned how wonderful I was through mutual friends and naturally I didn't try to disillusion her. She'd left her husband and besides, I wasn't serious about her. I wanted a sponsor in Chicago."

"A sponsor?" echoed Verity.

"As good a name for it as any," replied Halifax. "I had to be financed while I tracked down the Marsh secrets. I plan to pay back all the money I owe Gail. But when the suicide wave began, I became worried."

"And why?" asked Verity.

"Corland had shut up like a clam," answered Halifax. "Besides, I saw the crystal skull down at the Hotel Harbison. I asked Gail to buy it and we framed a clever way to get it by proxy. I wanted to find out how it operated and why, but somebody grabbed it ahead of me."

Halifax's eyes shifted to The Shadow. Though he still smiled, Halifax was delivering what amounted to a look of accusation. Then:

"It was wild, perhaps," said Halifax, "to hook the suicide wave with Marsh's pupils. But I decided to perform what Marsh magic I had, on the chance that some of them, if desperate, would contact me. I appeared as Chung Loo to keep my identity secret, so I could dodge any danger. I found that a chap named Cranston was also doing Marsh magic and figured he was playing a game similar to mine.

"Also, I saw your work, Miss Joyce. I'd heard once that Professor Marsh had a niece, his only living relative. I phoned you, saying I was Chung Loo. Regan was just dumb enough to think I'd called you as John Halifax, because he saw me leaving for the Mirror Grill, where you went later. That was why he was the only person who guessed my dual identity."

A whispered laugh came from The Shadow and Halifax promptly caught its significance. Still smiling, he bowed.

"I mean Regan was the only dumb person who guessed that I was Chung Loo," corrected Halifax. "Anyway, I don't suppose you guessed, Mr. Shadow. Probably you just knew."

Then, concentrating upon Verity, Halifax said steadily:

"I followed Cranston from the Mirror Grill to protect him. I took him for a Marsh pupil, who must be in danger. You followed him because you mistook him for a murderer. That was why I snatched the gun from your hand in the Planetarium. I recognized it as a dummy after I grabbed it. I had to take a clout at Cranston to quiet everything, because I was afraid the place was full of killers."

Verity's lips tightened. Halifax was correct about the opinion she had held of Cranston. It gave Halifax's whole tale the ring of truth. To dispute that point, Verity tried a few more questions:

"Why did you try to steal Gail Tyburn's necklace?"

"I didn't," replied Halifax. "I needed money and she hadn't any more. The necklace was the answer, so I told her to see Chung Loo. When I met her as Chung Loo, I told her who I really was. I thought that would fool Regan. Anyway, Gail gave me the replica and talked her husband into letting her wear the original. That was so she could lend it to Chung Loo and get the imitation back."

"But when Regan started to spoil your game, you killed him!"

"With that brass Chinese gun? Impossible! You're the person who should know that, Miss Joyce. You took the gun to your dressing room on the right side of the stage. When Smedley came after me, I jumped from the left, to head for the garden. I never had a chance to get back to the stage as Chung Loo. Somebody else fired that shot, somebody close by me in the garden."

That ended Verity's questions, but Halifax had more to tell.

"I bought these taborets from Corland," declared Halifax, "and they were all he had. Somebody must have planted another in his place to frame me. Tonight, when Lester Tyburn began telling Gail about antiques she had bought, I realized that Corland might have been keeping Marsh's equipment and could have shipped it here. I was right; here it is." Halifax turned to gesture about the room. "Some of it was already set up, like this big frame." With that, Halifax took a few side paces and stepped forward through a full-length metal frame that was riveted to the floor. "I must admit, it puzzled me a trifle, finding some of the apparatus set up. Particularly a frame"—Halifax let his smile go slightly sour—"because if anybody was framed, I was."

Something singular was occurring in back of Halifax. As he stepped forward, his figure seemed to form a double image. It couldn't be the lights in this room; recognizing that it wasn't an illusion, The Shadow veered sideward, then forward with his gun, too late.

By the time he'd got out of line with Halifax, The Shadow saw that the figure behind the smiling magician had risen to full height from a fast-operating elevator in the floor. As Halifax wheeled, he saw it, too, and so did Verity. Behind the frame, wearing a leer that made Halifax's smile seem as mild as a Mona Lisa painting, stood Lester Tyburn, also with folded arms.

There was a difference, however, between the poses of Tyburn and Halifax. Poked from each of Tyburn's cross-draped hands was a glittering revolver.

"Framed is right," taunted Tyburn. "You are all framed. Even I am framed, but in a way I like. A sheet of bulletproof glass rose with me in this metal frame, when I came up through the floor. If you want to test it, Shadow, you are welcome."

Tyburn's tone rang with a peculiar echo, proving

that a glass did partially block his voice. Instead of falling for Tyburn's invitation, The Shadow swung full about, aiming both of his automatics toward the attic's open door. He was just in time to cover a group of men who were moving in with guns while Tyburn tried to draw attention in the other direction.

The group consisted of Webster, Morse and Chaffin, the watchdogs of these premises. They were backed by Skip Hagathorn. Given a few seconds more, they would have assumed control, but The Shadow had caught them flat-footed in what amounted to a stalemate.

It was The Shadow's challenging laugh that held them. If The Shadow had opened fire, they would have spurted bullets in return. With Tyburn ready to spring to action behind him, The Shadow would have had to wheel among the boxes, leaving Verity and Halifax helpless in the line of fire. As it now stood, though the murder crew knew that they might win through force of numbers, none was willing to be the first to taste the leaden slugs from The Shadow's big guns.

With the echoes of The Shadow's laugh, there came a spasm of ugly mirth from Tyburn.

"Suppose we hold matters in abeyance," suggested Tyburn, in his ringing tone, "while you tell us, Shadow, how much you really know."

Somewhat to Tyburn's surprise, The Shadow accepted the challenge.

"You played the alibi business too heavily, Tyburn," declared The Shadow, still facing the men at the door. "You phoned here to Longwood from your apartment soon after Skip Hagathorn jumped off the bridge, playing he was William Brett, and joined these others when they faked a rescue act from the tugboat *Bluebird*. Nobody answered that call. You simply faked it."

"And that," retorted Tyburn, "would be difficult to prove."

"When Fleer died," continued The Shadow, "you were out here at Longwood, Tyburn. You phoned stating that your hired men were also here. There was only your word to prove it." The Shadow paused a moment.

"My word is still good," asserted Tyburn.

"You used Inspector Smedley as a stooge," continued The Shadow, "the night you sent this band of killers in to murder Corland. They established his death at nine forty-five, the time it actually happened."

"I thought that one out carefully," came Tyburn's ringing voice.

"When they returned here," added The Shadow, "you promptly sent them on another job, directed at a man named Lamont Cranston. You kept Inspector Smedley out at a roadhouse until you were sure they were back home again."

"And that," claimed Tyburn, "was the neatest touch of all."

"It was the giveaway," returned The Shadow, "because it ended on the lakeshore. It proved conclusively that your crew was using a super speedboat to cut the time of their trips in half. They couldn't have got away from the beach by the Planetarium in any other fashion. The alibis are ruined, because the time element no longer stands."

The men at the door shifted uneasily and Tyburn saw it. Before Tyburn could decide what to say, The Shadow spoke:

"Your own predicament is worse, Tyburn. You have no alibi at all for the time you tried to kill me in the cellar locker with the crystal skull. Tonight, when you killed Regan, you were the only man who could have loaded and taken that Chinese gun from the dressing room where Verity Joyce left it."

"Unless you took it, Shadow—"

"But nobody saw me go back stage, Tyburn."

"Somebody is going to find you here," snarled Tyburn. "This time you actually will be dead."

"It's lucky Lamont Cranston will still be alive" was The Shadow's answer. "You know, Tyburn, the alibis you fixed for your murder crew depend somewhat on him."

That was something Tyburn hadn't thought about, early in the game before he began to identify Cranston as The Shadow. The night of Brett's death was a particular case in point. The men at the door knew it and began exchanging glances among themselves.

"You're bluffing, Shadow," declared Tyburn, savagely. "My methods have been too well geared. I happened to be a Marsh pupil myself. In fact, I could show you a few tricks if my hands were not so full of guns. I wanted all this wealth of inventive genius for myself"—Halifax and Verity watched Tyburn unfold his arms and wave his gunhands to indicate the paraphernalia on display—"and I ferreted out Corland before Halifax did.

"I discovered that Marsh was ill in Canada. I opened an account for my wife in Corland's antique shop. I bought some odd items and stopped by one day to tell Corland how my wife frequently bought crates filled with antiques and stored them in the attic without ever looking at them. It gave him the idea of a good place to send the crates that Marsh had left with him. I was worrying Corland with anonymous calls that made him think someone was after the professor's stuff." Tyburn chuckled, harshly. "And someone was. Myself."

The men at the door were showing signs of their former bravado; nevertheless, The Shadow waited for Tyburn to conclude his tale.

"Corland decided to change the keyword that would make the skull speak," declared Tyburn. "Instead of the word 'skull' he used 'Yorick.' He mailed a letter to Professor Marsh, telling him of the change and I intercepted it."

"That's why my uncle never sent me word!" exclaimed Verity. "I wondered why the skull didn't speak. But it must have spoken for you"—she was facing Tyburn defiantly—"you... you murderer!"

Tyburn accepted the compliment with a bow. Then Verity riveted as she heard The Shadow's whisper, so low that no one else could catch it.

"Those little figures," said The Shadow. "The musician and the archer. They have names—"

"Yes," undertoned Verity. "One is Hassan, the other is Athelstane."

"Ask Tyburn if he ever heard of them," whispered The Shadow. "Ask him very loudly. He can't hear well through that glass."

"Tell me, Mr. Tyburn," called Verity in a defiant tone. "Did you ever hear of Hassan and Athelstane?"

The little figures were beyond the big frame. Halifax had placed them there when he unpacked them. The Hindu musician sat near Tyburn's elbow, the mediaeval archer almost directly behind him. At the name "Hassan," the musician figure raised its flute. When Verity spoke "Athelstane" the little archer began to move.

"Those names mean nothing," declared Tyburn. "We shall end this travesty right now. The police will hear gunfire, when they arrive they will find three bullet-riddled bodies; those of Verity Joyce, John Halifax and a no longer mysterious character who calls himself The Shadow."

Tyburn finished with a mock bow that The Shadow could not see. Actually, it was a nod to the men at the door, for The Shadow watched their gun hands tighten.

Verity gave a quick undertone to The Shadow.

"Tyburn is pressing the glass with his gun muzzles," informed the girl. "I think it is moving downward, from the way the guns wave. I can't see the top edge, though."

As The Shadow whispered a slight laugh as though to say he had expected this to happen, the little figure called Hassan began to play its flute.

The balance between life and death hung thread-thin as Tyburn gave a sharp glance at the piping flute player. It was drawing his attention from Athelstane, the archer, behind him, but there was a chance that Tyburn might remember the cross-bowman and look around.

Instead, Tyburn pressed the floor with his foot. The figure of Hassan jogged slightly, for it was set a trifle over the edge of the elevator trap on which Tyburn stood. Thinking that a slight jar had set it off, Tyburn laughed.

"We have music with our murders," said Tyburn, his voice still carrying an echo. "Nice murders, these. The police will think that John Halifax killed Verity Joyce and then shot it out with The Shadow, who was coming to the rescue. We shall plant the right guns to prove our case."

Tyburn's guns were still pressing the glass, waiting for its invisible edge to pass them. While Hassan piped, the figure of Athelstane, hidden by Tyburn's body, was busily at work. From the quiver, the little archer was taking an arrow and attaching it to the crossbow. Slowly the mechanical hands were raising the bow to the level.

From his slight angle, Halifax could see all this and was on the alert. So was Tyburn, but his attitude was gloating.

"Too bad, Shadow." No longer did Tyburn's tone echo, for the bulletproof glass had slowly slid below his chin. "You will be found with bullets in your back. They will be mine unless you prefer to turn about and let my men provide them."

The Shadow began a slowly whispered laugh. It was rising as Tyburn's guns gave an upward jog, indicating that the edge of the glass had passed. Tyburn shouted two words:

"Give it!"

A trigger finger gave it. The mechanical finger that pressed the trigger of a miniature crossbow. An arrow was in flight as Tyburn shouted and the pointed missile found the murder master in the center of the back. Tyburn jolted upward as he fired both his guns. Their bullets ripped the ceiling.

Simultaneously, The Shadow's .45's thundered a more accurate message. They beat the men at the door to the punch, by instants. Expecting The Shadow to whirl, alarmed by Tyburn's sudden jolt, the members of the murder crew were belated in their fire. Their shots, too, went wide and high, for The Shadow was clipping them as they pulled their triggers. Flayed by repeated shots from the cloaked marksman, Tyburn's men spun toward the stairs and went diving, sprawling downward.

As Tyburn rallied from the arrow shot, Halifax met him with a dive across the sinking plate of glass. They spilled backward, upsetting the figure of Athelstane, while it was placing another arrow on the crossbow. Wrenching free, Tyburn rose to one knee and drilled a shot straight for the charging figure of The Shadow, whose own gun spoke only a split-second later.

Though Tyburn's shot was first, The Shadow's was the one that counted. Fired from a lower level, Tyburn's bullet flattened just under the edge of the sinking glass while The Shadow, aiming downward, cleared that edge with the slug that found Tyburn as its target. Rolling from Halifax's grasp, Tyburn spread-eagled motionless upon the floor.

Now Verity and Halifax were following The Shadow down the attic stairs, hurdling the sprawled men who lay there. Halifax nearly tripped over the writhing form of Skip Hagathorn, the speedboat pilot who had tried to frame him by planting an explosive charge in the bow of a boat that Halifax had tried out as a prospective buy. Of course, it would have gone harder with Lamont Cranston and Rick Smedley if Hagathorn's scheme had worked. Perhaps Skip would live to confess the crime and blame its inspiration on Lester Tyburn.

Police whistles were shrilling from the outer gate with answering blares along the barbwire fence, when The Shadow and his two companions reached the Oriental garden and found a speedboat moored in the deeper part of the canal. This was the getaway craft that Tyburn and his men had planned to use, the same boat that had whizzed murderers between Chicago and Longwood in twenty minutes flat. The Shadow motioned Halifax behind the wheel and thrust Verity in beside him.

As Halifax pressed the starter, the motor gave the quietest of purrs. The boat moved noiselessly down the canal, sneaking out beneath the Chinese bridges and the wire fence beyond. In a matter of mere minutes, it had reached the broad waters of Lake Michigan.

From back along the stream came the rising tone of a strange, weird laugh that reached a strident crescendo, then broke into shivery echoes. It was the triumph laugh of The Shadow, marking his victory over crime and accepting full credit for the scene that the police soon would find upstairs in the Tyburn mansion.

John Halifax gave the speedboat all that its accelerator would take. It roared along the moon-bathed waters of the lake, following the shoreline southward. As the dial climbed to the sixty-mile mark, Halifax felt a surge of his old nonchalance. He glanced at the girl beside him. Her black hair flowing free in the wind, the lake air bringing the flush to her cheeks, Verity Joyce looked like something that belonged with moonlight.

For a brief instant, Halifax's foot eased the accelerator pressure; then, remembering The Shadow's final laugh, Halifax again gunned the speedboat to the limit. The Shadow had timed one speedboat trip from Longwood to Chicago. He might be clocking this one, too.

There was no combination more fascinating than moonlight and a girl, but for once John Halifax, of all men, preferred speed and speed alone. Smiling John Halifax wasn't looking for an argument over any woman, and particularly Verity Joyce.

At least, not with The Shadow.

THE END

WALTER GIBSON'S MAGICAL JOURNEY by Will Murray

Walter B. Gibson first entered the wonderful world of magic in 1906.

"I was in Manchester, Vermont," he recalled, "and I went to a party where they gave you a string and you followed the string and found something at the end of it. I got a trick box at the end of my string, so I got interested in tricks there. *St. Nicholas* had some articles on magic too. In 1910 or 1911, I got a better trick box. By 1912 or 1913 I'd found a magic shop, so gradually I got more and more involved in it."

Magic inspired Gibson's earliest ambitions. In 1913, he visited an aunt who ran a business in Manhattan: "When she heard that I wanted to be a magician, she called the girls together and said, 'We've got a magician here. He's going to show us some magic.' I was sixteen years old. Well, I did my big act. I made a handkerchief vanish and did a couple of other tricks like that, and they were reasonably impressed.

"Then my aunt remembered a man who was now only working there part-time because he'd started working steadily doing magic shows at the Eden Musée, a famous waxworks museum on 23rd Street. It turned out to be Dunninger, the man who later became a famous mind reader. That was my first acquaintance with a real, professional magician." After showing him some new tricks, young Joseph Dunninger invited Gibson to his show. A lifelong friendship thus began.

But Gibson was only beginning. He soon got a taste of the life of a working performer. In 1914, while still in high school, he teamed up with Howard Rippey to do shows. With another friend, Howard Kenner, he went on to even bigger performances. Before long, Walter Gibson was a solo act, doing card magic, coin tricks, vanishes and other examples of close-up legerdemain.

"Magic was my hobby and I did a magic act as a specialty with the musical clubs when I was at Colgate (Class of 1920)."

Gibson's magical circle continued to expand. He joined the Society of American Magicians in 1919, receiving membership card #586 signed by SAM's then-president, Harry Houdini.

"I had been writing tricks for different magic magazines," Gibson remembered, "including *The*

Howard Thurston and Walter Gibson in 1922

Sphinx, which was published in Kansas City. When I wanted to join the Society of American Magicians, one of my sponsors was Oscar Teale, who later became Houdini's secretary. I met people like Houdini and Thurston when I went to meetings in New York."

The following year brought new magical connections. "When the opportunity came for me to perform illusions in a carnival—known as Ruppel's Greater Shows—I jumped at the opportunity and performed magic on a platform all around New Jersey and Long Island," The Shadow's raconteur explained.

Connections led to new conjurer contacts. Introduced to Harry Houdini in 1920, they became friendly.

"Houdini sprang to fame with the rise of Vaudeville around 1900," Gibson noted. "He set records with his handcuff escape act, doing two shows a day on the Keith and Orpheum Circuits. After World War I, Vaudeville became more sophisticated, but Houdini still was a headliner with his escape from a 'Water Torture Cell'... It was the most spectacular escape act ever performed."

Magically speaking, it was a time of transition, Gibson recalled: "Vaudeville was low-grade entertainment. After World War I, it began getting aristocratic. Houdini was no longer a big attraction. He never set box office records after 1910.... The theater business was changing, Vaudeville was declining, but Houdini made out all right over the long period."

Gibson's first published book was on the subject. *After Dinner Tricks* was issued by the Magic Company in 1921. It was an offshoot of his *Philadelphia Ledger* column of the same name. This led Gibson to performing magic over radio station WIP in 1923. His magical star continued rising. In 1925, Gibson opened a magic shop in Philadelphia with publisher Bill Kofoed of *Brief Stories* as backer. Although short-lived, the shop put him at the center of local magical activities.

"I spent one whole summer touring with Thurston's entourage of 30 performers," Gibson recounted. "I wrote books for the show, such as *200 Tricks You Can Do,* authored articles for *Boys' Life* and other publications, and helped him work on his autobiography."

Thurston's *My Life of Magic* was released in 1929. It was Walter Gibson's first significant work on magic.

This led to working with the renowned Harry Blackstone, Sr., whom Gibson met in 1929. For Blackstone, he ghosted *Blackstone's Annual of Magic* and *Blackstone's Magic: A Book of Mystery,* as well as articles in *Popular Mechanics* and *Seven Circles* which ran under the famous Blackstone byline.

Gibson continued to perform. A performance of the Hindu Wand Trick intrigued Houdini, who planned to add it to his repertoire. Tragically, Houdini died in October, 1926, the trick unperformed.

"In his estate," Gibson recounted, "they found trunk loads of material explaining his escapes. I then did two books, *Houdini's Magic* and *Houdini's Escapes.* I was just finishing that job when The Shadow started."

The year was 1931. After a short period editing *Tales of Magic and Mystery,* and contributing to *True Strange Stories* and *Ghost Stories,* Gibson began leaning toward mystery fiction as his next world to conquer.

"During my period of fact writing I dealt considerably with magic," he explained. "It was a hobby that I turned into a business sideline. I was completing the second volume of magical secrets from Houdini's notes at the time I turned to fiction. I applied much that I had learned about a magician's technique when I came to devise situations in mystery fiction. I think that every writer can work a hobby or adapt specialized knowledge to fiction uses."

Gibson hoped to break into the hardcover mystery field. Fate altered his plans in a strange way. "I had been planning a weird and mysterious character with magical ways of getting out of problems," he explained. "At the same time, Frank Blackwell, editor of *Detective Story Magazine,* was looking for a writer to bring to life a sinister radio voice then featured on *The Detective Story Hour.*"

Gibson was familiar with The Shadow's laugh. He first heard it coming out of a radio speaker in Thurston's Long Island home. They were planning a radio show built around Thurston's act. But by the time that project reached

the air, Gibson was too busy with The Shadow to be involved.

The Shadow Gibson developed for Street & Smith was a mysterioso solver of crimes, an ebony-cloaked master of detection and misdirection. Faceless and enigmatic, he mesmerized 1930s America.

Gibson was told to concoct a pen name for his first pulp novel, *The Living Shadow.* For inspiration, he consulted a list of dealers in magical paraphernalia. Two names stood out: U. F. Grant and Maxwell Holden. "The choice was apt, for Max Holden specialized in Hand Shadows, casting lifelike silhouettes on screens or walls, while Gen Grant, as we called him, was the inventor of 'Walking Away from a Shadow,' a baffling illusion performed by the great Blackstone," Gibson once revealed. "Since these were both devices that I intended to attribute to The Shadow as a means of baffling or intimidating crooks, I felt that the pen name of Maxwell Grant would be appropriate; so I appropriated it, with due respects to Maxwell Holden and U. F. Grant."

The name of The Shadow's most famous alter ego also had a magical link.

"In going through Houdini's notes on magic," Gibson revealed, "I had come across a name: Baillie Cranston. It belonged to a theater owner in Scotland, and the 'Cranston' sounded good, though 'Baillie' seemed wrong. So I went through the alphabet, seeking a name to match it. When I reached the letter *L,* I hit upon 'Lamont,' which was about perfect. It sounded like a family name, which it was; and at the time it seemed to symbolize travel and wealth and standing in the field of international finance."

The first issue of *The Shadow Magazine* sold out. He wrote three more. Gibson was just beginning his fifth, when the world of magic called him back.

"As I began working on it, I received a telegram from Blackstone, the magician, asking me to go to Bermuda for three weeks and handle publicity for his show while it was appearing there. I accepted the offer and while there, I divided my time between the theater and a hotel room where I knocked out the fifth Shadow story, *Gangdom's Doom.*"

Gibson went on to finish *Houdini's Magic* and ghost *Modern Card Tricks* for

Harry Blackstone checks out *The Bunco Book* as Sidney Radner and author Walter Gibson look on.

Blackstone. In Reading, Pennsylvania, Blackstone played the Rajah Theatre. "It was at the time of the bank closings in Philadelphia. The show was a record sellout. Blackstone was paid in cash, from the box office receipts. I rode to Philly with him, carrying $3,000 in cash. When we arrived, he cashed checks for all his friends. It made a good newspaper story—'Magician Produces Money.'"

The Depression was just settling in, but between The Shadow and stage magic, Gibson found himself pulled in two directions: "During that period, "I attended a magician's conclave in Michigan, did magic at a Lion's convention in Toronto, and traveled to Atlanta and New Orleans with the Great Raymond, doing publicity for his show."

Within a year, Walter Gibson found that *The Shadow* was overtaking his life. Publisher Street & Smith bumped the quarterly magazine to monthly, and in the autumn of 1932, to twice a month. Gibson was forced to abandon most of his magical activities.

Instead, he poured his knowledge of illusion and escape into the series. According to friend and fellow writer Richard Wormser, Gibson tried to get into the act himself:

> Once, after The Shadow was a success, he came into the office with a helpful suggestion. He had worked out some suction cups for his feet and hands; if [they] would give him the money to buy an outfit like The Shadow's—big black hat, black cape swirling to his ankles—he would, when he came to confer at Street & Smith, enter by the outside wall, human fly style, instead of coming by the elevator. It would be a good publicity stunt, Walt felt.

The idea proved unnecessary. *The Shadow Magazine* kept selling.

Surprisingly, the pseudonymous writer of The Shadow discovered that prestidigitation and pulp fiction were not so far apart after all.

When Street & Smith decided to launch *Crime Busters* in 1937, Gibson created another mysterious detective in a black cloak—Norgil the Magician.

"Norgil was modeled somewhat on an earlier Harry Blackstone; his was typical of the grand Vaudeville acts," Gibson revealed.

Bits of Dunninger, John Calvert and Russell Swan also went into the mix. "For Norgil," Gibson continued, "I took the prototype of a traveling magician who was playing Vaudeville or lesser shows. Often, he would book towns because there was some crime to be discovered there. Norgil would often do odd feats of magic. I tried to do anything that I could to twist in magic. Most magic stories that people write, they tried to make the magician a little bit fabulous. But I was telling what was going on backstage. I didn't give away too many of the tricks."

The same year The Shadow returned to radio with Orson Welles—himself an amateur conjuror—playing the dual role. The new version would ultimately run almost 18 years.

"All of the radio scripts were adapted from my novels," Gibson said. "But actually, because of my heavy use of magic and visual illusions the novels are ideally suited for movies or television."

Gibson continued to exploit magical tricks and devices in *The Shadow. Serpents of Siva* was inspired by the title for a Shadow radio script Edward Hale Bierstadt planned to write. Gibson used the title for a springboard and filled the story with magical lore from his vast personal fund.

In 1940, Street & Smith entered the new field of comic books. For Blackstone's theater shows, Gibson was scripting program books in comics format.

"Street and Smith were always thinking of doing new comics at that time," Gibson related. "So, the deal I proposed was this: The comics were selling for a dime and would they give Blackstone returns at five cents a piece? That meant that Blackstone could order a thousand a week, hold a matinee on Saturday and the theater would pay five cents.

"So I called Street and Smith and talked to William DeGrouchy: 'How many do you have to print to make a comic book go over?' He said: 'We could get by with 50,000 returns and stash 50,000 or so.' I said, 'Fine, I've got your 50,000 for a year. Blackstone will buy them at a nickel a piece. At cost.' 'Oh, boy!' he says. 'That's great! You can't lose.' So we made a deal right then.

"I took a drawing room on the day train from Boston to New York and knocked out the first script to *Super-Magician.*"

Super-Magic Comics #1 was a sellout. With the second issue, it was retitled *Super-Magician*. Every feature was devoted to magic or magicians. Its success backfired on Gibson and Blackstone, however.

"They sold that so fast and did so well with it that they couldn't supply Blackstone with the copies he wanted," Gibson explained. *Super-Magician Comics* ran six years. Gibson scripted other magician-themed comics, such as *Ghost Breakers,* featuring Bill Neff, another model for Norgil with whom he once worked.

"Bill Neff's company had two men, himself and three girls. I traveled with him briefly; he put on a popular midnight spook show. In his regular act, he'd do 30 or 40 minutes of magic, with some weird stuff such as burning a girl alive. He'd put her in a coffin-like thing and set it afire, and her arm would flop out. He'd put it back in, and at the end, there was a skeleton in there and its arm flopped out.

"For the spook show, the lights would be out and ghost-things would be flying around on fishing

Magician/mentalist Dunninger met The Shadow in *House of Ghosts*.

rods; balloons would shoot out; and puffed rice was thrown onto the audience like 'fairy fingers'—it felt like spiderwebs on your face."

Through all this, the friendship between Joe Dunninger and Walter Gibson continued. Gibson made the mentalist and ghost hunter a supporting character in *House of Ghosts*, a 1943 Shadow novel featuring a mysterious mansion in which almost anything might happen—and did. Gibson recalled:

> The occupants themselves were confident that the place was haunted, and the only person qualified to decide that question was the master ghost-hunter Joseph Dunninger, who had become Houdini's acknowledged successor as a debunker of fraudulent psychic phenomena. I had known Dunninger for thirty years and was working with him on various projects, so his entry into *House of Ghosts* as a "guest star" appealed to us both.

A fictitious pair of performing magicians, Val Varno and Glanville Frost, showed up in two post-war Shadow mysteries, *Murder by Magic* and *Crime Out of Mind*. According to these stories, Lamont Cranston belonged to a thinly disguised version of the Society of American Magicians called the United Wizards Association.

In 1946, Walter Gibson ran into contract problems with Street & Smith over The Shadow. Finishing up a last story, he walked away. Simultaneously, his 12-year marriage collapsed. He was despondent. Then came an offer to join Harry Blackstone on tour. The world of magic had reclaimed him.

"Blackstone covered more distance on that tour than any other magician had ever done...," Gibson related. "I did special publicity for him, stories. I also worked backstage at the show. Once in a while, if someone was laid up, I took over. There were eight girls and twelve or so others in the troupe. We had it all set up so that if anyone left, someone else could move up and fill in."

It was an exciting period in Walter Gibson's eventful life. "One time a group of us were on the road and the car ran out of gas," he recalled. "No one seemed to be able to flag down a passing car for aid. Blackstone, wanting to help, stepped into the road and began plucking cards out of the air. A car stopped and the driver leaned out and asked, 'Why, Blackstone, what are you doing here?' It was someone who had been to the show."

In 1948, Walter Gibson returned to The Shadow, replacing his own replacement, a writer-magician named Bruce Elliott. Inspired by his travels with Blackstone, Gibson laid his new stories in the American cities he had visited. Set in Chicago, *The Magigals Mystery* centered on a real life troupe of lady magicians similar to the woman Gibson was about to marry. Litzka Raymond was the widow of the Great Raymond.

"I met Raymond in 1931," Gibson noted. "Litzka was with him then. She'd married him several years before. She was a lot younger than he was, twenty years. He died about 1948, and Litzka and I were married a year or so later."

Gibson knew most of the great performing magicians of the 20th century. He appraised them from the viewpoint of an insider.

"I think Dunninger, as well as Kreskin today, have a good ability to play their hunches. Dunninger was remarkably gifted at following a person's eyes and guessing their thoughts by how they reacted. And he was also a good hypnotist. I think he did have the ability to get an audience concentrating so hard

Walter Gibson's future wife Litzka (center) performs the famous "trunk trick" with the Great Raymond.

that a mass state of partial hypnosis was induced and people actually became confused by what he said."

Houdini ranked surprisingly low.

"He was a good lecturer," Gibson allowed, "with a powerful physique and a strong personality, but his knowledge of magic was less than either Thurston or Blackstone."

Gibson considered Thurston to be "the greatest magician of his time... Thurston was so much bigger than Houdini there was no comparison.

"Thurston had a troupe of 30 people and carried around his equipment in two railroad cars," he explained. "It took six men just to lift one crate, and he had hundreds of crates. For example, a top magician might carry around seven different backdrops for the stage to create different settings."

From a start as a sleight of hand specialist, Howard Thurston grew to become a premier stage illusionist. "Not content with merely vanishing people—as many as half a dozen at a time—he also caused lions, tigers, pianos, horses and even automobiles to come and go before the eyes of astonished onlookers," Gibson wrote in *The Master Magicians.* "Thurston ranks high among the 'greats,' because his show, if not the best, was certainly the biggest ever seen in America."

Harry Blackstone occupied a special place in Walter's heart, one that was apart from his vaunted conjuring skills. Blackstone's offer to take Gibson on tour probably saved his life. Theirs was a true magical friendship.

"Billed as 'The Last of the Great Magicians,' Blackstone invited comparison with memories of Herrmann, Kellar and Thurston," Gibson wrote in *Conjurers' Magazine.* "The reception he received in Philadelphia, where both Herrman and Kellar once owned their own theaters and Thurston was always popular, proved again that Blackstone and Magic are synonymous terms in the public mind."

But he held the Great Raymond in the highest esteem. "With the rapid expansion of steamship and railroad transportation in the early 1990s," Gibson explained, "it became possible to carry a full-sized magic show anywhere in the world, and the man who first turned this into a full-time opportunity was a young magician named Raymond. As a globe-trotter, he set the standard for a generation that was to follow, and wherever these newcomers went, they found the name of the Great Raymond

established as a master of modern magic.

"Raymond's program was so diversified that he could switch to any form of mystification; handcuffs, mind reading, hypnotism or straight magic.... Where magic is concerned, Raymond was indeed 'King of the World.'"

Gibson was fortunate to have lived during the Golden Age of Stage Magic—a world that became extinct with the postwar decline in stage performance venues.

"Early magicians depended a lot on trapdoors and a variety of other stagecrafts," he noted. "These devices were available when theater was still a major force, but are not so today.... They were virtually the entire show for two and a half hours. They often performed as many as 50 tricks and were on stage the entire time.

"But that is not to say that today's magicians are bad," he averred. "I think Mark Wilson, who used to perform in the *Pillsbury Magic Circus* and is now very successful in nightclubs, is one of the best magicians I have ever seen."

Gibson outlived virtually of all his magical contemporaries.

"Dunninger was rather aloof from other magicians, like Houdini," he mused. "Just before he died, the magicians decided to confer upon him the distinction of Master Magician at the Magic Castle out in Hollywood. Dunninger wasn't well enough to make the trip, so I made it instead; I accepted the award for him. Two days later—I was still there—he died. It was as if he'd been waiting until he got the award. I caught the next plane back and officiated at his funeral service."

In 1979, the Academy of Magical Arts awarded Walter B. Gibson a Masters Fellowship in recognition for his lifetime of magical works.

Of all the masters of magic with whom Walter B. Gibson was associated, the most astounding was the one he developed—the man of many faces known as The Shadow. A mysterious figure who dressed in an operatic black cloak and slouch hat—which he wore over elegant evening clothes—the Master of Darkness might have been a sinister version of a stage illusionist, who brandished twin .45s in lieu of a conjuror's wand!

"I never could imagine him doing a show," Gibson quipped. "Although I said to my wife the other day, maybe we should put out a book with The Shadow doing card tricks!" •

Walter Gibson had little to do with The Shadow *radio series. However, even the radio Lamont Cranston was drawn into the world of prestidigitation in "Death Comes to the Magician," a script by* The Shadow*'s most-prolific radio scriptwriter. Sidney Slon developed the radio character of Cranston's cabby Shrevvy (based on Gibson's pulp character, Moe Shrevnitz), but his most important contribution to the series was in the magical casting of his high school friend, Bret Morrison, who succeeded Bill Johnstone in the title role in 1943 and was the voice of The Shadow for more than a decade. "Death Comes to the Magician" was first broadcast October 4, 1942, and the script was reprised March 19, 1950 as "The Curse of the Great Nirvan." Neither broadcast is known to survive in recorded form.*

THE SHADOW
"DEATH COMES TO THE MAGICIAN"
by Sidney Slon

(MUSIC: "SPINNING WHEEL" - FADE UNDER)

SHADOW: (FILTER) Who knows what evil lurks in the hearts of men? The SHADOW knows. (LAUGHS)

(MUSIC UP…SEGUE BRIGHT THEME)

ANNR: Once again your neighborhood 'blue coal' dealer brings you the thrilling adventures of the SHADOW…the hard and relentless fight of one man against the forces of evil. These dramatizations are designed to demonstrate forcibly to old and young alike that crime does not pay.

ANNR: The Shadow, Lamont Cranston, a man of wealth, a student of science, and a master of other people's minds, devotes his life to righting wrongs, protecting the innocent, and punishing the guilty. Using advanced methods that may ultimately become available to all law enforcement agencies, Cranston is known to the underworld as The Shadow; never seen, only heard—as haunting to superstitious minds as a ghost; as inevitable as a guilty conscience.

(MUSIC UP AND OUT)

SHADOW: This is the tale of a magician's curse, and a feat of necromancy that leads in Kabalistic circles. This is the story of a magician whose conjurations had only been surpassed by that last great and final mystery known to man by the name…DEATH. Listen now as… "Death Comes to the Magician"!

MUSIC: CRASHES IN WITH HIGH WEIRD SPIRALING CHORD. ENDING ON A DISCORDANT PITCH)

HINDU: (ACCENT…AGE FIFTY-FIVE) (SUBDUED) Doctor…my master, how is he?

DOCTOR: Your master, Dham, is dying.

HINDU: No…no…he will not die…the great Nirvan will not die…he knows the secret of death…

DOCTOR: This is one secret even the Great Nirvan cannot solve, Dham. You had better go in to him, if you want to see him alive.

Bill Johnstone as The Shadow

HINDU: Yes, Doctor...I will go to him...but you will see you are wrong...Nirvan will conquer death.

(DOOR OPENS AND CLOSES)

NIRVAN: (OFF...HOARSE AND GRATING) Who is that? Who's there?

HINDU: (OK) It is I, Master. Dham, your humble servant.

NIRVAN: (FADES IN) Dham...come here...come here...I must speak with you...yes...yes...

HINDU: I am at your bedside, oh Great One.

NIRVAN: Good...good...listen carefully...there is not much time left. Tell me...have you obeyed my orders...have all my wishes been carried out?

HINDU: Have you forgotten so soon, my master? It was just this afternoon that the legal one was here...You commanded him to dispose of your property...it is all written down in your will!

NIRVAN: (LAUGHS WEAKLY) Yes, now I recall...this afternoon it was...My three tricks... (LAUGHS)...my three great illusions which no other magician can duplicate...will ever duplicate... When I am gone there will never be another to equal me...the Great Nirvan...

HINDU: You must not excite yourself, my master!

NIRVAN: NO, when I die...there will never be another. You see, Dham...I willed my "fire and sword" trick to Arturo, and to Bennington I leave my "Labyrinth of Sorcery" trick, but my greatest invention...my wall of glass and water"...

(LAUGHS INTO COUGHING)

HINDU: Please my master...

NIRVAN: ...That I will take to my grave. Then they will never be able to say...that any magician is as great as the Great Nirvan! (LAUGHS INTO COUGHING AGAIN)

HINDU: You must be quiet, oh Great One...it is the doctor's orders.

NIRVAN: Very well, I shall be quiet...now I am ready for death...Tell me, Dham...must the great Nirvan die alone? Have they all forgotten me?

HINDU: For two days, my master, many people have waited in the street outside the door. Many important people have requested admittance, but the doctor has refused.

NIRVAN: (PLEASED) Many have waited?

HINDU: You will not be quickly forgotten, my master...

NIRVAN: No...no...I will not be forgotten...

HINDU: One who waited has been more insistent than the rest...

NIRVAN: Who? Tell me who? No... no...don't bother...I know who it is...

(DOOR CLOSES OFF MIKE)

LORENZ: It is...Lorenz!

NIRVAN: You! Get out...get out, I say! I don't want to see you!

LORENZ: No? (FADES IN) But *I* want to see *you,* Nirvan! I must ask you something...

NIRVAN: How did you get into my house?

LORENZ: (LAUGH MALICIOUSLY) Is that a question for one magician to ask another?

HINDU: You must leave! As you may observe, my master is very ill.

LORENZ: Oh, I'll leave all right, after I've gotten what I came for...

NIRVAN: You want my three great tricks, don't you? Well, you'll never get them! Two I have willed to Arturo and Bennington...One to each of them...

LORENZ: And the third, Nirvan...the "glass and water" trick...

NIRVAN: That one. Lorenz, I take with me to my grave...

LORENZ: (PLEADING) No, you can't do that...you mustn't. You are great...you will always be known as the Great Nirvan...why must you be so jealous of your fame? Give me the third trick!

NIRVAN: No.

LORENZ: After all, I have earned it! Next to you I am called the greatest magician in the world...

NIRVAN: Self-named!

LORENZ: I see it all now...you've been afraid of me! I've come up too rapidly...I've even challenged your position as number one!

NIRVAN: You've stolen every one of my feats of magic...that is how you have come up, but three you will not have!

LORENZ: Very well, Nirvan....I will discover the secret of your tricks without your aid!

NIRVAN: Never!

LORENZ: (LAUGHS) Never? Well, "great" Nirvan, in exactly one year from tonight, I will perform your secret feats of magic for a select audience. Then I shall be acclaimed the greatest in the world! And you will not be able to stop me!

NIRVAN: (THREATENINGLY...SPEAKING WITH EFFORT) Listen to me, Lorenz! Listen to me well! I am versed in the arts of black magic!

LORENZ: (INSULTINGLY) Do you take me for a child, Nirvan? With all this gibberish about black magic?

NIRVAN: It is the truth! (COUGHS) I am dying...and I know it...but if you perform my great "glass and water" trick...if you even attempt it...I shall return from the dead and strike every memory from your brain!

LORENZ: (LAUGHS) (CONTINUES UNDER FOLLOWING)

NIRVAN: (RAGING) Stop! Stop that laughter! (TRYING TO RISE UP IN BED) Stop, I say! STOP! (LAUGHTER STOPS) (SLOWLY) I curse you, Lorenz...I curse you...may your mind be seized by rot...and all your efforts crowned by black failure...may you kill all you hold dear!

              (COUGHING FIT SEIZES HIM) (HE FALLS BACK ON THE BED)

HINDU: Master! Master!

NIRVAN: Water...wa....(STOPS)

HINDU: What is it? Speak, oh Great One...speak!

LORENZ: (QUIETLY) Your master will speak no more...the Great Nirvan is dead. (STRANGELY EXULTANT) The Great Nirvan is dead! Long live the Great Lorenz! (LAUGHS)

              (MUSIC TAKES IT AWAY)

WESTON: Of course, this whole business is ridiculous. I don't know whether to be insulted, or amused at being invited to the "Great Lorenz's" special performance.

CRANSTON: Well, personally, Commissioner, I'd be neither...I'd be interested...very much interested!

MARGOT: And just a little bit scared, Commissioner. Just think, Lorenz is defying the deathbed curse of the magician Nirvan and is going to perform his three great tricks!

WESTON: Miss Lane, it's just a publicity stunt...deathbed curse...bah!

CRANSTON: (LAUGHS) Maybe not, Commissioner. You know these magicians take themselves pretty seriously.

WESTON: Well, I don't, Cranston. Mr. Lorenz won't get me into the theater tonight.

CRANSTON: He may at that, Commissioner. I've got a hunch that something rather unusual is going to occur tonight.

MARGOT: You really think so, Lamont?

CRANSTON: Never can tell, Margot. Just look at the setup...Lorenz cursed by the Great Nirvan is going to perform Nirvan's feats of magic, in Nirvan's own theatrer...on the anniversary of his death.

WESTON: Humph! Nirvan's own theatre which he stipulated was to be closed and draped in mourning for him for a whole year. If this isn't a press agent's dream, I never saw one.

CRANSTON: Well, Commissioner, Margot and I are going, aren't we?

MARGOT: We are?

WESTON: Well, you'll go without me! I'd get more excitement out of a good Western story. That hocus-pocus gives me a good swift headache.

MARGOT: Oh, come along, Commissioner.

WESTON: Miss Lane, Cranston, this is definite…I am not going!

(MUSIC)

(SLIGHT BUZZ OF CONVERSATION AS IN THEATRE)

USHER: The fourth, fifth and sixth seats in this aisle, sir.

CRANSTON: Thank you.

MARGOT: You go in first, Lamont. I'll sit between you and Commissioner Weston. Is that all right, Commissioner?

WESTON: Humph!. Hocus Pocus, that's what it is…just a lot of hocus pocus publicity!

CRANSTON: (LAUGHS) Well, you can still go home and curl up with a good Western story, Commissioner.

WESTON: Yeah? Well, maybe it's not a bad idea…

MARGOT: Go on, Lamont…let's sit down.

CRANSTON: Right, Margot…(FADES SLIGHTLY) May we get through, please…Thank you…

(AD LIB GETTING SEATED)

MARGOT: We didn't get here a minute too soon, Lamont…the lights are dimming down…

WESTON: It's a darn good book, too…called *Pinto Pete Prepares.*

MARGOT: What does he prepare?

WESTON: How should I know? I haven't read it yet…thanks to you two!

CRANSTON: Sh…the curtains are parting…

(APPLAUSE FROM SMALL AUDIENCE)

LORENZ: Ladies and gentlemen… (OFF MIKE AND PROJECTING)

WESTON: (MUMBLING) It's a good story all right. Cardona says it about the best…

MARGOT: Commissioner…you're disturbing the people around us.

WESTON: Eh? Oh, yes…sorry…

LORENZ: (OFF) I shall not bore you with a long introductory address.

WESTON: (MUMBLES) Glad to hear that…

LORENZ: (FADE IN SLOWLY) I'm sure you all know pretty well my purpose in giving this performance. It is, in a sense, a challenge…a challenge made by the Great Nirvan on his deathbed…a curse that was a challenge to me. Tonight, I am going to perform all three of Nirvan's greatest illusions. I am defying him to return from the dead and punish me as he promised. (LAUGHS) You need have no fear that this will occur, ladies and gentlemen. In spite of his unquestionably great powers, the Great Nirvan will not solve the mystery of death…not tonight. Well, to begin. I call my two colleagues Arturo and Bennington to witness my performance. Will you both come on stage, please? Are they in the house?

(STIR IN AUDIENCE… SLIGHT BUZZ)

ARTURO: (OFF) Here. We're here.

LORENZ: Will you come up on stage please?

BENNINGTON: (OFF BUT CLOSER) (SARCASTICALLY) It will be a pleasure, Lorenz.

LORENZ: Thank you. Right up those stairs on the left there.

(FOOTSTEPS ON STAIRS)

LORENZ: And now, ladies and gentlemen, the famous "Fire and Sword" trick.

MUSIC: (UP FOR A FEW SECONDS) (INTO)

              (APPLAUSE)

LORENZ: Thank you… thank you.

              (APPLAUSE SUBSIDES)

LORENZ: Well, Arturo…Is that your "Labyrinth of Sorcery" illusion?

ARTURO: Yes, that is it.

LORENZ: And you, Bennington…did I perform the trick left to you by Nirvan, properly? The "Fire and Sword"?

BENNINGTON: (ANNOYED) Yes…yes…May I go now?

LORENZ: Not yet, my friend, not yet. You must also witness Nirvan's greatest feat…his famous "Glass and Water" trick…the secret of which Nirvan thought he had taken to his grave with him. But what man conceives…man can duplicate…now, ladies and gentlemen…the…

HINDU: (OFF) No…no…no…you dare not attempt that feat!

              (AD LIB SURPRISE FROM AUDIENCE)

LORENZ: (QUIETING AUDIENCE) Ladies and gentlemen…please…there is no need to be upset. It seems that the Great Nirvan's servant Dham has come to my performance after all…in spite of his reluctance to… (LAUGHS) see me destroyed by his master's curse.

HINDU: (FADING IN) Please, please…I begged you not to test the power of Nirvan's curse…Lorenz…I have come to make a last appeal to you!

LORENZ: You cannot stop me from going through with my plans, Dham.

HINDU: Then you are doomed…Nirvan will make you pay for your temerity.

LORENZ: I doubt that, Dham…but we are keeping my audience waiting. (CALLS) Open the curtains…

              (SOUND OF CURTAINS SLIDING ASIDE)

HINDU: (FADES) I will not wait…I cannot see you defy my master!

LORENZ: Very well. Ladies and gentlemen, I shall describe the great "Glass and Water" illusion for those of you who may never have seen Nirvan perform it. You see before you a huge glass tank filled with water… (STIRS WATER) the purpose of the trick is to pass through the tank…through the glass and water…emerging on the other side without breaking the glass or getting wet. These screens (FADES) will be placed on both sides of the tank. I will enter one side and will emerge on the other. (CONTINUED IN B.G.)

WESTON: (SOTTO VOCE…CUE) How does he do it…trapdoors in the stage?

CRANSTON: Stage is covered with a heavy canvas ground cloth, Commissioner. Trapdoors wouldn't help.

MARGOT: Lamont, I'm…kind of…worried…

WESTON: Say, you know…this is rather exciting…

MARGOT: Do you think that Nirvan's curse…

LORENZ: (OFF…CALLING) Are Commissioner Weston and Mr. Cranston in the house?

WESTON: (STARTLED) Eh? What? Did he mention my name?

CRANSTON: (LAUGHS) Yes, Commissioner. (CALLS) We're right here, Lorenz.

LORENZ: Oh, yes, Mr. Cranston, would you and Commissioner Weston be so kind as to assist me in this performance?

CRANSTON: (CALLS) Certainly, Lorenz. Come on, Commissioner.

WESTON: Me, too? Say, what is this?

MARGOT: (LAUGHS) Go on, Commissioner, it's your big chance to get on the stage.

CRANSTON: (LAUGHS) Not worried, are you, Commissioner?

WESTON: (ANNOYED) Worried? Who me? Say, it'll take more than this monkey business to worry me. Let's go.

LORENZ: (FADE IN) And now, ladies and gentlemen, Mr. Cranston and Commissioner Weston will be so kind as to manacle my hands and feet. You see, I want experts at this sort of thing...(LAUGHS) Will you examine the chains and handcuffs, gentlemen?

WESTON: (FADE IN) Be glad to...glad to... (RATTLE CHAINS) Hmm...they look solid enough. What do you think, Cranston?

CRANSTON: I agree, Commissioner.

LORENZ: Then will you lock me into them, please?

CRANSTON: Certainly. Give me a hand, Commissioner.

WESTON: Right.

               (RATTLE OF CHAINS AND CLICK OF LOCK)

LORENZ: Now, ladies and gentlemen, we have here on stage four eminent witnesses...Arturo, Bennington, Commissioner. Weston and Lamont Cranston. Will you gentlemen be so kind as to pull the screens around me? I will attempt to pass through the tank and emerge on the other side behind those screens there. Now, the screens...

               (SOUND OF SCREENS BEING PULLED AROUND)

ARTURO: Are you ready, Lorenz?

LORENZ: (BEHIND SCREENS) Ready. Start counting. By ten I shall have passed through the glass and water.

ARTURO: Very well. One...two...three...four...five...six...seven...eight...nine...

LORENZ: (BEHIND: SCREENS) (SCREAMS IN MORTAL TERROR)

               (AD LIB FROM AUDIENCE)

WESTON: What happened?

CRANSTON: (EXCITED) Give me a hand with the screens!

               (SCREENS PULLED BACK)

WESTON: Good heavens!

CRANSTON: He's gone...disappeared!

BENNINGTON: Nirvan's curse!

               (OFF MIKE AS THOUGH IT WERE COMING FROM SOMEWHERE IN THE DARK BALCONY OF THE THEATER...THE SOUND OF WEIRD DIABOLICAL LAUGHTER.)
               (MUSIC)

CRANSTON: You know, Margot, it's enough to make one believe in black magic. I don't know how Lorenz could have gotten off this stage without our seeing him.

MARGOT: I don't either, Lamont...and I...I don't like it. Let's get out of this theater...this place gives me the creeps.

CRANSTON: Wait till Weston gets back from his tour of inspection. He's got his men searching this theater from top to bottom.

WESTON: (OFF) (FADES IN) Cardona, I want you to get the names and addresses of everyone who attended the performance tonight and investigate them.

CARDONA: Right, Chief.

CRANSTON: There he is, Margot. (CALLS) Commissioner, did you find anything?

WESTON: Not a trace. That man Lorenz seems to have vanished into thin air.

CARDONA: We found a trapdoor under the stage, Mr. Cranston. My theory is that Lorenz escaped that way.

WESTON: But, Cardona, this big glass tank rests right over the trapdoor...It would be useless.

CRANSTON: And not only that, Commissioner, this heavy canvas ground cloth covering the stage would prevent Lorenz from using it.

WESTON: (SIGHS) Well, I don't mind admitting that this stunt has got me licked! What do you suppose happened to Lorenz?

MARGOT: I know it sounds rather silly, but do you suppose he's actually been made to disappear by Nirvan's curse?

CRANSTON: Can't say I blame you for thinking that, Margot…but I am beginning to see another motive in this whole business.

WESTON: What?

CRANSTON: Commissioner, who would stand to gain most by Lorenz's disappearance?

WESTON: Gain most?…

CRANSTON: Two men were ruined professionally here tonight by Lorenz's performance.

WESTON: (REALIZING) Why, Arturo, and Bennington…Lorenz did their tricks…

MARGOT: Oh, I see…do you think they'd try to get rid of him?

CRANSTON: They might, to protect themselves.

WESTON: Cranston, I think you've got something there! We're going to have a little talk with Arturo and Bennington!

(MUSIC)

(SOUND OF CAR RUNNING…BREAKS TO A STOP)

CARDONA: (SLIGHTLY OFF) This is Arturo's house, Commissioner.

WESTON: Okay, let's go in. Coming, Cranston?

CRANSTON: Right, Commissioner. Margot?

MARGOT: Have I ever refused?

CRANSTON: (LAUGHS) Can't say you have. Let's go.

(CAR DOOR OPENS)

WESTON: Wait here for us, Cardona.

CARDONA: Right, Chief.

(FOOTSTEPS ON GRAVEL WALK)

MARGOT: Gloomy looking old place, isn't it?

CRANSTON: Just the place you'd expect a magician would live in.

WESTON: Careful of the stairs, it's pretty dark…

(FOOTSTEPS UPSTAIRS) (THEN STOP)

CRANSTON: Here's the bell. Should we let him know we're coming?

WESTON: Why not? We've got nothing on him, yet. Ring it.

(BELL IS HEARD RINGING OFF MIKE)

(PAUSE)

Bill Johnstone in 1938

MARGOT: Maybe he isn't home yet.

CRANSTON: I can see a light in one of the back rooms through this window.

WESTON: Ring the bell again!

(BELL RINGS AGAIN)

CRANSTON: Guess, Margot, you were right about there being no one home…hello…what's this?

WESTON: What?

CRANSTON: The door's slightly open.

(CREAK OF DOOR SWINGING OPEN)

WESTON: Hmmn, that's strange…let's go in…

(FOLLOWING SCENE SOTTO VOICE)

(FOOTSTEPS ON WOOD ALONG CORRIDOR)

MARGOT: (WHISPERING) Doesn't seem to be anybody here…

CRANSTON: Let's take a look in that room with the light on!

WESTON: Fine thing for the commissioner of police to be doing…housebreaking!

CRANSTON: Here it is…

(OPENS DOOR)

MARGOT: I don't see anything out of pl… (SCREAMS) Oh…

CRANSTON: Don't look, Margot!

WESTON: Cranston, he's dead! Think it's suicide?

Kenny Delmar gives voice to Commissioner Weston opposite Marjorie Anderson as Margot.

CRANSTON: Can't tell, yet, Commissioner…help me cut his body down from that beam.

WESTON: Yes.

(SOUND OF CUTTING THROUGH TAUT ROPE) (BODY FALLS)

CRANSTON: Now, let's have a look at him. (PAUSE) Commissioner, Arturo has been murdered.

WESTON: Now, the question is, who hanged him?

(DOOR CLOSES OFF…SOFTLY)

CRANSTON: The door! Commissioner, I think we're going to have the answer to your question. Someone has just come in…Put out the lights in here!

(CLICK OF SWITCH)

Stand over here, Margot…Commissioner, you and I behind this door…now quiet…

(FOOTSTEPS APPROACH SLOWLY …UNCERTAINLY…)
(THEN DOOR OF ROOM CREAKS OPEN)

CRANSTON: Now, Commissioner! (STRUGGLE)

WESTON: I've got him, Cranston! Put on the lights!

(CLICK OF SWITCH)

CRANSTON: (SURPRISED) It's Dham…Nirvan's Hindu servant!

WESTON: And the man we're looking for! You murdered Arturo, didn't you?

HINDU: Murdered? No, I came to warn him of his danger…It is the truth…I swear it…

WESTON: Danger from whom?

HINDU: That I may not say.

WESTON: "May not say," eh? Well, I'll tell it…danger from you! You murdered him and were coming back to rob him!

CRANSTON: I don't know about that, Commissioner. If that's the case, why didn't he rob Arturo before…when he murdered him?

WESTON: I don't know, Cranston, but I'm going to find out…at headquarters! C'mon you! (FADES) Right this way!

HINDU: (FADES) But I am innocent…I know nothing of this…

(DOOR CLOSES AND CUTS OFF SPEECHES OF WESTON AND HINDU)

MARGOT: Are you going to police headquarters, Lamont?

CRANSTON: Yes, Margot, The Shadow would like to question Nirvan's servant. I have a theory that only he can give the correct answers to this mystery.

(MUSIC)

WESTON: Okay, Cardona, lock him up…maybe he'll speak after he's had a chance to think things over.

CARDONA: Right, Commissioner.

(CLANK OF JAIL DOOR CLOSING)

WESTON: (FADING) Let's go, Cardona…we'll talk to you in the morning.

HINDU: I will not speak…I am innocent… innocent!

(PAUSE)

SHADOW: (LAUGHS) Innocent? Dham?

HINDU: Who calls my name? I see no one!

SHADOW: It is The Shadow, Dham!

HINDU: Shadow? I have heard of you in my own land… they speak of the unseen one called Shadow. What do you want of me, unseen one?

SHADOW: Are you guilty of Arturo's murder?

HINDU: No…no…I came to warn him of his danger!

SHADOW: How did you know he was in danger?

HINDU: I know…

SHADOW: You are protecting someone, aren't you?

HINDU: I will not answer.

SHADOW: Your refusal tells me a great deal, Dham! It will go easier with you, if you make a clean breast of it!

HINDU: I will not betray, even if I myself am betrayed. I am guilty of betrayal once…I will not be guilty twice.

SHADOW: Very well, Dham…you've made your choice. Remember, The Shadow has ways of finding the truth!

(MUSIC)

WESTON: And that's the way the whole thing stacks up, Cranston…Miss Lane. We've gotten exactly nowhere. Lorenz disappeared into the blue…Arturo murdered…

MARGOT: You've got the Hindu servant, Commissioner.

WESTON: What good is that? We'll have to let him go today. We haven't enough evidence on him to bring him to trial.

CRANSTON: If only we could find Lorenz.

WESTON: Yes, "if"!

CRANSTON: What about Bennington…the other magician?

WESTON: Questioned him…he has an airtight alibi. He was with friends.

CRANSTON: Then finding Lorenz is our only chance of breaking this case.

WESTON: Hah! Fine chance! I'm almost ready to believe that he actually did vanish into thin air. I don't think we'll ever find him.

(KNOCK ON THE DOOR)

WESTON: (CALLS) Come in! (DOOR OPENS)

CARDONA: Sorry to bother you, Chief, but…

WE5TON: Didn't I tell you I wasn't to be disturbed unless it was very important, Cardona? Now, get out and…

CARDONA: But this *is*. important, Chief!

WESTON: What is it?

CARDONA: We've got him!

CRANSTON: Got who, Cardona? Arturo's murderer?

CARDONA: No! We've found Lorenz!

WESTON: You've found Lorenz? … Send him in! Well, don't stand there! Send him in!

CARDONA: Right, Commissioner. (TURNS HEAD) Come in, Lorenz!

             (FOOTSTEPS COME IN AND STOP)

CRANSTON: No doubt about it…it's Lorenz, all right.

WESTON: Where were you? What happened to you? (PAUSE) Why don't you speak, man?

CARDONA: He's not able to, Commissioner. There's something wrong with him.

WESTON: What? What are you talking about?

CRANSTON: Cardona seems to be correct, Commissioner…look at his eyes…

MARGOT: He looks like a walking dead man.

WESTON: Good Lord…that's right…

CRANSTON: (SLOWLY) I don't think he'll be able to give us much help, Commissioner…it appears that Nirvan's curse has been fulfilled!

             (MUSIC)

MARGOT: But, Lamont, you don't believe in black magic. How do you explain all this? How could Nirvan's curse come true to strike all memory from Lorenz's mind?

CRANSTON: I don't know, Margot. There are times when even the most rational mind will seek explanation in the art of black magic. However, I went down to Nirvan's theater today to have another look around…and I think I'm catching on to the trick…

MARGOT: The "Glass and the Water" trick?

CRANSTON: Yes. You see, the place was left just as it was the night Lorenz attempted…

             (BELL RINGS)

MARGOT: Now, who can that be?

CRANSTON: (LAUGHS FADES) I know a good way to find out.

             (DOOR OPENS)

CRANSTON: (SURPRISED) Dham?

HINDU: Come quickly…come…

CRANSTON: What? Where?

HINDU: Sahib, would prevent another death?

CRANSTON: Who's in danger?

HINDU: Bennington…he will die before this hour is out, unless you prevent it!

             (MUSIC)

             (CAR COMES TO STOP)

HINDU: We stop here.

MARGOT: But isn't this…where Arturo lived?

HINDU: Bennington is here.

             (CAR DOOR OPENS)

CRANSTON: You'd better wait here in the car for us, Margot.

HINDU: Sahib, there is more danger for her here…than inside with us…

Bret Morrison and Gertrude Warner costarred when this script was reprised in 1950 as "The Curse of the Great Nirvan."

MARGOT: Let me come along, Lamont.

CRANSTON: Very well...let's hurry...

(RUNNING FOOTSTEPS ON GRAVEL THEN UPSTAIRS)

HINDU: The door is open!

(DOOR CREAKS OPEN)

CRANSTON: Where is Bennington?

HINDU: He is waiting for you in the study.

(FOOTSTEPS ALONG CORRIDOR)

CRANSTON: Open the door of the study, Dham.

(DOOR OPENS SLOWLY)

CRANSTON: Go in. Now, switch on the lights.

(CLICK OF SWITCH)

"Death Comes to the Magician" was scripted by Sidney Slon, *The Shadow's* **most prolific radiowriter.**

MARGOT: Lamont! Look!

CRANSTON: Yes, we've gotten here too late, Margot. Bennington is dead!

(DOOR SLAMS SHUT BEHIND THEM)

LORENZ: I should say just in time, Mr. Cranston...Miss Lane...

CRANSTON: Lorenz!

LORENZ: Just in time for your own funerals... (LAUGHS)

MARGOT: Then you weren't struck dumb by Nirvan's curse! You were just pretending!

LORENZ: My performance was quite good...don't you think?

CRANSTON: What is your purpose in bringing us here, Lorenz?

LORENZ: To kill you both, Mr. Cranston.

MARGOT: Why? What have we done to you?

LORENZ: Let us call it a form of protection, Miss Lane. Now, you know definitely that I murdered both Arturo and Bennington here.

MARGOT: But we didn't know...

LORENZ: I am afraid that our friend, Mr. Cranston, knows something even more vital to me...the secret of the "glass and water" trick. Yes, Mr. Cranston, I was in the theater this morning while you were examining the apparatus used in that feat of magic.

CRANSTON: And you would commit murder for that?

LORENZ: Yes, Mr. Cranston, murder is a strange thing...it is difficult the first time...easier the second...after that it is quite simple. And I have so much at stake. Now, I am in complete and absolute possession of all three great tricks...I am the greatest magician in the world...only you two stand in my way. But not for long. Dham, prepare...

CRANSTON: (SUDDENLY) You're not going to get us without a struggle, Lorenz! I...

(TRAPDOOR OPENS AND LAMONT FALLS THROUGH BODY HITS BOTTOM)

MARGOT: Lamont!

LORENZ: (LAUGHS) (CALLING DOWN TO HIM IN PIT) You see, Mr. Cranston, I knew you would try that...that is why I had the trapdoor ready for you...

MARGOT: (ON) Lamont! You've killed him!

LORENZ: (SLIGHTLY OFF) No, Miss Lane, I think the fall into the pit has just knocked him unconscious. Dham and I will attend to him later... (FADES OUT SLOWLY PACING LINES) but now, I think we shall attend to you!

MARGOT: (SCREAMS)

(MUSIC)

LORENZ: (FADE IN LAUGHING) Our friend, Miss Lane, seems to have fainted, Dham. Too bad, we must kill her and dispose of her body. Would you suggest a shallow grave with quicklime, Dham, or do you think the furnace over there will do a thorough job? Well? I'm asking you your opinion!

HINDU: I have no appetite for this, Sahib...I am sick of this killing. I knew nothing of the Arturo's murder till after it happened—I tried to warn him—

LORENZ: You're not backing out now, are you? You're in too deep!

HINDU: I will have no more to do with it... I am going...

LORENZ: To the police?

HINDU: No...I will not betray you.

LORENZ: Suppose I make sure of that!

(GUNSHOT)

HINDU: (GROANS) (BODY FALLS)

LORENZ: There! Now, I am safe forever...nothing can touch me. As for you, Miss Lane, I think the pit of quicklime is more efficient. (LIFTS HER) UH...Now to...

SHADOW: (LAUGHS) There is one to stop you, Lorenz!

LORENZ: (TERROR) Wha......that voice...who said that? I can't see you!

SHADOW: It is the voice of The Shadow, Lorenz!

LORENZ: No...no...I know who you are...you are Nirvan! You've come back! (HYSTERICAL) Please, please forgive me...I...bribed your servant to get your feats of magic...I confess everything...don't hurt me...stay away from me.

SHADOW: You've been evil...and you must pay for your crimes!

LORENZ: I.confess everything, Nirvan...please don't touch me...

SHADOW: Come!

LORENZ: NO...NO...NO......(CRIES OUT AND FALLS TO FLOOR)

(MUSIC)

(CAR RUNNING...FADE TO B.G...UNDER...)

CRANSTON: Well, Margot. Commissioner Weston is satisfied that the case is solved. Lorenz in his mad desire to be the foremost magician in the world murdered both Bennington and Arturo...so that he would be sole possessor of the three great tricks.

MARGOT: But if he had the tricks by bribing the Hindu servant before Nirvan had died, why did he put on that special performance?

CRANSTON: Although he had the tricks, he wanted some means of advertising the fact...and the performance appealed to some weird dramatic streak in his make-up. Now do you understand?

MARGOT: Everything except how he was able to disappear from the theater.

CRANSTON: (LAUGHS) But I've explained that to you three times, Margo.

MARGOT: Would you try once more, Lamont?

CRANSTON: (AMUSED) Not that I think it will do much good, but here goes. In the "glass and water" trick, as you remember...the huge tank of water is on stage. The stunt is to pass from one side of the tank to the other through the glass and water...

MARGOT: ...without getting wet...

CRANSTON: That's right. Well, of course that would be. impossible...But it wouldn't be impossible to pass *under* the tank. You see, the great trick is really very simple.

MARGOT: Simple? How under the tank?

CRANSTON: Remember we noticed that the stage was covered by the canvas ground cloth?

MARGOT: Uh huh. Then you couldn't use a trapdoor.

CRANSTON: That's what I thought at first, Margot, but I found on examination that the tank was set right over a trapdoor. When the trap lowered, the ground cloth sagged.allowing just enough room under the tank for a man to squirm through. Now, do you understand?

MARGOT: I understand the trick, but how did Lorenz get out of the theater?

CRANSTON: There was a long thin slit in the ground cloth under the tank. Lorenz squirmed down through that into the trap and got away before we had a chance to search the theater.

MARGOT: It really is simple after all, Lamont. For a while, I was ready to believe it was done with black magic.

CRANSTON: You know, Margot, there is a little black magic in this case…

MARGOT: Oh, Lamont…

.CRANSTON: Seriously. When The Shadow trapped Lorenz in the cellar, Lorenz thought that The Shadow was Nirvan come back to wreak his curse. Lorenz in his fear suffered a stroke which has completely paralyzed him and made his mind a blank…

MARGOT: Lamont…Nirvan's curse…

CRANSTON: Yes, Margot…Nirvan said he would return from the dead and strike all memory from Lorenz's mind.

(CURTAIN)

ANNR: THE SHADOW program is based on a story copyrighted by Street and Smith Publications. The characters, names, places and plot are fictitious. Any similarity to persons living or dead is purely coincidental. Again next week THE SHADOW will demonstrate that…

SHADOW: (FILTER) The weed of crime bears bitter fruit. Crime does not pay. The Shadow knows! (LAUGHS) •

The 1940 Shadow cast (clockwise from top left): Keenan Wynn, announcer Ken Roberts, organist Elsie Thompson, director Wilson Tuttle, Arthur Vinton, Marjorie Anderson and Bill Johnstone

THE SHADOW'S RADIO MAGIC

After helping develop *The Shadow* radio series during. a 1937 plotting session with McKnight & Jordan radio writer Edward Hale Bierstadt, Walter Gibson had little direct influence on the radio series that showcased characters he had first introduced in the pages of *The Shadow Magazine.* Advertising executives complained that Gibson's novels contained too much "blood and thunder," though Gibson countered that the radio series featured too much "thud and blunder."

However, the solution to "Death Comes to the Magician" suggests that radio scriptwriter Sidney Slon had familiarized himself with the construction of Houdini's famous "Walking Through a Brick Wall" illusion, first publicly revealed by Walter Gibson in his 1930 book *Houdini's Escapes.* "The stage," Gibson wrote, "was covered with a large carpet of plain design and of heavy material, precluding all possibility of any openings. To make everything more convincing, a large cloth, inspected by the committee, was spread over the carpet. Then the brick wall was set in the center of the stage, and two threefold screens were placed against it, one on each side of the stage."

Behind the screens, "Houdini apparently passed through a solid brick wall, some eight feet in height, under the most exacting conditions. This effect seemed miraculous, as it was apparently impossible for the performer to go through, over, around, or beneath the wall." The secret lay in a large trapdoor, opened from below. "Both the cloth and the carpet,

which were large in area, sagged with the weight of the performer's body, allowing sufficient space for him to work his way through, the cloth yielding as he progressed. The passage accomplished, the trap was closed, and no clue remained." A variation utilized a rug with a secret opening concealed in the pattern.

Though Houdini was the first person to perform "Walking Through a Brick Wall" in the United States, he did not originate the illusion. During a British tour, the escape artist purchased American rights for the trick on May 4, 1914 from London magician Sidney Josolyne (though many believe that the illusion was originated by P. T. Selbit). Houdini soon dropped the trick from his act, preferring to focus on illusions of his own origination such as the more suspenseful Water Torture Cell.

Did Walter Gibson suggest the gimmick for "Death Comes to the Magician," perhaps passing it to Slon or the Ruthrauff & Ryan Advertising Agency via *Shadow* editor John Nanovic? Possibly, though it's more likely that the solution came directly from the intensive research that Slon was known0 for; the former *Shadow* cast member-turned-scriptwriter had even undergone painful decompression procedures while researching "The Sandhog Murders."

Sidney Slon helped develop the police procedural in *Shadow* scripts like "The Phantom Fingerprints." With "Death Comes to the Magician," Sidney Slon produced a radio rarity: an authentic magic procedural similar to those in Walter Gibson's pulp thrillers.

—Anthony Tollin

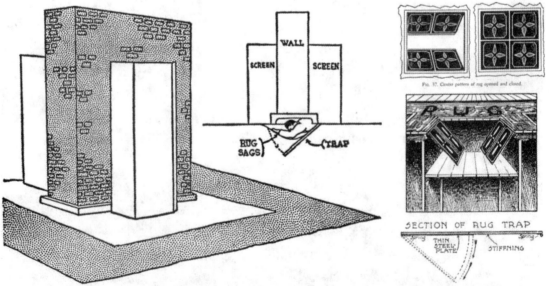

The secret of Houdini's "Walking Through a Brick Wall" illusion was first revealed in Walter Gibson's *Houdini's Escapes*. A variation, pictured in *Houdini's Fabulous Magic* by Gibson and Morris N. Young, utilized a trick rug with a function similar to the ground cloth in Sidney Slon's radio script.